THE SINGLE GIRL'S TO-DO LIST

By the same author

I Heart New York
I Heart Hollywood
I Heart Paris

I Heart Vegas – out Dec 2011

LINDSEY KELK

The Single Girl's To-Do List

HARPER

Harper
An imprint of HarperCollins*Publishers*
77–85 Fulham Palace Road,
Hammersmith, London W6 8JB

www.harpercollins.co.uk

This production 2012

First published in Great Britain by
HarperCollins 2011

ISBN: 978-0-00-793007-4

Set in Melior by Palimpsest Book Production Limited,
Falkirk, Stirlingshire

Printed and bound in Great Britain by
Clays Ltd, St Ives plc

MIX
Paper from
responsible sources
FSC® C007454

FSC
www.fsc.org

FSC is a non-profit international organisation established to promote the
responsible management of the world's forests. Products carrying the FSC
label are independently certified to assure consumers that they come
from forests that are managed to meet the social, economic and
ecological needs of present and future generations.

Find out more about HarperCollins and the environment at
www.harpercollins.co.uk/green

To all the single girls who gave hours of their lives, livers and lipgloss to research the ultimate to-do list, especially Rachael Wright, Sarah Donovan, Sarah Benton, Emma Ingram and Alicia Romano. Your sacrifice will not be in vain.

Thank you so much to Lynne, Victoria and the entire HarperCollins team, especially Ellie Portch, Kate Fitzpatrick and Sarah McPhee for being awesome amongst other things. Also, a special dose of international HC love to everyone at HarperCollins Canada – group hug. There aren't enough words, kittens or drunken hugs to express how much I love Rowan Lawton and Juliet Mushens at PFD for helping me stay sane (ish) and generally being the best agents on earth. To all my friends who dedicated their time and resources to trying to stop me ever finishing this book, thanks. I should also thank Enterprise car rental for letting me and Nana Wright hire a car for four whole days without any real driving experience (fools), Canada for letting us over the border despite the fact we were singing 'You Can Call Me Al' *very* loudly, Niagara Falls for being amazing and the WWE Universe for always being there.

Most importantly, THANK YOU to my new co-workers; aka my new buddies on Facebook and Twitter. You have provided me with hours of procrastination like no one before and for that, I love you all.

Four weeks earlier . . .

It had been an odd Sunday.

My boyfriend, Simon, had got up and vamoosed for football before I'd even considered rolling out of bed and onto the sofa for a three-hour *Friends*-a-thon. Even though it was late July, the weather was pretty mediocre and there was nothing compelling me to get up off the sofa other than a judgemental cat staring through the window and the intermittent need to pee. Usually I was mega-motivated on a Sunday. It wasn't too often I worked a regular five-day week, so Sundays were all together too often the only day I had to get anything done; but on that particular day, I couldn't bring myself to do anything more strenuous than to repeatedly text my gay best friend Matthew to ask 'how you doin'?'

I didn't care if it was a fifteen-year-old joke. It was still funny.

And so it was to me in my faded-to-grey Juicy Couture trackie bottoms, a Pokémon T-shirt I'd worn semi-ironically at university and a greasy topknot that Simon arrived home at four in the afternoon. I rolled onto my back and gave him a sexy grunt. Rowr. Rachel Sexpot Summers.

I knew things weren't right when, instead of giving me the standard kiss on the cheek and vanishing into the shower, Si sat down on the settee, elbows on knees, staring straight ahead and breathing loudly. After a couple of minutes, I muted Monica and shoved myself into a sitting position.

'You all right?' I asked.

'Do you want to go to the cinema or something?' He carried on staring at the fireplace. Not into it, just in front of it. As though he could see something I couldn't.

'I'm a bit knackered actually.'

So sue me. I wasn't being *that* lazy; I'd been working fourteen-hour days all week long. No rest for the wicked, or the make-up artist. 'Why don't we get a Chinese and watch a DVD or something?'

He was quiet for another minute. My finger hovered over the volume button while I waited for confirmation. Or at least the suggestion of an Indian.

Eventually, he spoke. 'OK. So I've been thinking.' Whatever was in front of the fireplace continued to entrance him. 'We should take a break.'

'We're going to Croatia in September.' I gave him a nonplussed stare and draped my legs across his.

'Yeah.' He stretched the word out almost all the way through an Asda commercial. 'No. I meant from . . . like . . . us.'

Now he had my attention.

'We should take a break?'

Whatever it was that was so fascinating in the empty space in front of the fireplace had apparently just started doing a jig. I couldn't remember the last time I'd seen him concentrate on something with such intensity that wasn't attached to an Xbox.

'Are you dumping me?' I pulled my legs up off his knee and curled into a semi-foetal position. I really wanted to brush my hair.

'No,' Simon shook his head. 'It's not that, I just need a bit of a break.'

'Sounds like you're dumping me.' I was trying very, very hard not to cry. I already looked bloody awful; tears were not going to help my case. But then, neither was talking in a voice so high and squeaky that it made dolphins sound like they were smoking twenty a day. 'What are you saying?'

'Stop freaking out. I just need to sort some stuff out in my head. I'm not breaking up with you.'

'Is there someone else?'

Oh my god, there was someone else. Five years, a mortgage, a co-signed car loan for a crappy secondhand Renault Mégane and he was seeing someone else.

'No,' he practically shouted. 'Of course there's not someone else.'

Fair enough.

'Is this because I don't want to go to the cinema?' I wrapped my arms around my knees.

'Do you want to go to the cinema?'

I shrugged, not knowing what else to do. 'I might.'

And that was it. We ended up going to see the new *Pirates of the Caribbean* film but, to be honest, it was a bit difficult to concentrate. And when Johnny Depp can't hold your attention, what chance does anyone else have? When we got home, I ran a bath and Simon moved his stuff into the spare room.

The next night, I got home from work to find a note on the bed to say he needed a bit of time to think and he was going to stay with a friend for a couple of days. But he did come home. Just as soon as I went away to work in Manchester for a week. And when I got back,

3

he'd gone away on a business trip. Then I spent a week at my mum's while she got to grips with a nasty broken leg. After that, he was off on a stag do. And then, one night, he just didn't come home.

But we weren't broken up. It was just a break.

A break that was rounding the four-week mark.

But still, it was just a break . . .

Four weeks later . . .

CHAPTER ONE

'If someone had told you, ten years ago, you'd be standing here doing this, you wouldn't have believed them, would you?' Anastasia asked, adjusting the strap of her lacy bra. She piled a mass of artificial blonde curls onto the top of her head before letting them fall perfectly around her slender shoulders. 'I mean, modelling? It's not something your career adviser usually recommends, is it?'

I glanced up from the ridiculously painful kneeling position I'd been locked in for the last fifteen minutes and stared daggers at the clueless blonde.

'Well, no, it's not,' I shuffled from side to side, trying to ignore the shooting pains in my kneecaps. 'But, to be fair, if someone had sat me down and told me I'd be spending most of my life covering bite marks on your arse, I might have found "model" more believable.'

'Yeah, sorry about that.' She shuffled her boobs around while I fought the urge to scrawl 'slag' across her bum cheeks in Ruby Woo lipstick. 'This new bloke's a bit kinky. Think I'm just going to stick with one boyfriend from now on. I mean, it might be dull as shit, but I'm thinking go with the one who isn't into all that weird stuff, you know? Thank god we didn't have this shoot last week – you'd never have been able to cover up the rope burns on my wrists . . .'

Breathing out, I blocked Anastasia's mid-Atlantic, Eastern-Europe-via-Essex drawl and focused on the job at hand. If there was one thing I was good at, it was focusing on the job at hand. Rachel 'Blinkers' Summers, make-up artist extraordinaire and queen of elective deafness. It was one of those jobs that sounded super fancy and terribly exciting but, in reality, being a make-up artist boiled down to getting up very early, standing around for hours, making someone else look beautiful and then going home very late. Glamorous.

But at least there was the all-inclusive workout. My kit currently weighed in at over thirty pounds, and lugging it backwards and forwards on the Tube had more or less replaced my weekly run. And there was a chance you might meet the odd celebrity, but all that really meant was that you too could experience the wonder of covering up evidence of sexual exploits so sordid that you could never watch *Coronation Street* ever again. There wasn't a soap star alive that wasn't into something weird. Happily, most days, I was just locked up in a studio in exotic Parsons Green, powdering body parts from dawn till dusk. It was hardly conducive to going home, whacking on the false eyelashes and glamming myself up for a night out with the celebs I'd been rubbing shoulders with all day. In fact, it was mostly conducive to going home, running a bath and passing out by myself while my boyfriend, Simon, watched TV.

I could never date a chef, I thought, sponging on one last layer of body foundation. He might be the best cook in the whole world, but he's not going to want to whip me up a seven-course tasting menu when he walks through the door. You'd be lucky to get spaghetti hoops on toast for two. Not that I even had that in the house, I lamented. It was Friday, which meant tomorrow was Saturday, and Saturday was food shopping day. It really didn't feel like a weekend unless I'd had my blood pressure tested by a run around Sainsbury's. Unfortunately that usually meant Friday-night dinner was a dodgy low-cal ready meal left over from my last diet, or pizza. Which explained why, on occasion, I needed the ready meals.

'Raquel, you're always so quiet,' Ana said loudly, arching her back to get a look at my handiwork. 'What are you thinking about?'

'Nothing,' I lied, stepping back to take a critical look at her now perfectly peachy arse. Not a trace of her sexploits to be seen; just as well seeing as this was a shoot for multipacks of high-street undies. I wasn't sure my mum would want to buy a five-pack of knickers that enticed wannabe rock stars to gnaw on your rear end. Or maybe she would: she and dad had been divorced for twenty years, after all, so it had been a long time since anyone had rocked her kasbah. I hoped. Ew.

'You're done.' I waved her off with one final flick of the bronzer brush. 'Go on.'

Ana clapped her hands together and skipped over to her happy place. In front of a camera. Behind said camera, Photographer Dan called out words of encouragement, snapping away while Ana threw herself around the fake bedroom set with all the gusto that I guessed had resulted in her getting bitten on the backside in the first place. It was pretty impressive stuff. I tucked my long blonde hair behind my ears and tried not to be jealous. It was a while since I'd been thrown around a bedroom.

I shook my head at the cavorting occurring in front of me. What did 'a break' even mean? Both television and movies, my most trusted advisors in life, had shown us that breaks were never actually a good thing. Fingers crossed, Simon was staying away from copy girls. This was, after all, the relationship all of our friends were jealous of because we were so incredibly sorted. Five years in and we were all set with the mortgage, a proper car, irritating pet names used in public, everything. I was certain he was going to propose. I actually had the odd wedding magazine stashed in my work kit, hidden away like girl porn. What's more, we still Did It relatively often, which as far as I could tell, was a pretty big achievement after five years. OK, so it wasn't like a Dita von Teese show every night (you try rocking stockings and suspenders when you've been up since six trying to make the latest 'celeb' kicked off *Strictly* look as though they haven't been on a forty-eight-hour bender), but it was good. We were still good. Or at least, I thought we were. It was possible my standards had lowered without me realizing.

'Make-up?' Photographer Dan shouted across the set.

Nodding obediently, I trotted over, wielding my powder brush, ignoring his elaborate tuts and sighs. Dan was one of my more regular partners in knicker-shooting crime and I was used to his 'artistic' temperament, but that didn't mean he wasn't a massive pain in the arse. However, spending six hours together in the middle of a desert, waiting for a fading supermodel to vomit everything she's eaten since 1996 so you can get one photo, really helps you bond with your work buddies. So I let it go.

'Take your time, Raquel.' Dan held his massive camera up in the air with one hand and gave me the filthiest look he could muster. 'It's not like anyone has anything else to do today, is it?'

I returned the politest smile I could muster while mentally flashing him a great big wanker sign. He knew I hated it when Ana called me Raquel. It was so bloody affected. She knew my name, she wasn't Eurotrash, she was from Basildon and her name was Anne Smith. I never bothered to point out that she'd gone to school with my cousin. Until she dropped out before her exams. Ten years on and she was lying about more than just her name. Twenty-two, Ana? I think not. Sadly, she and Dan were a frustrating combo, and killing them with kindness was the only way to get through the day. A row was usually exactly what Dan was looking for – he loved getting my back up, but I was nothing if not professional. Blowing the excess powder off my brush, I flicked it lightly across Ana's glowing (but not even slightly 22-year-old) skin, while she and Dan giggled at each other. Behold, make-up-artist-slash-invisible woman.

'Done?' Dan asked, checking I'd powered her boobs sufficiently. I didn't know for sure but I was pretty certain that, off set, Dan and Ana weren't being quite so professional as me. In fact, I was pretty certain he was one of the men who had been nibbling on her jacksy. I recognized the bite marks from the last time he'd eaten half my sandwich without asking. Well, maybe he wasn't the bottom-biter but he was definitely up to something with Ana. He was probably the dull one. Crazy sex romps with someone who was only interested in checking out his own biceps couldn't be much fun for a supermodel.

'Just a minute,' I confirmed, looking my model over from every angle. I might think Ana was a vacuous slapper, but I did care about my job.

But no, I thought to myself, stepping out of the bright

9

lights and back into the shadows, if someone had told me I'd be doing this in ten years, I really wouldn't have believed them.

'Goodbye, Raquel,' Ana breezed by in a flurry of air kisses, swathed in at least three pashminas. In August. 'And, Dan, it was so lovely to work with you again. I hope I will see you soon.'

The air kisses in his direction weren't nearly so breezy, and the subtlety of her charade was somewhat undermined by the fact that the stylist, Dan's assistant, Collin, and I all heard her 'whisper' that she'd be waiting for him in the car. Ah-ha. Suspicions confirmed. At least he had the decency to look embarrassed about it. I chose to take the high road and carried on packing away my kit. There was no way I was getting involved with this. In the six years we'd worked together, he must have shagged enough models to open his own branch of Victoria's Secret, but Ana was actually a name. Good for Dan, finally made it into the Premiership after years in the lower leagues. He was dedicated to his cause, if nothing else.

'Night, Rach,' he shouted across the studio, sheepishly heading out after his latest conquest. I gave him a quick wave before settling down in the make-up chair and pulling out my notebook. Cue satisfied sigh. Whizzing through page after page of my own handwriting, I finally found today's date, written in blue at the top of the page. My to-do list. Taking a black pen out of my handbag, I crossed off the tasks achieved with one straight, black line: drop off dry cleaning, buy toilet roll and knicker shoot. Still to go, buy wine, bikini wax, wash hair (it was almost down to my arse; honestly, it really was a task that warranted its own bullet point) and call my brother.

OK, so maybe my attachment to the lists was slightly unhealthy, and possibly the buzz I got when I crossed something off shouldn't be quite so satisfying (another indication that my sex life wasn't all that it should be?), but I had a system. Write in blue, cross it off in black, new list every day, don't go to sleep until they're all done or rolled over. I couldn't help it; apparently I had some sort of genetic defect that prevented me from achieving anything unless it was written down. I blamed my GCSE science teacher, who told me making lists would help with my revision. I might have failed double modular science but I passed obsessive-compulsive order development with flying colours. To be honest, I knew which had come in more useful over the last twelve years and it wasn't anything to do with a working knowledge of photosynthesis. Well, hopefully biology would come into play tonight because tonight I had bigger fish to fry.

Tonight, I was going to lure Simon back into the big bedroom.

CHAPTER TWO

Because no plan can succeed without the assistance of reliable wingmen, I had drafted in my best friends, Emelie and Matthew. Unfortunately, by the time we arrived at The Phoenix, Emelie was wasted. The queen of pre-partying had put away almost an entire bottle of red at my flat and was now trying to convince us to join her in a round of shots. And, for whatever reason, only known to himself, Matthew was encouraging her. Generally speaking, I didn't drink. Hangovers really didn't sit well with my job: there weren't many models or celebs that wanted a make-up artist stinking of gin, breathing on them for an hour at a time, and applying liquid eyeliner half cut is not something I'd recommend. That said, I was a pretty good drunk, more happy than emotional and, nine times out of ten, I managed to keep my kebab down. Emelie, however, was not blessed with that talent. Despite knowing that she was incapable of drinking so much as a shandy without vomming all over the night bus, she never gave up. Amazing tenacity, that girl.

'Come on, Ray, it's Friday,' she said, brandishing a shot glass, brimming with thick, sticky-looking liquor. 'And, you know, liquid courage.'

'One shot,' I warned, more an order for her than a promise to myself, then knocked it back in one. My throat scorched with sambuca afterburn and, by the time I'd prised my eyes open, she was ordering a second round. Too bad tonight would not be a night spent holding back her hair while she brought up half of Burger King.

'If you leave me with her, I will destroy you,' Matthew said, reading my mind. I shrugged, trying not to smile. He loved her really. Matthew (never Matt) and I had been friends ever since he walked out of a queer theory lecture at uni, declaring it 'a great big bag of wank'.

As his brand-new flatmate, I felt obliged to chase after him, and we spent the afternoon, evening and much of the early morning in the union, drinking pints and making up our own queer theories. Mine hung on the idea that men were just greedy, Matthew's on his belief that 'touching a vagina would make him vomit'. There was evidence to back both schools of thought. After that, we were bonded for life. It was a win-win for me – I never had to worry about him trying to get in my pants and he had a stand-in girlfriend to keep his grandmother happy. His mother had known he was gay from birth, by his account, but his grandparents weren't quite so accepting. Which was possibly why he wore a skintight, neon-pink T-shirt to his grand-father's funeral.

The poor lamb hadn't had an easy time of it as a kid. His dad had skidaddled before he was even born and only shown up again a year earlier, shortly before shuf-fling off his mortal coil and leaving Matthew an absolute ton of money, leading him to quit his air steward job and spend the last twelve months generally fannying around London with absolutely no aim in life. Even when he wasn't rich, he was pretty much a catch, however you looked at it. The boy was huge, well over six feet tall, and broad with it. Handfuls of thick blond hair dropped into his dark blue eyes and his skin was always tanned, despite my constant sun-bed warnings. Looks-wise, he was somewhere between Hitler's Aryan dream and Louis Walsh's wet dream. Personality-wise, definitely erred more on the side of fascist dictator than Gary Barlow. Which was pretty much why I loved him. That and because he came over and killed my spiders when Simon wasn't around.

It was still early, only just after ten thirty, but the club was already busy. Over in a dark corner of the small, sweaty basement, my brother and his friends were cooing over some guest DJ's vinyl collection and debating which records to play. I raised a hand when he looked up. They ran this night every month, mostly so they could hang around the DJ booth and look cool to girls. The things boys did to get laid. Said the girl still trying to find a way to get comfortable after her speculative Brazilian.

'Have you said hello to Paul yet?' Em asked, distributing the second round and looking at my brother with puppy-dog eyes. 'We really should.'

I threw back the shot and shuddered. 'We really shouldn't,' I disagreed. 'Actually, you really shouldn't. Seriously, Em. No.'

'I'm just saying we should say hello,' Em said, absently licking a drop of sambuca from her little finger, completely oblivious to the fact that every man in the bar was waiting to offer to do that for her. 'As if I fancy your brother.'

Emelie Stevens and I knew everything about each other. We were each other's secret-keepers. She knew I hadn't lost my virginity until I was 22. She knew I couldn't get to sleep at night unless I knew where my childhood teddy bear was. She knew I accidentally ran

14

over Matthew's cat when I was supposed to be looking after it. I knew she had spent several years of her childhood starring on a Canadian children's TV show. I knew she had got a pregnancy test in the first year of uni after she let John Donovan touch her up behind halls after the Halloween party. And I knew she'd had a crush on my brother since he came to collect me for Christmas break in the second year.

It was ridiculous, really – Emelie was beautiful. As in, I worked with supermodels day in and day out and I still thought she was beautiful. Medium height, medium build, slightly more than medium boobs, from the back maybe you might think she was a regular girl, but then she would turn around and you would literally stop in your tracks. She had the longest, thickest auburn hair and offensively green eyes that were lined with the thickest, flutteriest eyelashes this side of Bambi. Her outfits were always faultless and she could make a bin-bag look sexy if she wanted to. If that wasn't enough, Em had grown up in Montreal and, even after ten years in London, had an adorable lilting French-Canadian accent that slipped out when she was stressed, or angry. Or on the pull. As a package, she was unbelievable. Unfortunately for mankind, she was ridiculously unattainable.

While I hadn't been single since I was 16, Em hadn't been in a serious relationship in, well, ever. It wasn't for the want of offers, she went through men like I went through pickled onion Monster Munch, but they never lasted more than a couple of weeks. Either they liked her too much, they didn't like her enough, they were too rich and showy, they were too poor and boring. No one stood a chance. She constantly rattled on about how she was looking for 'the one', how she'd know him as soon as she saw him and that there was no point wasting time on losers, but Matthew had another theory: that she was so hopelessly in love with my slag of a brother, no one else stood a chance. As pop psychology went, it wasn't a bad call. Unfortunately, my brother wouldn't dare mess about with her. Paul's feckless womanizing was a badge he wore proudly and, while he'd made his intentions towards Emelie quite clear over the years, I had intervened at every opportunity. My best friend was not another notch on his bedpost. Not that there could be a lot of bedpost left by now. Oh universe, why would you surround me with so many manwhores?

'Did you get the email from uni?' I changed the subject while trying to convince my hair to stay behind my ears. There was just So Much Of It. 'About the ten-year reunion?'

'Got it, read it, deleted it,' Matthew nodded, pulling my hair loose again. 'They just want money.'

'I just can't believe it's been ten years since we started.' Emelie was trying to catch the bartender's eye for some proper drinks. Luckily, the bartender was a woman so it was taking longer than her usual three seconds. Almost a whole thirty before a bottle of white wine was in front of us. 'It doesn't feel like ten minutes ago.'

'And look at you two now,' Matthew replied, wrapping an arm around Em to physically remove her from the bar. 'Top make-up artist and super-successful . . . what exactly is it that we call you?'

She made a face and wriggled out of his bear hug. 'I'm a graphic artist.'

'You're a what?'

'She drew a picture that someone put on loads of stuff and then lots of little girls bought it,' I clarified for Matthew. 'A picture of a cat.'

'Got it,' he clicked and pointed, ignoring Em's 'I'm

not amused' face. As always. 'You're the one that weasels kids out of their pocket money.'

'You can both fuck off, I'm a graphic artist,' she started defensively. 'And Kitty Kitty isn't a picture of a cat, it's a brand. And it's one of the most successful tween brands in the UK.'

'Tween,' Matthew smirked. 'Stop making up words.'

'Em, we know.' I pulled out my Kitty Kitty wallet and waved it in her face to prove my point before she went for Matthew. 'He's jealous because he's unemployed.'

'Taking a sabbatical,' he corrected, spying an empty sofa and crossing the dance floor in three strides to bag it before a group of girls could hurl their handbags onto the table. 'You're only unemployed if you're broke.'

'Run that one past me again?' Em asked with faux innocence.

Matthew closed his eyes and pinched the bridge of his nose. His 'I'm calm, really' pose. 'I'm taking time out until I work out what I want to do.'

'For the last year,' Em said, not quite quietly enough.

'For the last year,' he repeated pointedly, in her face. 'Maybe I should just draw a crappy cat and stick it on lunchboxes instead of doing something worthwhile.'

'Because serving people chicken or pasta at fifty thousand feet was worthwhile?' Em snapped back.

'No, you knob, that's why I'm taking a sabbatical!'

'For the last year—'

'Children,' I said loudly. 'Inside voices?'

Matthew narrowed his eyes while Em stuck out her tongue before they both turned to look at me, argument forgotten. Really, I spent far too much time feeling like a primary school teacher on a field trip than was healthy. Which was one of the reasons I needed Simon back so badly. Perfect, adult, sensible Simon. The one thing in my world that reminded me I was a grown-up.

Well, Simon and my tax return, but I really didn't like to put the two of them in the same category if I could help it.

'So tonight's the night?' Em asked, inching down the hemline of her tiny black Topshop dress. 'With Simon?'

'Yes,' I confirmed, forcing my hair back behind my ears again. 'Tonight is the night.'

'Is there a plan?' Matthew asked, flicking my hair loose again. 'Don't put it behind your ears, you look like a sad mouse. And no one wants to shag a sad mouse.'

'Thanks,' I glared at the floor rather than at my friend and took a deep breath. 'And no, no plan. I'm just going to go over with a drink and say hi to his friends because you know, his friends love me.'

Em and Matthew nodded encouragement. His friends did love me. I was the cool girlfriend. The one that thought it was hilarious that they went to Spearmint Rhino after their Christmas party. The one who made bacon sandwiches the morning after when they passed out on our sofa. The one who understood the offside rule. Or, at least, I was the one who tolerated the strip clubs, made the bacon sandwiches to sober them up and pretended to understand the offside rule. And elaboration on those facts was completely unnecessary.

'And then you're going to pull him to one side and tell him he's the love of your life and this break stuff has only made you realize how badly you need him and that you want to have his babies?' It would be an understatement to say that Emelie had something of a romantic nature.

'Or pull him to one side and tell him that tonight's the night he gets to go where no one has ever gone before?' Matthew's sensibilities were not quite so romantic.

'Firstly, Matthew? Ew. And Emelie, your relationship

advice is not required.' I started to brush my hair behind my ears but stopped myself just in time, much to Matthew's delight. 'I'm just going to tell him that I think that the break has been really valuable, I've had a lot of time to think about what I want and that now I think we're ready to move on to the next level.'

'Babies?'

'Anal?'

'Oh my god.' I pressed my hand to my eyes, hoping they'd have disappeared when I opened them again. But no. Still there. 'No. To both. But especially Matthew. God.'

Matthew shrugged and took a deep swig of his drink. 'I'm just saying, if you really want to get his attention . . .'

'I don't think we need to pull out the big guns just yet,' I said, checking my watch for the millionth time that night. It was almost eleven. Why wasn't he here yet? He always came to The Phoenix on Paul's nights. 'I'm just going to suggest we talk. We've been together for five years, we finish each other's sentences, we're supposed to be together.'

'Yeah, because blokes love talking on a Friday night,' Matthew said to Em, who nodded in agreement.

'He's right,' she agreed. 'I mean, not about the back-door proposition; although, actually, he's probably right about that too. Men are weird.'

'This just makes more sense,' I replied. 'Simon isn't good at planned one-on-one situations. He thinks I'm trying to give him an appraisal. I don't want him to feel like I'm bullying him into a deep and meaningful, it's just going to be a "hey, how's everything?" casual chat during which he will remember how fabulous I am and how much he misses me, then it's back home for mind-blowing sex and we're done.'

19

'And then he'll forget all about whatever underlying reasons there are for this break bollocks and you'll live happily ever after?' Matthew stared at me and shook his head. 'Piece of piss, Rach.'

'I appreciate your input, really,' I stood up and calculated my route to the bar. A drink would shut them up. It wouldn't be my problem when Emelie had to pay a fifty-quid taxi-cleaning bill again. 'Despite one of you being incredibly homosexual and the other not having had a boyfriend for more than two weeks since you broke up with Adam Rothman in Pizza Express three years ago because he finished your fudge sundae while you were in the lav. More wine?'

'Touchy,' Matthew drained his glass. 'And yes.'

'Well, you look good,' Em said. 'I mean, you know, like you've tried.'

I tried not to punch her in the face. 'I have tried.'

'And you can tell.' She gave me an encouraging smile, as though she really did think she'd just paid me a compliment.

'I think what our dear friend is trying to say, is that you look even more amazing than usual,' Matthew corrected. 'Seriously, you look great.'

After turning my entire wardrobe out onto my bedroom floor, I'd settled on skinny jeans and a low-cut black vest that were both just tight enough to pass as sexy-tight and not too-many-pies-tight. I hoped.

'I know this isn't what you want to hear right now, but are you sure about tonight?' he asked. 'About getting back with Simon and everything?'

Brilliant. We were going to have The Talk. Again. Matthew had been ready to punch Simon in the face ever since the break was agreed upon. It wasn't that I didn't appreciate his loyalty, but I really didn't want it to be weird when we got back together. It's never fun to be the person that bitched the ex out to high heavens and then the couple gets back together. I should know; I'd been that person on several occasions.

'We're not getting back together because we're not broken up,' I reminded him. 'But yes, I am sure about tonight.'

'We're just worried about you,' Emelie said, wearing her best concerned face. 'You've just been so miserable lately.'

I had?

'And should you really have to be trying so hard?' Matthew stared before I could interrupt. 'He should be begging you to take him back after this "on a break" rubbish. Are you sure you wouldn't be better off maybe making the break a bit more permanent?'

'I'm sure,' I said quickly. 'He's my boyfriend. We own a flat. We're going to get married. We're going to have babies. How many times do we have to go over this?'

'I just don't think your soul mate should spend a month in the spare room while he "works things out".' Matthew loved his air quotes. 'I'm not saying you weren't happy before, but you're not happy now. Things change, you know, that's not always bad.'

'Please don't start on about soul mates.' This was my least favourite part of the conversation and we'd had it enough times. Between them, Matthew and Emelie were keeping Clinton's Cards in business – hopeless romantics the pair of them. 'And it hasn't been a month yet, so don't exaggerate. I don't have a problem with it so you shouldn't. He just needed a little bit of time to . . . you know . . . just to work stuff out. Isn't he better than the others?'

'Yes but honestly, love, the others weren't up to much,' Matthew examined his fingernails to avoid looking at me. 'You don't have the best taste in men, you know. But I don't want you to throw yourself after this just because it's familiar.'

'Seconded,' Emelie piped up, clutching an empty wine glass. Going to the bar was definitely going to be the easiest way out of this. 'Too many people stay with blokes that are past their sell-by date out of habit.'

'It's not that at all.' I stood up and looked around again. No sign. 'He's got a good job, he'll be a great father, he's not a wanker and I love him. Now who wants what to drink?'

Emelie raised her hand.

Matthew folded his arms. 'Glad you got to the most important part first. Clearly he's the one.'

'If you'd had my parents, you wouldn't believe in "the one" either,' I replied. 'Now, disgusting house white all round?'

I turned on my heel to head for the bar, trying not to lose my temper. There was a reason Matthew was being so unnecessarily emo so I had to let this go. Aside from the fact he was just looking out for me, his 'soul mate', Stephen, had left him six months ago for a 24-year-old underwear model and he still wasn't anywhere near over it. I'd never seen such a messy break-up in my life and pretty much avoided mentioning Steven, models and underwear at all times. Which sort of limited our conversation this evening. It wasn't that he didn't want to talk about him, it was just that whenever he did, he went sort of catatonic for a few hours and then I got a phone call three days later to say he'd woken up in Mexico and needed me to feed his cat. Well, that was when he'd had a cat. The joys of being a former trolley dolly who was currently burning through a pretty hefty inheritance. Most people I knew broke up with someone, went out, got drunk and woke up on a night bus in Peckham. Matthew got drunk, went to Heathrow, got on a plane and woke up in Rio. With someone called José. We still didn't know very much about José but they were Facebook friends, so that was nice.

I twisted and turned through the growing number of bodies on the dance floor and weaselled into position at the bar. I placed my order and turned to look back at my best friends, now gesturing wildly at each other and cackling like witches, harsh words forgotten. They left me exhausted. And I wasn't quite sure what I'd do without them.

'All right, sis?' Paul sidled up beside me, winked at the girl behind the bar and started sipping his pint before I'd even opened my mouth. 'Emelie's looking fit tonight.'

'Don't bother.' I ordered the wine and gave him the sternest look I could muster. 'Aren't there any other lucky candidates ready to catch whatever you're passing round this evening?'

'Oh god, yeah, loads.' He turned around and leaned against the bar. 'But none of those would piss you off quite so much, would they?'

'You're so funny.' I grabbed the bottle and headed back to the table. With Paul hot on my heels. Well, flats.

'Matthew,' he nodded, before slipping onto the seat closest to Emelie. 'Em.'

I pretended not to see her blushing for the sake of my own sanity.

'So, what are you doing sitting down?' Paul asked. 'This DJ's amazing.'

'We were just counselling your sister.' Matthew took the wine from me and topped up everyone's glasses. Ahh, the great British Friday-night tradition of binge-drinking. 'That's a serious job, you know.'

'She won't listen,' he replied. 'Don't waste your breath.'

'Rach.' Emelie tore her eyes away from my little brother just long enough to spy Simon arriving. I looked up to see him roll through the door and straight up to the bar with a group of people I didn't recognize.

Simon. My Simon.

I couldn't believe it was four weeks since I'd laid eyes on him. Half of me felt as though he'd kissed me on the head on his way out this morning, and the other, like I was looking at a complete stranger. He was still in his smart jeans-and-shirt ensemble that he wore to work on casual Fridays. If he'd been stuck in the office late, he'd be wanting a drink. Probably a whisky and Coke, even though I knew what he really wanted was Malibu and lemonade. Given his sloped shoulders and slight stagger, it seemed as if he'd had a couple of drinks already. He looked tired. It made my heart hurt not to be able to go over to him and kiss him hello. But that wasn't part of the plan.

Sitting at a table, moping into a glass of wine wasn't going to win him back. I forced my face to put on a smile for the first time in what seemed like forever and took hold of Emelie's arm. 'Come on, I want Simon to think we're having fun.'

'Any chance we could actually just have fun?' she asked. 'Because that's probably more believable than pretending.'

'Just dance with me,' I slid my black leather clutch under my arm and pulled her towards the floor. Matthew and Paul followed, Matthew never one to miss an opportunity to get his dance on and Paul presumably sensing an opportunity to touch Emelie up a little bit. As Smokey Robinson blared out of the speakers, conversation was no longer an option, so I closed my eyes and started to move, hoping that Simon was watching. After a decade of dancing together, I could feel Matthew and Emelie without needing to open my eyes. Em was leaning against my back, partly to try to look sexy and partly because she was already too drunk to dance without support. Matthew would have his hands thrown in the air at the side of me, singing along, his fast footwork lost in the throb of bodies. I felt Em drift away and a pair of man hands gripped me around my waist. I put my head down, smiled to myself, not wanting anyone to see and leaned back into Simon's chest.

'Hi.'

Of course it wasn't Simon. It was a complete stranger. And not one you would want touching you. I stopped suddenly, giving him just enough opportunity to spin me around and dip me low on the dance floor. Emelie and Matthew were too busy busting their own moves to notice, and my brother had adopted the official 'I can't see this so it isn't happening' tactic, as was the way when someone was having a crack at your sister.

'Oh my god, get off.' I tried to wriggle free but my suitor must have been almost a foot taller than me. And five stone heavier. He simply picked me up and held me in the air. I placed my hands on his shoulders to steady myself as my shoes slipped off my feet. Which didn't stop me landing what could have been a very, very painful kick if it had hit two inches to the left.

'I don't think so.' I pulled my hand back and cracked him right across the face. Fair, given that I'd missed the kick to the balls. Another good reason why I had no interest in breaking up with Simon.

Bending down to grab my shoes, I ignored the 'oohs' that echoed around me and pushed my way towards the bar just in time to see Simon heading up the stairs, towards the street.

'Simon!' I shouted, trying to get my shoes on before I got outside. 'Wait, Simon!'

'Rachel?'

I whirled around to see Simon accepting a cigarette from a man I didn't recognize in the smokers' corner on the side of the street. He looked surprised to see me. And also a little bit like his form tutor had just caught him out behind the bike sheds. Not the impact I was hoping for.

'Simon,' I said, staring at him trying to hide his cigarette behind his back. 'You're smoking.'

'Uh, no, I just, well, one.' He waved the Marlboro Light around as though it was a magic wand. 'I had a really shit day. Were you inside?'

'You, you didn't see?' I asked, wrapping my arms around myself. It was a little too cold to be outside without a coat. 'You didn't see us dancing?'

'Dancing?' Simon looked confused. 'With who?'

'No one, not with anyone,' I said, taking a step towards him. 'Matthew and Emelie. And Paul.'

He took a step backwards. 'Right. I didn't know you'd be here.'

I stood and looked at him for a moment. This wasn't how this was supposed to go. This wasn't why I'd worn my best underwear. This wasn't why I'd been through the agony of a bikini wax.

'Simon, can we talk for a minute?' I asked, taking another step towards him.

'Can we do it tomorrow?' he countered. 'I know we need to talk about stuff, I've just had a really shit day and I've been so busy and——'

'I haven't seen you in four weeks.' I lowered my voice as subtly as possible. 'Can you give me five minutes?'

'It's just because, I think we're leaving, Mark's friends are at this other place and we're probably going to go there . . .' He trailed off, looking back towards someone named Mark who still wasn't looking at me. Whoever Mark was.

'I just need a minute,' I said, trying to remember my speech. 'I wanted to talk about the break thing. I've had enough.'

'Oh.' He dropped the cigarette and stamped it out. ''Oh, OK. Let's just get it over with then.'

Get it over with?

Before I could start on the next part, he walked over, put his arm over my shoulder and led me over to the railings across the street.

'I'm sorry I haven't been around.' He left his hand on my shoulder for a moment before looking at it and pulling it away, jamming it deep into his pocket. 'I did want to talk but things have been mental. Work's mad, I'm training up this new assistant and he's shit and then there was the stag do and, sorry, I'll shut up. Shoot.'

'You wanted to talk?' I asked, wishing I'd put on lip balm before I came outside. From the corner of my eye, I saw Matthew stick his head out of the door, then slide back in once he'd clocked me. 'I've wanted to talk about it too.'

'Yeah?' Simon didn't look happy. 'I thought having time away would make this easier. Doesn't though, does it?'

'Doesn't what?' I rubbed my arms briskly. It really was cold and my bra was not adequately padded enough for such temperatures. 'Look, Si, like I was saying, I've wanted to talk since you left. I think the whole break time thing was totally OK and it's been good to have some space but I'm done with it. The whole break thing.'

'OK. Good. OK.' He fumbled around in a pocket for his cigarettes. 'Is there someone else?'

'Is there what?' I pushed my hair back again and

tried to ignore Matthew standing across the street, motioning for me to pull it forward. 'Why would there be . . .? Look, Simon, I'm over this whole break thing. I just want things back to normal.'

Simon lit another cigarette and looked at the floor. 'Sorry Rach, I've had a couple of drinks, I'm not following. What are you saying?'

'I don't want to be on a break.' I reached over and took the packet of cigarettes out of his hand. 'Will you look at me, please?'

He inhaled deeply and blew out a long stream of grey smoke, shaking his head. I stepped closer until we were toe to toe and placed my empty hand on his arm, pulling the cigarette away from his mouth.

'Simon, you don't smoke.'

'I smoked before we started going out,' he said quietly.

'We've been going out for five years,' I replied in a voice just as hushed but, regardless of volume control, I could see a small audience with ears pricked across the street.

Suddenly our private conversation felt very public.

'Five years is a long time.' Simon pulled his arm away from me, stepped back and took another drag. 'And I don't want to be on a break either. So we're agreed that the break isn't working.'

'Simon, I'm really not following,' I was totally lost. This was really, really not how this was supposed to go. We were supposed to be halfway to doing something indecent in the back of a taxi by now, not rambling in the middle of the street while Matthew pretended not to be watching from the doorway of the club. And, oh brilliant, Em was there as well. At least Paul had stayed downstairs – oh, wait a minute, nope, there he was. Just what I needed.

'I know I haven't dealt with the whole break-up very

well, but I don't want to make it any harder than it is already.' Simon shrugged. 'It's not been easy for me either, you know.'

'What are you talking about?' I grabbed his arm tight and got as close to his face as was humanly possible given his cigarette breath. This was supposed to be seductive, not confusing and gross. 'Can we please just go home?'

'I'm not coming home.' He shook off my arm and stepped backwards. 'This isn't a break, Rachel.'

Simon looked pale and awkward and it didn't really matter how cold it was any more.

'I don't want to be on a break because I want to be with you,' I said softly, staring steadily at his shoes. 'It's just a break. We're not, you know, we're not. Not on a break.'

For a few moments, he didn't say anything. I didn't say anything. Across the street, I could hear people talking, laughing, even some shouting a couple of doors down, but it seemed as if it was miles away. I coughed, just to check I could still make noise.

'Simon, I love you.'

Nothing.

'Simon?'

Still nothing.

I pressed my lips together to try and stop the tears that were tickling the corners of my eyes, blurring the bright red postbox into a red slash to the side of me.

'Simon, please.' I tried to keep my voice even but I was having enough trouble getting the words out at all. 'You're my boyfriend.'

Simon took one last drag, dropped the cigarette butt and ground it into the pavement with a brown leather shoe I didn't recognize. Looking up at the sky, he blew out his breath loudly.

'You're not the one.'

I folded my arms tightly, pressing my fingernails into my bare arms.

'I'm sorry, Rachel,' he said, looking quickly back down at the street. Anywhere but at me. 'I'm wasting your time. You're not the one.'

'I'm not . . .' I cleared my throat and started again. 'I'm not the one?'

'No,' Simon replied.

'Is someone else the one?' I asked, afraid to hear the answer. 'Are you . . . is there . . .?'

'No,' he said, finally looking somewhere just to the right of my nose. Still not quite at my eyes. 'Honest. It's just, I thought about it and I care about you, I do, you're just not the one. We're not going to work out in the end.'

'Any reason in particular?' I couldn't believe what I was hearing. 'What did I do?'

'You didn't do anything,' he shrugged. 'I just woke up one day and I knew. I thought the break would help but . . .'

'You thought the break would be easier than out-and-out breaking up with me,' I revised for him. 'And that I would get the hint or something?'

'I'm sorry, I haven't done this very well.' He went back to his pocket for the cigarettes but they were still in my hand. Impetuously, I threw them into the road and under a car. 'Rachel, I just don't, I'm not, god this is shit. I'll always love you, I'm just not, you know.'

'I don't know actually.' I shook my head and felt my hair fall around my shoulders. 'Because I love you.'

'Jesus, Rach.' Simon reached an arm out towards my bare shoulder and laid his hand against my skin. It should have felt warm and reassuring but instead it stung. 'I'm sorry.' He pulled his hand away and shoved it back into his empty pocket.

I took a step backwards, blinking until the tears slipped over my eyelids and ran down my cheeks. At least I wasn't wearing any mascara. Nothing like panda eyes to make a girl look utterly pathetic. I looked at him. His short dark-blond hair was darker in the street-light and his eyes were red and tired. The strangest thing was looking at his lips. And letting the fact that I wouldn't be kissing them ever again settle in my mind. They were off-limits. He was off-limits. No longer mine. Another step back and I took him in completely. All five feet nine of ex-boyfriend. Ex. What a horrible sound. This wasn't my Simon; this was a stranger. I stepped back again, stumbling off the kerb and into the road.

'Rachel!' Someone shouted sharply and I turned around just in time to see a black cab whirr past me, beeping his horn, the driver shouting something like 'stupid cow' out of the window. Even though I was still standing in the road, I couldn't seem to move. Instead, I sat down. Which seemed like a sensible idea.

'Rachel,' another voice said, softer this time but closer. I felt several arms wrap around me and pull me to my feet before hearing raised voices and scuffling behind me.

'Get her in a cab,' Matthew's voice commanded someone. 'I'll sort these two out.'

I was more interested in my shoes. I loved these shoes. How long had Simon had those brown shoes? How come I hadn't seen them before? He'd probably bought them earlier – only a boy would go out dancing on a Friday night in new shoes without knowing whether or not they'd rub. Which of course they would; all of his shoes rubbed.

'Rachel, are you OK?' Em's voiced asked.

I nodded.

'Me and Matthew are coming home with you.' Her voice was coming from somewhere above me but I couldn't quite focus on it.

I shook my head.

'Yes, we are.'

'No,' I said steadily. 'I just want to go home and sleep. Really. Just come over in the morning. I'll need you in the morning.'

'I really think we should come home with you, just me or just Matthew, whoever you want. This is not open for discussion.'

I shook my head again and stretched my arm out to an approaching black cab. 'I'm fine.'

Before she could do anything, I shook Emelie off and opened the cab door, slamming it shut behind me, hitting my leg in the process. I didn't feel it.

'Amwell Street, Islington?' I leaned forward until I saw the driver nod and then slouched back while he did a U-turn. Out of the window, I saw Emelie throwing her hands up at Matthew who was holding his own hands over his face. Behind them, Paul was holding his nose but I couldn't see Simon. Until we stopped at a traffic light. Then I spotted him. On the floor at Paul's feet with Mark the Stranger at the side of him.

Well, would you look at that?

CHAPTER THREE

By the time the cab dropped me off at home, I'd replayed our conversation over in my head so many times, it felt like something that had happened to someone else, or that I'd seen on TV. The exact words used were hazy, each gesture exaggerated or traded in for something that didn't happen, but the end result was always the same, no matter how many times I ran through it. I'm not the one. He doesn't love me. He doesn't want me.

It took me far too long to get my keys in the door, and when I finally managed to force my way in, I flipped on the lights only to illuminate five years of happy memories lining our hallway. Holiday snaps, concert tickets, napkins from restaurants, postcards from holidays, everything we'd collected over the duration of our relationship, mounted, framed, hung, down to the receipt for the drinks on our first date. He'd kept that and given it to me the day we'd moved in together. There was no way this was actually happening.

Exhausted, I turned the light out and turned into the bedroom, kicking off my shoes and scrambling out of my vest and jeans as I went. I'd made the bed before

I left, hoping to be falling into it with Simon and not tearstains and a scraped knee. Despite the fact that I'd been sleeping on my own for a few weeks, this was the first night since 'the break' that I'd felt lonely. This was the first time I was alone. I swapped my uncomfortable underwear for an old T-shirt of Simon's that I kept hidden inside my pillowcase along with a dodgy old pair of boxer shorts that had no elastic left. I lay on my back and stared at the ceiling, Simon's words buzzing through my brain as if I'd left the TV on. Sleep wasn't coming but the most ridiculous things kept popping into my mind. My credit card payment was due. I still had two episodes of *Glee* to watch on Sky Plus and it was running out of memory. Tonight would be the first night I hadn't washed my face in over four years. This was why I had to write lists. Regardless of my relationship status, no one wanted to work with a spotty make-up artist. I slid off the bed, hitching up the baggy boxers as I went.

In the hallway, I reached out to touch my favourite photo of us, taken at Emelie's birthday the year before. Simon was laughing at something Matthew had said and I had my arms linked around his neck, my face leaning into his shoulder. He looked handsome, I didn't look fat and we were happy. The perfect picture. I could feel the sobs building in my chest when I heard scuffling at the front door. Turning on the lights, I peered through the glass. It was Simon. I waited a couple of seconds, my mind completely empty, before I flipped the lock and swung the door open.

His left eye was already turning purple and, although someone had tried to clean him up, his nose was bloody and his lip was bust. Between his messed-up face and my seductive ensemble, this was so far removed from the perfect picture, I could have smiled. Could have.

'The lock needs some WD-40 or something,' I muttered, one hand holding up my shorts.

'I'm sorry,' Simon was still hovering outside the door.

'Not your fault,' I shrugged. 'It's been sticky for ages.'

'No, I'm sorry,' he said again.

I moved away from the door to let him in, my back pressed against the wall of photos. He paused right in front of me and opened his mouth to say something before changing his mind.

'Simon?'

He stopped, turned around and looked me up and down.

'Is that my T-shirt?' he asked.

'Yeah,' I pulled at the frayed hem. 'It's comfy to sleep in.'

'I thought you'd thrown it out,' he replied.

Feeling my bottom lip start to tremble, I shook my head. I squeezed my toes and feigned a yawn so I could push back the tears.

'Right,' he said, his hands deep in his pockets.

I nodded. He just stood there, battered, bruised, miserable and staring at the shoes I'd never seen before. I knew I had to say something and say it now. By the morning, it would be over. Relationships like ours always died quietly in the night; we weren't ones for violent, bloody deaths played out in public. Far too English for that. But my tongue was tied up with too many questions and my heart was already playing dead. Swallowing hard, I opened my mouth, no idea what was going to come out.

'New shoes?'

For a moment, I really didn't know what was happening, I was still staring at Simon's shoes as they came over and then his arms were around me, his hot, damp face on mine. It wasn't until I felt a picture frame digging into my shoulder blade that I realized we were kissing, that his hands were running up and down my back and then tangling themselves in my hair and back down again.

'I'm sorry,' he said into my hair. 'I'm so sorry.'

Instinctively, my arms went up around his neck and my lips took his kisses on autopilot, but the sharp corner of the photo was still cutting into my back. It was only when he moved the kisses from my mouth down to my throat that I realized my eyes were open and my mind was completely quiet. What was wrong? This was the plan. Simon paused and looked up at me with a new expression on his face, half confused and half desperate to get his end away. I'd seen them both independently of each other enough times over the last five years but this was a new combo.

'Rach?' he panted. His concern was reasonable: firstly, kissing my neck was the surefire way to get into my pants, as he well knew; and secondly, I'd wanted this so badly for so long, I ought to be responding at least. Something was just off. 'Rach, honest, I'm sorry.'

'Stop. You can stop saying that,' said a voice that sounded like mine. If he apologized, that meant he had something to apologize for and I couldn't deal with that right now.

'OK.' He reached around my neck and scooped my hair over one shoulder, a gesture so familiar my stomach dropped through the floor. 'OK.'

I nodded and closed my eyes when he leaned in to kiss me again. I kissed him back, trying not to hurt his split lip. But he didn't care about his split lip. For the first time in a month, he wanted me, so I let him turn me towards the bedroom door, push me onto the bed and I felt the comfortable weight of his body on top of me. I didn't need to think, I didn't need to act, his hands started on their regular route around my body, lips making their way across my collarbone, my left leg curling up around his waist. I'd missed this so much. I'd missed him so much. My body should be screaming for him, not just reacting. It was just weird because it had been so long, that was all. And so I ignored the little voice in my head, intent on chanting 'not the one, not the one, not the one' over and over and over. Instead I closed my eyes and began playing my part. I had him back. And that was what I wanted. He was what I wanted. And he was mine again.

The next morning came like any other, the sun streaming in through the too-sheer curtains on the bedroom window that I never bought blackout curtains for, because Simon liked to wake up to natural light. And, as though he'd never been away, there he was beside me, that natural light illuminating his dark blond hair until it was almost golden. I lay on my side, a few inches away from him, just watching him sleep. Last night had been strange, I hadn't been able to quite shake off the feeling that we should have talked before Simon jumped back into my bed, but this morning everything felt right. We were back on track. Whatever madness he'd been suffering, he was over it.

I turned onto my back, trying not to wake him and smiled to myself while I thought about my daily chores. Perhaps I could let myself off the list today: the post could wait at the post office until Monday and I'd get Matthew's birthday card tomorrow. But I did need to go to the supermarket – we were out of everything. I slid off the bed, not budging the mattress, and grabbed last night's jeans and tank top that were still lying in a sad puddle on the floor. I got dressed in the hallway, grabbing my phone, cash card, keys and a cardigan on my way out through the door, pausing just for a second to straighten the frame we'd dislodged the night before. Nothing was really aligned, but to see it there, cockeyed and nudging the next photo, made me come over all OCD. I put it back where it had been before but it still didn't look right. Instead of fannying around and making too much noise, I took it down and propped it against the wall, making a mental note in my temporary to-do list to put it back up later on. After breakfast. After whatever Simon wanted to do today. I'd rewrite the list for tomorrow. OCD assuaged.

It was super-early for a Saturday and London was mostly still asleep, but buses bustled by and weekend workers walked on, heads down, earphones in. I dabbed on lip balm, tenderly touched my chafed chin and wrapped my hair around itself into a relatively controlled knot on the back of my head as I wandered down the street. I really had to get it cut; I really had far too much hair for just one person. But Simon liked it long. And I was used to it. Even if Dan did call me Cousin It whenever I wore it down on set.

I couldn't believe Paul had punched Simon. It was the nicest thing he'd ever done for me. Totally made up for the time he'd cut the hair of every single one of my My Little Ponies. Well, maybe not all of them. I should call him and let him know we'd worked things out, otherwise it was going to be incredibly awkward at my dad's wedding in a couple of weeks. Right now, I needed to think about getting pastries, coffee and cream. And probably some stain remover to try and get the blood out of Simon's shirt. And they say romance is dead.

The supermarket seemed strangely busy, full of people on their way to work, buying tuna sandwiches for their lunch break, early risers doing their shopping, and more than one creased-looking gentleman with a terribly self-satisfied expression on his face.

'All right?' Something reeking of YSL Kouros nodded at me over the croissants. 'Heavy night?'

'Something like that,' I said, without eye contact. Didn't he realize he was in London? We didn't talk to strangers. We didn't even talk to our neighbours for the first five years unless it was to complain about the noise or errant pet shitting in our garden.

'Yeah, trick is to get out before the 'wake-up,' he said, filling up a plastic bag with cinnamon Danishes. 'But I always leave a note. You've got to leave a note. Just out of order not to.'

'Right,' I gave him a tight smile and backed away slowly towards the queue for the till.

And he followed.

'Always felt bad for girls,' he went on. 'You know, you see a bloke on the walk of shame and everyone thinks, "Get in there, son!" but you see a girl walking down the street at six a.m. on a Saturday in last night's clothes and everyone just thinks "slag".'

'Yeah,' I said, flicking through the items in my basket for a moment before I realized what he'd said. 'Sorry, what?'

'Not me though,' Kouros Man flung out his hands, spilling his already opened can of Red Bull. 'I do not judge. And it's not like you've got your skirt up your arse and tits hanging out like some of them, is it? Good outfit.'

Brilliant. Not only was this charmer still drunk, he thought we were one-night-stand kindred spirits.

'You should probably give me your number, you know, in case you ever need company.' The stale stench of whatever he'd been drinking/spilling down himself last night combined with the overabundance of intense aftershave came closer, making me gag.

'I have a boyfriend,' I said quickly, holding the basket between us. 'So no.'

'Right, course you do,' he replied, fingering a packet of Durex for a moment before adding it to his booty. Double gag. I turned my back, hoping he would just go away, but I could still smell him. I had a feeling it would be a lingering odour. Thank god Simon had come to his senses. That was the first man in five years to ask for my number and I really didn't feel like he was a keeper.

I paid for my breakfast bounty and vamoosed back out onto the street, so enthralled by my iPhone that I couldn't even hear Kouros Man muttering loudly after me. Muttering something that sounded suspiciously like 'bitch'. No, he didn't judge.

August never guaranteed good weather in London, but that morning was beautiful. Bright, cool sunshine and a clear blue sky. I bounced back along Upper Street, scanning text messages from Matthew and Em. They wouldn't appreciate a blow-by-blow phone call pre-seven a.m., so I tapped out an 'everything's fine' text, deleted the torrent of abuse aimed at Simon, and kept the effusive messages of love. Never hurt to have them around.

I locked my phone and slipped it into my back pocket. I wasn't particularly good at expressing emotion and I had never been particularly free and easy with the 'L' word. I loved my parents, I loved my brother, I loved Matthew, Emelie, Simon, Galaxy chocolate, Alexander Skarsgard and Topshop Baxter Jeans. And I really, really loved my flat. I'd lived in a wild assortment of shitty bedsits and tolerable house-shares since university but this, our beautiful two-bedroom first-floor flat, snagged for a song in the middle of the recession, was my home. The last eighteen months had been spent feathering our nest. Mostly with piles of clothes I never got around to ironing, but still. Home. I climbed the five steps up to the royal blue door and paused for a moment. I was nervous. What if Simon was awake? Maybe I should have attempted to make myself look half decent before I left. What was I going to say to him? Maybe we could just pretend last night never happened.

'At least he won't be wearing Kouros,' I said to myself, and sort of to a passing dog walker, as I stuck my keys in the lock.

The flat was still quiet when I passed through the door and I slipped off my shoes so as not to wake Simon. OK, I would brush my teeth, make coffee and then whatever would happen, would happen. Setting breakfast down on the kitchen countertop, I made a beeline for the bathroom. Whatever would happen *would* happen. And so what? I thought as I splashed my face with cold water. One awkward conversation and then back on the road to marriage, babies and bliss. Everyone had bumps in the road; everyone had their little moments of madness. What relationship was perfect? I grabbed my toothbrush and reminded myself that the happily-ever-after myth was just that. A myth. Hmm, no toothpaste. Automatically, I reached into the cabinet beside the sink for a new tube. Real relationships were difficult and required work. They needed understanding and compromise. You couldn't just run away when things got tough, you had to . . .

The toothpaste.

There wasn't a new tube of toothpaste in the cabinet beside the sink because I'd started a new tube of toothpaste the day before. But it wasn't in its holder. And neither was Simon's toothbrush. And his razor was gone. Still clutching my toothbrush, I padded back through to the hallway and stopped outside the bedroom door. Even though I already knew what I was going to find, I just couldn't open it. I felt sick. And angry. And stupid. I pushed the door open with my big toe and peered inside. At the empty bed. I stepped backwards and felt something hard and cold under my foot, followed by something sharp, stinging and hot. The photo from Emelie's birthday. Simon must have knocked it over on his way out. In his rush.

Toothbrush in one hand, phone in the other, I slid down the wall, knocking every other photo onto the floor on my way down, and watching my blood trickle out onto the laminate flooring Simon had so lovingly laid, the day after last year's FA Cup final. Simon always said there was no DIY during football season.

I slid the lock off my phone and pressed the last call button.

'Matthew?' I said quietly, trying not to flex my toes. 'He took my toothpaste.'

CHAPTER FOUR

'I'm going to kill him,'

I nodded.

'I mean, I'm going to destroy him. Hold him down, punch him in the face and then rip off each limb before beating his face in with the soggy ends.'

''K,' I agreed.

'And then I'm going to—'

'Emelie,' Matthew interrupted, reaching down to scoop me up from the floor. 'You're not helping.'

I leaned into my friend and squeezed my toothbrush in one hand, my phone in the other.

'Want to give me that now?' he asked, holding out his hand. I gave him my phone.

'And the toothbrush?'

I reluctantly passed it over.

Matthew and Emelie had crossed London in record time and made it to my door before I'd even moved. I had called Matthew, he had called Emelie and she had called Domino's but they weren't delivering yet. But the thought was there. I'd given them the abridged version of what had happened since I'd got in the cab, punctuated by sniffling, sobbing and general self-pity and, in turn, they'd filled me in on what had happened at their end which basically consisted of Paul knocking Simon on his arse, Matthew watching with admiration and Emelie landing a kick to the crotch while calling him something terrible in French that didn't really translate. When the police were called, my three musketeers had scarpered to the nearest McDonald's and Simon had crawled into a cab. Which was where my story took over.

'It never occurred to me that he would come here,' Matthew said, stroking my hair as I sat on the sofa. 'We were going to come over but you didn't answer the phone so I assumed you were asleep. You always reply if you're not asleep.'

'I did sleep,' I said. 'I'll be all right.'

'I know you will,' he said. 'Of course you will be. You're well rid of that arsehole.'

Was I rid of him? Surely he was the one who had got rid of me? And I wasn't an arsehole. I didn't think.

'You're so going to be all right.' Em was brewing enough tea to quench the thirst of Bristol. 'How about a bath? A bath might feel good.'

'I don't know.' How did someone not know whether or not they wanted a bath? Oh good, I'd gone mad.

'Well, whatever you want to do, just tell us.' Matthew kissed the top of my head and looked at me expectantly. 'Or, you know, sit there in silence and we'll just talk at you. Either way.'

The clock on the DVD player said it was 10.00 a.m. The *Mad Men* DVD has gone from the top of the DVD player. How could it only be 10.00 a.m.? Your life wasn't allowed to go down the shitter before noon on a Saturday, surely. Simon must have taken the *Mad Men* DVD. I should get changed. I actually should have a bath. But a bath would make my foot hurt. I cut my

44

foot. And what was I going to get changed into? Pyjamas would be too pathetic; clothes seemed too optimistic. Maybe I could go back to sleep. It was still early. If this was a normal Saturday and I hadn't just been completely screwed over by the person I thought I was going to spend the rest of my life with, I'd probably still be in bed.

'Rachel, are you thinking things and not saying them out loud?' Matthew asked.

Oh, I was.

'He's taken the *Mad Men* DVDs,' I said eventually. My voice sounded thick and tragic.

'Had you finished watching them?' he asked.

I shook my head.

'*Fils de pute*,' Emelie breathed. 'It's one thing to take a girl's toothpaste, it's another to take her Don Draper—'

'Right, bath first,' he said, giving Emelie the nod. She immediately stopped refilling the kettle and hotfooted it into the bathroom. Taps turning, water running, Emelie swearing when she scalded herself on our hot tap just as she always did. 'OK?'

I really couldn't do much more than nod. It was like I was asleep with my eyes open. Somewhere between two and twenty minutes passed before Emelie called that the bath was ready. Matthew helped me up and gave me a gentle push towards the bathroom.

'You'll feel better, really.' He shut the door before I could start stripping off. Amazing best friend though he was, Matthew was wildly uncomfortable around female nudity. He had been very clear from the outset that he had no interest in seeing so much as a boob from either of us. Emelie had, of course, flashed him within three weeks of living together, but I'd managed to retain my modesty. 'Amazing what a bath can do.'

'It's ready.' Em manoeuvred her way behind me in

my tiny bathroom and pulled as much as my hair as she could into a ponytail on the top of my head. 'Do you need anything?'

'I'm good.' I peeled off my vest and dropped it on the bathroom floor. Five more minutes and it probably would have crawled off my back itself. The skinny jeans were more committed to sticking with me. It took me a good couple of attempts to wrestle my way out of them before Em stepped in with one good hard tug and yanked them down over my knees. Hanging onto the sink, I watched her scoop them up, flash me a grin and then shut the bathroom door behind her. Standing in front of the mirror in my bra and pants, hair piled in a giant pineapple on top of my head, crying, with a bottom lip so low you could hang coat hangers off it, didn't make me feel pathetic at all. Have a bath, Rachel. You'll feel better, Rachel.

Tearing my eyes away from the sex bomb in the mirror, the actual bath itself looked amazing. It was full and overloaded with bubbles, and the steam scented the room with a relaxing, clean smell – lavender and something. All I had to do was get in. One foot, then the other and, soon, I'd smell clean and fresh too. My skin would be pink and soft, the bubbles would tickle the back of my neck and, whether I liked it or not, my muscles would relax and I probably would feel a bit better. Only, I didn't want to feel better. I wanted to wallow and mope and run the events of the last twelve hours over and over in my mind. I didn't want tea; I didn't want baths; I didn't want sympathetic friends. I wanted my boyfriend back. But if I didn't get in the bath, a) Matthew and Emelie would know and b) I would smell. Couldn't hurt to show willing. That was, of course, unless the bath was scorching red hot and took the skin off my foot.

Outside the bathroom, I could hear my friends' emergency summit. The joys of cheap Nineties renovations: the walls in this place were paper thin.

'Right, I'll strip the bed and you take the photos of him down,' I heard Matthew directing. 'I'll bloody boil-wash the bedding. I want every trace of that shit out of this flat before she gets out the bath.'

'Done and done,' Em replied. 'I can't believe he's done this.'

'I know,' he said. 'I really thought this one was going all the way.'

Me and you both, I thought. Me and you both.

'Then thank god he's done it now. Imagine if they'd actually got married.'

'I know, I mean, how do you pretend you're happy for someone marrying a knob-head?'

I sank back into the bath. My friends thought Simon was a knob-head? But we'd been together for five years and they'd never said anything. I knew I was never at risk of either of them trying it on with him – aside from the fact he had a penis, he really wasn't either of their types, but still. They hated him so much they were pleased we'd broken up?

I held a bright pink foot out of the water and checked my toenail polish. It needed changing. Theme of the day. Turning on the cold tap with my toes, I tried to come up with reasons as to why Em and Matthew would dislike Simon so much. Admittedly, they didn't have that much in common. Simon was pretty much a full-time bloke. He watched football, played video games, enjoyed the work of Will Ferrell, the body of Megan Fox and the music of Coldplay. That didn't make him a bad person, just a straight 29-year-old man. Maybe he hadn't always been completely comfortable around Matthew in the early days, but that was just because he didn't have that many gay friends. And maybe he'd been a little too comfortable around Emelie on occasion, but she could hardly pretend she wasn't flattered by his clumsy flirting. And he was a good boyfriend. He cooked, mostly because I couldn't. He did all the man jobs, brought me flowers when he'd worked late, always remembered my birthday, never cancelled on plans, came to every last wedding, birthday and christening I dragged him to without complaint. He wasn't selfish or greedy, he didn't cheat or lie; he was a good man. We were happy. We had a routine. And apparently I wasn't alone in thinking this was going to end in a ring and a white dress and a rousing rendition of 'Oops Upside Your Head' on the floor of a nice hotel somewhere in Surrey.

But no. No ring. No white dress. No group dance number. No explanation. Maybe if I spoke to him. Maybe if I got a real explanation, we could still talk this through. I could still get him back.

After what I hoped was a decent amount of time, I heaved myself out of the still-hot water and towelled down. Matthew wouldn't appreciate the show of skin but, as my dressing gown was in the bedroom, this was the best I could do. I just wanted to put on some clothes, pick up the phone and get this sorted. Matthew and Emelie were standing in the living room, my bedding dumped on the floor between them.

'What now?' I asked, feeling all my newly acquired get-up-and-go get up and go. 'What happened?'

'Nothing.' Emelie looked up, panicked. 'Wow, you look better. Why don't you go and get dressed?'

'I look like shit,' I said, tightening my towel around me. 'What's going on? Did something happen? Did Simon call?'

'No,' she said. Matthew slipped something into his

back pocket and stepped behind Em. 'Get dressed then we'll go and get something to eat. You must be starving.'

They were the worst liars ever.

'What did you just put in your pocket?' I asked Matthew.

'Nothing.' His voice was higher than mine.

'OK, give it here.' I held out my hand. 'Whatever it is, give it.'

Matthew and Emelie looked at each other. Giving him her best Care Bear stare, Em shook her head but he just nodded and pulled a piece of paper out of his back pocket and bit his lip.

'Matthew,' Em put her hand on my shoulder, holding me back, 'don't.'

'Why don't you get dressed first . . .' he started, but I was too fast. Pushing Emelie onto the sofa, I narrowed my eyes, tightened my ponytail and checked the towel. Before jumping onto the sofa and leaping onto Matthew's back. With one arm around his neck, I grabbed at the piece of paper in his hand while he ran around in circles, squealing like a woman.

'Get her off!' he shrieked, lapping the room like a headless chicken.

Emelie rolled back on the sofa, tucking her legs underneath her, hands pressed against her face. I wasn't sure if she was laughing or crying and I really didn't care. All I knew was that I was getting that bloody piece of paper. Matthew was on his fourth lap of the living room when I finally managed to snatch it out of his hand. At the exact same time as I lost my towel. Ignoring the fact that at least three of my neighbours were watching me take a naked piggyback ride around my living room on a six foot four gay man, I slid to the floor and quickly scanned the note.

Matthew came to a standstill, panting far too heavily for a man who worked out as often as he did. 'Jesus H Christ,' he wheezed, eyes wide and a look of complete horror on his face. Em composed herself quickly and wrapped my towel around me. But I wasn't too worried about being naked at that moment. I was far more concerned with the contents of the note.

It was pale and blue and lined with raw, torn edges down one side where it had been ripped from a notebook. My notebook. Someone had been in my bag, ripped a page out of my notebook and left me a very brief message.

Rachel,
I'm sorry. It's not going to work. I'm away with work this week and then I'm moving out.
   Sorry.
   Simon

I read it three more times before looking up at my friends. Matthew's expression was somewhere between traumatized and apologetic. Emelie just looked so incredibly sad. I opened my mouth to say something, anything to break the tension, but all I could manage was a sharp intake of breath. This was it? This was all I got? The note scrunched up too easily, until it was just a few sharp corners in my palm, and when I opened up my fist, it sat there like a tiny ball of nothing. When I opened my eyes, it was still there. A tiny, innocuous piece of paper that had just completely broken my heart.

'What time is it?' I asked.

'Half eleven?' Matthew guessed.

'Is the pub open?'

'It's London,' Em picked up her handbag. 'There's always a pub open somewhere.'

I nodded and clutched my towel closed around me. 'I'll get dressed then.'

Happily, we didn't have to search for long. Within the hour we were safely stashed away in a dark corner of a dark pub up the road from my flat. With a bottle of white wine on the table and three orders of posh fish fingers on their way, we were set up for the afternoon.

'So your options are, we can get drunk, slag him off and stagger home with a kebab.' Matthew ticked off the options on his fingers. 'Or we can get drunk, you can cry and embarrass yourself horribly, then we stagger home with a kebab.'

'Tell me there's an option three.' I tried to stop myself from poking my finger through the hole in my leggings. I'd blame my shoddy ensemble on the speed with which I'd got dressed, but really, most of my clothes were either entirely too much or just a bit shit. No one cared what the make-up artist was wearing on set and I'd developed something of a black leggings, white T-shirt uniform over the last couple of years. Didn't take too much thinking about when you were rummaging in the drawers at five a.m.

'Option three, we get drunk and plan your fabulous new life and then stagger home with a kebab,' Matthew finished.

'Do I get a vote?' Emelie waved her hand in the air. 'I want option three. And I'd also like to suggest pizza instead of kebabs.'

'No, it's got to be kebabs,' Matthew declared. 'This is the only time I can eat one without hating myself afterwards. All calories consumed within forty-eight hours of a break-up are null and void.'

'Any more rules I should know about?' I asked.

'Oh god, loads,' Em chimed in. 'You're allowed two sickies from work, three late-night phone calls to me and himself without any complaining, as much ice cream as you can humanly consume. You get to go on a credit-card-trashing spending spree as long as you only buy completely ridiculous things you'll never wear in six months' time. What else?'

'You're allowed to shag someone completely inappropriate as long as they're really fit,' Matthew added. 'And you never have to call them again.'

'Probably give that one a miss for now,' I said, checking out my split ends. 'I've had a bikini wax, maybe I could just get vajazzled for you?'

'I don't even want to know.' Matthew plucked his iPhone from the selection on the table as it began to vibrate. He took a quick look, swiped at the screen and stared for a moment.

'Are we keeping you from something important?' Em asked so I didn't have to.

'You're always keeping me from something important,' he replied. 'But I still love you. But back to Ms Summers. Have you got a busy week?'

'Working on Monday, the shoot will probably run over to Tuesday,' I shrugged. 'More knicker work. More Ana. More Dan.'

'Then we haven't got long to get you started on the road to recovery.' Em took a tentative sip of her wine. It was a little bit early, even for her, but god bless her for giving it her all. 'And over your hangover.'

'I can't believe he's just gone.' I rested my elbows on the table. 'Is that what usually happens? They just leave?'

'Never had one stick around long enough to answer that question with credibility,' Em admitted. 'I lean towards just not answering calls and texts until they stop trying.'

'And you know, I personally favour the screaming row complete with plate smashing, potential violence and optional public scene at three in the morning,' Matthew said. 'Leaving a note seems terribly middle class and straight to me.'

'What do I do though?' I knocked back half the glass of wine. Start as I meant to go on and all that. 'I mean, after the wine and the kebab. How am I supposed to be single?'

'This isn't your first break-up. You know you're going to get through it.'

'Not my first break-up, but it is the first time I've been dumped.'

The table fell silent. There was a chance I'd lost the sympathy of the room.

'Oh my god, it really is, isn't it?' Matthew breathed. 'You've never been dumped before.'

'And actually,' Em set down her glass and brushed her wild red hair behind her ears, 'what's the longest amount of time you've been single?'

'It's not like I haven't had my fair share of shits,' I defended myself quickly. 'I just always managed to get in there first with the whole "ending it" thing.'

'But you've never really been single, have you?' Matthew was pulling his 'I'm thinking' face. 'You've been with Simon, what, five years?'

'Yep.' I tried to swallow as much wine as I could before we opened the ex files.

'And if I recall correctly, you broke up with Jeremy on the morning of Fat Theresa from Media Studies' wedding and met Simon at the reception.'

Poor fat Theresa from Media Studies – we'd graduated how many years ago and she still couldn't shake the nickname? Actually no, scratch that, she was fat and she was married, why should I feel sorry for her? I wished I was fat and married.

'And before Jeremy it was, who, Will?'

'Will the wanker?' Em clapped her hands. 'Oh, he was funny.'

'No he wasn't, he was a wanker,' I corrected. 'He was cheating on me with about twenty-five different people.'

'And yet you insisted on giving him a chance.' Matthew narrowed his eyes. 'And then another chance. And then another one. I really never understood that one. He wasn't even that hot.'

'I think it was because he wasn't Martin,' I theorized.

'Martin. Lovely, lovely Martin,' Matthew smiled. 'I miss university boyfriends. They were so simple.'

'Yeah, except lovely Martin was shagging his English lecturer,' I reminded them, refilling my wine glass. The booze was definitely necessary.

'And me,' he added. 'But not until afterwards, obvs.'

'I just never thought about it before,' Em waved to the waiter who was aimlessly wandering around the pub with our fish fingers. 'How is it possible that you've never ever been single?'

'Because I'm awesome?' I ventured.

'Aside from the obvious,' she replied. 'Everyone's single at some point.'

I chopped a fish finger in half and dipped it in far too much tomato sauce. Few things made me happier than ironic menus in trendy London pubs because really, nothing made me happier than fish fingers. Why hadn't I ever been single?

'It isn't like I line blokes up,' I said. 'Otherwise we wouldn't be sitting here now, would we?'

'Suppose not,' Matthew was only half paying attention as he built a shaky fish finger sandwich. 'So this is all going to be new to you. Wow.'

'I just can't believe it,' Fish fingers and Sauvignon Blanc went together surprisingly well. 'I thought I was going to be engaged by the end of the year, now I'm just going to be one of those crazy women on the bus wearing too much blusher, carrying a cat in a bag.'

'No you're not,' Em tugged my messy ponytail. 'You're going to be fine. Better than fine. Single and amazing.'

She didn't sound terribly convincing. 'But I just want my life back to normal.'

'No such thing,' Matthew pointed out. 'This is normal now.'

Dropping my fish finger back on the plate, I felt my entire face fall. 'That is so depressing.'

'No it isn't, being single is awesome,' Em said. 'You just have to get through the shitty break-up stuff and then it's going to be great.'

'She's right,' Matthew confirmed. 'When you have a serious boyfriend you just plod on because that's what you do. But it doesn't mean you're happy. Now you've got a chance to find out what makes you happy, not what makes him happy or what you like "as a couple". This is going to be good for you.'

'I just wish there was a guidebook,' I sulked. 'I'm not good with change.'

'There are loads of guidebooks,' he pointed out. 'Millions. It's just, they're all shit. And anyway, you don't need one. You've got us and we're two of the most fabulous single people in London. We're like . . . mentors. We could totally get funding from David Cameron: he loves a mentor.'

In the interests of getting a couple of minutes of

peace and quiet to eat my lunch, I bit my tongue and bit into a chip. I did feel better for getting out of the house, just as I'd felt better for my bath. And I felt better for the wine and for sitting here with two fabulous friends. But I still didn't want to feel better, I just wanted Simon back. Feeling the tears trying to make a comeback, I tried to concentrate on something else. Anything else. It was Saturday: what needed doing?

Since Simon had raped and pillaged my to-do list for his heartfelt 'fuck you' note, I had to start a new one. Pushing aside my lunch, I started to scribble down everything that needed to be done before I went back to work on Tuesday. I still had to go to the post office, still had to get Matthew's birthday card and present. I needed to call someone to look at that damp spot – what, a plasterer? And I should probably call my dad, tell him Simon wasn't going to be coming to the wedding.

'Uh, Rachel?' Matthew piped up.

I looked up, end of the pen in between my teeth. 'Yuh?'

'What exactly are you doing?'

I looked from Matthew to Emelie and back again. Both had forks full of food paused mid-air and both were staring at me like I might be slightly mentally unstable.

'Writing my to-do list?'

'To do what?'

'Stuff?'

'Right.'

I looked at my friends once more then went back to my list. 'It makes me feel better, OK?'

'As long as it includes "get wasted" and "do a rebound guy", I'm fine with it,' Em said after a moment.

'And put "give Emelie all of Simon's *Peep Show* DVDs" on there as well.'

'You can have the DVDs,' I promised. 'But these are actually things that need doing, not a fantasy break-up list.'

'You're already pretty far along the break-up list,' Matthew commented through a mouthful of chips. 'The actual deed is done, someone's punched your ex in the face and you've even had the break-up sex. I usually take ages to embarrass myself with that one.'

'Me too,' Em nodded. 'Break-up sex is the thing that usually drags this out. You're doing very well. Everything ticked off already.'

'Just need to crack on with the being single to-do list then.' I scratched at the label on the wine bottle, trying not to pout. 'Stop shaving your legs, get hammered, die alone with cats.'

'Oh, Rachel,' Em's eyes glittered. 'That's it. We'll write you a to-do list. A single girl's to-do list.'

I tore off a big long strip of label.

'What?'

Em's face was lit up like Blackpool. 'We'll write you a list. Everything you need to do as a single girl. Everything you should have done by now but haven't because you've been hanging around with that twat.'

'It's not a bad idea actually,' Matthew said. 'I'm assuming I'm allowed to contribute despite not actually being a single girl?'

'I don't know,' she mused. 'If I thought you were going to say sniff a bunch of poppers, go out dancing all night and then make out with a hot stranger in a public bathroom, I'd let you have more of a say in this, but you won't because you're a rubbish gay.'

'We don't make out, dear, we're in England.' Matthew topped up her wine while giving her the glaring of a lifetime. 'And just because I'm not falling out of a sauna in Vauxhall at six a.m. every morning having blown three closeted Tory MPs doesn't mean I don't have valuable insight into how to be successfully single.'

'If it'll stop you two from squabbling like children, I'm in,' I relented. 'Come on, then, what's going on this list? Besides cry myself to sleep on Valentine's Day and shag a stranger in the toilets at Inferno's?'

'Oh, I think we can do a lot better than that,' Em promised. 'Much, much better.'

CHAPTER FIVE

After six bags of crisps, three bottles of wine and two hours of heated debate, we were both incredibly drunk and also getting somewhere with The List. And there wasn't a trip to the post office to be seen.

''K, 'K, 'K, let's go through it one last time.' Matthew held up the last napkin on the table that wasn't already covered in discarded drafts of my to-do list. The definitive top ten things I needed to achieve before I could fully declare myself single. I was still unclear as to why Emelie thought learning to juggle would make me a more successful singleton, but still, they were trying. Matthew cleared his throat and – with some ceremony – began. 'Number one, makeover.'

'Not a makeover,' Emelie interrupted. 'It's like, a complete transformation. We're changing your hair, your clothes, your make-up; we're redecorating your flat. Everything.'

'I do need a haircut,' I admitted. And, more importantly, the living room totally needed painting. If I just kept my mouth shut, there was a good chance I was getting two free painter's mates out of this list. Result. 'What's next?'

'Exercise regime,' declared Em to a chorus of groans, taking the pen from Matthew and writing it down. I'd been trying to get this one off the table since two bottles of wine ago. 'No arguing. It's important; you're skinny and shit now but you do not get off your ass unless someone makes you and one day you're going to wake up fat. Trust me, you'll feel amazing.'

'Sitting on the sofa after a long day at work or dragging my arse down to a horrible sweaty box filled with horrible sweaty people who judge me for not being able to do the treadmill for more than ten minutes without falling over and then charge me sixty quid a month for the pleasure?' It was an excuse I'd used on myself for many years. Unfortunately, it looked as though I was much easier to convince than Emelie.

'Then no gym but, dude, this is staying on the list.' She threw her hands out in front of her. 'No arguing. That's the rule. You can't argue with the list.'

'Can't argue with the list,' Matthew concurred. 'Which brings us to point number three. Do something extreme.'

'I think I'd just be happier . . .' Pause to hiccup. '. . . if all the points of the list were more specific. That one's open to a lot of interpretation. And what I consider too extreme might be totally normal to him.' I pointed at Matthew with my glass. Why did my arm seem so heavy all of a sudden?

'Let's not go there,' he shook his head. 'Let's be honest, I have done some truly terrible things with some truly terrible people.'

'It means bungee jump or skydive or something.' Em tried to pull the subject back. 'Not move to Australia or shave your head.'

Bungee jumping. Really? I was beginning to doubt the legitimacy of the list.

'I'm supposed to get over a lifelong fear of heights and do a bungee jump within two weeks?' I dropped my head onto the table. Ew. Sticky. 'This is hard.'

'It's not meant to be easy.' Matthew pulled my head up by my ponytail. 'It's meant to teach you what you're capable of.'

'I thought it was meant to be fun?'

'It will be fun,' they chorused.

Me plus heights did not equal fun. It equalled the need for adult nappies and therapy. I couldn't even go on the rides at Alton Towers without being drunk first. Which, incidentally, it turns out they frown upon. Nothing like throwing up on Oblivion to find out you're not allowed to bring alcohol into an amusement park.

'And you'll be a billion times stronger for it afterwards,' Em said. 'Besides, you're the one who said you wanted to get it all done by your dad's wedding, not us.'

My dad's fourth wedding was coming up in two weeks and I needed a date. There was no way I was going on my own so that my evil Aunt Beverley could ask me where my boyfriend was then go on to tell me all about my cousin's three fabulous children. I was certain she was the one who had told my grandmother on her deathbed that I was a lesbian. But I'd applied that timeframe on the second draft of the list when it still included 'wear high heels every day for a month' and 'learn to cook', not when it involved me risking my life for my friends' amusement. Maybe it would be easier just to rent a male prostitute for the wedding. Maybe we'd fall in love. Maybe it would be a wonderful story to tell our children. Maybe I'd catch something dreadful from him and I'd never be able to actually have children. Hmm. Might just stick with the list.

'Whatever, number four?'

'That's a perfect one actually,' Emelie said. 'Find a

date for your dad's wedding. Let's get you right back out there.'

I had sort of been planning on asking Photographer Dan to do the deed but I let her add it to the list. It had taken an entire packet of Kettle Chips to bargain her down from anonymous sex with a stranger to a date with no required physical contact, so I was just going to shut up. It would still count if it was Dan, wouldn't it? It would still technically be a date to the wedding.

'Number five. Do something he wouldn't approve of,' Em declared. 'And you can't double up on activities so the bungee jump can't count as something he wouldn't approve of. It has to be something totally different.'

'I'm doubling the bungee jump up with number five, scare myself to death.' I pouted for a moment. Simon wasn't a big rules and restrictions kind of a boyfriend. If anything, he was too lazy to try to stop me doing anything, and there wasn't anything I'd ever wanted to do so badly that I'd have tested that. Except . . .

'I want to get a tattoo,' I took the napkin and added it to the list. 'Simon hated tattoos. I worked with this model once and she had this gorgeous cherry blossom thing up her back and ever since then I'd always wanted one but I never got one in case he didn't like it.'

'See? This is such a good idea.' Matthew raised his glass with more success than Emelie before writing 'tattoo' on the napkin. 'Congratulations, you're getting a tattoo.

'Six,' he shouted. We were so embarrassingly drunk for the middle of the afternoon. Sod it: I'd had a very bad day. 'Buy yourself something obscenely expensive and selfish.'

'Like a Vespa scooter you drive once?' I asked as innocently as possible. My hair felt heavy. I needed to stop drinking.

'Exactly like a Vespa scooter you drive once. I don't

62

feel guilty. Think about all the money you're saving in birthday and Christmas presents. And trips to see his shitty family. Wedding presents for his shitty friends. You're completely entitled to buy something that benefits no one but you in the aftermath of a break-up.'

'Can I buy myself something too?' Em asked.

'No,' Matthew replied. 'You're already utterly selfish.'

'Moving on,' I said quickly. 'What else?'

'I still think you need to write the letter.' Em was too drunk to care about Matthew's insults at this point. Thank god. 'I know we took it off the last draft but I think it's a good idea. It's closure.'

'Fine,' I waved my hands in defeat. 'I'll write the bloody letter.' I really didn't want to do this one. Why spend a perfectly good evening stirring up exactly what the rest of the list was trying to suppress? I was supposed to be getting over Simon, not sobbing into a piece of Basildon Bond over how he didn't love me any more. But if it was on the list, it was happening. 'But I get to pick the next one. I want to travel.'

'You can have that.' Em stood up suddenly and not at all steadily. 'I need a wee.'

'That's nice,' Matthew took back the pen as she climbed out from her spot at the back of the table with all the grace of a drunken giraffe and wandered off across to the bar. 'You can have travel but you have to go somewhere you've never been before. Where do you want to go?'

'Can we have this as one of the slightly vague ones?' Names upon names of places tumbled through my mind. There were so many places. 'I only have two weeks after all. And I'm guessing Milton Keynes won't count.'

'You've got to use your passport,' he replied. 'That's the only stipulation. Got to get the stamp in your passport.'

Throwing myself out of a plane to my inevitable squishy death was one thing but travelling somewhere that required a passport inside two weeks? That was ridiculous. And sort of exciting . . .' How am I supposed to manage that?' I challenged, hoping he had a viable suggestion that didn't involve us waking up drunk on a ferry to Norway.

'I don't know, can't you get a job abroad or something?' he shrugged. 'Travelling isn't hard.'

The truth was, I'd been passing up international jobs for so long that my long-suffering and foul-mouthed agent, Veronica, had stopped putting me forward for them. It wasn't as if there was a lack of work or lack of demand for my talents (no point being modest, I was drunk), but I hated to be away from home when Simon was alone. Which seemed really quite stupid now. Maybe I could put in a call. Couldn't hurt.

'I thought of one while I was in the lav,' Em yelled with delight, and threw herself across Matthew to get to her seat. 'You need to buy a vibrator.'

Despite how red my cheeks already were from All The Booze, I felt myself colour up from head to toe. How did she know I didn't have one already?

'How do you know she doesn't have one already?' Matthew asked. Part of me was delighted that he'd read my mind, but part of me was just sort of shocked he hadn't passed out with shame. He must be more drunk than I could tell.

'Trust me,' Em shook her head. 'She doesn't. You don't, right?'

'It's not going on the list,' I said. 'It's not. Going. On. The list.'

'Then you pick one,' she slumped back in her chair. 'I'm out of ideas. Or drunk. Or drunk and out of ideas.'

I knew she was still sulking about not getting

rebound shag on there, but there was no way I was writing that down. I wanted to show willing but I didn't want to have to drop my knickers for some random. In fact, I was fairly certain that there was going to be no knicker-dropping for some time. God, this was getting depressing. Maybe I should reassess my need for a vibrator.

'How about contact my first crush?' I suggested. 'That might be a fun one. There was this boy I was totally in love with when I was fifteen and then he moved away. That would be a learning experience, wouldn't it?'

Em was still pouting but Matthew looked interested. 'I like it,' he declared after a couple of sips of wine. 'Sort of like coming full circle. Show that there was life before knob-face and that there will be life after.'

'I think it's lame,' Emelie said, but it was too late. It was on the list.

'So,' Matthew was counting on his fingers. 'We have makeover, exercise, bungee jump – or similar, tattoo, date for the wedding, buy something obscene that isn't a vibrator, write a letter to knob-face—'

'Do we have to keep calling him that?'

'Yes,' they said simultaneously.

'Buy something, travel somewhere you've never been before, hunt down your first crush—'

'And give him one.'

I spat a mouthful of wine across the table.

'Emelie, you're not helping.' Matthew looked appalled. 'And that's nine.'

'It has to be ten,' I said. 'Can't have nine.'

'You are a mental OCD cow,' he replied. 'Fine. One more.'

We sat staring at each other around the table while my mind ticked over. Learn to play the guitar. Appear on a reality show. Swim with dolphins. Run the marathon. Date someone from each of the armed forces. Shag a boy in a band. Get a pet. Volunteer for a charity. Wow, I really was getting desperate. Before either Matthew or I could venture a suggestion, Emelie broke the silence.

'Break the law,' her eyes glittered. 'You have to break the law.'

'Don't be ridiculous.' I didn't even look up from my lovely, lovely wine. 'I'm not going to break the bloody law.'

'Actually . . .' Matthew said quietly.

'Oh shut up,' I gave him the look. 'I'm not breaking the law. I have never broken the law. I don't even go over the speed limit. You know this.'

'Which is exactly why you're going to do it,' he said, adding it to the bottom of the napkin. 'Amazing.'

'I can't believe you're going along with this.' I rubbed my eyes in disbelief. And to try and make them focus more clearly. 'Seriously? Matthew?'

'We're on the verge of an all-new Rachel Summers,' he replied, dramatically shaking the list to dry the not-even-slightly-wet ink. 'Devil-may-care law breaker and international playgirl, Rachel Summers.'

'Don't forget the tattoos,' I reminded him. 'If I'm going to be crossing over to a life of crime, I'm going to need the prison tats.'

'This is going to be so much fun.' Emelie poked at the last surviving bag of crisps. 'So. Much. Fun.'

I took the napkin from Matthew and studied it carefully before slipping it inside my bag. What was I signing up for?

'For me or you?'

He looked at Em, who, with a little difficulty focusing, looked back.

'Definitely us,' he said, both of them nodding. 'Definitely us.'

Once Emelie had finished drinking the last drops of wine directly out of the bottle, we agreed that was a sign it was time to leave. Helping each other out of our seats, I tried to stand as steadily as possible, walking in something akin to a straight line out of the pub, blinking into the late afternoon sunshine. I looked up at the sky, not quite understanding why it wasn't dark. I'd been up for ages. It had been some time since I'd been this drunk in the day, but I had a horrible feeling that this was the beginning of something, rather than a one-off. I also had a horrible feeling that I was going to puke.

Against all odds, the three of us managed to stagger home in one piece and collapsed on the sofa. Within five minutes, Em and Matthew had passed out. I sat back in the middle of the sofa – Emelie snoring her head off on my shoulder, Matthew curled up against the arm, his feet in my lap – and stared into the mirror in front of me. Nothing had changed. The sofa was still red, my grandmother's mirror still hung over the fireplace and the patch of damp in the corner of the room still needed taking care of. Nothing had changed but everything was different.

Easing myself out of the drunken BFF sandwich, I tiptoed into the kitchen to get some water. Glasses still in the cupboard, cold tap still not really cold enough. I drank one glass straight down, filled another and leaned against the kitchen counter. Everything had seemed OK in the pub. We had my list to think about, fish fingers to eat and, most importantly, wine to drink. But now I was home . . . now it was real. For some reason, I'd half expected Simon just to be lying on the sofa watching *Final Score* and eating Doritos like it was any other Saturday. But he wasn't. The flat was empty. Just like it would be from now on. Almost as soon as the thought settled in my mind and the water had hit my stomach, I felt it coming right back up.

Thank god the flat was small enough for me to make it into the bathroom in time. There were very few things in life I disliked as much as throwing up, which was one of the reasons I really didn't drink that much. Bracing myself against the sink, I washed my face and stared at my reflection in the mirror, trying to convince myself that the hot tears streaming down my face could be easily explained by the fact I'd just puked.

'That's it,' I told myself quietly. I might be drunk at four on a Saturday afternoon but I didn't really want anyone to hear me talking to myself. 'No more tears.'

Granted, that was a statement that carried a lot more credibility on a bottle of Johnson & Johnson's Baby Shampoo, but I had to make myself believe it. I was not going to waste any more tears on someone who had left me a note. I was not going to make myself sick over someone that thought five years could be written off in fewer than four sentences. I was not going to break my heart over someone who could break my heart and still think it was OK to take my toothpaste at the same time. I was done. Heading back into the living room, I curled up on the armchair and shook my head at Drunk and Drunker. It had been a hard day for the both, clearly. Trying not to wake them, I pulled the to-do list out of my bag and read it over again. I would never do any of these things. Never in twenty-nine years would I have considered any of them. I wasn't the kind of girl who would do any of these things but I couldn't help but wonder what kind of girl would.

And I couldn't help but be a little bit excited to find out.

CHAPTER SIX

'Morning.'

I rolled over to feel something soft on the other side of my bed.

'I thought you said no same-sex experience on the list?' Emelie mumbled.

'If I went gay, it wouldn't be with you,' I replied.

Why was Emelie in my bed? Where was Simon? Why did my brain feel as if it had been taken out, tumble dried without so much as a sheet of Bounce and shoved back up my nose?

Oh.

Right.

'It's too early,' I rolled back over and mumbled into my pillowcase. Maybe if I lay face down long enough, I'd smother myself into a coma. That would be a nice long nap, wouldn't it? A lovely, lovely coma. Alternatively, I realized, opening my eyes, I should get up and be with other human beings as there was every chance I wasn't terribly mentally stable. Wishing yourself into a coma isn't usually A Good Thing. 'I want a lie-in.'

'It's almost ten, that is a lie-in,' Em said, bouncing

up and off the bed like an Andrex puppy. 'Today is the first day of your single life. That's exciting. Get. Up.'

I felt the sunshine on my face and made a mental note to pick up some blackout curtains as soon as humanly possible. Silver lining number one.

'I feel like shit.' I pushed my legs over the side of the bed, hoping they would somehow catapult the rest of my body over there. 'Is this part of being single?'

Em stretched and nodded. 'We need to work on your alcohol tolerance. I'll put the kettle on, see if he's up.'

After passing out on the sofa, the rest of last night was a bit of a blur. I remembered waking up around seven, throwing up again, drinking tea, ordering a pizza and playing 'guess who's going to die?' when Matthew turned on *Casualty*. Afternoon hangovers were the worst. Once it had been established that I wasn't going to cry myself to sleep, Matthew and Em had allowed me to slope off to bed. Still, it made a change from my regular Saturday rituals of doing the washing, watching DVDs and going down to Pizza Express early enough to be home for *Match of the Day*.

Yawning, I combed my hair out of my face and tethered it behind my head. Was it weird that yesterday had probably been more fun than any other Saturday in years? Maybe fun wasn't the right word. It was definitely the most interesting.

The hardwood floor in my bedroom was never warm, not even when the sun was streaming in, like it was this morning, but only one foot was cold as I forced myself to stand up. Glancing down, I saw that was because one foot was standing on something white. Something soft. I dropped back onto the bed, releasing the fabric. It was Simon's T-shirt. It must have got thrown under the bed during our Friday night sexcapades. Closing my eyes, I held onto the worn cotton tightly and tried to breathe slowly. The main reason I hadn't cried myself to sleep the night before was that I was just exhausted. My body's first line of self-defence was to shut down and go to sleep, but that wasn't an option today. I was going to have to do something.

'Do you want shower or tea first?' Em stuck her head round the door. 'Matthew's in there now but you can go next if you want?'

I shoved the T-shirt into my pillowcase and stood a bit too quickly. The afternoon hangover had definitely become a morning hangover, bleurgh.

'Shower.' I was desperate to get out of the room, to put some distance between me and that T-shirt. 'Definitely shower.'

Sitting down and drinking tea would inevitably lead to conversation. Conversation would inevitably lead to talking about Simon. Talking about Simon would inevitably lead to my brain exploding. I needed a distraction. A six foot four gay man in a towel wasn't quite what I was thinking about, but that was what I found in the living room. And I supposed it was technically a distraction. Just not as good a distraction as the other thing I found in the living room. My single girl's to-do list.

'Jesus, how much did we drink last night?' Matthew pinched the bridge of his nose and leaned his wet hair back against the sofa. 'Or, actually, all day? I haven't felt this shit in ages.'

'Apparently we need to build up our alcohol tolerance,' I said, trying not to catch sight of myself in the mirror. The glimpse of the scarecrow-cum-crypt-keeper I'd got before I could avert my eyes was bad enough. 'I don't know how she does this.'

I picked up the knackered napkin and took a pit stop on the sofa beside Matthew. His skin was still hot from the shower and he smelled clean. I smelled like evil.

'Planning your bungee jump?' he asked, eyeing the list.

'Maybe not today,' I replied, considering each point. Hmm.

'We really do have some bright ideas when we've had a drink, don't we?'

Makeover. Exercise. Bungee jump. Tattoo. Date for the wedding.

'Still, kept you from slitting your wrists – and, you know, avoiding that in the first twenty-four hours is pretty important.'

Buy something. Write a letter to your ex. Travel. Find your first crush. Break the law.

'Are you safe in the shower this morning or do you need a buddy?' Matthew was still talking. 'I can see from here your legs need shaving and I don't know if you're safe with a blade.'

'I'm safe,' I promised, placing the list on the coffee table and heading purposefully into the shower. 'Trust me.'

The mirror was still misty from Matthew's shower – that boy was always in there for a lifetime, but one quick swipe with my hand revealed just how bad my situation was. Straw-like ponytail, dull skin, yesterday's T-shirt. As a make-up artist, I was used to scrutinizing faces, looking at every different angle, settling for nothing less than perfection, but I never turned that same gaze on myself.

If I was being entirely objective, what did I see? My skin was grey and dull, my eyes red and swollen and the angles of my face were lost in the shadows of my hair. My hair . . . I would never let a model go on set looking this way. It was horrible. Awful. And Simon loved it. Suddenly I couldn't bear the weight of it dragging me down for another second. Without one more look at the girl with the long blonde hair, I opened the bathroom cabinet, grabbed the scissors out of the first-aid kit and hacked away at the ponytail, right underneath the hair tie. When I looked back in the mirror, I had a pair of scissors in one hand and a two-foot-long ponytail in the other.

'MATTHEW.'

'What?' He peeked through the door cautiously. 'Are you naked? Is there a spider? Are you naked?'

I held up both hands as the ponytail holder slipped out of my newly bobbed hair and hit the floor. My new do fluttered defiantly above my shoulders. And not in a good way.

'Oh sweet baby Jesus.' Matthew slapped his hand over his mouth, eyes a mirror of mine. Wide, confused and slightly insane. 'What have you done? EMELIE.'

I could feel my bottom lip starting to tremble but I couldn't let go of the scissors or the hair. And now I'd turned away from the mirror, I didn't dare look back.

'I don't know,' I whispered. 'Have I gone mad?'

'It's a bit *Girl, Interrupted* but it's fine,' he said, reaching out for the scissors. 'Why don't you give those to me, Angelina?'

'Does it look awful?' I already knew the answer to that.

'Rachel,' Emelie appeared behind Matthew. 'Your hair.'

'Looks great,' Putting the scissors on the shelf, high out of my reach, Matthew took the poor ponytail out of my hand. 'I'll just, um, I'll take this.'

'I can't go outside,' I said in a tiny voice. I was too

73

afraid to touch it, in case it fell out. 'I look like a boy. Oh god, I look like Justin Bieber.'

'He looks like a girl anyway,' Em said, putting her arm around my shoulders in a gesture that was both supportive and, ingeniously, kept me away from the mirror. 'It's cute. Really. And you needed a change.'

'I did need a change,' I repeated. My head felt so light, as though it might float up off my shoulders and fly away. 'It was on the list anyway.'

'List?' Em ran her fingers through the ends of my hair. 'You did this because of the list?'

I nodded.

'Riiiight,' she tugged manically on Matthew's sleeve.

'Before you start bungee jumping off the roof, just shower, wash your hair and get dressed,' Matthew commanded, patting Emelie's arm. 'It's going to be OK.'

'Yes, it's going to be OK,' Emelie agreed, poking the ends of my hair. 'Actually, this will save us a lot of time on blow drying.'

Silver lining number two.

Once I'd showered, shampooed and stopped staring at myself in the mirror, I slipped into my fluffy towelling dressing gown and prepared myself for whatever intervention would be waiting for me in the living room. Matthew and Emelie were sitting silently on opposite ends of the sofa, the napkin from the night before in between them.

'So,' Matthew pointed towards the empty armchair. I sat obediently. 'You're taking this list thing seriously, then?'

'Yes?' I shrugged. 'I didn't realize it wasn't serious.'

'You're really going to do a bungee jump? Even though you're so scared of heights I have to come over and change your light bulbs when Simon's out?' Em asked. 'And you're actually going to break the law?'

'Bungee jump or similar,' I reminded them. 'And I suppose so, yes. Somehow. I mean, I'm not going to plan an armed robbery but there must be something faintly criminal that I can get away with. If it's on the list, I'm going to do it. And since you're responsible for most of these, you're going to help me.'

'Rachel, I have to tell you something.' Emelie leaned forward and took my hand in hers. 'I have never in my entire life been so incredibly proud to know you.'

Matthew held his head in his hands. 'As much as I of course second Ms Stevens' support, are you sure this is a good idea? I mean, it's not like I don't know how hard break-ups can be, but throwing yourself into something dramatic might be a bit much.'

'I think I need to throw myself into something a bit dramatic,' I replied. 'I haven't thrown myself into anything even slightly dramatic in a very long time.'

'As long as you don't take such a drastic approach to breaking the law.' He didn't look convinced. 'I don't want to see the two of you on the news after a failed bank heist.'

'We could totally pull off a bank heist,' Em pouted.

I switched from chair to sofa and wrapped my arms around my best friends. 'Which is why I need your help with this,' I explained. 'I want to do this. You're both right, I've never been single, I don't know how to be single. I don't want to walk into my dad's wedding looking like some feeble tramp who spent a fortnight listening to Power Ballads '89 and watching *Bridget Jones's Diary* over and over, crying "that will never happen for me" and eating ice cream until I lapse into a diabetic coma.'

'That would be quite dramatic given that you're not

even diabetic,' Matthew replied. 'You could just not go to your dad's wedding. It's not like there won't be another one.'

'It's just too tragic that it's his fourth and I'm not even engaged.' I ran my fingers through my short, wet hair. 'I'm twenty-eight. Everyone's going to ask if I turned up alone. And you know my brother is going to appear with some random slag he's picked up the night before and everyone's going to think it's charming.'

'Um,' Em coughed awkwardly. 'About your brother.'

'Not now, Stevens,' Matthew gave me a sturdy side hug. 'Right. In that case, we've got a lot of work to do, haven't we?'

'We really have.' I heaved myself off the sofa, catching sight of my hair in the mirror. 'We really, really have.'

One of the benefits of being a make-up artist was a wealth of helpful connections in the beauty world, connections I'd never really taken advantage of before. But with just a few texts, I'd called in enough favours to get an appointment at a great salon with a great stylist inside the hour. Given that Matthew had less than no interest in hair, make-up, clothes or anything else that happened on or to girls, he'd been left in charge of clearing Simon's influence out of the flat: getting the locks changed, clearing out his stuff and preparing for redecoration. I was on a mission. By the end of the day, I wanted to feel like a new woman. If he didn't want me in his life, I didn't want him in mine. There was some debate over whether or not changing the locks was overkill, but the idea of Simon just being able to let himself in whenever he wanted actually made me feel sick to my stomach.

Which was more or less the reaction Tina Morgan,

hair stylist to the stars (if you counted the cast of *Hollyoaks* as stars) had to my hair.

'Fuckin' hell, Summers,' she barked with cigarette-scented laughter as I dropped down in the styling chair. 'Who did this?'

'I did,' I replied, trying not to regret my decision. I'd known Tina since college and she was amazing with hair. Her make-up work erred more towards drunk Pussycat Doll, but when it came to hair? First class.

'Right, you never did do well in the hair modules, did you?' She pulled the strands through her fingers, measuring out the lengths. 'I've been dying to get my hands on your hair for years. Well, you've fucked this up good and proper, haven't you?'

It was a shame that her talent was matched with an almost complete absence of social skills, which I supposed was why she was still curling WAGs' extensions in a salon off Regent Street on Sundays, instead of tending to the A-list in LA. Happily, that was working in my favour today. White-blonde hair, hot pink lipstick, skintight blue jeans and a mouth the size of Guernsey. And I was putting myself in her hands.

'Yes I have, but here's your chance.' I took a deep breath and forced the words out of my mouth. 'I want a complete change. Do whatever you want.'

Tina stepped back from the mirror. 'Anything?'

'Anything,' I said, closing my eyes. 'Just – I want to look good.'

'One guess,' she stepped up to the plate. 'Break-up?'

I bit my lip. 'Not to be a dick, but I don't really want to talk. I just want to look amazing.'

'As if I'd let you leave here looking any other way.' She slapped me round the back of the head. 'So colour, cut, long, short?'

'I want to look completely different,' I said, catching

Emelie's eye in the mirror behind me. She was totally chatting up one of the other stylists. She gave me a surreptitious thumbs-up and carried on. Shameless. 'Just make me look different.'

'Oh, this is going to be fun.' Tina could hardly control the joy in her voice.

One last look at what was left of my long, blonde hair and I closed my eyes. 'Yeah. Everyone keeps telling me that.'

It was another three hours and forty-five minutes of sheer torture before Tina managed to say something that made me smile.

'And you're done.'

Never one to miss an opportunity for drama, she'd had the mirror at my station covered until she'd decided she was finished. Given how much hair I'd lost already that day, I had been a little alarmed to see chunks falling all around me, but not nearly as concerned as I'd been by the variety of colour processes that had been burning my scalp. My hair had never been exposed to anything more aggressive than Sun-In before today. I'd always been a blonde. Not a sexy Brigitte Bardot blonde or anything but definitely blonde. I wasn't mysterious enough to carry off brunette and highlights needed too much attention. What had she done?

'Can I see?' I asked, not sure I actually wanted to. If she pulled the towel off the mirror and my hair was purple, I was going to have to go the full Britney. Shaved head, trashing her car with an umbrella, barefoot eating Cheetos in the loo, everything.

'Ta-da,' she pulled away the towel with a flourish. Woah.

My almost waist-length blonde hair had been

replaced by a short, red bob that bounced around my chin. I hadn't had a fringe since I was a little girl but now there were long, sweeping strands framing a pair of bright blue eyes. Were my eyes always this colour? My hair was red. Really, really red. I looked like someone else. And she looked amazing.

'No way!' Em leapt out of the seat she'd been occupying for the last hour or so while every straight stylist in the place pawed at her in between appointments. 'You're a redhead! Like me!'

'I'd say you're more auburn,' Tina sniffed, still picking up pieces of my hair and dropping them down by my ears. 'Sort of drab your hair, isn't it?'

'*Pouffiasse*,' Emelie remarked with a tight smile.

'Can I touch it?' I asked, raising a tentative hand to my new fringe. 'Is it permanent?'

'It is and you can,' she confirmed. 'You know what, I'm really bloody good at my job.'

I had to admit she was right. 'You are,' I agreed, eyes locked on my own hair, a smile spreading across my face. 'I can't believe it.'

'You're going to need to come in for the roots doing about once a month, same for fringe trims and I'll show you which shampoo and conditioner you need . . .'

Tina continued to outline the aftercare my new hair required but I really wasn't listening. I was too busy imagining my new do swishing around town. Redhead Rachel sipping cocktails at Bourne & Hollingsworth. Redhead Rachel laughing with friends on Primrose Hill. Redhead Rachel and her sophisticated date enjoying dinner at . . . well, somewhere I hadn't been before because I'd never been on a date with a sophisticated man. While she debated with herself over the benefits of a colour-depositing shampoo over a colour-preserving conditioner, I reached into my handbag and pulled out the tatty napkin. Makeover. Done. I placed a very large, very satisfying tick beside Matthew's scrawl and smiled happily. Genuine happiness. It felt strange. And nice.

'Wow. You look amazing.'

Oh. A very handsome man appeared in the mirror at the side of me.

'Seriously, you look beautiful.' He reached out to run his hands through my hair, making me jump. This also felt strange and nice. Behold the power of the list! A strange, hot man was touching me without prompting! So what if it was only because he had a vested professional interest?

'Yuh-huh,' something that was supposed to sound like a laugh but came out sounding a little bit more like a sneezing donkey. Always attractive.

I wasn't good at accepting compliments. It had been a while since I'd had one that wasn't from my mum. OK, so he obviously worked here and was obliged to tell me my hair looked nice, but still. 'I looked shit before.'

'OK then.' His smile faltered slightly. Well, this was only stage one of the transformation. Fail.

'I think you look stunning.' Emelie sidled up to him, slipping her hand up his arm and putting on her best Bambi eyes. 'Doesn't she look beautiful? Doesn't she look as though she was born to be a redhead?'

'She does.' The light reappeared in his eyes at Em's touch. How did she do that? How did anyone flirt successfully? It really was a mystery as to how I'd ever snagged Simon in the first place. Oh wait a minute, no it wasn't. Wedding reception, open bar, awkward snog and then, before I really knew what was happening, we were watching *EastEnders* at his parents' house on Christmas Day. One of my friends was going to have to stop being so bloody selfish and get married soon or I'd be stuck telling hot hairdressers I looked shit until some middle-aged divorced neighbour took pity on me and marched me down the register office.

I went back to marvelling at my hair while Em flirted with Hot Hairdresser, leaving Tina to fuss around with the ends of my new do.

'Seriously, Tina, thanks so much.' Standing up was challenging, after three hours on my arse. My legs felt like jelly. 'If there's anything I can do for you, just let me know.'

'Actually,' she tapped glossy navy blue nails against her fuchsia lips, 'there is something. Dan Fraser. You two are big mates, aren't you?'

I wrinkled my nose. Ooh, even that looked cute with my new hair. More like a playful minx and less like a truffle pig. 'I wouldn't say big mates, but we work together a lot.'

'You've got his number though? He never answers on Facebook.'

I genuinely couldn't cover up my surprise. 'You want Dan's phone number?'

'I want more than his phone number,' she replied. Ew. 'I've had my eye on that for years, but whenever I've managed to get a job with him, he's been in a serious relationship.' She stuck her fingers down her throat and gagged. 'Criminal.'

What was the polite way of telling the woman who'd just totally transformed your hair for free that Dan Fraser hadn't had a girlfriend in the six years I'd known him, serious or otherwise. Mostly because he was too busy shagging every model stupid enough to fall for his lines. Unsurprisingly that was quite a lot of models.

'Yes. He has had a number of very serious girlfriends.'

81

If in doubt, lie.

'But I just thought, you know, fuck it. May as well send him a text outlining exactly what I'm offering. Nothing to lose at this point.'

Oh dear god, she was disgusting. I needed to be more like this.

'Right. Despite his very serious girlfriends?'

'I heard he was shagging Ana now. That can't be serious, can it? She's a right slag.' She pulled the smock from around my shoulders. My T-shirt looked so sad next to my fabulous new hair. 'More of a slag than me.'

'Yeah, she is,' I waited for Tina to be offended. I'd have been waiting a long time. 'She's a massive slag.'

At last, something that wasn't a lie.

'So you've got his number?' Tina raised an eyebrow and pulled an iPhone out of her back pocket. Against my better judgement, I took out mine and read out Dan's number. I knew I felt bad for facilitating this, but I wasn't sure for whom. Tina, who was going to get shot down, or Dan, who was going to have to do the shooting. All I knew was that I really wanted to listen in on the phone call.

'I think maybe the Ana thing might be a bit serious, so don't get – you know – upset if he doesn't reply.' It was the best I could do without screaming 'you deluded cow' in her face. 'And he's not very good at replying to texts.'

Aaand right back to the lies.

'You could always put a good word in for me,' she suggested. 'Tell him how amazing I am.'

'Why not?' Redhead Rachel was a natural. I'd already started lying, may as well carry on.

Hot Hairdresser was giving Em his card, presumably not to organize a shampoo and set, and Tina was already busy texting Dan while I stood quietly in the corner, clutching my bag and hoping the popular girls would hurry up. Oh dear god, it was Year Ten all over again. Except this time I had a bright red bob instead of Sun-In streaks. This was a vast improvement.

'All right, bye then.' I gave Tina an awkward half-hug and grabbed hold of Em's hand. 'Thanks again.'

'You can be my bridesmaid.' She fluffed up my hair one more time. 'As long as you've never shagged him, obviously.'

'Obviously.'

I had more chance of marrying Dan than she did. Matthew had more chance of marrying Dan than she did.

Regent Street on a Sunday. Usually, central London at the weekend was my idea of torture, but this time every single bum-bag-wearing tourist was just another admirer, put on Earth to give my hair a second glance. Those lucky, lucky people. I skipped through the crowds, Emelie pulling me along as she scooted off to some undeclared destination. After a couple of busy minutes, she dragged me down a considerably quieter side road, just off Carnaby Street.

'Dude, that hairdresser was totally into you.' Em wrapped her arms around my neck, after we'd found a few feet of space to claim as our own. 'Didn't you think he was cute?'

'Yes,' I breathed in deeply, trying to get the scent of hair dye out of my lungs. 'But I didn't know what to say. And he was only talking to me to get to you, anyway.'

'Whatever.' She jumped on my back in a half-piggy-back. Which was difficult given that she was at least four inches taller than me. 'You need to get more confidence. That hair does not blush at hot men and fade into the background. It doesn't wear baggy-kneed leggings and drink cheap white wine in The Lexington.'

I looked down at my regulation leggings and T-shirt uniform. She had a point. Oh dear god, there was going to have to be shopping.

I was terrified of shopping.

'Even if we just get you a pair of jeans?' Em bargained.

Jeans were the hardest thing! Nothing was designed to destroy your self-esteem like the purchase of new denim unless you were six feet tall and a size zero.

'Rach, the hair wants new clothes.' She placed a convincing hand on my arm. 'It wants pretty things. It wants to have fun. Your outfit wants to go back to some sort of eastern European country and eat potatoes. Do you feel good about that?'

'There does seem to be a bit of a mismatch.' I caught the coppery tones out of the corner of my eye. My hair was red. 'Maybe a tiny little mini bit of shopping? But not jeans.'

Before she could reply, I spotted a not-at-all unattractive man nudge his not-at-all unattractive friend and give us the eye. Men! Men were looking at us! And not a man who was contractually obliged to compliment me on my hair just because he worked in the salon where it had been coloured!

'Right, this is happening then,' she linked her arm through mine. 'I'm fairly certain that list of yours says complete transformation You look amazing. You look like cocktail dresses, dirty martinis and never paying for dinner. I like.'

'Who knew hair could say so much?' I asked, checking it out in a shop window. Yep, still there. Still red. As was the amazing azure blue silk shift dress staring back at me on the other side of the glass. 'Em, my hair says it wants that dress.'

'Yes it does,' Em agreed. 'And who are we to say no to it?'

Stepping inside the store was like travelling back in time. My experience of shopping in central London was usually limited to a smash and grab through M&S's lingerie department, a speedy spin through Topshop or standing outside Primark while Emelie took one for the team. I wasn't qualified for Primark. This place was something else. Rows of beautiful block colours lined one wall while the other was covered in a million different patterns, each and every one of them glistening silk or crinkling crinolines. It was clearly vintage heaven. And if I was out of my depth in Primark, I wasn't even experienced enough to cross the threshold of this place. Nope, I told myself, daring to press a finger against a delicate lace glove hanging elegantly out of a battered old suitcase. Old Rachel would never have come in here. New Rachel would totally come in here. Which made a lot of sense given that I was actually already inside and someone was going to have to rein in Emelie and her overspending.

'Everything is so beautiful.' My mother had always been a huge advocate of the 'look but don't touch' school of shopping when said shop did not have visible price tags. This was such an establishment, but I just couldn't keep my mitts off the beautiful, beautiful things. 'I just want all of it.'

'The hair has spoken.' Em held up a gorgeous sky blue dress. It looked like silk, square neckline, sleeveless, tiny fitted waist and a flirty flared skirt. It was the kind of dress a girl who always curled the ends of her hair would wear. A girl who matched her handbag to her shoes. In other words, any girl who wasn't me. 'Try this on.'

'Can I open a fitting room for you?' The girl I'd just

described in my head appeared from nowhere and took the dress from Emelie. Resplendent in a coral polka-dot wrap dress, Mary Jane shoes and white ankle socks, she gave us both a grin and nodded for us to follow. 'Are you looking for anything in particular?'

'Everything,' Em answered before I could open my mouth. 'We're in the middle of a bit of a style overhaul.'

'I just coloured my hair,' I added. 'I'm just looking to try some new stuff, dresses aren't usually my thing.'

'We'd better get to changing that quickly then.' The shop girl opened a large wooden door and shooed us inside the changing room. Not that you could really call it a changing room; it was like walking onto a set, all duck-egg blue walls, three huge freestanding mirrors and a pair of overstuffed chaise lounges. My hair was perfectly at home but oh my, how my outfit let me down. I looked back at the dresses hanging outside the changing room. How was this bigger than the entire rest of the shop? It was like a fashion Tardis. 'You've got a great shape for vintage, everything tends to run a little bit small. Let me pull some pieces. Just dresses?'

'Anything you think would work.' My heart raced at the idea that being a short-arse would be paying off for the first time ever, and at the sight of all the different colours being pulled from the racks out front. For someone who only really wore monochrome, this was like taking couture LSD. I saw ice blues, pale yellows, jade greens, stripes, spots, florals and solids, all coming my way.

'Most of these are vintage.' Shop Girl transferred the outfits from her arms to the hanging rail in my changing boudoir. 'But there are a couple of new pieces as well. There's nothing too out there, it's all very wearable, I promise.'

Apparently she could see the fear in my eyes.

'I've just never worn anything so pretty before,' I blushed. It was shameful. 'I don't know when I'd wear it.'

Shop Girl looked as if she understood. Or at least as if she really wanted to make a sale.

'Every day when I get dressed, I think, what do I wish would happen today? And I dress for that. I'd never forgive myself if Johnny Depp walked by and asked me to join him in Monte Carlo for the weekend and I was wearing jeans. I would totally get over being in the queue for a lottery ticket in high heels.'

You couldn't argue with the woman, really.

'I'll be outside, give me a shout when you're done.' She closed the door behind her and left me and Emelie alone to play dress-up.

'Get this one on before I buy it first.' Em threw the sky blue silk at me. 'It might be the prettiest thing I've ever seen.'

Disappearing behind the curtain and trying not to be too ashamed of my old underwear, I slipped into the new dress. The sensation of the cool silk against my skin combined with the sight of my bouncy bob in the mirror was enough to draw out a gasp. The dress was beautiful. My hair was beautiful. My big dark circles and dull skin were not beautiful. But still.

'Oh Rach.' Emelie stuck her head around the curtain. 'You look like a girl.'

'Thanks,' nothing like a backhanded compliment to make you bounce up and down with joy. 'I feel like a girl. It's weird.'

But some sort of girl-instinct kicked in and, before I knew it, I couldn't stop twisting backwards and forwards at the waist, making the dress flare and kick out. I was like a little girl in her birthday frock. Not that my mother had ever put me in a birthday frock for fear of me scratching out her eyes. Even though I was the older sibling, I'd spent most of my childhood in Paul's hand-me-downs. Jeans were much more practical for climbing trees and riding bikes. It was a mystery to everyone how I'd ended up as a make-up artist. Made total sense to me; I'd been living vicariously through my models for years but now I was done with vicarious living. Time to give actual life a go.

'It's beautiful,' I said to the mirror as much to Emelie. 'I just can't imagine wearing it.'

'What's to imagine?' She snapped a pic with her phone. 'You're wearing it. Now take it off and get the yellow one on.'

Emelie and the world's best shop assistant had a point. Just because I'd never worn a dress down to Tesco before didn't mean I couldn't start now. Probably wouldn't pop down to the post office in the floor-length emerald green silk gown Em was admiring at that second, but I could see myself chowing down on a tuna niçoise at Pizza Express in this cute little sundress.

'Oh, look at you,' Shop Girl reappeared at the door. 'Betty and Joan all rolled into one.'

'We're not doing *Mad Men* references right now.' Em drew a finger across her throat. 'But you're so right.'

Betty and Joan all rolled into one? That was a lot of pressure on a girl who wasn't even a Peggy twelve hours ago. The stress must have registered on my face.

'Try on the stripes.' Shop Girl pointed at a black and white number hanging on the rail. 'Your friend and I can pick out some shoes.'

Without even knowing, she'd used Emelie's magic word. That girl would leave me to burn in a fire at the first sniff of a kitten heel. Alone for the first time since I'd GI Jane'd myself, it was strange not to have the buzz of reassuring chatter around me. And it was even stranger to see myself with new hair, a new dress, a new look in my eyes. Time for another professional appraisal. The hair certainly looked better and the dress really did fit me wonderfully. The full fitted skirt was sympathetic to the Christmas weight around my thighs (Christmas weight I was still carrying around in August) and gave me a waist that really wasn't there. The colour, a pale dandelion yellow decorated with tiny white swallows, was so delicate, and the fitted bodice, with its tiny little tie-up straps, would really only work on someone who didn't have much in the way of boobs, e.g. me. At last, a reward for suffering the nickname 'Two Backs Summers' all through Year Eleven. I could honestly say, in this dress, I looked pretty. And since the biggest compliment I could pay any of my old outfits was 'I'm not naked', that pretty much meant I was sold. On pretty much everything.

A couple of hours and one awkward conversation with the credit-card company regarding 'unusual activity' later, Emelie and I fell through my front door, heavy on shopping bags and light on cash.

'What do you want to do now?' Em asked, cheeks flushed with the fever of her own spending spree. 'Dinner?'

'Nope,' I yelled from the hallway. 'Matthew, bin bag.'

Without stopping to take off my shoes, I marched straight into the bedroom and pulled open my wardrobe door. I was a woman on a mission. Jeans. T-shirts. Baggy jumpers. Old dresses that were too big, too small or just OK. Not a single thing I'd want to be seen out in should I run into Ryan Reynolds down the post office. Which meant they all had to go in the bin. Where was the point in chopping my hair off, going red, buying enough new dresses to clothe India and then falling back into old, sloppy, knackered habits? With one swoop, I scooped all my old clothes into the bag Matthew was holding open, before moving on to the drawers. I didn't flinch once. There wasn't a single item that tugged at my heartstrings and begged to stay. Nothing sentimental, nothing so pretty it begged for a second chance. Every single item accepted defeat gracefully. It didn't take long before everything baggy and saggy and slightly grey was gone, replaced by a rainbow of pretty dresses, each and every one worthy of an A-list lover. It was a miracle.

In the living room, Matthew had worked a miracle of his own. By the time Emelie and I arrived home, the locks had been changed, all of the photos had been taken down and every single thing of Simon's was stashed in bin bags in the basement. If only he was down there with them. It was impressive; the place was spotless. Turned out I actually owned a vacuum cleaner. You learn something new every day . . .

'You really do look great.' Matthew made me do one more spin in the last outfit of my impromptu fashion show before patting the seat next to him on the sofa. I really didn't want to sit down: my new hair had made me slightly hyper. 'I love it.'

'It's not too Cheryl after the divorce?'

'Not even,' he reassured me. 'You feel all right?'

'Good actually.' I looked around the room trying to work out what had been hidden away. It was strange, like playing that party game when your mum takes something away from the tray and you have to remember what's gone but you can't see it, you just know something is missing. 'Honestly, really good.'

'Hold that thought,' he lied. 'So, while you were out, Simon called.'

And just like that, I felt like shit again.

'Did you speak to him?' I tucked my hair behind my ears. Dress schmess.

'He wasn't really up for a chat.' He immediately brushed my hair out from behind my ears. 'He wants you to give him a ring.'

'Right.'

I peered down at my shoes. I needed new shoes to go with my new hair. And a new boyfriend to go with my new shoes. And we'd fall madly in love, get engaged and have a baby and then bump into Simon at a mutual friend's barbecue and he would realize what a mistake he'd made because I was so wonderful and then he would throw himself off a bridge. Now who could I get to have a barbecue?

'You don't have to call him,' Matthew interrupted my fantasy. 'I could call him. Or you can just text him or something.'

'Or I could call him and tell him what a massive bastard he is,' Em shouted from the kitchen. I could hear the kettle whistling already. She was ever so good. 'Please let me call him.'

'No, I can do it,' I stood up. And sat back down. And stood up again. 'I can call him.'

There was no question as to whether I physically had the ability to call him, but the mental strength? Turned out to be something else altogether. As I dialled the number, I started to feel a little bit sick. But it had to be done. Not calling him now I knew he'd been in touch meant it would just be hanging over my head. My pretty red head. I could do this. Redhead Rachel could absolutely do this. Emelie delivered my cup of tea and Matthew sat beside me on the sofa, a warm, heavy hand on my shoulder. It was only a phone call. Just because the last words we'd exchanged were during awkward break-up sex that I'd thought was awkward reunion sex at the time, why would this be strange?

'Simon speaking.' He answered, as always, on the second ring.

'S'me.'

Eloquent to the last.

'Rachel?'

My voice was a little bit quieter than I would have liked but I wasn't crying. Because I had red hair. Redheads didn't cry. Probably.

'Yep, Matthew said you called?'

If only we had videophones. He couldn't even see how amazing I looked. Actually, this was an iPhone, we did have videophones . . . could I still hang up and call back?

'I can't actually talk at the moment,' he sounded tired. 'I'm busy now. I called you an hour ago.'

'Well, we could maybe get a coffee later or something?' I replied before I lost my nerve. That's what people who weren't about to slash their wrists because their boyfriend had callously abandoned their five-year relationship did, wasn't it? Coffee. Coffee or gin. Or whiskey. Mmm, whiskey.

'Or a drink?'

'Tonight?' he asked.

'Yes. Tonight.' Was it me, or did he sound a bit annoyed?

'Can't. Busy.' Definitely sounded a bit annoyed.

This was an interesting turn of events.

'Right, because Matthew said you wanted me to call you back.' I tried to control my increasing rage. Redheads had fiery tempers; this absolutely was not my fault. 'What's going on?'

'I'll email you tomorrow, I'm at the cinema,' he

hissed. 'And I'm going away on this work thing tomorrow so it'll be the afternoon probably.'

He was at the cinema? He was at the bloody cinema? He had run out on me *and* stolen my toothpaste and now he was at the cinema? Couldn't help but wonder what he was seeing.

'I don't want an email, I want you to talk to me.' Red Rum. Red Rum. 'What is going on, Simon?'

'Look, I'm hanging up,' he upgraded from a bit annoyed to pissed off. 'I just wanted to stop round and get some stuff but it's a bit bloody late now. There's nothing to talk about.'

'There's nothing to talk about?' Ooh, that was a bit shrill. 'Five years together, you suddenly up and decide you're done with it and there's nothing to talk about?'

'Rach, we're not getting back together,' he replied. 'There's no point trying to get me out for a drink, thinking I'll change my mind and come home. So just give it a rest.'

I was actually lost for words.

But Simon clearly wasn't. 'I'm twenty-nine. I don't want to "talk about it",' he ranted. For someone who didn't want to talk to me, he seemed to have a lot to say right now. 'I don't want to go to Sainsbury's because it's Saturday; I don't want to have tea with your mum because it's Monday, and maybe, I don't want to get married, knock out two kids and die from complete and utter boredom. Now I've got to go, I'll email you tomorrow or we'll talk when I get back.'

I hung up before he could and handed my phone to Matthew.

'What a knob.' Matthew tightened his grip on my shoulder. 'What a complete and utter knob.'

'Calm down, Matthew, he can't talk, he's at the cinema,' I replied with bitter sarcasm.

I didn't know what to do with myself. I could call back but he'd probably just turned his phone off. I could go to every cinema in London and check every single screen until I found the bastard, but then what? Obviously there was always physical violence but I'd heard that was never the answer. Even if it did feel like it would give me some degree of satisfaction.

'I know what to do.' Em passed me a cup of tea and a bottle of Jack Daniel's. I held both for a moment. Whiskey was the last thing I needed but I'd seen *Mad Men*. Or at least some of *Mad Men*. Redheads didn't drink tea when they were angry, they drank whiskey. 'Get your laptop.'

I pulled out my ancient MacBook, inherited from Paul two upgrades ago, and passed it to Em before alternating sips of tea and bourbon. Hmm, interesting. Tennessee Tea. Probably wouldn't catch on.

'Matthew here has done a fabulous job of getting all knob-head's stuff out of the flat but now it's exorcism time.'

'Are we going to burn his stuff?' I asked hopefully.

'We're not going pyro just yet.' She opened up the computer and brought up Facebook. 'We're going to erase him.'

'You're going to kill him?'

'Not quite,' she replied. 'You're going to wipe him out of your digital existence. You don't want to be logging in and seeing his face every two seconds. Oh. Ah.'

'What's up?' Tetley's and Jack Daniel's actually went together better than I'd expected.

'He's sort of beaten me to it.' She turned the screen to face me.

Simon Mitchell is no longer listed as being in a relationship.

Simon Mitchell is now listed as single.

I couldn't stop staring.

'He's changed his relationship status on Facebook?' I said. 'What is he, fourteen?'

'You've got quite a lot of messages.' Matthew pointed to the little red icon at the top of the screen. 'Maybe we need to go on a bit of a PR offensive.'

'No.' Another swig. 'I'm not lowering myself. I just want him gone.'

'Done and done.' Em started tapping away at the keyboard.

It was one thing for him to want to break up with me; it was another thing for him to tell the entire internet. It was just so final, so public. Surely I should be allowed to tell people in my own time? Now 417 people had all been told that I'd been dumped without my knowledge. I hadn't even told my mum. Bloody Facebook – and to think I'd enjoyed *The Social Network*. Clearly Mark Zuckerberg was the devil. Why was there no official rule about this? Or at least an episode of *Sex and the City*? There was an episode about what to do when your boyfriend has skid-marks; there should definitely be one about this. It's not as if they achieved anything else in the second movie – surely ten minutes could have been spent clarifying what happens when your boyfriend tells the entire internet that he's finished with you. Carrie Bradshaw, you selfish cow.

'What can we do?' Matthew asked softly.

It took me a moment to realize that the strange raspy sound I could hear was my own breathing.

'Not a lot anyone can do, is there?' I bit my lip. 'I'm just going to have to get on with things.' One more swig. 'And get drunk.'

Forty-eight hours ago I'd been a blonde with a

boyfriend. Now I was a redhead with a drinking problem. By Saturday, I was set to be a bald smackhead.

Amazing.

By the time I'd calmed down, Emelie had removed any and all traces of Simon from my computer. Matthew had blocked his number from my mobile and I was drunk. Em had said I needed to build up my alcohol tolerance.

'I need to go to bed,' I announced, halfway into the third episode of *Come Dine with Me*. 'I have work in the morning.'

'Me too.' Em rubbed her forehead, looking a little the worse for wear. She'd really gone above and beyond and joined me in the Jack Daniel's fest. 'I have a meeting. Somewhere. About Kitty Kitty lunchboxes. I really should go home and get some clothes.'

Matthew was reading text messages on his phone and pulling a concerned face. I knew better than to ask who they were from and what they were about. I rarely ever felt better for the graphic detail he was happy to share.

It hadn't even occurred to me that Emelie hadn't actually left my side since Saturday morning. Matthew as well. If I hadn't been feeling so shit, I'd be feeling pretty lucky.

'You don't have to stay, either of you.' I barrelled into her, face first, with a massive hug. 'I'll be fine.'

'I don't have work – if she's leaving, I'm staying.' Matthew looked at me, looked at his phone and then back at me. 'You're stuck with me tonight.'

'I do love you.' I clambered across Em to give him a hug all of his own. 'You're both amazing.'

'True,' he said, ruffling my hair. 'It's definitely bedtime for you though, red.'

'I have red hair,' I said, rolling off his lap into a graceful pile on the floor. 'It's pretty.'

'And tomorrow you're going to have a hangover.' He picked me up and carried me off into the bedroom. If only he were my lovely boyfriend and not a giant homosexual. Sob. 'What time do you need to get up?'

'Dan's collecting me at ten,' I said with a hiccup. 'S'fine.'

'I'll get you up at nine then.' He deposited me on the bed and kissed me on the forehead. 'See you in the morning.'

'Night,' I whispered to the empty room. All I wanted to do was sleep. Sleep and have the room stop spinning. I rolled onto my front and shoved my face into the pillow. My fingers found the soft edges of Simon's abandoned T-shirt and curled around it, holding on tight. This would be the first night I was actually sleeping alone. I mean, Simon hadn't been in my bed before Friday for weeks, but he hadn't moved out. His things were there even if he wasn't. I'd never felt alone. The bed had never felt so big and cold and empty. These were the things I was going to have to get used to. Going to bed alone. Getting up alone. Remembering to buy loo roll because no one else would. All my single friends complained about these things endlessly but I'd never given them a second thought. Food shopping stopped being a trolley full of ingredients just waiting to become a wonderful shared meal, and instead became an embarrassing Ben & Jerry's, Lean Cuisine for one basket full of shame. There was no one to drive you to the doctor's. You missed endless movies because you had no one to go with. Not that singledom had slowed Simon's movie-going habits down.

Accepting that sleep wasn't coming any time soon, I turned on the bedside light and grabbed my handbag from its home on the back of the bedroom door. The bag had been my mum's in the Eighties. It was electric blue, slouchy leather with an endless number of pockets and ridiculously long shoulder strap that meant it bounced around my knees when I walked. Emelie hated it. Matthew once referred to it as a transsexual horse's nosebag. I loved it. I had ever since my dad had given it to my mum for Christmas when I was four. It had gone in the loft after the divorce, along with everything else that meant bad memories, but she'd finally handed it over two years ago during an epic clear-out and I hadn't let it out of my sight since. It might have helped if my sight had been a bit clearer at that exact moment. I swung the bag off its peg with more momentum than necessary, succeeding in not only getting the bag free but also knocking myself in the nose and flat on my back across the bed into the bargain. I should probably stop carrying around three different books in there when I blatantly wasn't reading any of them.

'Bugger,' I muttered, pressing my palm against my eye.

The pain slipped away quickly, either because it wasn't as bad a knock as I thought or because I'd drunk half a bottle of bourbon – either way, I opened my eye and peered inside my bag. Inside, safely tucked away in one of the many zippered pockets, was my list. As far as I could tell, I had two options. I could lie here in the dark, drunk and depressed, and ultimately cry myself to sleep, or I could remind myself that I wasn't a hopeless, boring loser. Or, at least, that I didn't have to be.

There was something a little sordid about changing your life based on notes scribbled on a wine-stained napkin but, right at this second, it was either Simon's T-shirt or Rachel's list. And, to be fair, I'd had my life changed for me already. This was just a case of taking control. Today the hair, tomorrow the world.

I took my phone from the nightstand and quickly snapped a photo of myself in all my red-haired glory. God bless the iPhone 4 and its frontal camera. Why was I even so upset? Hadn't I cut off my hair today? Hadn't I coloured it red? Hadn't I called Simon without breaking down and begging him to come back to me? I wasn't boring. I wasn't whatever he thought I was. With one last hiccup, I pulled Simon's T-shirt out from under the pillow and tossed it to the end of the bed. Tomorrow, it was going in the bin with all the rest of the rubbish. Clutching the list to my chest, I lay back and closed my eyes. I'd fall asleep eventually, I just had to lie here and . . .

CHAPTER SEVEN

'Come on, Red, get up.'

Being violently shaken by a gay man was never one of my favourite ways to wake up on a Monday morning, let alone when I'd consumed half a bottle of Jack Daniel's the night before.

'No, Nana needs her rest,' I groaned, pulling a pillow over my face. 'Jesus Christ, my head hurts.'

I prised open one eye to see a man's hand setting a mug of tea down by my face. Trying to open the other eye only resulted in a shooting pain all the way down my cheekbone. And I was fairly certain there was some drool. Definitely a little drool.

'Oh. My. God.'

'Yeah,' Matthew said slowly. 'You might want to have a shower and, I don't know, put on all your make-up before you leave the house.'

'I never wear make-up for work,' I protested, trying to sip the tea without making the throbbing in my eye socket any worse.

'I know,' he replied in the same voice. 'Little bit of cover up here maybe.'

He reached out and poked my face.

'Shit!' I wailed, spilling the tea all over the floor.

'What did you do to yourself last night?' Matthew pulled back one of the curtains to get a better look at my eye. Not that there was a shortage of offensively cheery sunshine in the first place. 'Looks like you snuck out to Fight Club.'

'I don't know, hit myself with my bag,' I groaned, trying to turn over on to my back but feeling like an upturned cockroach. No, a cockroach was too good for how I felt. Maybe if someone had stood on that cockroach with a Doc Marten boot and pulled three of its legs off before kicking it across the room. And this was why I never drank whiskey. 'What time is it?'

'Just after nine?' He squinted at the clock on my phone. 'You've got an hour.'

'But I need to sleep.' I tried to sit up too quickly and got a wave of nausea for my trouble. Back down, Rachel. 'Or be sick. And then sleep.'

'Want me to call in sick? You know you get a couple of freebies in this sitch.'

I tried to imagine Dan's reaction to my pulling a sickie an hour before the shoot was due to start. If he didn't come round here and kill me, my agent surely would.

'No, I have to go.' My stomach churned promisingly as I writhed around onto my back. 'Did Em get home OK?'

'Em didn't get home, she's on the sofa,' he replied. 'It's not pretty. I'm cutting you both off the whiskey.'

'Doesn't she have a meeting?' Bed was so lovely. Why couldn't we all just live in bed? Just because it hadn't really worked out for John Lennon didn't mean the idea wasn't worth revisiting.

'Oh, she's up,' Matthew said with a smile. 'She's been up most of the night. I recommend that you try not to breathe on your way through the living room. Or use your eyes. Or make any noise. In fact, it might be worth going outside and breaking in through the back window.'

With a sour expression, I rolled off the bed and into the living room, immediately regretting my decision.

'Oh, Emelie.' I couldn't quite believe the sight on my sofa. Her long curly hair was a tangled mess and her face was actually grey. I chose not to look in the bucket tucked away round the corner.

'Oh god,' Em actually put her hand up to her mouth. 'You look like shit.'

That, coming from her?

'Have you seen yourself?' I asked. 'Pot. Kettle. Black. Look into it.'

'I've banished all reflective surfaces.' She closed her eyes and pointed towards the hot pink throw she'd tossed over the mirror above the fireplace. 'Don't make too much noise. Or, you know, any. I don't want to have to kill you.'

'Understood.'

Pinballing from wall to wall, I thrust myself forward towards the bathroom. Maybe I should have opted for the no-mirror too. There wasn't a lot of time to do anything with myself: Dan was supposed to be picking me up in less than an hour. I gently washed my face and then set to covering up the bruise under my eye. It wasn't too bad. After a couple of minutes with my civilian make-up kit – some Laura Mercier Secret Camouflage, a dab of Touche Éclat and far too much Nars Orgasm blush to perk up my deathly pallor – and I was passable. At least I hadn't had to bust out the hard stuff, no face and body foundation necessary. I did not look good, but at least I didn't look as though I'd been punched in the face and then spent all night awake, drinking whiskey.

* * *

'Fuck me,' Dan said, staring straight at me and not even slightly at the road. He'd arrived dead on the dot of ten and, so far, it was all I could do not to puke in his car. 'What happened to you?'

'I cut my hair, I dyed my hair and I got drunk,' I burbled, leaning into the cool glass of the window, trying to maintain short, shallow breaths. 'Next?'

'It's just, you know, a new look,' he pointed out. 'Not that it's not good. Who did it?'

'Tina Morgan,' I replied. 'It took three and a half hours of Tina Morgan.'

'That's weird.' He was still paying slightly more attention to my hair than I would like given that we were in a moving vehicle. 'She left me the most bizarre voicemail yesterday. Seriously, like, obscene.'

I didn't have the energy to laugh but I did force out a smirk. 'I think she likes you.'

'Well, she's not really my type,' he replied, looking out through the windshield just long enough to hurl abuse at the Ford Mondeo in front.

'Not everyone can be a supermodel, Daniel,' I said, closing my eyes behind my giant Aviators. It couldn't be much further. It couldn't be much further.

'What makes you say that?' he asked.

'Because you're shagging Ana?' I waited for a cheeky shrug or sarky comment but it didn't come. In fact he didn't say anything.

'Because you flirt with every single model on every single shoot?'

We drove in silence for a few minutes. Happily, I was too hungover to feel awkward.

'Flirting with the models is part of the job,' he said eventually. 'There's nothing to it; it's just on-set banter.'

'And off-set shagging,' I added.

We paused at traffic lights and he turned in his seat to face me. 'Who exactly am I meant to have shagged?'

'Aside from Ana?' I challenged.

'Aside from Ana,' he replied.

'So you are seeing her then?'

Another long pause, another set of traffic lights. Driving through London really was an arse-ache.

He put the handbrake on and stretched one arm out of the window, the other out behind my headrest. 'What if I am?'

'What if you are?' I said, staring at the road ahead. Well, there went my easy date for dad's wedding. Arses.

'You're always bouncing around, telling everyone how wonderful it is to have a boyfriend.' He pulled off as the lights changed. 'Ooh, me and Simon are going to Croatia; ooh, me and Simon are decorating the spare room; oh no, I couldn't possibly come out for drinks, I have to get home to Simon.'

I had to say, I did not care for his impression of me.

'Do I really do that?' I was actually fairly certain I didn't say 'ooh' half as often.

Dan shrugged and pushed his curly brown hair out of his eyes. 'I don't know. You must or I wouldn't say it, would I?'

'Well, no need to worry about that any more,' I muttered into the window. Why weren't we there yet? I just wanted to get through the day, go home and look at my list. I had thought maybe today was an 'angry letter' day, but perhaps it was more of a 'breaking the law' sort of a Monday. Putting a photographer through his own windscreen face first was illegal, wasn't it?

'Dumped you, has he?' Dan laughed.

'Yes,' I said simply. 'Don't you read Facebook?'

Dan let out a noise that sounded suspiciously like someone had kicked a seal in the face. I turned a tiny bit in my seat to take a look at him. I'd never, ever seen that man look more uncomfortable. And given that I'd seen him shooting several extraordinarily homoerotic D&G underwear campaigns, that was quite the statement.

He looked at me, staring through the darkened lenses of my glasses for just a second too long.

'What?' I asked. I would have shrugged for effect but I definitely would have vommed on him.

'Nothing.'

He looked away and turned the radio on. I closed my eyes and concentrated on remaining vomit-free for the rest of the journey.

Against all laws of god and man, I managed not to throw up in the car and Dan managed to get us to the studio on time. Far more predictably, Ana was, as always, late, and after our fun in-car conversations, two minutes' peace was wonderful. But not nearly long enough.

'Raquel!'

Before I'd even had time to crack out the Vita Coco, all six feet of supermodel blew into the studio, ignoring all of the lackeys and hangers-on who were paid to tolerate her, and flew right at me. Her perfume was almost enough to push me right over the edge – super-models still wore Angel? As she got closer, I stopped being able to smell it and actually began to taste it. And if she hugged me any tighter, my children would be born smelling of it.

'Oh, honey, I feel a-maze-ing this morning.' She released her vice-like grip, shook her coat off onto the floor and dropped into my chair. Why had I designed the make-up as a neutral lip and a smoky eye? There was absolutely no need for her to shut up. Aside from it being polite but, obviously, social graces had passed this one by. 'So you know I was seeing that guy? The one with all the money? Well, I decided I couldn't be arsed with him any more, called him Friday night to tell him we're over and he shows up at my flat with this!'

She thrust her hand into my face, almost taking my eye out with an offensively large rock: a large, sparkly, clear diamond mounted on an equally sparkly, diamond-encrusted band. It took me a couple of minutes to focus on it for fear of being blinded. I drew back and switched my attention from the giant engagement ring to her ridiculously beautiful face.

Now was it possible to choke someone to death with a foundation sponge?

'Of course, I told him I'm not marrying him because, you know, I'm maybe in love with someone else.' She gave me a knowing look and then craned her neck around to sigh loudly in Dan's general direction. 'But he would not take it back. Idiot. But it's so pretty. What do you think?'

I had nothing. I opened my mouth a couple of times and closed it again. No snappy comebacks, no congratulations, not even an angry rant. I was dry. All those years of working on zoning out and, finally, my brain was doing it automatically. A-maze-ing.

'Hey Ana, can I please get you on the bed to block out some shots?' Dan placed an arm in the middle of her back and guided her away.

'You know you can get me on a bed to do anything,' she purred at Dan before casting me a filthy look. First-class flirt she might be, but she was still pissed off she was having to block out her own shots and I could tell she somehow knew this was my fault, even if she wasn't sure how.

'Thank you,' I mouthed at Dan, sitting myself in the make-up chair. He nodded and turned the cameras on

Ana, who was already tossing back her hair and contorting herself into positions entirely inappropriate for a multipack of white cotton hip-huggers.

Don't let this get to you, I told myself; this is just how she is. It's not as if I really want to tear off her eyelids with a Shu Uemura eyelash curler or anything. Except I sort of did. How could anyone want to marry her? And not just anyone, but someone who could afford to put on her finger a diamond big enough to host an episode of *Dancing on Ice*. Ana was beautiful but she was also a cheat, the world's most fickle woman and – not to be a bitch but – she was also really, really stupid. I was loyal, faithful and not *that* stupid. I wouldn't be challenging Stephen Hawking to a game of *Countdown* or anything, but I wasn't a thicko. Still, I couldn't even hold down a boyfriend who bought me a Nintendo Wii for Christmas. At least I could understand her and Dan: they were the male and female equivalents of each other. But imagine someone normal and rich wanting to marry her?

Trying not to freak out, I opened up my make-up case and concentrated on pulling out various bits and pieces. Primer, foundation, concealer, blusher, bronzer, highlighter . . . there was an awful lot of make-up involved in making a girl look like she was naturally beautiful, and today it was going to feel like awfully hard work.

Two cartons of Vita Coco, a Berocca and two ibuprofen later, I was feeling, if not looking, something like human, and Ana was back in the make-up chair, considerably more subdued. She dropped her chin and looked at me as if I was a three-legged dog.

'Dan says you're sad,' she said, sporting her 'concerned' face. 'And that I'm not supposed to ask you about it.'

I gave her a half-smile, pushed back her hair and

started cleansing as gently as possible given my limited coordination.

'So why are you sad?' she asked after half a second.

'I broke up with my boyfriend,' I said, methodically sweeping at her face with a cotton-wool pad.

'Is that why you're wearing a wig?'

God, Allah, Buddha, Angelina Jolie and all the saints, someone give me the strength not to punch this woman in the face.

'It's not a wig, it's my hair.'

'Ohhh.' She tugged on a strand just to make sure while a very high-pitched squeal went off in my brain. 'Well, that sucks. And I'm here waving my beautiful, beautiful ring in your face. I'm so dumb.'

'You weren't to know.' I calmly moved on to moisturizer. And failed to correct her.

'It is definitely over?' She peeped at me with one eye.

'It is.'

'Good,' she clapped her hands together and giggled. Faintly heartless but – as I'd already established – she wasn't the sharpest knife in the drawer.

'You were with that guy for way too long,' she explained, catching my wrists in her hands. 'I have so many boyfriends for you. Rich ones. Or hot ones. I am not sure if there are any hot, rich ones who would want . . . be your type. Which do you prefer?'

I breathed out and reminded myself how incredibly in control I was.

'Ana, leave it.'

'No, really, you should just like, totally hook up with some random guy,' she went on. 'You're not ugly or anything. Just let me call one of my guys. I'm a one-man gal from now on anyway. They'll totally take you out if I ask them to, don't worry. You need a really good seeing-to, that's all.'

'For fuck's sake, can you shut up?' I asked her quietly.

'Raquel?' Ana looked up at me with wounded eyes. 'I'm only trying to help.'

'Well, you're not fucking helping,' I said in a much, much louder voice. So loud, in fact, that everyone in the room seemingly looked up at once. 'I don't need you telling me what I need, you overpaid, oversexed, vacuous cow.'

It was hardly a noisy set before I went the full Christian Bale, but you could have heard a pin drop after I dropped the F-bomb. Ana cowered in the chair in front of me.

'Raquel?'

'Oh, just fuck off.' I threw my hands up into the air, showering her in loose powder. 'My name is not Raquel. It isn't. You know it isn't. My name is Rachel. You know my name is Rachel. Why, oh why, oh why, do you insist on calling me Raquel? You stupid, stupid woman. Have all those laxatives finally eaten away at your brain?'

I'd seen Ana burst into tears over a broken nail twice, so I was relatively impressed that it took her until my laxative comment to crack this time. Of course that could be because that was the one that really hit too close to home. With a quivering lower lip, she instinctively held a finger under each eye to protect her eyelash extensions and ran wailing from the set.

'What?' I spun around, managing not to fall over. Score. 'Have I missed something? Is she off the laxatives?'

'What are you doing?' Dan was at my side in a heartbeat, as both stylists, the hairdresser and even Collin ran after Ana. 'What was that?'

'Don't,' I warned. 'She was totally out of order.'

'No, you're out of order, you can't talk to the model like that – you know that.'

We stared each other down for a moment. I had no idea what Dan was thinking but I was genuinely considering kicking him in the balls. I'd had enough.

'But she can talk to me however she likes?' Instead I kicked the loose powder pot right across the set and slammed my open make-up kit shut. 'Not any more. I'm not a doormat, Dan. Do you know how incredibly boring it is putting up with everyone else's shit?'

'Oh what, so you've dyed your hair red and now you're all feisty?' he scoffed. 'Whatever.'

'Maybe I'm just bored of smiling and nodding,' I ranted. 'Maybe I'm bored of listening to her brainless shit. Maybe I'm bored of putting up with your twatty attitude. Maybe I'm bored of being bored by all of this.'

He grabbed hold of my wrist as I turned to walk away. 'Twatty attitude?' Dan's brown eyes were as wide as saucers. 'I've got a twatty attitude? Can you hear yourself?'

'Forget it, Dan.' I shook him off without a second thought. 'I'm out.'

Grabbing my make-up case, I followed in Ana's footsteps out through the door, ignored the desperate sobbing coming from behind the bathroom door and took a sharp turn to the right. It took a moment, but eventually I found a quiet spot in the car park, hidden behind two giant SUVs, and just sat for a moment. In the background, my brain was still whizzing around at a million miles an hour but, right in the front of my mind, everything was blank. I had no idea what I was doing and I *always* knew what I was doing. That was my thing! But even though I was confused and scared and was almost certain I was going to puke, somehow, somewhere, I felt good. I felt strong. I felt as if I could do anything.

'Yo, Red, what's up?'

And as if by magic, the universe stepped in to trample all over my rage buzz. Tina Morgan stood over me, packet of Marlboro Lights in one hand, lighter in the other.

'Having a fag?' She and I had studied together, worked side-by-side at shows and generally competed for work since college. I knew her shoe size, her natural hair colour and her mother's middle name, but she hadn't paused for breath long enough to find out I didn't smoke.

'Nope,' If I refused to make eye contact with it maybe it would just go away.

'Hair still looks good.' It was a compliment directed more at herself than me.

'Thanks.' I knew I was being rude but I just didn't have the patience.

'Hot in there today.' She kicked my foot repeatedly until I looked up, at which point I was greeted with a big cheesy grin and a dramatic wave. 'Earth to Rachel, 'kin hell woman, look lively.'

I smiled.

'Gotcha, not in the mood.' She parked her sizeable arse down next to mine and sparked up. 'Smoke?'

I shook my head.

'I can't be arsed today if I'm honest.' She took a long drag and exhaled upwards, a light summer breeze springing up just in time to blow it back in my face. 'Thank god I'm done for the day. I hate doing studio shit when it's nice out.'

I nodded.

'Wouldn't mind so much if I were you, though. Can't believe you didn't tell me you're working with him today.' She gave a low groan that quite frankly made me feel incredibly uncomfortable. 'He's bloody beautiful. His arms are like the size of my thighs. And I do not have skinny thighs.'

I shrugged.

'Seriously, you must have had a go on it, though?' She pursed her heavily coloured-in lips and narrowed her eyes in what I took to be an expression of lust. God help any man on the receiving end of that face. It was terrifying. 'Or is he a blondes man? He hasn't replied to my voicemail yet.'

Combo shake and shrug.

'He's here today though?' she asked, fluffing out her crop. 'Maybe I should just go and see him?'

'Actually, you could do one better,' I said, my brain suddenly remembering what it was for. 'I just got a call about a thing and I need to leave. Could you fill in for me? Dan would love you for it.'

'Seriously?' Tina looked at her watch, at me and then back at her watch. 'Why do you have to leave?'

'My dog is dead,' I said without thinking.

'Shit, god, yeah, go.' She stood up, stamped out her cigarette and hustled me to my feet. 'Was it sick?'

'Yes. She had TB.' My eyes were wide with wonder at my own lies. TB? Really, Rachel?

'Dogs can get TB? In London?' Tina asked, following me back into the studio. I passed her the make-up design sheet and threw everything into my case. It wasn't as if she was that bad a make-up artist. No really. Sort of. 'Do you have it?'

'No,' I looked at her like she was stupid, then remembered I was the one who had just lied about my nonexistent dog dying of TB. 'Anyway, thanks for this. I'll make sure you get paid for it, obviously.'

'Obviously,' she muttered, clearly regretting her magnanimous moment. 'I'll email you.'

'Thanks so much,' I said, dragging my half-zipped case out behind me on one wheel. I just had to get out of there. I wasn't sure exactly what I was going to do but I had to leave. But of course, for that to happen, the universe would have to be on my side in some small way. I had just made it out of the car park, and was hiding beneath a staircase waiting for a cab, when I spotted Dan stomping up the road, clutching a packet of Monster Munch with a face like thunder.

'What are you doing?' He pointed to my case with his non-pickled onion-y finger. 'We're not even nearly done and you've got some serious apologizing to do before she'll even come back out of the bog.'

'I'm really sorry but I have to go.' I clutched my phone tightly. Could an iPhone double up as a weapon? I had a feeling there wasn't a bludgeoning app. 'I can't do this.'

'Rachel, you're working,' Dan explained slowly. 'You can't just leave. Remember? You make the model look pretty, then I take the photos and then we all get paid.'

'I found a replacement,' I said, ignoring his hilarious tone. 'She's got my directions, she's fine. You'll be fine.'

'This morning you said you were fine,' he countered, still not happy. 'And now you're screaming at super-models. I can't believe you're being so unprofessional.'

Which was the straw that broke the camel's back. Stupid camel.

'Shut up.' I felt hot tears pouring madly down my face from nowhere. 'I turned up today, I did my best and I fucked up, I know, but I've sorted it out, OK? Just let me go home, you arsehole. I can't be here right now.'

'Thank god you're going,' Dan shouted as I pushed past him to the shiny black people-carrier that was pulling up on the pavement. 'Seriously, I don't want you on my set in this state. Sort yourself out, woman.'

I turned to stare at him, open-mouthed. This was a new height of dickishness, even for him. 'Oh my god, you absolute bastard.' I marched over, yanked the bag of Monster Munch out of his hand and stomped on it with what I hoped was a defiant and not-at-all crazy stare. Before I could deliver what would doubtlessly have been an epic one-liner, he reached out and pushed my hair back from my face.

'Did he hit you?' he said, touching my cheek.

'What?' I couldn't help but be a bit confused. Did who hit me? Why was he touching me? Why was my cheekbone tingling?

'You have a black eye. Did he hit you?' He let go of my face and made fists with both hands. Very manly. 'Your ex?'

If it was at all possible, Dan looked even angrier than he had before I trod on his Monster Munch. I just wished I'd stolen them to eat in the car. My stomach was screaming out for a tasty corn snack.

'What are you talking about?' I was very, very concerned that Dan had gone insane, until I went to wipe wet face and came away with a handful of Touche Éclat. Ah. Black eye.

'No one hit me.' I had been trying so hard not to touch my make-up, I'd completely forgotten about the actual injury. Apparently YSL was not waterproof. Which you'd think I'd know. 'I'm a moron. I hit myself. With a bag.'

Dan eyed me suspiciously for another moment. 'That does sound like something you would do,' he relented. 'But, you can't just fucking leave. Just have a minute and we'll get this done as soon as, then you and I will go to the pub and get hammered and,' he reached out and took hold of my hand, 'we'll talk.'

'I told you, I got a replacement.' I shook him off and pushed my case into the back seat of the taxi. 'I don't need to get hammered, I just need some sleep and I'll be fine tomorrow.'

'Rachel, you can't go.' He grabbed hold of the car door as I threw myself in after my case. 'I mean, if you go now, I don't want you on my set tomorrow.'

'All right Dan, can we crack on?' Tina hung out the door and pouted. 'I don't know how much longer I can talk about The Hills with this brainless tart.'

I shook my head at the speed of Ana's recovery.

'That's your replacement?' He didn't even turn around to look at her. 'Myra Hindley?'

I was fairly certain he was just making a very unfortunate reference to her hairdo so I ignored him.

'Did she tell you about her dead dog?' I could see Tina was trying to look sympathetic, but she was wearing so much make-up, she just sort of looked like a sad tranny.

'Get out of the car,' Dan demanded, kicking the bumper with his Adidas Sambas.

'I'm sorry, I won't do this again.' I could feel the tears threatening again. I wasn't sure if it was the hangover, the humiliation or Tina's face, but I had to leave. 'I'll be back in the morning.'

'No, you won't, because you're off my set.' Dan slammed the door shut. 'You're fired.'

'What?' I spluttered out the window. 'You can't fire me.'

'All right, maybe I can't fire you, but I can throw you off my fucking set. Now do you mind, me and Andy Warhol here are going to be busy correcting your mistakes.' He turned and vanished back inside, Tina giving me a thumbs-up and following.

CHAPTER EIGHT

'That arsehole.' My mum dropped a slightly floppy slice of Pollo ad Astra pizza back onto the plate and stared at me, mouth hanging wide open. 'Why didn't you ring me?'

My mother and I had a standing Monday evening dinner date at Pizza Express. We varied location to mix it up a bit but, like her daughter, Sarah Summers was a creature of habit. On the odd occasion, we'd have company, Simon, Emelie or Matthew usually. If it was a blue moon, my brother might come too and, given my circumstances, he had promised he'd come along this evening. We'd been there for an hour. No sign of him.

'Because you would have called him an arsehole and then spent the next three hours telling me how you always knew he wasn't the one for me and how this would just be the universe's way of making room for my soul mate,' I said, dunking a dough ball in garlic butter. Really, there were times when Pizza Express was all you needed in life. I'd picked the relatively swanky Kentish Town restaurant to try and make it feel like a slightly classier occasion. It wasn't really working.

'I would not,' Mum denied vehemently, still not ready to tackle her posh chicken pizza.

'Really?'

'I may, *may*, have suggested that everything happens for a reason,' she relented. 'And actually, I know you're going to tell me to shut up, but your Saturn return is due to start very soon so this does make a lot of sense. Clearing the decks, presenting you with the problems you need to solve. Saturn always brings important life lessons.'

I was always being told how I was the double of my mum – and it was true. Or at least it was before my makeover. We had the same blonde hair, the same blue eyes, and I'd inherited her short stature, small boobs and dry sense of humour. What hadn't been passed down was her inexhaustible ability to believe the best in people. She and my dad had met as teenagers, fallen hopelessly in love, married within months, knocked out me and my brother and then, after fifteen years of heart-warming bliss, my dad met a new soul mate – his secretary – and sodded off to start a new family. Five years later, he did it again. In two weeks, he'd be on to 'The One' version 4.0. Despite this, Mum remained the eternal optimist and they were still best friends. Seriously, he regularly popped round for a cup of tea and, on occasion, she had been known to babysit my step-siblings. It was too weird for me but they seemed pretty happy with the arrangement. Didn't mean she wasn't completely mentally imbalanced though. Once upon a time, my mum was just a generally chipper person. Then she started saying things like 'everything happens for a reason', followed by 'the universe always gives you what you need as long as you are open to its energies'. For the last two years, she had moved onto the hard stuff – astrology. It wasn't a pretty addiction but my brother refused to be involved in the intervention. I had explained that his 'whatever makes her happy' rationale would only lead her onto worse things – Tarot cards, Ouija boards, psychics – astrology was clearly a gateway drug.

'He was always going to be a problem though, you knew that,' she said after a couple minutes of silence/ me ignoring her last comment.

'I did?'

I did?

'Don't you remember when I did your charts? You being a Virgo and him a Scorpio, it was never going to work out. Opposite ends of the spectrum: nightmare.' She tucked back into her pizza, much happier. It was the astrological equivalent of 'I told you so'.

'If we could knock off the Mystic Meg shit, that'd be fab,' I said without really thinking.

'Rachel Lulu Summers,' Mum replied just as fast. 'We don't swear in restaurants.'

My mother's appalling taste in music meant that I had suffered for twenty-eight years. Literally a handful of people knew my middle name and two of them were dead. Natural causes, though: I hadn't done anything dramatic.

'It's not a restaurant, it's a Pizza Express,' I sulked. I was a *South Park* T-shirt and pair of DMs away from reverting to my 15-year-old self. If I wasn't careful, she was going to stop my pocket money. Or cry. Which I just couldn't take.

'I'm sorry,' I said, taking a deep breath. 'I'm out of order. You're right, it is for the best.'

She faux-yawned and wiped at her eyes. In case I didn't feel horrible enough.

'And I won't swear if you won't use the "L" word.' I pushed the plate of dough balls over to her. The most dramatic apology known to man.

'So you're all right then?' she asked, giving her nose a scratch. 'I know you've got Emelie and Matthew and whatever, but you don't have to pretend with me.'

'I'm not all right,' I admitted quietly. 'And it's the first time I haven't been, which is why it's horrible. But I will be. Got to be, haven't I?'

'I don't know where you get that attitude from,' Mum marvelled, sitting back in her seat and smiling. 'You've always been so rational. So level-headed.'

'Your stellar parenting, I'm sure,' I smiled back, nabbing one of the dough balls.

'I'm sure.' She raised an eyebrow.

'I thought I was the sarcastic one.' I chased the dough ball with a bite of her pizza. I always got the worst food envy.

'Everything I know I learned from you,' she promised. 'But seriously, it's definitely over? With Simon?'

'Definitely definitely.' I looked around the room at all the happy couples enjoying their mid-priced Monday-night pizza extravaganza. Bastards. 'I mean, he's gone. He left a note. We talked yesterday.'

My mum really didn't need to know about our pre-note activities. If only because she'd probably hunt Simon down and kill him like a dog. Which might be fun but I'd hate to have to go and visit her in prison. They were always in the middle of nowhere.

'I just can't believe he'd be so heartless.' She shook her head, tight blonde pixie crop shimmering under the overhead lighting. 'But you know Scorpios, emotionally detached. Cold.'

'Mother.'

'Sorry.'

I stared at the last dough ball until Mum sighed and pushed the plate back over to my side of the table. 'I don't know why you bother ordering anything else.

You haven't touched your salad.' She pointed with her fork. Manners. 'You are eating, aren't you?'

'I am,' I said, actually trying to think when I'd last consumed solid food. That wasn't pizza. 'Matthew and Emelie are taking care of me. They're not going to let me starve or fall asleep in the bath or do anything silly.'

'Yeah, I can see that with the hair,' she replied, spearing a giant piece of tuna from my plate. 'I can't believe you did that to yourself.'

'You don't like it?' I modelled my new bob, flourishing my hands for full effect. 'It's been a bit of a hit with everyone else.'

'Well obviously it looks lovely,' Mum backtracked. 'I meant I'm not convinced they're going to stop you from doing something stupid. As evidenced by the fact that you just told me you hacked your own hair off with kitchen scissors. Your lovely hair.' She sighed loudly and took a moment's silence for my butchered mullet.

'First-aid scissors,' I corrected. 'And it's fine. It's on my list.'

'You and your silly life.' She looked lovingly across the table. For one silly minute, I thought it was at me.

'Get into an argument with your hairdresser?' I felt a hard slap on the back of my head. 'Or are they retraining Freddie Krueger? Care in the community or something?'

'Paul,' I greeted my brother with the enthusiasm he deserved. Given that he was ninety-seven minutes late.

'All right Mum?' He ducked down to give our beaming mother a kiss on the cheek. While Mum and I could stand in for Doc and Dopey if the panto was running out of dwarves, Paul was the opposite. He was massive, almost as tall as Matthew and, given that Matthew was practically a genetic freak, that was big. But his height was about the only thing he'd got from our dad. Two sets of bright blue eyes looked at me from across the table now, and Paul's blond crop was almost the same style as our mum's. Which was a bit weird actually.

'So, she told you she's been dumped?' Paul picked up a fork and started on my salad. And Mum's pizza. At the same time.

'Paul, try and be a bit more sensitive to your sister.' Mum slapped his arm and tried not to smile. I tried not to point out that she hadn't told him not to swear in the restaurant. I also tried to remember I wasn't 15. 'She's had her heart broken.'

'Yeah Paul, I've had my heart broken,' I parroted, taking my salad back, even though I didn't want it. I had sharing issues with him, dating back to a LEGO incident in 1989. 'Piss off.'

'Language, Rachel.'

'Yeah, language, Rachel.'

The last time I'd laid eyes on Paul he was knocking Simon on his arse outside The Phoenix but despite that Neanderthal display of brotherly love, he was clearly not giving an inch tonight.

'So how's your young lady?' Mum asked politely, signalling the waiter so Paul could order a drink. Young lady was code for 'that girl whose voice I heard in the background the last time I called you and I can't remember her name probably because you didn't know it'. 'Well?'

'Uh, fine,' Paul evaded the question and stretched with a yawn. 'I'm knackered. Work's been a bitch lately.'

'You work in a shop selling skateboards,' I said flatly. 'And said shop doesn't open until midday. How are you knackered?'

'Busy time of year?' He gave a waitress a grin as she delivered his beer. It was horrifying to watch him in action. Until he was 21, Paul had been a skinny runt of a boy, obsessed with computer games and *Lord of the Rings*. Then something terrible had happened to him – the combination of a pneumatic blonde called Theresa and some late-blooming testosterone. For the last ten years, he'd been burning through girls faster than he'd read the Harry Potter books. Both activities that took place under cover of darkness, in his bedroom and away from prying eyes.

'Hang on, I need to answer this,' Mum pulled a buzzing mobile out of her handbag and waved it at us. 'I've applied to go on this goddess workshop in Glastonbury this weekend. I think this is the head of the coven.'

'The coven?' I repeated loudly and not with love. Paul kicked me under the table and shook his head, but Mum hadn't even noticed. She was too busy running for the door, the phone to one ear, her hand pressed against the other.

'The coven?' I hissed at my brother. 'Seriously? And you don't think she's going too far with it?'

'You are so hard on her,' he said between mouthfuls of tuna. 'I don't know why you can't just let her do what makes her happy.'

'Because she's not really happy, it's a distraction,' I replied. 'How can she be happy on her own, still convinced that Dad's going to wake up one day and be like, "ooh, I think I might actually still be in love with Sarah, goodbye current wife".'

'You say it like it would be the most random thing he's ever done,' Paul deadpanned.

'Touché,' I said, turning my glass of wine thoughtfully. 'But I just wish she would find somebody. I hate her being on her own.'

'Maybe she doesn't want to be with somebody. Some people don't,' he replied. 'I don't.'

'You're always with someone,' I argued. 'I've never ever known you without a girl.'

'Not the same,' he said, still eyeing up the waitress. 'I like having someone around, yeah, but I'm not knocking myself out to get married. I have fun and when it stops being fun, we're done.'

'And you wonder why I won't let you go out with Emelie,' I said, looking him hard in the eye.

'Who's to say I wouldn't feel differently about her?' He was enjoying this far too much.

'I so don't understand why someone wouldn't want to be in a relationship. Isn't it better to have one person to share your life with? To be there at the end of the day?' I leaned over the table and nicked a cherry tomato back. 'Someone who puts you first?'

'I put me first,' Paul said. 'And there's always someone there when I need them.'

'Yeah, I don't mean the first lucky girl to answer your "who wants a shag?" text on a Friday night.' I pulled a face when he laughed.

'It's not always a Friday but they are lucky. A quality collection of London's finest ladies, handpicked for their high IQs, conversational abilities and readiness to turn up at mine at one a.m.'

'You are disgusting, you know that don't you?' I took my salad back. Maturity be damned.

'Whatever,' he said, grabbing the remains of Mum's pizza. 'I'm just saying, not everyone wants to be you. Not everyone needs a boyfriend or girlfriend to be happy. We're not all after two-point-four children and a semi in the suburbs.'

'I like having a boyfriend,' I said defensively. 'There's nothing wrong with that.'

'And there's nothing wrong with Mum wanting to be on her own.' Paul finished the pizza and wiped his hands on his jeans. 'And there's nothing wrong with me playing the field until I decide otherwise.'

'As long as you're not playing the field with my best friend, I don't care.' I handed him a napkin. 'It's this whole "I hang around until it's not fun" attitude. That's not how relationships work, you know.'

Paul shook his head and tore his eyes away from the waitress for a moment. It looked as if he was about to give me the benefit of his extra years of dating wisdom. Or burp.

'I get it, I do. We haven't got the best parental role models as far as relationships go, but you can't go around telling everyone you're right and they're wrong just because you don't want to be on your own.'

'You make me sound like a monogamy nazi,' I complained. There was no way he was going to Psych 101 me on this. Just because I didn't like the idea of casual dating didn't mean I was a complete mental.

'Your walk does have a touch of goose step to it,' he said, standing up. 'At least she's not on her fourth wedding. Are you going?'

'I've got to, haven't I? You're not going to bail?'

'No, I'm going.' He looked as though he'd been caught with his hand in the biscuit tin. 'You haven't talked to Emelie?'

'Of course I've talked to Emelie?' I narrowed my eyes. 'Since when do you talk to Emelie?'

'Just the other night.' He waved off my glare. 'After I'd punched your boyfriend in the face, we were talking.'

'No, that's fine.' Mum wandered back up to the table and absently stroked my head as she sat down, knocking half my hair down. 'Yes, tomorrow. Blessed be.'

Blessed bloody be.

I necked my wine and then smiled as genuinely as I could. Which probably wasn't very.

'Anything you want to say?' Mum asked.

'Paul ate all your pizza.'

'Rachel thinks you need a boyfriend.'

'Children,' my mum sighed, rubbing her forehead. 'I should have just had cats.'

'Couldn't agree more,' Paul raised his glass.

'Or at least stopped at one,' I replied. 'Definitely just stopped at one.'

After Paul had finished eating everyone else's dessert and I'd spent a thrilling twenty minutes on the 214, trying to avoid making eye contact with a scary-looking tramp obsessed with singing the entire score of *The Little Mermaid*, I arrived home to an empty flat. A Post-it from Emelie explained she'd had to go home to pick up some stuff she needed for work and that she'd be back late. An overly complicated note from Matthew told me he needed to pop home to do something but to call if I needed him, which I assumed meant he had a date and didn't know how to tell me. Well, I had to be home alone sooner or later.

Sitting on the sofa, staring at the blank TV screen, my brain immediately started flitting around. I wondered what Simon was doing, how I was going to pay the mortgage on my own, when I was supposed to start my next job, why I still hadn't bought Matthew a birthday card for Saturday. There was only one way to shut myself up when my brain started messing around like this. Picking my handbag up from the floor where I'd dropped it, I fished around for my notebook. A list would help. I had so much to do. Except, well, I didn't. Without a boyfriend to look after, there really wasn't anything that *had* to be done – besides my to-do list.

Feeling one of Emelie's promised horrible lows

coming on, along with an almost overwhelming urge to call Simon and beg him to come back to me, I picked up my phone. My hair couldn't take another funny turn. And he had said to call if I needed him.

'What's up?' Matthew answered on the first ring.

'My mother's a witch and my brother's an arsehole.'

'That's a terrible thing to say about your mother.'

'She's joining a coven,' I said, holding the list up in front of me. I was literally itching to put a line through something. 'I got fired today.'

'Did you finally punch Dan?'

'I called the model a vacuous oversexed cow,' I yawned.

'Is she?' I heard some skittering around in the background, hushed words not meant for me.

'Yes, but that's not the point,' I replied. 'I'm blaming my hair. It makes me do things I would never do. Is someone there? Is this a bad time?'

'Yes but no, I can talk.' He clearly didn't want to go into more detail than that so I let it go. 'And you're missing a vital fact here. You did do them. Maybe you've always been a redhead at heart. Have you done anything on the list today?'

'No,' I admitted. 'I really wanted to, but what with work and dinner with my mum, today just sort of got away from me.'

'It's not too late: go out and rob an off-licence,' he half joked. 'Are you OK?'

'Yeah, I thought I might do some online shopping or something.' I pulled my laptop out and rested it on my belly. 'I still need a dress for my dad's wedding. Because I need all the dresses now. And, you know, actual clothes.'

'You did get a bit brutal on the clear-out,' he replied. 'Women have got the internet all wrong, though. You know it's really only there for porn, don't you?'

'And for ex-boyfriends to humiliate you in an international public forum.'

'And for that,' he admitted. 'You haven't been stalking him, have you? Take it from an expert, it's really not worth it.'

In the first few post-break-up weeks, Matthew hadn't taken his eyes off his phone. He was constantly checking for status updates, new photos, comments on friends' notes. Anything that would give him a clue as to what was happening in Stephen's life now that he was no longer a part of it. It was like cyber self-harm. And only now could I completely understand the draw.

'You know what we could do.' I opened Facebook, hovered over the search box and then began typing in a name. 'We could stalk my first crush instead.'

'Oh, we could.' Matthew suddenly sounded animated on the other end of the line. 'That would be fun and nonviolent.'

'I was sixteen,' I reminisced. 'His name was Ethan, he was gorgeous and I was completely obsessed with him. It was all very late Nineties David Beckham. He was the trumpet player in this summer orchestra thing I went to.'

'You were in an orchestra?' I could hear him trying not to giggle. I hoped it was at me and not as a reaction to anything else that might be happening in his flat. 'What did you play?'

'Violin. Badly.'

'Did that put Ethan off?'

'I can't imagine it helped. I sounded like I was trying to abuse a guinea pig. I'm not musically gifted.'

'I know, I've heard you sing.' Matthew yawned again. 'So tell me all about Ethan. I'm determined to get you giddy about boys again.'

'I'm going to get giddy over someone I haven't seen in twelve years?'

'Can't hurt, can it? Little bit of catching up, maybe some online flirting. This is what Facebook is for.'

'I thought it was for your boyfriend to let the entire world know you're a used-up old hag who he wouldn't spit on even if you were on fire.'

'What's his surname?'

'Harrison, Ethan Harrison.' I tapped his name into the little box at the top of the page. 'He was blond. And gorgeous.'

'Like me.'

I let that one sit for a moment.

'Did you kiss him? Did he touch you up behind the bike sheds?'

'Sadly not.' I refused to look at the numbers racking up underneath my shopping cart. 'He wasn't interested, I think he thought I was a boy. I did look a bit like a boy, to be fair. It was all very traumatic, lots of longing looks through the music stand, scribbling his name inside my composition books.'

'I've got about seventy-five thousand Ethan Harrisons,' Matthew complained. 'Can we narrow this down a bit?'

'Yep,' I nodded, looking at the same search page. 'He went to a different school to do his A levels and then I heard he'd moved to Canada with his family, so try that maybe? I must have cried for about a month after he left, just lay in my room listening to "Eternal Flame" on a loop.'

'Mine was Ryan Smith,' Matthew replied. 'He was such a thug. I've never been able to listen to "My Heart Will Go On" since. What a heartbreaker. Are you still looking?'

'Yes,' I was down to five possibilities. This was actually quite exciting.

'Well? Which one is he?'

'He's the beautiful one,' I said, clicking on a photo of my schoolgirl crush, all grown up. 'He's the really, really hot one. Dark blond hair, Labrador in the background, father of my future children.'

'You had good taste as a teenager,' he whistled down the phone. 'He is hot. And I never agree with you on boys.'

'What do I do?' I was actually stroking the screen. 'What do I do?'

'I don't know,' Matthew admitted. 'If you were gay, you'd just send him an obscene photo and hope he sends one back.'

'You're such a cliché.' I refused to let him sully this moment with the love of my life. 'But since I can't whizz off a picture of my genitals, what should I do?'

'Cold shower and bed?' Not a bad suggestion given the circumstances. This was when I realized the more open-to-interpretation items of the to-do list were going to be dissatisfying. Objectives should always be clearly defined.

'Do I message him?' I couldn't get anything out of his profile other than this single pic, but already I'd painted an entire life for him. The photo was just him and the dog, so I'd decided he was definitely single and the dog meant he was loving and outdoorsy. I could be outdoorsy. If I put my mind to it. The shorts and T-shirt combo didn't give a lot away and he'd cut his hair, which was fair, given that curtains weren't really a big trend in the twenty-first century. Thank god. But his eyes were the same. His smile was the same. I suddenly had a very strong urge to start doodling Rachel 4 Ethan and listening to 'Hit Me Baby (One More Time)'. Not that I'd bought that single. Or subsequent album. Cough.

'Do you want to message him?' Matthew asked.

'I want to marry him I replied.'

'Maybe save that for the second message,' Matthew advised.

I was still filling in Ethan's life story when I heard a key in the door. 'Emelie's home,' I told him. 'I'd better go and put the kettle on.'

'I know when I'm not needed,' he said. 'Use me up then cast me aside as soon as your wife gets home.'

'Oh, just go back to whatever sordid scenario you were working up to before I called,' I cackled down the phone. 'Bye Matthew. Bye nameless, faceless stranger.'

'Quite, love to the wife.' He hung up.

I closed up my laptop and took out the napkin. I was going to have to be careful with it – only two days old and it was already looking a little fragile. But then, it was only two days old and I had already completed two of the tasks. My transformation was well under way and I had found my first crush.

'Em?' I shouted from the sofa. 'What are you doing in the morning?'

'Sleeping,' she said, clutching the doorframe as though she was about to collapse. 'I had to go to that Kitty Kitty meeting this afternoon. Honestly, I thought I was going to die. Pretty sure I would have approved Kitty Kitty branded nukes today if they'd painted them Pantone 264 and stuck a cat on them. You?'

'I called a supermodel a vacuous oversexed cow and got kicked off the set,' I said, twisting around to see her properly.

'Fine,' she turned around and disappeared into the spare room. 'You win.'

CHAPTER NINE

'I can't believe we're doing this,' Emelie groaned, her head between her knees as she stretched out in Regent's Park. 'Exercising is on your to-do list, not mine.'

'You're being supportive,' I reminded her. 'And besides, I said I'd come to your crappy charity do with you tomorrow night so shut up and run.'

'It's not even nine a.m., you torturous mare.' She pulled an incredibly unattractive face and then set off ahead of me. 'Why running? Why not something nice and relaxing like yoga?'

'Do you recall when we destroyed my excellent credit rating inside two hours on Sunday?' I reminded her. 'When the lovely man in Topshop had to call my bank to confirm it was in fact me who was determined to bankrupt myself in such a short space of time?'

'I have never been so proud of you,' she nodded.

'Well, be proud of the fact that I already owned trainers and this doesn't cost us anything.'

She twisted her head from side to side. 'Fair enough.'

I hadn't been enthralled by the idea of running, but the list had to be obeyed and it was the only exercise that didn't involve exorbitant expenditure or swimsuits.

And, as it turned out, an early run through Regent's Park was lovely. Generally speaking, I was not a morning person. Or an athletic person. But this was just lovely. All of London laid out around us, waking up to another beautiful summer's day. It was amazing; we'd had more than three in a row. Still, it was forecast to piss it down all next week, my mum had rung to tell me. The BBC and her shaman had both told her so. No Rachel, I told myself, now is not the time to think about whether or not your mother is going to end up working the mines of a Temple-of-Doom-style cult. Now was the time to concentrate on the new you. On your wonderful run. Shake off the cobwebs, get the blood pumping. The park really was beautiful: trees, grass, the odd friendly dog walker to say hello to on the way. Brilliant. This was how every day should start. In fact, I decided, this was exactly how every day would start from now on. The new me was a runner. A redheaded runner who didn't take shit from anyone and had filthy dreams about doing it with Ethan Harrison in the music room.

'So my brother said something a bit random last night.' I ran a little faster to catch up to Em. Damn her ever-so-slightly longer legs and considerable fitness levels. 'We were talking about my dad's wedding and he asked if I'd spoken to you about it.'

'Weird,' she replied, stepping up the pace a little. Running was fun. Well, maybe not fun but still. 'Maybe he thought you had forgotten about it and I would have to remind you.'

'Maybe.' I was starting to pant a little bit. Good, feel the burn and all that. 'I just thought maybe you'd talked about it on Friday night.'

'Well, that would make more sense, wouldn't it?' She stared straight ahead, her face hidden behind her giant swinging ponytail. 'Because you're hardly likely to forget your dad's wedding, are you?'

'Why are you being weird?' Ooh, bit of stitch there. Not to worry, run it off.

'I'm not being weird,' she said, sprinting off even faster. 'Shut up and run.'

'Then why is your voice so high that the dog over there is covering his ears?' My calves were burning but I was not giving up. Not on the running or on what was going on between Emelie and my brother.

'It's nothing.' Em slowed down a little bit until we were shoulder to shoulder. 'Paul just suggested that I come to the wedding to keep you company.'

'To keep me company?'

'Uh, yes.'

'And did he extend this gracious invitation to Matthew as well?'

'Uh, no.'

I jogged slowly on in silence for a few minutes, my muscles starting to loosen up. Em slowed down and trotted along behind me, saying nothing.

'And what did you say?' I asked once we'd been overtaken by a couple of pensioners. Not embarrassing at all.

'I said I would go,' she said quietly.

'And in what capacity exactly would you be attending?' I focused on the path in front of me. The muscles that had been loosening up were feeling really rather tight all of a sudden. That was normal, wasn't it?

'As Paul's date,' she replied. 'He hadn't got round to asking anyone yet so I said I'd go.'

I wasn't sure if it was the sudden sick feeling in the pit of my stomach or the agonizing cramp that got me first but, before I knew it, I was on my arse at the side of the footpath, making some very unattractive noises and gripping my bulging calf. That part, at least, was probably the cramp.

'Oh shit.' Em was on her knees in a heartbeat. 'Rub your calf. It's just lactic acid, you must not have warmed up properly.'

'You're actually going to my dad's wedding with my brother?' I asked, tears streaming down my face. 'Despite, well, despite having met him more than once?'

'I won't if you don't want me to,' she covered her face with her hands. 'I just wasn't thinking. It was after the whole Simon thing and he asked and I said yes and then I didn't know how to tell you and . . . you know I'm an idiot. And that I sort of like him and I never like anyone and I know it's awful because it's Paul but still, I . . . I don't know what to say.'

'He's my little brother,' I wailed. 'He's disgusting.'

'I know,' she wailed back. 'I'll cancel.'

As the pain in my calf started to subside, I looked up at my best friend. She looked gutted. But my brother was such an arsehole. Why was the universe testing me? Wasn't it enough that my boyfriend had declared me boring and discarded me after one lacklustre shag and taken my toothpaste, without my brother stealing away my best friend? I lay back on the grass, narrowly avoiding a dog turd, hidden carefully from view. Ew. Maybe running wasn't that lovely. I sat up, shook my head. They were both grown-ups. I couldn't tell her not to go out with him. Jesus, as if this wedding wasn't already going to be the shit show of the century, now I was going to have to watch my brother paw my best friend all day long. Aunt Beverley was going to love this.

'Don't bloody cancel,' I sulked. 'I just can't believe you've got a date for my own dad's wedding and I haven't. And don't you dare say ask Matthew because that's just sad.'

She threw herself at me in a massive hug and beamed happily. 'There's got to be a million people you could ask.'

'I'm going to have to come up with someone soon,' I said, clambering upright and trying not to vom. I would just run it off, the cramp and the brother/best-friend-related nausea. Run it off all the way to Starbucks and drown my sorrow in muffins. 'Any ideas?'

'A million.' Em nodded at me to start walking. Bloody leg. Bloody exercise. Bloody list. 'I could take you to a bar tonight, get a drink and you could go home with absolutely any man in there. Picking up boys isn't hard – it's one hundred per cent confidence. But walking up to a stranger and saying, "Hey, want to be my date to my father's wedding in less than two weeks?" isn't exactly a big turn-on to most men. Unless you pitch it in stockings and suspenders and pair it with blow-job vouchers. Even then—'

'But I put it on the list,' I whined. 'I have to do it.'

'How's that going?' she asked. 'The list? Where are we?'

Pulling a face, I tried to pick up my pace a little. Nope. Not a natural runner after all. Shit.

'It was great on Sunday,' I said. 'With the hair and the clothes and everything, I felt amazing. Every time I get dressed in my new stuff it's like, yeah, I can do this today. And I know it sounds stupid but I really don't think I'd have told Dan exactly what I thought of him if I hadn't done it. And I found Ethan on Facebook last night, that was cool.'

'Wedding date candidate?'

'Probably a bit far for him to come from Toronto.'

'Ahh, a fellow Canadian.' She tightened her giant ponytail. 'Did you message him?'

I shook my head. 'What's the point? The list said I

135

had to hunt him down, that's all. And honestly, just looking at his photo was enough to send me head over heels in crush with him; I don't think I could cope with actually talking to him. And it's not like we were best friends or anything. Wouldn't it be weird?'

'Not at all, a little online crush could be just what you need,' she reasoned. 'Clear the emotional decks, a little flirting practice.'

'Maybe.' I was getting much better at being noncommittal. 'I've got a lot of other stuff to worry about anyway. We only have ten days for me to get a tattoo, bungee jump, break the law, find a real live date to my dad's wedding, write Simon a letter explaining what a knob he is, buy something obscenely expensive with no money and travel to a country I've never visited before.'

'Nothing dramatic then,' she suddenly sprinted off ahead. 'We'd better get cracking, hadn't we?'

Running lasted exactly seven more minutes before Emelie declared she'd had enough and diverted our course from Regent's Park to the bus stop. I couldn't say I was against the idea; there was a slight chance I wasn't quite the natural runner I'd hoped. And besides, today was going to be a busy day. Today was all about the list. Since Matthew had cleared out everything tainted with Simon's influence, my flat felt incredibly empty, but at least it meant I could actually sit at the desk in the spare bedroom without tripping over his trainers, a half-empty bottle of vodka or, god forbid, twice-worn pants. Why were men incapable of finding their own way to the washing machine? I'd heard terrible rumours that in New York they didn't have washing machines in their apartments. I pitied the poor girls forced to date boys who had to actually go out to a laundrette to wash their underwear. They probably crawled down the street all on their own.

Pulling aside the curtain so I could see the summer sunshine outside, I set my to-do list, my laptop and a steaming cup of tea down on the desk. OK, I meant business. I felt like tying back my hair and putting on some glasses, only my vision was twenty-twenty and my hair was too short to tie back now.

'Right, where am I?' I studied the list carefully. Nope, hadn't changed. Sipping my tea, I pulled my best Carrie Bradshaw pondering face and peered out into the garden. The point of the list was to catch me up on everything I'd missed out on, to show me how much fun it could be to be single and widen my horizons. So far, it had drained my bank balance, stained three white pillowcases red and given me the subconscious horn. Maybe they were important milestones on the road to becoming successfully single. I wasn't entirely sure where getting fired for the first time in my life came into it but, surely, there was a lesson to be learnt somewhere. I wanted to believe it was 'I'm mad as hell and not going to take it any more' but 'keep your mouth shut or you'll be bankrupt and homeless within six months, you complete mental' was more likely.

I picked up my phone and scrolled through the missed calls. One from my mum, accompanied by a well-meaning voicemail; one from the bank, presumably to ask why I thought it was a good idea to spend All My Money on Sunday, and three from my agent, the first one dating back to precisely one hour post-Anagate. I could do this. I was a big girl. I was in control of my life. I was master of my own destiny. I was ready. Taking a very deep breath and then a sip of tea and then scrolling through a few pages of Asos. com and then another deep breath and one more sip of tea for luck, I pressed redial.

Then hung up immediately and opened Facebook.

Ethan's profile hadn't changed in the slightest in the last twelve hours but, given that I could only see one picture and see that he lived in Toronto, that was hardly surprising. The 'send message' button on the right-hand side of the screen winked at me.

'Go on,' it whispered. 'What's the worst that can happen? Worst-case scenario, he doesn't reply. Best-case scenario, he could be the one!'

My finger was poised on the wireless mouse. One click. One message. It was just a message. How many Facebook messages had I had from people I went to school with? People I went to primary school with? And yes, I'd ignored most of them, but still, I hadn't shared a Twix with them during a trip to see the London Philharmonic on the fourteenth of August, twelve years ago. That was something. He'd remember that. He'd remember me sitting across the aisle and two rows behind him on the bus. He wouldn't think I was a freak. But, just in case, I immediately went through my Facebook pictures and untagged any and everything that could be conceivably considered to be unattractive. Gone were the Halloween pictures of me dressed as a Fraggle. Gone were the pictures of me tossed over Matthew's shoulder. Gone were the pictures of me in a bikini – he could make his mind up about that situation as and when he came to it. Just one message.

I opened up the dialogue box and typed 'hi' into the subject. Hi. That was OK, wasn't it? There was nothing potentially crazy about hi? There was nothing bunny boiler about a simple hello.

Now, for the message. Hi Ethan, I began, I don't know if you remember me, we were in orchestra together when we were kids.

'Eurgh,' delete, delete, delete. When we were kids? Because now I'm a dried-up old crone whom no one wants and so I've been reduced to hunting you down online because you're my last chance at love! How's it going?

'They're always saying Facebook ruins marriages in the *Daily Mail*,' I whined out loud. 'Why is this so hard?' Maybe Matthew was right; perhaps photos of genitals were the way forward. Hey Ethan, Check these out – they're my boobs. Love Rachel xoxo. This was just too difficult. There was no way to send a message without looking like an obsessive stalker or a sad loser. Until I'd decided which of those was preferable, I'd just keep looking at his manly photo. And keep opening a photo of me right next to it so I could see what we'd look like together. We looked good. And this would be a funny story to tell the grandkids, wouldn't it? Guess what, before your nana and granddad got together, your nana may or may not have cut herself out of a picture from her dad's second wedding where her bridesmaid dress looked a bit like a wedding dress and then pasted it into a picture of your dad. Simon once told me loads of guys he knew used Facebook as a porno substitute when they were having 'a quiet five minutes alone'. I wasn't sure which was worse, masturbating over the girl in accounts' holiday photos or Photoshopping pretend wedding photos. Yes I did. Yes I did.

Thoroughly ashamed, I accepted that it was time for my punishment. I picked up the phone.

'Veronica Mantle,' she answered right away. 'Can I help you?'

Uh-oh.

Now, I knew for a fact that Veronica recognized my number. And for the six years she had been my agent, her response to seeing that number on her screen was exclusively 'what the fuck do you want?' or 'darling,

I have fantastic news', so either she'd had a recent head trauma and developed a completely new personality, or this was some hilarious joke. That only she was in on.

'Veronica? It's Rachel.'

Nothing.

'Rachel Summers?'

'No, it can't be,' she replied. 'She's dead.'

Double uh-oh.

'Um, no, definitely not dead.' I tried a nervous laugh but it just came out as a faint squawk. 'Felt it yesterday though.'

'Right.' Veronica did not return my squawk. 'But if Rachel wasn't dead, she would have returned my calls before now. Or fled the country before I came over to her house to kill her.'

The last two words were so carefully enunciated, I actually turned in my seat to see if there was a Tarantino-esque hit man at the door.

'Yeah,' I mumbled into a steadying sip of tea. 'Not dead. Dumped, not dead.'

'I haven't dumped you yet.' Her voice was worryingly breezy. 'Oh god no. If this in fact is Rachel and she isn't dead, I won't be dumping her until she's had the mother of all roastings, cried like a baby and begged for my forgiveness. Then, if she's really lucky, then I'll dump her sorry arse and she won't fucking work another day in her hopefully very short life. Have you got any fucking idea what sort of damage limitation I've had to do because of your fucking temper tantrum? How many arses I've had to kiss? I thought I was going to have to suck Ana's dick to calm her down at one point. And she doesn't have a dick, Rachel. So how was I going to do that? Tell me how?'

Veronica never had been one to mince words.

'I don't know?'

'So no, I haven't dumped you yet. I suggest you start your grovelling apology now and I'll let you know when to stop, you fucking knob.'

'I meant Simon dumped me,' I whispered. And I'm sorry. Very, very, very, very, very, very, very—'

'What the fuck?'

Was cutting me off mid-apology the same as letting me know when to stop?

'Rachel, what did you just say?'

'Simon dumped me?'

'When?'

'Saturday?'

'And you went to work on Monday?'

'I did.'

'Even though you knew you were going to have to work with that ridiculous twat?'

Did she mean Dan or Ana?

'Yes.'

'In that case, what can I do for you today, my love?'

I held my phone away from my ear to check the number. Had I just redialled my mum by mistake?

'Really?' It wasn't that I wanted to push my luck, just make sure I hadn't been whacked and then slipped into some sort of personal heaven where life suddenly became easy.

'You should have fucking called me before now.' She dialled her volume down from eleven to somewhere around eight and a half. A good sign. 'And you should never have fucking gone in the first place but since you haven't fucked up ever before and that, as of right now, you are my own personal bitch, I'll let this one go. Did you know she's fucking Dan?'

'I did.' I stopped waiting for the barrel of the rifle to pop through the letterbox and turned my attention back to my tea. 'They're going to have to come up with a new kind of STD for them to give each other.'

'Well, you owe him a thank you,' Veronica replied. 'He talked her down. I'd say send flowers but maybe a box of assorted condoms would be better. Barbed-wired for her pleasure.'

'Nice,' I winced and crossed my legs.

'You've also got a "let's go out and get twatted on expenses" voucher to redeem. You free later?'

She really was a great agent. If it weren't for the fact she'd told my mum that all she really needed was to go out and get properly shagged at my twenty-fifth birthday party before blasting out 'I Touch Myself' on karaoke, I'd have even called her my friend.

'I think I'm still hungover from Saturday. And Sunday.' Still far too soon for alcohol. 'But there is something you could help me with.'

'You do know I can't actually have anyone killed, don't you?' She lowered her voice. 'Not that I want that getting out to the masses.'

'I assumed people just killed themselves on your command.' I touched the list for good luck. 'No, I was hoping you could get me some international work. I really want to travel for a bit.'

'Hmm.' The keys of her keyboard clicked for a few moments. 'I'm not just going to be able to pull something out of my arse for you on this, you know? There aren't that many people out there who know you. Which is entirely your own fucking fault.'

'I know,' I said, turning my profanity filter up a notch. I hardly ever even heard it any more. 'But I really want to get out there. I don't care if it's shows or shoots, studio, location, whatever.'

'You haven't done anything on location in years.'

If she hadn't been an agent, Veronica would have

made a fantastic mechanic. She was a teeth-sucking away from, 'And I don't like the look of that head gasket one little bit'.

'Now, if Dan weren't fucking furious with you, he's got a job booked in Sydney in a couple of weeks. I could have pulled some strings and got you on that if he'd insisted. The editors love him.'

Oh, fuck a duck.

'Give me a couple of days, yeah?' She sounded confident enough. 'And just take it easy until then. Go out, get twatted, shag some ridiculously fit moron who won't be able to follow you home. Never been a better time to be single, Rachel. Women have the dicks now. We're the men. We say who, we say when, we say where and we say how. Who wants a boyfriend when you've got bigger balls than they have?'

I said my goodbyes, chugged my cold tea and spent the rest of the afternoon trying not to think about the size of Veronica Mantle's balls.

CHAPTER TEN

'Raaaa-cheeeeel.' I felt a hand lightly tapping the top of my head. 'Waaaaaakey-waaaakey.'

As long as I lived, I would never, ever forgive Matthew for waking me up in the middle of a dream involving Ethan Harrison, a music stand and certain acts that 16-year-old Rachel would have been horrified by because her mum said they made you a loose woman. And that was when the term 'loose women' still meant you were just a bit of a slag, not Jane McDonald, a former *Coronation Street* barmaid or a Nolan.

I really didn't feel like getting up. After speaking to Veronica, I'd spent the rest of the day cleaning out my cupboards, trekking all my crap down to the charity shop and carting three tins of emulsion, two roller trays and a selection of paintbrushes back from B&Q. Of course, by the time I'd got home and stuck masking tape all round the doorframe, I was too knackered to do anything else. I blamed my run. Marathon, practically.

'What time is it?'

'It's almost ten.' He pulled the cushion out of my hands and started bashing me over the head with it.

'Get your arse up. We have to be there by half eleven; it was the only time they could fit us in.'

At least Matthew brought coffee to accompany his violence. I shuffled into a sitting position and held my hand out for caffeine-y goodness before I could even open my eyes properly.

'Excellent work on the sugar-to-coffee ratio,' I mumbled, glugging it down.

'Since you're still in the first few days of this process, you're allowed a lie-in,' Matthew grabbed an arm and pulled. 'But really, we have an appointment.'

'You're not getting me fitted for some horrifying contraceptive device, are you?' I rubbed the sleep out of my eyes. 'Where are we going?'

'If I tell you, it won't be a surprise, will it?' He snatched my coffee and held it over his head.

Totally cheating.

If there was one thing Matthew loved, aside from doing it with boys, it was a surprise. Once he'd prised me out of bed and dragged Emelie away from her computer, he refused to part with any details of where we were headed. All we knew was that it was twenty minutes away and we were headed there on foot. I was so knackered by the time we came to a halt outside a pair of big black wooden doors, I was pretty certain I'd agree to whatever he had planned as long as it meant I could have a sit-down.

Which was a bit of luck actually.

The three of us were standing outside a tattoo parlour.

'Am I really doing this?' I asked, looking from one to the other. 'Seriously?'

'Totally serious,' Matthew nodded. 'But not you, us. I was thinking about the list and you're right. There's no joy in sitting around moping, so I wanted to help. This was pretty much the only one I could organize at short notice. Looks like bungee jumping is going to take a few days.'

I launched myself at him in a giant hug. 'Jumping off a bridge with a skipping rope tied to my ankles aside, I'm actually really excited.' I could feel all my hair giddiness rearing back up. Times a million. 'I can't believe we're getting tattoos.'

'Why do I have to get one?' Emelie dug her hands into the pockets of her cardi. 'I really, really don't like needles.'

'Because we're doing this together.' Matthew pulled her into the hug against her will. 'And because you've already sodding well got one anyway.'

She responded with her middle finger.

'So what are we getting?' I asked, half desperate to get in there and get inked before I lost my nerve, half terrified. If Em already had a tat and was behaving like this, just how much was it going to hurt?

'I thought, we should get something very deep and meaningful,' Matthew started. 'Like James Franco's face. But then my artistic talents didn't extend beyond this.'

He held out a piece of paper showing three five pointed stars intertwined with delicate twirly bits. There really wasn't a word for twirly bits but it was gorgeous.

'Where?' I asked.

'Chest.' Matthew tapped just above his heart.

'Shoulder,' Em sighed. 'I suppose.'

'Really?' I tried to imagine the design on my bare skin. Shoulder didn't seem right.

'Not as tacky as a tramp stamp,' Matthew said, pulling up Emelie's T-shirt to reveal an elaborate scroll design at the base of her back. 'See?'

'Piss off.' Em yanked her top back down until it reached her barely there denim shorts. 'I was seventeen, everyone was doing it.'

'That's how the Nazis got into power, you know.' Matthew looked away as he spoke. 'Let's do this.'

'It hurts,' Matthew wailed ten minutes later. 'I can't do it.'

Emelie was seated on a stool in the far corner of the room, in silence, burly tattoo man number one starting on her third star, while Matthew lay on a bed in the middle of the room and was far from silent. 'It really, really hurts,' he began whining again.

Burly tattoo man two sighed and pulled away the needle. 'I did tell you this was a sensitive area. I'm almost bloody done. So either shut up and let me get on with it or I write pussy across your forehead.'

Matthew gritted his teeth and nodded for him to continue, the self-sacrificing trooper that he was. I sat quietly beside the bed, letting him try and break my hand while I waited for one of the artists to finish up. Did all tattoo parlours have to be painted red? And did all tattoo artists have to have aggressive haircuts? The walls were covered in the artists' previous works: seemingly there was a huge preference for crosses, roses and boobs amongst London's tattooed community. Where were the pretty tattoos you saw on celebrities? Was the wall art some sort of test for the people who just wandered in for a Tweetie Pie on the ankle?

'Right, I'm done,' burly tattoo man number one announced over by Emelie's stool. 'Let's have you over here.'

'Let go,' I hissed, wriggling my hand out of Matthew's grip and walking bravely over to the stool. Em shuffled across to an empty seat, a little pale but at least she wasn't screaming in agony. Unlike some people.

'It was fine,' she said, wincing as the tattoo artist laid the dressing over her fresh ink. 'Not nearly as bad as I thought.'

I explained to the artist what I wanted – the same design as Emelie and Matthew, on the inside of my left wrist – and closed my eyes as he took a disposable razor to the area. Then he wiped it down with antiseptic and laid out his tools. Fresh needles. Fresh ink. Bloody great big buzzing power tool that was about to scar me for life.

'Just breathe; it'll only take a minute,' he reassured me with a smile. Underneath his lack of hair and assorted skull and naked woman tattoos, he actually seemed quite lovely. 'Really, it's not that bad, just a scratch.'

'I'm fine,' I said, trying to ignore my increasing heart rate and squeezing my eyes shut. To be honest, the razor bothered me more than the needle. At least it did until I heard the needle power up. It was like a dentist drill. A dentist drill was about to be applied to the delicate skin of my inner wrist. 'I'll be fine.'

And I was for the first couple of seconds. Then the stinging started. Followed by the undeniable sensation of a needle cutting into my skin. So it was true. Tattoos were not pricked on by unicorn horns. Damn it.

'Are you all right?' I heard Matthew ask. The lack of sobbing coming from his general direction suggested he was finished.

I nodded in response but couldn't quite make words. This really wasn't as pleasant as sitting in a salon and having someone fuss all over me for an afternoon. But I was getting a tattoo. Me, a tattoo. Next up, swearing at the teacher and smoking behind the bike sheds.

'Well, while you're incapacitated, I have some exciting news.'

Oh god. What could it be? He was moving to Mexico with José. He was going on *Britain's Got Talent*. He was pregnant.

'So, you know how me and Emelie both know your Facebook password?'

'Leave me out of it,' she shouted across the room. Burly tattoo artist number one frowned at the raised voices. He was obviously a delicate thing.

'I did not know this Matthew, no.' I gritted my teeth and prepared myself for the worse. I had a horrible feeling – a feeling that had nothing to do with the needle being dragged through my skin – that I knew what he was about to say.

'It's nothing really. Nothing that wasn't going to happen anyway, I've just sped things along a little bit. I might have messaged Ethan,' he backed away until he was out of kicking range, 'as you.'

'As me?' My voice was unnaturally squeaky. But then, there wasn't anything natural about having needles dragged through your skin, was there? 'What have you done?'

'Nothing, I just sent him a message asking if he was the Ethan Harrison you used to go to orchestra with and, you know, hello. That's all.'

I didn't need to see his face to know he was lying.

'And what else?'

'Nothing! Really.'

'Matthew?'

'Nothing. But, well, he replied.'

Burly Tattoo Man Number One finished up with a smile.

'All done,' he said, wiping off the tiny drop of blood and excess ink. 'Keep it clean, put a dab of antiseptic cream on it a couple of times a day and you're golden. Then kick him in the balls, that's a proper shit thing to do.'

I thanked him with a hug, which admittedly might have been a bit much, but the post-tattoo endorphins were starting to buzz around my body. If I felt good for getting a haircut, I felt amazing for getting a tattoo. It was suddenly very clear to me how people got addicted to this.

Once we were all done, I couldn't stop looking at the white bandage on my wrist. Matthew was looking very pleased with himself. Emelie just looked as though she was going to throw up.

'Let's get you outside.' I put my arm around her waist and walked her towards the door.

'I'll pay, don't worry,' Matthew called after us.

'Oh, you'll pay,' I promised. 'Don't you worry.'

After Matthew had settled up, we headed out for the freshest air we could find to revive Em. I led the wounded soldiers to a couple of empty benches outside the Tate Modern in complete silence. I had no idea what I wanted to say to Matthew. I knew exactly what I wanted to do, but say? Nuh-uh. It had taken a little over an hour to do all three tattoos and by the time we made it over to South Bank, the sun was high in the sky, behind London's landmarks.

'I cannot believe you did this.' I clutched at my dressing, focusing on that fresh tattoo buzz and not the rising homicidal tendencies I was experiencing. 'What were you thinking?'

'You know I try not to think where men are involved,' he shrugged, sitting down beside me while Em took the neighbouring bench alone. She looked as if she needed a minute. 'I thought it would be good for you.

He's cute, you already know him, he's in another country. It's totally safe flirtation.'

'Just tell me exactly what you said,' I sighed.

'Not a lot.' Matthew flung his leg over the bench, narrowly missing clubbing Em in the face. 'Just the usual, good to hear from you, what are you up to, I'm doing this, blah, blah, blah.' He passed out cans of Diet Pepsi he'd picked up en route.

'You don't get to blah-blah over the details when you hack into my Facebook page and email boys,' I said, holding the cold can of cola to my bandage. 'What exactly did you say? Word for word.'

'Wouldn't it just be easier for you to read it?' Matthew suggested. 'I can't remember what I said, you've got an iPhone.'

'No, you need to read it out loud so I've got my hands free to punch you at the pertinent parts. I can't do that if I'm holding a phone and a drink.' I huddled up next to Emelie, who was still sitting quietly, can unopened in her lap. 'And be quick about it, it's not warm.'

'Fine.' He pulled his phone out of his jeans pocket. 'Just remember before you start getting shitty, I did this for you.'

'Whatever, just read it.' I hugged Em a little closer and stared across the water, watching buses run up and down the roads, St Paul's peeping out above them. Pretty.

'Hi there, I'm not totally sure if you're the right Ethan Harrison, it's been so long! But if you are, I'm Rachel Summers and we were in an orchestra together when we were younger. I was just messing around on Facebook and thought I'd look you up. Give me a shout if this is you! Would be great to be back in touch. Rachel, kiss kiss kiss,' Matthew took it upon himself to read the message out in a hilarious girl voice. Which was, of course, hilarious.

'And he replied?'

'He did, right away.' He traded his girly voice for a terrible Canadian accent despite a) being seated next to a native Canadian, and b) that he was well aware that Ethan had grown up in bloody Surrey. 'Hi Rachel! Yes it's me! It's so great to hear from you!'

'You don't need to exaggerate the exclamation points quite so much.' I couldn't deny it, my heart was pounding. Ethan bloody Harrison. Ethan Harrison thought it was great to hear from me. Or from a 29-year-old gay man masquerading as me.

'Whatever, what straight man is so excited about life? "Hi Rachel, yes it's me, it's so great to hear from you. How's it going? I tried to look for you on here once but I couldn't find you. Seems like there are a lot of Rachel Summers in the UK. So what's going on with you? Married? Kids? Still in Surrey? I moved to Toronto after A levels when my dad got a job out here. It's pretty awesome. I'm a high school music teacher now – who'd believe it after how bad I sucked in orchestra, right? Lol!"'

'Lol?'

'Lol.'

Hmm. Wasn't sure the father of my children would Lol.

'And then just "Write me back, I'd love to hear from you." Which is nice.'

'I ought to throw your phone in the bloody river,' I said. Ideally I wouldn't have been grinning ear to ear as I spoke, but beggars can't be choosers.

'Do it, I need an upgrade.' He gave me a nudge.

'You ought to be shot.' I picked at the edge of my bandage. 'You reckon I can take it off yet?'

'Yeah, it's been ages.'

It hadn't even been an hour.

Matthew pulled at the neck of his shirt, unfastening a couple of strategic buttons to peer at his own. 'Ew, it's been bleeding.'

'You woman.' I tried not to wince as I pulled away my own dressing. Three little black stars sat out in sharp contrast to my pale skin. 'I can't believe we got tattoos.'

'I know,' Matthew replied, sticking his bandage back down. 'We should go and get some cider and drink it in the park while we smoke a pack of Lambert & Butler or something.'

'Behold people, item number four. Bloody busy couple of days.'

'A toast,' Matthew raised his Diet Pepsi to mine. 'Do you feel any different? Now that you're a third of the way along the road to being a real singleton?'

'I feel amazing actually,' I said. 'Like I could do anything.'

My wrist hurt. My head buzzed. I wanted to look at my tattoo. Because I had a tattoo.

'You can,' he replied, rubbing my back. 'That's the point of this list, isn't it? To help you realize that.'

'It is,' I nodded slowly. 'And I cannot tell you how pleased I am to have my OCD validated.'

'I don't think it would be that good an idea to try and bungee jump off Westminster Bridge. Two's enough for one day, don't you think?' Matthew let his arm settle on my shoulders.

'Simon hated tattoos,' I said. 'He would hate this.'

'Well, you didn't do it for him,' he reminded me. 'You did it for you. Because you wanted to do it. That's how you're making all your decisions from now on. Remember that every time you look at it.'

'And I can totally cross it off the list.' I was delighted. Being terribly careful about my wrist, I pulled out the scabby napkin, found my black pen and dutifully ticked off 'Get a tattoo'.

'And you've already got your crush, your makeover, and Emelie tells me you attempted to exercise,' he said, ruffling my hair. 'You're doing so well.'

'You as well.' I gave him a nudge in the ribs. 'Just exactly who were you entertaining last night?'

Since StephenGate, Matthew hadn't actually allowed a man over his threshold. Not that he hadn't been over theirs; he just couldn't mentally deal with the idea of someone else in his and Stephen's place. It was understandable, or at least it was now.

'Just a friend.' He dismissed my question out of hand. 'We'll do me when we've done you, don't worry.'

'Well, I'm thirty-three-and-a-third per cent more successfully single than I was on Saturday, so I've got thirty-three-and-a-third per cent more time to worry about you,' I said with some pride. 'We're getting down to the tough ones though. Might have to wait until tomorrow. Apparently Em and I are going out tonight, some charity thing, and she says I have to dress up. Could take some time.'

'Sounds tough,' he replied. 'Dress up like a girl?'

'Like a girl. And not just put on a dress, the whole shebang,' I confirmed, stashing the napkin carefully back inside my handbag. 'Em, you ready to head home? I'm feeling a tub of Marks and Sparks Rocky Road bits coming on . . . oh shit, Matthew.'

On the opposite bench, Em was slumped forwards, her head tucked between her knees and a very attractive puddle of puke on the floor by her feet.

'Emelie, are you OK?' I asked as I rushed over, crouching down at the side of her; being very, very careful not to get near the vom. New shoes. New suede shoes. 'Em?'

'I puked.'

'You did,' I pushed her hair back from her face. She had not puked in her hair. Result. 'But it's OK.'

''Bleurgh,' she whispered. 'Puke.'

'Matthew!' I called back to the bench but I'd been replaced by a tall, combat-short-wearing man who was preening himself and trying to give Matthew a piece of paper. Dear god. It would all have been terribly cute. If our friend hadn't been throwing up in front of the Tate Modern. 'MATTHEW.'

A little giggling, acceptance of the piece of paper, followed by an awkward handshake, followed by a face like thunder stomping over in my general direction.

'What?' he demanded, looking at Emelie unimpressed. 'What's wrong with her?'

'She's sick,' I said, stroking her hair. The universally approved action for consoling a pukey friend. 'We need to take her home.'

'Excellent timing.' He bent down and scooped her up, tossing her over his shoulder. Which was when she threw up down his back. 'Brilliant.'

I followed dutifully, trotting behind and knotting her hair into a bun on the back of her head. 'And she's not even drunk.'

CHAPTER ELEVEN

'I can't believe we're doing this,' I said, hobbling slightly in my high heels. 'I look ridiculous.'

'You look hot,' Emelie replied. 'Now just be quiet. Chin up, tits out and follow me. Let me show you how we do this.'

Following her public pukeathon, Emelie had spent two hours in my bathroom and emerged looking as if she'd had a full night's sleep. It really was disgusting. Her hair was glossy and curled, her skin soft and scented and, once I'd been at her with my make-up kit, she looked like a goddess. I'd tried my best. My red hair was shiny and smooth, I'd gone all out with my make-up in that I was actually wearing some, and I'd added my new black platform heels to make me feel more ladylike. Somehow, it was sort of working. I had to admit, we looked good.

'*Bonsoir.*' She batted her eyelashes and laid the accent on thick for a group of very well-dressed smokers outside The Savoy. 'Light?'

All three men began patting themselves down feverishly, staring at Emelie's skintight red dress. Eventually one held up a lighter, triumphantly shoving the other two out of the way.

'It's crazy inside, right?' She placed the cigarette between her lips and nodded for him to light it. The flame lit up her perfect make-up and he was done. Completely smitten. 'We had to step outside for a break. It was just getting so . . . sweaty.'

I didn't know where to look. She was shameless. But so, so effective. It was some sort of charity do, an auction of original artworks to raise money for, well, something depressing. Em had donated an original Kitty Kitty sketch. Not being eleven, I sometimes forgot about Kitty Kitty. To me it was that cat cartoon she used to do when she should have been studying, the one Matthew would inevitably redraw to make it obscene. To the tweens of Great Britain, the Netherlands, Brazil and Germany, it was the highest grossing non-media brand for girls under fourteen. Quite impressive really. And happily for me, that income kept her in designer outfits for me to borrow at times like this. Declaring the event a mission, she had pulled the two tightest dresses from her wardrobe and declared the evening on. We were going to find me a date to my dad's wedding if it killed us. It was a charity do, after all: surely some well-meaning man with too much time and money would take pity on me?

'I don't think being outside has helped me at all,' Em announced to the assembled gents. 'Perhaps you would like to get me and my friend a drink?'

She ground her unsmoked cigarette into the ground and smiled brightly. Partly because she didn't smoke and partly because, as she'd explained on the way, this was all part of her plan to teach me the art of flirting. Her role was to chat up likely suspects. Mine was to shut up, look pretty, and do as I was told. I believe it was Meatloaf who had said two out of three ain't bad . . . The dress she had chosen for me was genuinely beautiful. I'd actually gasped when she held it out. Narrow black straps at my shoulders cut into a super low V neck that on Emelie must have been indecent. Given my comparative lack of charms, I had convinced myself I made it look elegant. At least, judicious use of double-sided sticky tape meant that I wasn't going to make it look pornographic. The tightly fitted top half billowed into layers of ruffles that I could just about manage not to trip over if in the platforms. Of course, they provided their own problems. I was not going to be able to drink. Or I was going to have to drink a lot, I wasn't sure which. I'd gone for neutral lipstick and my most carefully applied winged liquid eyeliner – maximum drama, minimal touch-ups. Definitely elegant.

Em, on the other hand, did not look elegant. She looked stunning. Her red strapless gown clung to her curves like it had been made for her and the skirt fell all the way to the floor in a cascade of delicate pleats. Every time she moved, it moved with her, a deep slash in the front of the skirt revealing yards of leg right up to her thigh. A slash of MAC Russian Red lipstick lit up her entire face and she'd somehow managed to tame her curls into Veronica Lake-style waves. It was ridiculous. If it hadn't been woefully inadequate, I'd have said she looked like Julia Roberts going to the opera in *Pretty Woman*, except she was twice as beautiful and somehow managed to give the impression that she'd be better in bed than a pro. It was quite impressive.

The owner of the winning lighter held his arm out to Emelie. 'Let me get you that drink,' he beamed like a lottery winner. His friends accepted defeat, looked at each other for a moment before one of them held his arm out to me.

'Charmed,' I muttered, taking him up on his offer. Whether he liked it or not.

Within five minutes of sailing through the doors of the hotel ballroom, Emelie and I had lost our escorts and were merrily quaffing champagne at the free bar.

'This is amazing,' I said, staring around with wide eyes. 'How do you not come to these things every night?'

'They're usually really boring.' She accepted a questionable-looking canapé from a very handsome waiter. 'But we should do this more often, girls' night out. You're not that likely to meet the love of your life in a dark room in Vauxhall.'

'Don't,' I shuddered. First and last time I ever went to Fire Nightclub with Matthew. Do not, I repeat, do not open the wrong door in that place. Terrifying.

'I can't remember the last time we did a girls only night.' Em sipped from her champagne flute delicately. I tried not to chug. As much fun as this was, I still felt wildly out of place. The easiest cure for that, of course, was booze. I was pretty sure Shakespeare said something similar. Probably used more words though.

'The last time we were out properly on a Saturday night was last Christmas.' She smoothed down a stray strand of my hair and smiled. 'At that thing with Matthew and Stephen.'

'How is that even possible?' I returned the favour and brushed a touch of loose eye shadow from underneath her eye. I was a perfectionist. 'That's months ago. And we've totally been to The Phoenix since then. Loads of times.'

'Two hours in the basement of a pub once a month is not the same as "out",' she explained. 'I'm not complaining, I know when you're with someone you don't want to be trekking around London in high heels when you could

159

be at home watching *The Inbetweeners* with your boyfriend but, from an entirely selfish perspective, I'm really happy you're here now. I've missed you.'

I didn't really like the picture Em was painting. Maybe I had abandoned her a little bit over the last few months. In days gone by, even when Simon and I first got together, we would be out round town more often than not but, once we'd bought the flat, I'd started to hibernate a little. Having her as a constant presence for the last few days had felt so natural. I'd totally taken our friendship for granted.

'I've been so pathetic,' I moaned. 'Honestly, I don't deserve you to be this awesome. I'm so sorry.'

'Shut up,' she pulled me into a hug and brushed away my apologies. 'I'm always here for you whenever you need me. And yeah, so we haven't seen each other as much as we used to, but that's what happens. You were always there for me when I needed you. That's what matters.'

'I've missed you too,' I said with an awkward half-hug. 'Time just got away from me. Now everything's changed, I feel a bit like I've been sleepwalking the last couple of years. If I'd opened my eyes to the situation sooner, maybe I wouldn't be here now.'

'Hindsight is a fine thing.' Emelie nodded towards two tuxedo-clad guys at the bar. 'As is that. Blond or brunette, which do you want?'

I considered the options. They were both attractive; the blond guy was chiselled, clean cut, tall. The darker-haired guy looked more like the Geography teacher everyone has a crush on in Year Eight.

'Brunette.' My mouth felt dry. My armpits felt sweaty. Perfect pick-up combo. 'Remind me again what this is? In case it comes up?'

'Charity thing; they're always charity things,' she

hiccupped as she finished one glass of champagne and readily accepted a second. I really wanted to tell her to calm down; there was no way she was chucking up on the night bus looking like that. 'I want to say children's charity.'

'You are a great philanthropist.' I couldn't help but stare at all the attractive men around us. Granted, they were in tuxedos and everyone alive looked hotter in a tuxedo. It was just a stone-cold fact. Just as the man coming up to us was a stone-cold fox. The blond.

'Ladies.' He nodded to us both but I knew before he even started which of us he had come to talk to. I wasn't even offended. At this point, I was very close to adding 'go gay with Emelie' to the to-do list. 'Would you like to dance?'

Ever the good friend, Emelie looked to me for approval before accepting his arm and venturing towards the dance floor. I waited for the Geography teacher to make his move, but instead he held position a few feet away, staring somewhere off to the left of my ear. Oh god, what did I have to lose?

'Hi,' I held my hand out and prayed he would take it. After an incredibly uncomfortable couple of seconds, he did. 'I'm Rachel.'

'Asher.' He didn't quite smile but he didn't turn and run either. 'I'm sorry, I just really hate these things. Tim dragged me along; his wife is pregnant and she's not feeling well and he didn't want to come on his own and I hate wearing a suit and it's been a really long day and . . . Well. Hmm. Quite.'

Because it wouldn't be enough for one of us to be socially awkward, would it? Nothing like a bit of verbal diarrhoea to get things off to a good start.

'What do you do?' I asked, watching married father-to-be Tim whisk my friend around the dance floor.

Funny how he wasn't wearing a wedding ring while he danced with the prettiest girl in the room.

'I'm a yoga instructor.' He sounded much more comfortable in familiar territory. 'Tuxes aren't my usual uniform.'

'Suppose not,' I gave him a supportive smile and tried not to imagine him in a downward dog. Champagne wasn't good for me. 'Where do you teach?'

'Oh, all over London.' He picked up a glass of champagne from the bar and knocked half of it back in one. Good boy. 'Do you practise?'

'I dabble.' I'd been to one class, refused to accept that bending could be difficult and immediately put my back out. 'I'm more of a runner.'

I'd tell him that was a lie after he proposed.

'You should come to one of my classes.' He coloured up a little bit underneath his heavy glasses. I liked it. 'One class and I promise I'll convert you.'

My brain told me to laugh girlishly and accept. Instead I made a sort of snorting noise, blushed from head to toe and sank an entire glass of champagne.

'Could you excuse me for a moment?' Asher backed away slowly. 'Back in a minute.'

Of course you will be. I watched him all but run towards the exit. Of course you will be.

I managed almost an entire minute before I began to feel conspicuously alone on the edge of the dance floor. Rubbing my bare arms, I accepted a refill on my champagne and decided to take a turn around the room. My experience of balls was limited to the dances attended by Meg and Jo in Little Women and Jane Austen adaptations. They were always taking turns around the room. Not that this event could really compare; for starters there wasn't a bustle in sight and I couldn't see a Judi Dench anywhere.

Following a sign for 'silent auction', I headed down a darkened hallway, my heels sinking into extraordinarily plush carpet. Since I'd already sank three free glasses of champagne and blagged a free ticket from one of the patrons, maybe I felt obliged to donate something somehow. Didn't seem like it would be the kind of event where I could chuck a tenner in a bucket at the end of the night, and I was almost certain no one was walking around selling raffle tickets.

The auction room was almost empty; just a few partygoers wandered around looking at the paintings and photographs on display, occasionally pausing to write on slips of paper and pop them into envelopes beside each work. I stopped in front of a black and white photograph. It was beautiful. A wide desert sky, clouded over, with someone kneeling in the lower left-hand corner, her face in the shadows. It was one of those moments where someone is caught completely off guard and isn't trying to be anyone. It felt raw and honest and just very special. And according to the guide price, the charity was expecting to get five thousand pounds for it. No wonder it was a silent auction, I thought. That direction was presumably to stop me shouting 'bloody hell, how much?' out loud.

'You like it?'

I was so busy trying not to look shocked at the price of the photograph, I didn't see him coming. And even if I had, there was no guarantee I would have recognized Dan in a tux in the first place. Wow. Never having seen him in anything other than jeans and T-shirts, the transformation was startling. The intense black fabric of his tux contrasted with the sharp white shirt, making his light tan glow, and the perfectly fitted formality of his outfit clashed against his slightly too long brown curly hair. He really was not a bad-looking man. Tall, broad, gorgeous dark brown eyes . . .

'I love it.' If anything was going to tear my attention off that picture, it was going to be him. Something winged and fluttery was happening in my stomach. But this was Dan, couldn't possibly be butterflies, more likely killer moths. 'What are you doing here?'

'And good evening to you too,' he replied. 'I work with the charity. I'm assuming you're here with Emelie?'

'Yes?' OK, so I'd been a bit rude, but really, he'd taken me by surprise. 'How did you know?'

'Because I was the one who got her involved with the charity in the first place. I introduced her after your birthday party two years ago?'

Blank stare.

'At karaoke?'

Blank stare.

'Karaoke Box? Smithfield?'

'Ohhh,' the penny finally dropped. He really did have a good memory. 'Well, it's a great photo anyway.'

'It's one of my favourites.' He handed me a small stiff card programme. Desert series number four, Daniel Fraser. It was his picture. 'You were on the shoot, don't you remember?'

'Oh my god, I was.' I took another look. Dan took this? 'Morocco, isn't it? What, four, five years ago?'

'Four,' he nodded. 'You look beautiful by the way. I wasn't sure it was you at first.'

'Same.' I wasn't quite sure what to do. The last time we'd spoken, it was with raised voices. And then there was the terrible Monster Munch hate crime. Still felt bad about that. 'So.'

'So,' he took my arm in his. 'Walk?'

This was the second time in two days I was positive someone was going to kill me. When I had a boyfriend, I could go weeks without fear of homicide, months even. I really hoped this was just teething trouble and not a regular part of singledom. We walked out of the gallery in silence, up a sweeping staircase and stopped once we reached a grand balcony, overlooking the ballroom. Phew, witnesses. I spotted Emelie in her red dress right away. I was so proud of her; she looked as if she was having the time of her life.

'Should we be up here?' I looked around nervously. I was pathologically terrified of Getting into Trouble and the balcony was all but pitch-black, only lit by the dance floor below. Didn't seem like somewhere we should be.

'Should you be here at all?' Dan asked. Thankfully I could hear the hint of a smile in his voice. 'Don't actually remember seeing your name on the guest list.'

'I'm Em's date,' I reminded him. 'I was on there, just under my other name, plus one.'

'So you'll go gay to get into parties just to see me, but you can't be arsed to stick around and finish a job?'

I took that to assume he wasn't mad at me any more.

'I want to say sorry for Monday.' Deep breath, genuine-sounding apology, beg him to take me to Sydney with him, go and get more champagne. You can do this, Summers. 'Everything went a bit blank. She opened her mouth and I just saw red.'

'So I see.' He responded by taking a strand of my hair and running his fingers along to the end. As it dropped back onto my neck, a shiver ran down my spine and all the way back up again. 'Did the red hair make you crazy or did the crazy lead to the hair?'

'The list led to the hair.' I mentally slapped myself

165

around the face. Dan Fraser did not make me tingly. Dan Fraser made models and morons tingly and I was neither. Most of the time. 'As you've probably noticed, I can't be trusted to take care of myself, so Em and Matthew have made me this list to . . . oh god, it sounds so stupid saying it out loud.'

He turned around to rest his back on the banister and gave me his best Roger Moore eyebrow. It worked well with the tux.

'It's a list of things to do to help me deal with the whole being single thing,' I confessed before I could stop myself. So that was how James Bond got so many women. It was all in the tux.

'Explain please.'

This was fine. I would let him take the piss for five minutes and then he would agree to get me on the Sydney job and then it would all be worth it. Dignity was overrated anyway.

'I've never really done the single gal about town thing.' I examined my rush-job manicure while I spoke and resisted the urge to start peeling. 'I didn't really know what to do when Simon, well, when Simon dumped me.' It was still bloody difficult to say. 'And I'm always writing lists for whatever and so, the single girl's to-do list was born.'

'And what is on this miraculous list?' he enquired. At least he wasn't laughing. 'Apart from drastic hair alterations and getting fired?'

'Getting fired wasn't on there actually.' I pulled the list out of my tiny beaded evening bag. I didn't imagine for a second I'd need it but my OCD had developed a new symptom that apparently required me to carry it with me everywhere. It was my very small, very delicate, very close to disintegrating blankie. 'See? Makeover, exercise, bungee jump – or similar, tattoo, date for my dad's wedding, buy something obscenely expensive and selfish, write a letter to your ex, find your first crush and break the law.'

He took the napkin from my hand and studied it for a moment. A long moment in which my heart almost stopped. Then he handed it back.

'You're going to do a bungee jump?' Dan did not look convinced.

Or die.

'Or similar.'

I stashed the list safely away, looked back at Bond and prepared to start begging.

'So I was talking to Veronica and she said you were going to Sydney,' I began.

'Yeah, next weekend. It's really over with Simon? This isn't just some distraction until you get back together?' Dan stared ahead into the darkness beyond the balcony.

'Definitely,' I confirmed. Talking about just exactly how dumped I was wasn't aiding me in my plan to be nice to him. 'Thanks for making sure.'

'But you're never single,' he said quietly. 'I've known you for six years and you've never been single.'

Without the light of the ballroom on his face, I couldn't make out his expression without staring at him. So I did that.

'First time for everything,' I replied. 'You're the professional bachelor. Maybe I should have come to you for advice? What are your top tips on surviving singledom?'

'Don't be single,' he replied instantly.

Oh. Awk-ward.

'Maybe I need to be on my own for a bit,' I replied, feeling ten times more uncomfortable than I had in the bar. 'Given that I haven't been before.'

'I give you a week.' He turned back to face me, his

usual slightly mocking smile back in place. 'I know you, you're not the kind of girl who can be on her own.'

'Thanks for the vote of confidence.' I rubbed my tattoo with my thumb. 'I already crashed and burned once tonight and I'm supposed to be finding someone to take to my dad's wedding, not hiding from the cool kids with you.'

'We're not the cool kids?' he asked, taking my wrist in his hands. 'I can't believe you got a tattoo. How far are you down this list anyway?'

'Hmm, makeover, exercise, tattoo, crush, all ticked off,' I counted in my head. 'So four down, six to go.'

'Crush?' He traced the pattern of ink along my wrist. There was that shudder again. Oh balls. No, I was not going to have girl feelings for Dan, three glasses of champagne and a little light stroking or not.

'This boy I went to school with.' My voice was involuntarily shaky. Stupid ovaries making decisions without me. 'I found him on Facebook, he lives in Canada now.'

'Oh, right.'

I turned my attention back to finding Emelie, but she wasn't on the dance floor. And neither was married-with-children Tim. Not ideal.

'Didn't your dad get married last year?' Dan asked, leaning over the balcony at the side of me. He was so close, I could smell his shampoo. Nice that he'd showered especially. Not that I was thinking about Dan in the shower. 'Or was it the year before?'

'Year before.' Score five points for remembering. 'It's a fairly regular thing, a bit like a leap year.'

'You didn't think to ask me?'

I smiled and shook my head. 'I actually did.'

'But?' He was so warm. How was he so warm? It was freezing on that balcony.

'But you're dating Ana.'

Never in six years had I known Dan to be lost for words. It must have been a full moon. Or a blue moon. Or the apocalypse.

'I'm dating Ana,' he repeated eventually. 'So of course you wouldn't have asked.'

'That, and the last time I saw you, you fired me and then I stomped on your Monster Munch.' I tipped my head to one side. 'Not a euphemism.'

'But you would have asked if I wasn't?'

'For the want of anyone else to ask, yes.'

'Fuck off.' He closed his eyes and smiled to himself. Smug git.

'You're such a charmer.' Down on the dance floor I spotted Emelie twirl back onto the dance floor, thankfully *sans* Married Tim.

'Leo,' he held out his hands. 'Obviously.'

'Virgo,' I replied. 'Obviously.'

'Most beautiful sign in the zodiac.' Dan turned to look me straight in the eye for the first time that night. He tucked my hair behind my ear and left his hand resting on my cheek. 'That colour really does suit you.'

'Aren't I the make-up artist?' I tried to laugh at the cheesiness of his lines but all I could think about was that hand on my cheek. His skin was warm but mine was burning. 'I'm the one who's supposed to be worried about colours.'

'I would have been a great make-up artist.' He dropped his hand. Hmm, maybe I didn't want him to move it after all.

'It's not like you're a bad photographer.' Wasn't there a point to this conversation when we started it? I was definitely trying to get somewhere and I was certain that the original destination was never into Dan's pants. 'But make-up is probably the only other profession that would have given you access to more women.'

He squinted at me through a few unruly curls, smile vanishing. 'You really do think I'm just a massive slag, don't you?'

I wanted to say no, because he obviously wanted me to say no. But I really did. Even if I felt terrible about it. Ish.

'I don't think you're a massive slag.'

Diplomacy was, after all, just socially acceptable lying.

'Just a regular slag?'

'I think you've "dated" a lot of models.' I made air quotes around dated and got a foul look for my efforts. 'And I think you have a very flirty attitude with the rest of the models.'

'Like I said, Leo,' he leaned forward again. 'Can't help that.'

'I'm fairly certain that you can't blame your star sign for your behaviour when you're thirty.' I tried to lean over the balcony beside him without flashing the entire dance floor below. 'You are what you are.'

'And what are you?' Dan asked. 'Aside from a border-line OCD totally judgemental cow?'

Right back on track. Awesome.

'Aside from that?'

'Aside from that.'

I watched Emelie dancing just a few feet below, laughing as she spun from man to man. It was a mystery to me how she hadn't been fooled into shackling herself to someone before now. Maybe she really did love being single. Maybe there really was something to it.

'I don't know what I am. I'm good at my job. I'm a good peacekeeper, contrary to what's happening right now. I know all the words to every Destiny's Child song on record and a couple that aren't.' I rubbed my bare arms. Along with the lights, someone had forgotten to turn the heating on up here. 'I want a family. I want a dog. I'm always cold. I can recite the entire script of *Who Framed Roger Rabbit* when I've had more than three whiskeys. What else do you want to know?'

'*Who Framed Roger Rabbit* is a criminally underrated movie.' He slipped off his jacket and placed it around my shoulders. 'Better?'

It might have buried me and it was so warm from where it had been moulded to Dan's body but, in all honesty, I wasn't warmed through from the shared body heat so much as the act itself.

'Better.' I slid my arms through the sleeves and looked at my fingertips peeping out of the ends, before I let them dangle down. 'Thanks.'

'You're welcome.'

The music that had been so loud downstairs was just an echo up on the balcony, a pulsing beat that counted down the seconds of silence between us.

'That really is a beautiful picture,' I said, just to say something. 'In the gallery.'

'I love what I do.' He accepted the compliment with a graceful nod. 'The magazine stuff pays but that's what makes me tick.'

'Yeah, I love doing the editorial stuff,' I agreed. 'I'm definitely going to start pursuing more of that side.'

Sydney. I had to convince him to take me to Sydney. 'Which reminds me, the Sydney job.'

I was fully prepared to launch into all the reasons why he should take me to Australia with him when I felt his hand lightly brush my shoulder. First I looked at the hand, then at his face, back to the hand and again at the face. He wasn't smiling any more. His lips were slightly parted, eyes trained on mine, as though he was waiting for permission. Not having the words to deal with this situation, I bit my lip and stayed completely still. Taking my silence as assent, his fingers slid down my bare skin until they reached my hand where they curled around mine. My other hand gripped the banister tightly while his other hand found its way onto my cheek. This was too weird. As his head leaned in towards mine, I took a tiny step backwards, breaking his hold on my hand, on my face. He pressed his hands to his sides, looking at the floor.

'What are you doing?' I asked once I'd made it a safe distance away.

'Nothing,' he replied, taking his own step backwards and banging his fist against the solid oak banister. 'Just me, isn't it? Can't help myself.'

I pulled off his jacket and hurled it in his general direction before I turned and headed for the staircase. I couldn't be there. I could do this. Whatever it was. Bye-bye Sydney, I thought as I clomped all the way down to the bottom. What an arsehole. And I thought I'd fucked things up by shouting at him. Not even nearly.

'Hey, there you are,' a worse-for-wear Emelie greeted me at the bottom of the stairs. Her eyes weren't quite focused, but best friend telepathy made it quite clear that I wasn't in the world's best mood ever. 'What's wrong? Do you want to leave?'

'I'll tell you later and yes.' I grabbed one last glass of champagne and sank it in a one-r. 'I just need to use the loo.'

Em nodded and pointed down the hallway. 'I'll call a cab,' she scrabbled around in her clutch for her phone. 'We wouldn't make it off the night bus alive dressed like this.'

'That or we'd make a lot of money,' I reasoned, trying to calm down. 'But I don't really want to have to put "high-class hooker" on my tax return this year.'

'So 2009,' Em agreed.

Promising myself she was joking, I scuttled off to the loo, desperate to be out of my beautiful dress and back in my pyjamas so I could go to bed, wake up tomorrow and pretend the evening had never happened. But, of course, that would have been too easy.

'Raq – Rachel?'

Ana stared at me from the doorway of the toilets. It was strange to have someone more than a foot taller than you cowering in your presence. She was here? She'd been here the whole time Dan had been doing whatever it was he was doing? He was such a scumbag. As soon as he decides to commit to something, he has to bust a move on the closest single girl he can get his hands on. Actually, that was giving him too much credit; he probably wasn't too arsed about the single thing.

'OK, fine,' I said more to myself than Ana. 'I'm sorry about the other day; I was totally out of order. Now I really need a wee. Can I get past, please?'

She pushed herself against the wall, creating enough space for a Chieftain tank and a double-decker bus to get through side by side.

'Thanks,' I muttered. 'Dan's upstairs.'

'I know you're just jealous,' she said once I was a few feet away. 'Of Dan and me. With your "poor me, I've been dumped" sob story.'

I stopped in my tracks and turned slowly.

'Seriously? You think I'm jealous of you and Dan?'

The two girls standing at the sinks suddenly fell silent and began to wash their hands in slow motion.

'I know you are,' she pouted. 'He's always talking about you. You're obsessed with him. It's sad.'

'He's always talking about me and I'm the one that's supposed to be obsessed with him?'

That one didn't make sense, even for Ana.

'Ana, Dan and I are friends,' I explained slowly.

Veronica had given me a pass once, I wouldn't get a second one; I could not lose my temper. 'We've been friends for years. The reason I lost my temper on Monday was because I'd just broken up with my boyfriend and I was a bit hungover. I'm sorry, I was out of order, but trust me, I am not obsessed with Dan.'

Although you did quite like it when he stroked your arm, you schlaaag, an unhelpful voice in my head reminded me.

'Whatever,' she dismissed, standing up straight. 'It's just kinda sad, don't you think? You get dumped, fuck up your hair and then go after someone else's boyfriend?'

Had to say, I much preferred her afraid.

'Although I wouldn't have thought you had it in you,' Ana fluffed her long blonde hair so that it settled around her bare shoulders. Her skintight gold Hervé Léger bandage dress made my formally racy black number look like I'd borrowed it from the Queen. 'You're just so boring.'

'Boring?'

Don't hit her, don't hit her, don't hit her.

'Dull as shit actually. No wonder your boyfriend dumped you. Probably shagging your nan for some excitement.'

I couldn't hit her. I'd be fired. And she was from Bas Vegas after all, probably pretty handy in a fight. And those two cows who had been washing their hands longer than Lady Macbeth were hardly likely to help me out in a pinch.

'Probably,' I agreed, stretching my arm out towards her. I was pleased to see her flinch.

'Tattoo, Raquel?' She slipped back into her coquettish laugh. 'Who do you think you are, Angelina Jolie?'

'Hardly.' I reached across her face and punched the fire alarm as hard as I could. The sirens and the sprinklers kicked in immediately. 'I don't steal other people's men.'

Well, that cleared the loo pretty quickly. Ana ran out screaming, closely followed by the two witnesses. Emerging back onto the dance floor, I saw a full evacuation was in full flow. Hmm, maybe I should have thought about this one a bit more carefully.

'Rachel, come on, it's a fire alarm!' Emelie grabbed my arm and pulled me towards the door. 'This is insane. Did you see Ana? And Dan?'

'Did you?' I looked around, panicked. Sure enough, there was Ana sobbing on Dan's shoulder and bleating at a man in an orange high-vis vest. Oh dear. Before I could leg it, she was pointing at me and shrieking hysterically. I caught Dan's eye for a moment and realized he was trying not to laugh. I paused and felt a small smile on my lips. I had to stop drinking. And getting tattoos. And dying my hair red. Actually house arrest from now on might be for the best.

'Excuse me, miss.' An authoritative voice to the side of me got my attention as the sprinklers stopped. The ballroom was almost empty, save for me, Emelie, Dan, Ana and a couple of fire wardens. And a policeman. 'This young lady tells me that you set the fire alarm off.'

'She does?' I was still watching Dan. The arsehole was enjoying this.

'She did it,' Ana wailed at the top of her voice, all pretence of a pretty accent vanished. From here on in, the only way was Essex. 'She facking did it.'

I was delighted to see whoever had taken care of her make-up for the evening hadn't bothered using waterproof formulas. She looked like a blonde, bedraggled Alice Cooper.

'Aren't you Anastasia Smith?' Emelie stepped forward, looking oddly starstruck. 'The model?'

'Yes,' she resumed character flawlessly, a beat too late. 'I am.'

'The overpaid, talentless old slag who is too stupid to remember someone's name?'

Oh, Emelie.

'Right, that's *it*,' Ana pushed Dan to one side and launched herself at Emelie. In the blink of a false eyelash, I was in the middle of the world's sexiest catfight. It was just a shame we weren't streaming it live, directly to Perez Hilton: we probably could have made some money. Ana lashed out with her acrylic claws but Em was right in there, punches swinging. All my money was on the redhead. As long as that redhead wasn't me.

'Bugger,' I yelped, taking a swipe to the face and falling to my knees.

'Friendly fire! Sorry!' Em panted as the policeman pulled her off, Dan tackling Ana at the waist.

And so it was, piss wet through, the skirt of my dress all torn up and with my second black eye of the week, that I was carted off to the police station.

'Em?' I whispered, torn between hoping my mum would never find out about this and wishing they would turn the siren on.

'Rachel?'

'Do you think I can count this as breaking the law?'

She sighed and rested her wet head against the back seat.

'Yeah, Rach.' She held up her handcuffs to gesture towards mine. 'I reckon you can.'

CHAPTER TWELVE

Matthew had been delighted when we'd called him from the police station but less amused when we called asking him to bring our ID in. The problem with tiny evening bags was that they didn't really facilitate the carrying of passports. Not that I'd been planning on getting arrested.

'When we put "break the law" we meant nick something,' Matthew yawned in the taxi home. He really hadn't needed to come down in his pyjamas but I was grateful regardless. 'Break the speed limit. Put a cat in a dustbin. Not set the fire alarms off at The Savoy and punch a supermodel in the face.'

'Emelie punched the supermodel in the face,' I clarified. 'And I didn't set the fire alarms off at The Savoy. There are no witnesses, only Ana's word against mine and, as the lovely police officer pointed out, she's a bit mental. It was clearly an accident.'

Em sat silently between us. She stared straight ahead, dazed and confused.

'I'm glad you're taking the new you thing seriously,' he replied. 'But maybe, when you write the letter to Simon, you don't do it in the blood of a sacrificial virgin, OK?'

'OK.' That sounded like a fair compromise. 'Oh, and Dan tried to kiss me.'

'What?' Emelie snapped out of her catatonia and Matthew spat his coffee all down the back of the driver's seat.

'Sorry.' He gave me a full Exorcist turn across the back seat of the cab. 'Dan tried to kiss you? Before or after your *Ocean's Eleven* impression?'

'Before,' I rubbed my shoulder, thinking about the shiver down my spine when he'd touched me. 'We were talking and then he just leaned in a boom. Busted a move. And Ana reckons he thinks I'm obsessed with him?'

'No one's obsessed with him but himself,' Matthew scoffed. 'Hot or not, he's a totally self-absorbed knob.'

'I know,' I nodded thoughtfully. 'She says he talks about me all the time.'

'Ew,' Em chimed in, 'that's so weird. And, more importantly, was he a good kisser?'

'I didn't actually kiss him.' And I absolutely did not regret that fact, I reminded myself. 'I stopped him.'

'Oh,' she looked disappointed. 'Oh!' And then strangely happy.

'That guy at the bar, he was looking for you.' She shone the light of her phone into her clutch. 'He said he went to the loo and when he came back you were gone. He gave me his number. Ashley or something?'

'Asher,' I said, taking the slip of paper. Wow. He actually had gone to the toilet. I'd walked away from a cute yoga instructor that told the truth to narrowly avoid kissing an arrogant photographer who was full of bullshit. 'Wow.'

'The miracle of the list.' Em waved her hands around and made spooky noises. 'Call him. Tomorrow. Or I will.'

'Think you two have done enough communicating on my behalf,' I said, resting my head on Emelie's shoulder and watching the lights of London rush by. Strangely enough, I was quite tired. 'I'll call him.'

Thursday morning came around altogether too quickly. When I finally came to around eleven, I lay in bed for an hour, trying to work out just what exactly had come over me the night before. Just what had come over Dan. And whether or not I would ever work again. At least I had one welcome distraction. A Facebook friend request from Ethan. I lay looking at my phone, happily scanning through his photos and rejoicing in the lack of an apparent significant other. If it weren't for the fact he openly specified that he was interested in women, I'd have been worried. As it was, I was just taking in all the different action poses. Ethan rock climbing. Ethan running in a race. Ethan walking his dog on a beach. Thank you Mark Zuckerberg, all is forgiven.

I tapped out a short message, enjoying the fluttering feeling in my stomach.

'Hi Ethan, great to hear from you too. I can't believe you're in Canada, but I can absolutely believe you're a music teacher. You were always the best in orchestra.'

Too cheesy? Nah, I rolled over onto my belly, I was leaving it in. It was true, and weren't you supposed to flatter boys' egos?

'Unsurprisingly, my career didn't take a musical route. I'm a make-up artist now, living in London. I share a flat with my best friend in Islington, it's fun.'

Technically that was true. Yes, Emelie had her own place, but she hadn't spent a night there since Simon had and 'I live alone because my boyfriend abandoned me but my best friend is temporarily staying with me on suicide watch' just didn't have the same devil-may-care ring to it.

'Do you still have family over here?'

Roughly translated as the world's worst version of 'do you come here often?'

'Loving the pictures of your dog. I think about getting one all the time. Anyway, must dash, busy day – speak soon!'

And round off the message with three out-and-out lies. Perfect.

After five more minutes of Facebook stalking, I rolled across the bed to locate my handbag and pulled out my notebook and pen. The single girl's to-do list was coming along a treat, but today it was time for a more common-or-garden variety of list. It was bizarre; I hadn't gone a day without making a to-do list since 1998. I'd even made one every day on holiday, even if all it said was go to beach, drink lurid-coloured cocktails and pass out. In fact, they were some of my favourites, even if Em tried to piss on my chips by complaining that diarizing a hangover didn't make it any easier to deal with. Figuring it would help my brain stop thinking mad thoughts about moving to Toronto and having beautiful children who played ice hockey and pronounced about 'aboot', I started on a new list. Matthew's birthday was on Saturday and I was contractually obliged to throw him some sort of party. Usually this took place in the pub, due to my general lack of hostess skills and Simon's general grumpiness at finding king prawns from the Iceland party platter down the back of the sofa a week later.

But not this year. This year I was throwing him the party to end all parties and there wouldn't be an Iceland platter in sight. Oh no, this year we were M&S catering all the way. M&S catering and enough booze to put

Mel Gibson on his arse. Or that one from Girls Aloud who liked a drink. I never could remember her name.

First things first: online invite. It really was true, nothing actually happened now until it happened on bloody Facebook. So what if it was only two days to the party, it wasn't like anyone had anything better to do, was it? We were 28: Saturdays weren't for having fun. They were for X Factor and family events you were obligated to attend. Once I'd sent a desperate plea to everyone Matthew had ever met, I went to work on the real list. I'd basically been falsely imprisoned the night before; after all, I deserved a treat. And oh what a treat. Food shopping list, booze shopping list, present shopping list. And I still had to buy a dress for my dad's wedding. The purple silk Warehouse sale number that I trotted out to everything just wasn't going to cut it any more. If only I had a lucrative and high-profile job in Sydney to look forward to . . .

For the first time in I couldn't remember how long, I actually had to put some thought into getting dressed. All my new ensembles were hung up along the curtain rail, out where I could see them and where they could block the bloody sun out of my bedroom. It looked like some kind of very glamorous branch of Oxfam. What to wear today? Now, was Thursday more of a stripy sundress day or a floral Fifties option? I opted for the floral number and tiptoed into the living room to check myself out in the mirror. Being a short-arse, I had to climb on the sofa to get the full effect. And it wasn't horrible. My new bob skirted around my shoulders and the pretty patterned dress squared up my skinny shoulders with adorable cap sleeves. The biggest miracle was that, somehow, the dress had created a waist where there was No Waist. On anyone else, it would have been criminally short, but my midget proportions worked in my favour on this occasion. It looked good. I, on the other hand, did not. Unless waxy corpse was the 'in' look of the season. And, as a professional, I was pretty sure it wasn't. Ever.

Settling on the sofa, I opened my make-up kit and started to play. A little foundation, a lot of blusher, some mascara, maybe a flick of blue eyeliner? I didn't know if it was just because the girl in the mirror was gradually beginning to look human, or because I hadn't had to do this professionally for all of three days, but making myself up was fun. I looked lovingly at the colourful pots of MAC eye shadow, stroked the rubberized casing of my Nars blusher, smiled sweetly at my Lancôme lip gloss. I had to stop thinking of make-up as drudgery, just like everything else. Maybe if I was a better ad for my own work, I'd get more editorial stuff. I didn't need Dan to take me to Sydney; I was bloody good at my job. Veronica should just put me forward and the editors could make a call based on my book. Redhead Rachel had spoken.

Before I left the house, I put a couple of minutes' thought into Matthew's birthday present. Usually, buying for old friends was an easy job, but he was impossible. He despised shopping for himself but he hated when people bought him clothes. If you gave him skincare products, you were calling him old. He was a foodie but he had a nut allergy. He loved sweets but if you got him chocolate, you were trying to make him fat. And even though he loved music, he was a terrible, terrible muso snob and so CDs were out of the equation. Possibly some vintage vinyl but, even then, it had to be mint. And not ironic. So vinyl was an option. There was only one thing I could be certain he would love and that was a clone of himself. If all else failed, there was his annually requested gift, a bottle of whiskey and gay porn. The gift that kept on giving.

Vinyl.

Simon's vinyl.

I shot up off the sofa and catapulted over to the music stand in the corner of the room. Simon had insisted on buying a turntable a couple of years ago and ever since had been collecting rare vinyl to show off whenever my brother or any of his muso friends came over. As far as they were concerned he specialized in the Sixties. In reality, I knew the only music that ever got any play on his iPod was Lady Gaga's first album and Coldplay's last record. Not even *Parachutes*. There it was. His treasured ultra-rare Beatles record. The one he'd held to his chest and whined like a baby until his mum had given it to him. Hmm. Couldn't hurt to get it valued, could it? I'd probably be doing him a favour. And if I had something very valuable on the premises, I could be robbed. He'd feel awful if I was robbed and murdered in the night because he'd left me here alone with a rare Beatles record. I should get it valued. I was going to Soho anyway. Popping it into a protective sheath fashioned out of two issues of *Heat*, I slipped the record in my bag and left the house, feeling strangely elated.

Soho always seemed like a strange part of London to me. Close enough to Oxford Street for tourists to wander in accidentally, mingling with the middle class 'meedja' types who weren't cutting edge enough to have moved their business out east, and of course gay man upon gay man upon gay man. Not literally upon each other obviously. At least not in daylight hours. Most of my time on its cobbled streets was spent either in one of the classy hotels on shoots or hanging out in the Friendly Society with Matthew and Stephen in happier times. In unhappier times, it was the O Bar for an hour until he'd pulled, at which point I'd go and repeat the process with Emelie at Floridita before meeting Simon for a Wagamama's round the corner. Maybe I was a bit boring. But today Soho only meant one thing: birthday shopping. Determined to redeem myself for last year's boxer shorts and beer combo (I'd been very busy. And very lazy), I headed into Vinyl Junkies, looking for something special.

Record shops aren't made for girls. This was a fact. Just like comic shops, Dungeons & Dragons tournaments and reading the newspaper on the toilet, record shops, especially specialist vinyl stores, were property of the Y-chromosome. I felt uncomfortable the second I walked through the door, just wishing I'd gone for jeans and trainers instead of a dress and eyeliner. The two middle-aged men, one bald, one overly hirsute, both misogynists, had me pegged as a novice before I'd even opened my mouth.

'Hi.' I gave them my best please-don't-laugh-in-my-face-or-rip-me-off smile.

They gave me their best you're-shit-out-of-luck-darlin' nods in return.

'I'm looking for a record,' I squeaked. 'For a birthday present.'

They exchanged a look.

'Course you are,' Bald Music Shop Man replied. 'We've got lots of records, though. Anything in particular?'

Great. They had confirmed that I was a moron. Why hadn't I asked my brother Paul to come with me? He was probably best friends with these arseholes.

'My friend's a bit of a muso,' I elaborated, scanning

the glass display cases behind the counter. 'He really likes . . .'

Oh dear god, my mind was completely blank. Why? Why? Don't say it Rachel, don't you dare say it.

'He really likes music.'

Neither Bald Music Shop Man nor Hairy Music Shop Man had an answer to that. OK, there was only one way to save this. Delving into my bag, I pulled out my *Heat* sheath.

'Don't think we've got anything they're reviewing in that, darlin',' said Hairy Music Shop Man. This was the funniest thing Bald Music Shop Man had ever heard.

With a tilt of the head and a small smile, I peeled away the Cheryl Cole cover and revealed my bounty. Oh, would you look at that? Suddenly I had the attention of both muso men.

'While I'm here, I was wondering if you could have a look at this for me.' I laid the record on the counter very carefully. John, Paul, George and Ringo looked up and gave me a smile.

Obviously, these were men who weren't able to communicate in a non-sarcastic fashion and so I took their silence as approval.

'It's my mother's,' I lied unnecessarily. 'I want to get it valued for her. Obviously I've looked online.'

I hadn't looked online.

'Um, well.' Bald Muso Man went to pick it up but paused, looking to me for approval. I gave him a nod and quietly enjoyed the power trip. 'I don't know, it's rare.'

'Sleeves in good condition,' Hairy Muso Man began giving it an automatic once-over. 'Mirror vinyl, Canadian import. Very nice.'

Maybe it's a sign, I thought to myself, while they

ummed and ahhed: all roads lead to Canada. Maybe I was supposed to sell this and use the money to fly to Ethan where we would fall in love and immediately get married. That made sense, didn't it?

'I reckon we could do you about five hundred quid,' he said, not letting go of the record.

Until that second, the proudest moment of my life had been when I'd picked up the keys to my flat. Or the time I did not dry-hump James Franco in the make-up chair. As of that moment, it was not snatching the money out of Hairy Muso Man's hand and running for the hills. Five hundred quid? Really?

'Oh,' I shrugged and held my hand out for the record. 'I can probably get more than that on eBay. Thanks though.'

'Eight hundred,' Bald Music Shop Man said quickly.

'Hmm.'

'Eight-fifty. Best I can do.'

I tried very hard to look unconvinced while I weighed up my options. On one hand, there was a chance that this was sort of technically stealing. But at the same time, Simon was an evil scumbag who had callously abandoned me with the record, which sort of somehow suggested that he wanted me to sell it. Didn't it? And I would very much like eight hundred and fifty pounds.

Hairy and Baldy were literally on the edges of their seats. Pursing my lips, brushing off the skirt of my stripy sundress and hitching my handbag back up on my shoulder, I shrugged.

'Done.'

Walking back out into the sunshine, I felt a little dazed. I had nearly nine hundred quid in my handbag. I pulled out my notebook, checking my shopping list to try and ground myself, but instead of seeing a list of tasks, I just saw £850, written about seventeen times. The worst thing was, I didn't even feel bad. Not a jot of remorse. He hadn't picked that record up since bringing it home two years ago; he would never even know it was missing. I hoped.

Dodging a fruit and veg stall set up in the middle of the street, I headed back up Berwick Street, narrowly avoiding walking face first into a stupidly hot man. We danced around each other for a moment until he laughed and hopped into the street.

'Sorry,' I said. I hated the left-right swerve game – why couldn't we just agree everyone would walk on the left, like on Tube escalators?

'No worries, angel,' he smiled back. Why couldn't everyone be as friendly as a gay man wandering around Soho in the middle of a Thursday morning, I wondered, almost immediately encountering an identical situation with an angry looking man in a suit. Gays were lovely.

Unless you forgot to buy their birthday present. Oh bugger. There was no way on god's green earth I was going back into the record shop, not now I was winning. Which left only one option. Looking up, I spotted exactly where shorts guy had come from. Prowler. Lovely Soho and its gay sex supermarkets . . .

Ten minutes later, I was back on the street, clutching a gay porn parody of *Jersey Shore* and a selection box of Trojans just to be a bit fancy. Matthew would love it. Done with Soho for the day, I prepped myself and my eight hundred and fifty pounds to brave the sprint to the Northern Line at Tottenham Court Road. And I really was just about to leave when I spotted a glass-fronted shop off to my left. In the windows were two dummies, decked out in nothing more than nipple tassels and top hats. It was hardly a shocking sight in Soho but this shop made me stop in my tracks.

Because this wasn't just any shop. This was Agent Provocateur.

Emelie had been a devotee of luxury lingerie since she'd opened the floodgates in La Senza in the second year. Since then she'd graduated through Elle Macpherson Intimates, Cosabella and Calvin Klein and now she was onto the hard stuff. La Perla, Coco de Mer and of course, Agent Provocateur. It wasn't that I didn't like pretty things; I did, but Em earned an awful lot more money than I did. Two hundred quid on a bra? I just couldn't do it. She'd spent several years trying to convert me, insisting that spending that much on something created exclusively to make you feel like a sex kitten could only be good for you, but I could always think of at least five other ways to spend that money. But now, newly single Rachel was going to have to Do It with someone new for the first time in years. And I wasn't twenty-three this time. Sure, new Rachel had already proved she was confident and potentially certifiable – but sexy? It just wasn't a word that sat well with me. A confidence boost couldn't hurt, could it? And I didn't have to spend two hundred quid. I could just look. Probably.

'Hi, can I help you with anything?' asked a painfully beautiful pin-up-a-like as I walked through the door. Clad in a short pale pink dress and black stockings, she gave me a smile with deep red lips. Speaking as a professional, it was a great make-up job. Speaking as a normal girl it was wildly intimidating.

'I'm just browsing, thanks.' My plan was to make a polite lap of the store, pick up two things, check the prices and then go for a tactical exit. Until I saw it. Pink silk, black lace overlay and oh my but it was beautiful. Just seeing the bra hanging there made me want to have sex; I couldn't even begin to imagine the power it might wield on an actual person.

'The Françoise. My favourite.' The pin-up spoke in a quiet voice. Her reverence was entirely appropriate. 'Would you like to try it on?'

'Yes,' I nodded. 'Yes please.'

Looking at myself in the dressing-room mirror was an extraordinary experience. My boobs hadn't got any bigger, my thighs hadn't got any slimmer, and I hadn't suddenly developed Jessica Rabbit curves, but suddenly I was sexy. I was wearing nearly five hundred quid's worth of lace and elastic and I'd never felt more incredible. Not that I'd be able to get into the stockings and suspenders ever again without the shop assistant's help. But when was I going to wear it? I asked myself, turning around, holding up my hair and checking out the back view. It was entirely pointless. I could get just as nice stuff from M&S. Probably. Just because I'd sort of stolen nearly a grand from my ex-boyfriend didn't mean I was made of money, this was ridiculous, this was . . . I stopped striking ridiculous poses in the mirror for one second and carefully removed the single girl's to-do list from my handbag. Buy something. And unless I was very much mistaken, the addendum to that decree was 'something obscenely expensive and selfish.' Like designer lingerie. Like five hundred pounds' worth of designer lingerie. With the money you just made from selling your ex-boyfriend's ultra-rare Beatles record. Well, his mum's Beatles record but she had it coming as well. The cow never had given me her chocolate cheesecake recipe and I had asked for it time and time again. Maybe she kept it from me because she knew we were never getting married and she wanted it to stay in the family. Cow.

'Everything OK?' Pin-Up Gal asked outside the changing room. 'Can I get you anything else?'

'Do you have any more of the knickers in stock?' I

said, letting redhead Rachel take over. It was just easier if she dealt with these decisions.

'Absolutely,' she confirmed through the door. 'Just the briefs?'

'All of it,' Redhead Rachel confirmed. 'I'll take all of it.'

And from that moment on, with Dita von Teese as my witness, I vowed I would never wear a greying bra with no elastic and a little bit of plastic underwiring poking out, ever again.

Having spent the morning buying designer underwear, hanging out in gay sex shops and selling expensive records that didn't belong to me, I felt like the afternoon belonged to tasks my mother would have approved of. Stashing my ill-gotten gains in the bedroom, I changed out of my dress, into a T-shirt and started painting. More people than I'd anticipated had responded to my Facebook invite to the party on Saturday, presumably pity acceptances given that they'd all seen my newly single status on FB. Not that I cared. Pity popularity was still popularity. Of course that meant I couldn't really leave the living room in its current state – masking tape around the light switches wasn't avant-garde, it just looked stupid. As Em had pointed out. Yes, oddly enough, neither she nor Matthew were available to help me out when I'd called to see what they were up to. In Emelie's defence, she was working. Dead-Dad rich Matthew however, had no such excuse. He was just AWOL. As he had been a lot over the last couple of days. If he wasn't with me, he wasn't giving up where he was. Pushing away my concerns that there was no estranged dead dad and that he was turning tricks somewhere in South London, I got back to the job at hand. Hands on hips, I stared down the tins of paint in the corner of the room.

'It's just you and me,' I said out loud, plugging in my iPod dock and putting it on shuffle. And then skipping when 'Love Me Do' came on. Maybe just a bit of Madonna. Me, Madonna and two tins of Dulux Sexy Pink silk emulsion. What could go wrong?

About a month or so after we'd moved into the flat, Simon and I had been scoffing spaghetti bolognese on the sofa, watching Kirstie and Phil, when it happened. Laura the journalist was looking for a London crash pad and, after several misses, Phil eventually found her a beautiful studio in Clapham. And inside that studio in Clapham was a hot pink wall and a red leather sofa. My eyes had lit up in a way that scared the pants off Simon. I hadn't even said anything before he declared a loud, clear 'no', got up, put the kettle on and refused to listen my pleas. Eventually, I got my red leather sofa but he wasn't having any of the hot pink wall. Well, fuckadoodledoo, Simon; now it was my living room and I was having my hot pink wall. And I was listening to Madonna while I did it. In a T-shirt and my knickers. Mostly because it was really hot but also because who cared? Who knew how long I'd be able to stay here if he decided he wanted to sell, but for every last second I had in the flat, it was going to feel like home. My home. Checking the sofa and all immovable furniture was properly covered, I stood back, paint tray in hand, and made sure I was ready to start. It was a big day for proud moments. Having actually used masking tape was the kind of achievement that made me want to call my dad. It was Facebook status update big.

Singing very loudly, I merrily started slapping paint on the wall, beginning with the edges and then moving onto some more experimental designs. Such as writing 'Simon is a dick' in two-foot-high letters right in the middle of the wall. I stopped to take a quick snapshot with my phone before beginning to paint over it. Utterly absorbed in the task at hand, my mind started to run away with itself. Maybe I could stretch out from make-up design to interior design. I was clearly a natural. Perhaps I could put some colour in the bedroom. Maybe some red. Maybe blue. Caught up in redesigning the apartment, and halfway through a vital reinterpretation of 'La Isla Bonita', I realized the doorbell was ringing. Missing out on anything being one of my greatest fears in life, I turned down Madge, dashed to the front door and pressed the buzzer to let them up, only then remembering I wasn't wearing any trousers. Oh well, I told myself, probably a Jehovah's Witness, they wouldn't mind. Regardless, I was already on shaky ground with the commandments as it was, so one of heaven's reps turning up while I was semi-naked was hardly likely to be the crucial black mark against my name. As it turned out, I would have been much happier with a Jehovah's Witness. Or even a Coldseal Windows salesman. Or Hitler. In fact, I'd have been happier with pretty much anyone but Dan Fraser.

CHAPTER THIRTEEN

'Hi.' Dan stood in front of me, back in his regulation jeans, T-shirt and trainers, looking far more confident than he had any right to. 'Can I come in?'

I peered around the doorway and attempted to stare him down. It was easier with the tins of paint. 'Why?'

'Because?' He ran his hand through the back of his hair, making his curls flop forward into his eyes. Not that I was noticing his eyes. Or his curls. Or the way his bicep curled against the white fabric of his T-shirt when he bent his arm. 'Rachel, just let me in.'

I considered slamming the door in his face for a moment before relenting and opening it fully. Redhead Rachel was going to have to go back in her box for ten minutes. 'I honestly have absolutely no idea why you're here,' I said, closing the door behind him. 'Unless Ana sent you to kick my arse.'

'Ana could kick your arse all by herself.' He walked through to the living room and surveyed my handiwork. 'Maybe not Emelie though. You're painting? Or just graffiti-ing your own house?'

I looked at the oversized abuse on the wall and shrugged. 'He is a dick.'

'Definitely, definitely all over then?' he asked.

'We've been through this. I think it was just before your girlfriend went mental in the bogs of a very classy event.' I sat on the arm of my chair, keeping a safe distance in case he came down with a case of the kisses again. Kissing Dan would be awful. Genuinely terrible. I really hadn't given it a second thought and I absolutely hadn't lain awake thinking about how our almost-kiss made my heart race and lips tingle. 'Apparently I'm boring.'

'Couple of things.' He still had his back to me as he picked up a paintbrush and began painting around my eloquent message. 'Firstly, she's not my girlfriend. Secondly, you were the one who ended up being carted off in a police car and, thirdly, no one can call you boring. As evidenced by my secondly.'

Why hadn't he mentioned the fact that I wasn't wearing any trousers? Why hadn't he acknowledged that he'd tried to kiss me? She wasn't his girlfriend? Which pants was I wearing again? Why was he here?

'I wasn't at my most stable,' I admitted, picking up the second paintbrush and starting on the other wall. 'Things are a bit up in the air at the moment. And she was such a . . . such a—'

'Such a dick?' he interrupted.

'Well, yes,' I looked over to watch him happily painting away with a smile on his face. I supposed it would have been a shame to have those biceps in the neighbourhood and not put them to good use. The biceps and the lovely back muscles that moved under his too tight T-shirt every time he stretched up. And I wasn't sure how his backside was helping, other than temporarily putting me into a trance every time he bent down to reload his brush. 'I'm sorry, I know you two are, well, whatever, but I can't deal with it any more. She's a moron, Dan.'

I wasn't able to engage my tact muscles at the same time as my perving muscles, apparently.

'Yeah, she is a bit,' Dan agreed, making short work of the white wall. 'I don't know what I was thinking.'

'It's possible that you weren't,' I suggested, slightly relieved that he hadn't walked out before finishing that difficult bit up by the ceiling. I hated stepladders. 'As usual.'

'How's the list going?' he turned quickly, catching my checking him out completely.

I blushed and turned back to painting my wall, hoping that he could only see one set of cheeks blushing.

'Fine.' I really didn't want to go into my lingerie purchase with him right now. He was seeing all he was going to see of my underwear there and then.

'Good.'

We painted along to low levels of 'Crazy for You' until I decided enough was enough. We weren't going to talk about the fact that he'd tried to kiss me the night before? I put my brush back in the tray, checked they were in fact decent, full-coverage knickers and cleared my throat.

'Dan?'

'Rachel?'

'Without wanting to sound ungrateful, why are you here?'

He stopped painting, turned around and pulled a face.

'It's a good question actually,' he said, pink paint dripping onto his white trainer. 'I was at a camera shop in Old Street and I was walking back to Angel then the next thing I knew, I was here.'

'Right.' I noticed a smudge of paint on his cheek and fought the urge to rub it off. Redhead Rachel was clearly insane and she did not like being put in a time out.

'Thought I'd check to see whether or not they'd sent you down.' Dan spotted the paint on his shoe and sat down cross-legged on my hardwood floor to wipe it off. 'I just wanted to see if you were all right.'

Well that was nice. Really nice.

'You could have called,' I suggested. 'Sent a text?'

'I could,' he agreed.

Right, I needed trousers. The overwhelming urge I had to knock Dan onto his back and find out just what that kiss would have felt like was entirely being-in-my-knickers-related, obviously.

'Back in a minute.' I dropped my paintbrush on a dustsheet and pelted into the bedroom. I just needed a pair of trousers, shorts, anything. A pair of knackered cut-offs that had somehow survived the cull won the race and I slipped them on while giving myself a stern talking-to. This was Dan. This was my friend, Dan. OK, so yes, when you very first met him you thought he was cute, but as soon as he'd established that you were the hired help and not a model, he'd turned off the charm, turned on the bullshit and any thoughts of an office romance were quickly banished. He probably just felt sorry for me because I'd been dumped. Or maybe Veronica had told him I wanted the Sydney job and he was here to let me down gently. Either way, hanging around my flat looking cute and helping me with the painting . . . well, it wasn't a crime but he needed to leave. It was too weird.

'You know, I've never actually been inside your flat before,' he called from the living room. 'It looks like you.'

'Thanks,' I said, striding back in with a great sense

of purpose. A sense of purpose that was somewhat shaken when I saw that Dan had taken his T-shirt off. Oh. My God.

'I didn't want to get paint on it,' he explained, pointing to his shirt on the chair, like butter wouldn't melt. It was one thing to see your attractive co-worker in far-too-tight-for-a-straight-man jeans and T-shirt, and one thing to see him looking gorgeous in a tuxedo, but to have him half-naked in your living room was quite another. Had he always had that body? Yes, the great arms I could understand, he was always lugging camera equipment around, but actual abs? Muscles that I could see and count? Not that he was body-builder bulgy, just nicely defined and perfectly tanned. And while I'd always thought I preferred Simon's smooth chest, the curly brown rug that perfectly matched the hair on his head wasn't hurting. We weren't talking Tarzan and the apes, just a light dusting right across his broad, broad chest.

Shi-i-i-t.

'All right, Fabio.' I picked up his T-shirt. 'I've put my clothes on; you put on yours. It's time to leave, I've got plans.'

'Fine, but I think you're going to want another coat on this unless you want people playing *Catchphrase* on your wall.' He set down his brush and pulled on his shirt. Promptly getting pink paint all over it.

'Say what you see, Dan,' I said, holding the front door open. 'I'll talk to you later.'

'Wait.' He paused on the top step. 'What are you doing Saturday?'

'Day?'

'Night?'

Ruh-Roh, Scoobs.

'I'm actually having a birthday party for Matthew,' I stammered. 'Here.'

'Oh.' He picked at the paint on the front of his shirt. 'That sounds like fun.'

'You can come if you want.'

The words were out of my mouth before I'd had time to think them through. Damn you, Redhead Rachel. I needed to be careful; this whole split personality was all going a bit *Black Swan*. Except I was not Natalie Portman and no one was going to be giving me an award for going mental. 'Nineish?'

'Done,' he gave me a grin and vanished down the stairs. 'See you Saturday, Summers.'

I didn't know what I was most worried about. The fact that I was going to see him on Saturday or the fact that I was super excited about it. Preventative measures had to be taken.

Back in the living room, I sat down for a second and stared at my freshly painted pink wall. What exactly had just happened? Completely weirded out, I dragged my handbag across the floor and pulled out my phone, the scrap of paper with Asher's phone number on it coming out too. Right. I was supposed to call him. Maybe a palate-cleansing date with the cute Clark Kent-alike yoga teacher was exactly what I needed. Because Dan hadn't asked me out on a date. And even if he had, I wouldn't have said yes. Probably. I tapped the numbers in quickly before I could go any further down that line of thought.

'Hello, Asher speaking,' he answered right away, which was nice.

'Hi, Asher.' I wasn't good on the phone; texting had been invented for a reason. 'It's Rachel? We met at the thing at . . .' Where was it that I'd set the sprinklers off and caused thousands of pounds' worth of damage and watched my best friend punch a supermodel in the face? Oh yeah. 'The Savoy last night.'

'Oh, hi.' He didn't hang up! He actually sounded

happy! He didn't know that I was the psycho who'd probably cost him his deposit from Moss Bros! 'I didn't really think you'd call.'

Oh.

'But I'm really glad you did.'

Oh!

'Did you get out OK? How mad was that scene with the sprinklers?'

'Yeaaah.' I was very glad he could not see my face. 'Mad. Totally mad.'

'I was thinking, do you have plans tomorrow night?' he asked straight out. Wow! A date! This is what happened to Emelie all the time!

'I don't,' I said, trying my best to sound flirtatious. This was, after all, the potential father of my children. Christ, my mother would die from happiness if I told her I was marrying a yoga teacher. Although, as we hadn't even been on one date yet, there was a chance I was putting the cart a little bit before the horse.

'Brilliant,' he definitely sounded happy. 'I'm teaching a class in Islington and I thought you might like to come along.'

Really? He'd gone to the trouble of giving Emelie his phone number so he could recruit me into one of his bloody yoga classes? Sorry Mum.

'And then maybe we could go and get a drink?'

The wedding was back on.

'That sounds lovely,' I lied through my back teeth. The drink sounded fantastic; the yoga sounded like sheer torture. 'Can't wait.'

He gave me the time and whereabouts of the class, we said quick goodbyes and I hung up. Yoga date. Either this was a brilliant idea – lots of potential for touching and hilarious stories for the kids, or a terrible idea – I would end up back on muscle relaxants and we'd only have kids because we kept dating out of a weird sense of obligation since he'd injured me and I was embarrassed. Once again, I had that cart rolling well ahead of the horse.

While I was on a roll, I checked Facebook for any new messages from Ethan and giggled like a little girl when there was one waiting.

'Hey again,' he started, 'I can't believe you're single.'

I took one look at the ever more obvious 'Simon is a dick' on the living-room wall and struggled to see his difficulty.

'You're still ridiculously cute – remind me why we never got together? You could have been my first kiss instead of Verity Smith. Have you seen her on here? Not a pretty picture . . .'

What? Still cute? There had been a level of cuteness previously established?

'Sorry, that's awful. But yeah, sucks that you're not with someone awesome. If you were here or I was there, I'd totally be asking you out. You never thought about emigrating? Toronto is great!'

Obviously I hadn't thought about emigrating to Toronto but, as of that second, I was mentally packing my bags. I could live in Canada. So what if it was a bit cold. So what if I didn't know anyone there except for the love of my life. It was close enough to New York that I could get good, high-profile work – and it wasn't as if there wouldn't be work there. I was fairly certain people wore make-up and read magazines in Canada. At least, Emelie did, and she was Canadian. Technically.

Giving up on the painting, I ran a bath and thought about the items left on my list. We were more than halfway along now and it was getting tricky. I still had everything crossed that Veronica would be able to get me on the Sydney job, which would cross off the travel requirement. Writing the letter to Simon was something that needed doing while I was in a more stable mental state. Or a less stable state. One or the other. Which only left finding a date for my dad's wedding and bungee jumping. Or similar. I wasn't sure which was more worrying. Not that anything was as worrying as the fact that I could not stop thinking about Dan's chest hair. Sinking into the deep bubble bath, I closed my eyes and tried not to picture his arse as he bent down to pick up the paintbrush. A bungee jump would definitely be less trouble than this.

It was Friday. And what a difference seven days could make. It was like I was living in not quite a Craig David song, although I sincerely hoped I'd be chilling by Sunday. Except without actually saying chilling, because I could never get away with saying that. What with me being 28, middle class and white. In an attempt not to think about the fact that I had my first date in five years later that day, I'd started the morning off with a run marginally more successful than the last, in that I didn't fall over; then put another coat of paint on the living-room walls and been out to buy food and booze for the party Saturday night. I'd even made my very own chocolate cheesecake in lieu of the forbidden royal iced sponge that Matthew had outlawed. No one had dropped by uninvited, no one had thrown up and no one had dumped me. So far it was one of my better Fridays in recent memory.

Emelie and Matthew had finally surfaced to come and wish me well on my date, in that Emelie was texting Paul, halfway through troughing a giant chicken vindaloo and Matthew was texting 'nobody' and had just spent over an hour trying to get the hottest photo of his new tattoo for Facebook (he said Facebook, I was pretty sure he meant Grindr). Oddly enough, neither of them felt up to coming to yoga with me. I wasn't asking them to come on the date, just the yoga class for a bit of moral support, but when six thirty rolled around, I was standing at the front door in a pair of Emelie's tight little workout trousers and a hot pink vest that just didn't cover nearly as much as I would like and clutching Matthew's yoga mat. Alone.

'But I don't want to.' I went to my last line of defence: whining.

'What if Asher is your soul mate?' Emelie asked through a mouthful of naan bread.

'He's probably not though,' I whined again.

'Em said he was hot,' Matthew said without looking away from his phone. 'Get out of the house.'

'Have fun on your date.' Em waved her hand around randomly, her eyes trained on the X Factor auditions repeat. She was certainly doing her best to fill the Sky Plus box up with as many anti-Simon shows as humanly possible.

'I hate you both.' I let myself out with a huff. 'I'm going, aren't I?'

'And you're going to be late,' Matthew pointed out.

'Fuck off.'

'I'll leave condoms by the bed,' Em called.

Turning on my ballet flats, I stomped out and slammed the door. As much as you can stomp in ballet flats. Which it turned out was quite a lot if you really put your heart and soul into it.

Predictably, the bus was late, meaning I only just made it to the yoga class in time. Asher, sitting up at the front of the room, gave me a relieved smile and a wave as I dashed in, clumsily unrolling my mat and clobbering two other students round the head with my foam blocks. Thank god I hadn't picked up the wooden ones.

'Good evening everyone,' Asher began. I sat cross-legged and tried to look as serene as possible. Out of his tux, Asher was still very cute, although I sort of missed his geeky glasses. Hopefully they'd be reinstated for drinks. His yoga outfit was thankfully not made of Spandex. Perhaps he was the one? Perhaps we'd end up living on an ashram with our beautiful bendy children Clover and Paxo. Hang on, that was the stuffing.

'Shall we start tonight's practice with three ohms and quiet the voice in our mind?' Asher called out to the class in a disturbingly calm voice. Maybe he could tell I was considering naming our first-born child after a Christmas dinner table staple.

I closed my eyes and took a deep breath, but the little voice in my mind refused to play along. Instead of ohm-ing, it seemed to be tutting loudly and whispering something that sounded rather a lot like 'Christ? Really?'

Yes brain, I replied unhappily, really.

'How did you find it?' Asher asked at the end of the session. I sat on the floor, red-faced and sweaty, rolling up my mat and praying that I would never unroll it again. I stared up at him, not quite able to believe he was asking. I'd spent half the class in corpse pose, silently crying, and the other half tearing my hamstrings off the back of my legs, audibly crying.

'It was challenging,' I said, after spending at least half a minute trying to think of an answer that wasn't a lie and didn't include the words 'fucking horrible'.

'Wasn't it?' he beamed. 'So what do you feel like doing?'

Sitting on the floor, looking up at his open, happy face, I had a sudden vision. Asher and I in perfect warrior poses with two identical little Ashers trying to copy us and falling over in adorable bundles of geeky, glasses-wearing joy. Snapping back, I bit my lip.

'Drink?' I suggested.

'And then I called her a vacuous cow,' I said, finishing up my hilarious 'the day I shouted at a supermodel story' and my second glass of red. 'And marched off.'

'Right. Wow. That's um, yeah. Wow,' Asher said for the umpteenth time, finishing up his third beer. He drank a lot for a yoga teacher, I thought. That wasn't a tick in the 'future father of my children' column.

'But you know, onwards and upwards. My round.' I stood up. 'Another of the same?'

'Right. Yes,' Asher said. 'Another.'

Standing at the bar, I looked back at our table. OK, so he was a bit quiet, but he seemed nice. And he couldn't be evil or anything if he taught yoga, surely? After class, we'd ducked into The Lexington, my theory being that if my hamstrings gave up, I'd be able to crawl home. Jamie, the bartender, nodded acknowledgement and lined our drinks up on the bar.

'All right, Rachel?' he asked, taking my twenty.

'Not so bad.' I returned his smile and took my change. 'Busy night?'

'There's a band on upstairs so it's pretty quiet actually,' he said, nodding slightly over to where Asher was sitting playing with his phone. 'What's all this?'

'Oh, new . . . friend,' I pulled a face. 'Simon and I broke up.'

'Bloody fast worker,' he replied. 'I suppose there's no point messing around.'

'He seems all right,' I nodded.

'Well, I'd hold out for better than all right, if I were you, but as long as it's fun.' He gave me a half-smile and moved down the bar to serve the next punter.

Fun. Hmm, was I having fun?

'So how long have you been into yoga?' I asked, setting Asher's beer down on the table in front of him. His long legs were folded up underneath his chair, yoga mat off to the side.

'Cheers. Been a couple of years now,' he said, pushing his glasses back up his nose. 'I love it.'

I nodded. Good, healthy lifestyle. Tick. 'What made you start?'

'Actually an ex got me into it,' he admitted, sipping his pint. 'He'd be practising for years and it was like, if I ever wanted to see him, I had to go to bloody yoga class. I'm glad I did now, though – much happier having yoga in my life than him.'

I felt my eyes widen against my brain's command and very slowly spat my wine back into my glass. For some reason, I was not quite able to swallow . . .

'Your ex was a *him*?' I was sure my voice wasn't quite as high-pitched as it sounded in my head.

'Yeah, oh god, that's not a problem, is it?' He looked nervously across the table. 'I forget some people aren't always totally OK with, you know, that.'

Before I could answer, a strapping six-foot yoga god wandered into my vision, pushed me over onto my arse and swooped in to give Asher a great big kiss. I sat on the grass weeping while my fantasy children sobbed, 'why, daddy, why?'

'Totally OK with that,' I said, having another, considerably more successful go on the wine. 'Totally.'

'Phew.' He jokingly wiped a hand across his forehead. 'Like I say, ex. Long time ago ex.'

I was fine with it. Really. Who wouldn't be in this day and age? Aside from my dad. Again, big tick in the yes column from my mum probably. But I was fine with it.

'I did the teacher training after we broke up.' Asher

sat back in his chair and stretched out his legs. I couldn't even move mine. Still. And it had been two hours and three glasses of wine since I'd even attempted a downward dog. 'Can't believe my distraction ended up changing my life.'

'I can kind of understand that.' I sipped my wine. 'Really.'

'Good to know.' He leaned forward across the table and looked around before nodding for me to come closer. I put down my wine. Was he going to kiss me? Was this the start of something wonderful? 'I know we've only just met, but I actually run a naturist class on Saturdays and then some of us kind of get together afterwards. At my house. You could come along tomorrow if you wanted to?'

I sat back, pressing my lips in a thin, white line.

'Is that the loo over there?' he asked, pointing towards the doors at the side of the room. I nodded silently, staring ahead and not moving. All that time on corpse pose had come in handy after all.

As soon as he disappeared into the toilet, I whipped my phone out of my bag to send Em our agreed 'get me the hell out of here' text message. I'd had enough. I glanced up at the toilet door. No movement.

'I'M A CELEBRITY, GET ME OUT OF HERE' I typed as quickly as I could and kept my phone in my hand.

I had a text from Dan. My thumb hovered over the open button for just a moment. Most likely he was going to say he couldn't make the party, that Ana had tightened the chain on his balls and summoned him home. Try as I might to pretend otherwise, I felt a bit disappointed.

'Can I bring anything tomorrow?'

Huh. It was a nice text. But I still had no idea what was going on and I hated not knowing what was going on. Matthew's best bet was that it was exactly that, a bet; while I didn't like being the subject of a wager, I was prepared to accept it was a likely option. And also, as Em immediately pointed out, I was perversely sort of flattered. As long as it wasn't a pull-a-pig sort of bet. That wasn't flattering to anyone.

I was brief in my reply. 'Just yourself. And booze. Loads of booze.'

'Checking in?' Asher retook his seat. 'Or just letting your friends know I'm not a serial killer?'

'Well, I don't know that yet, do I?' I really didn't want to be on a date with the naked yoga orgy-meister any more. 'No, I just got a text.' I waved my phone around in the air, just to illustrate the point.

'Anything exciting?' he asked, trying to readjust the boys subtly. He was unsuccessful, I noticed immediately. This was one of the major problems about a post-yoga date. Spandex or not, his ensemble left very little to the imagination – and I wasn't even that imaginative. And that would have been embarrassing even if we weren't sitting in my local surrounded by men in jeans and other assorted normal-person outfits.

'Just a friend,' I stuttered over the word slightly. 'A guy I work with.'

'He's a make-up artist?'

I thought he sounded a little bit too amused by the idea of a male make-up artist for a bisexual yoga-teacher.

'He's a photographer,' I clarified. 'We work for the same agency.'

'I've never met a make-up artist before,' he mused. 'Can't imagine spending all day touching up someone's lipstick.'

I smiled politely and threw back half my glass of wine. It was drink it fast or throw it over him and I didn't want to cause a scene. Where was Em? Where was my phone call?

'What made you want to do it as a job? The make-up thing, I mean.' Asher rubbed the end of his nose. Had it always been that big?

'Well, I used to like art at school but I was no good at it and I was always doing my friends' make-up.' I had the short answer down pat. It was a question I was asked a lot. 'The more I did it, the more I really loved the idea of making something beautiful, using make-up to transform someone. That's it really.'

'It's interesting because obviously you don't look like someone who wears a lot of make-up,' he said while I sat on my hands. 'It's probably because I'm a man but, really, I just don't understand the thrill of covering your face in crap. No one looks better like that. I mean, the other night? All those women done up like complete tarts? No thanks.'

'Well, I don't go around covering people's faces in crap,' I said. 'Thank goodness.'

'It's just a weird job though, isn't it?' He just didn't know when to stop. 'Did your parents never freak out and tell you to get a real job?'

'Nope.'

'And the whole "artist" thing. Really? Make-up *artist*? I mean, if you were a real artist, wouldn't you be offended?'

'Nope.'

Despite the fact that my glare could have frozen the seventh circle of hell, he carried on.

'Always fancied being a photographer though.' He laid his phone on the table to show an entirely unremarkable shot of London from Waterloo Bridge. 'I've always had a good eye.'

I couldn't count the number of times I'd seen Dan

deal with amateur photographers. Putting them down with a look was one of his gifts. Occasionally it took a patronizing smile or polite laugh. I understood; we both had jobs everyone thought they'd be able to do. After all, I was just touching up someone's lipstick and putting crap on their face.

'I think it's probably a more difficult job than people realize,' I said diplomatically, ignoring his phone. 'Dan is really talented.' I thought back to the photo in the gallery the night before. He really did have an amazing eye for creating something stunning. When he wasn't taking pictures of Ana in her knickers.

'Yeah, if I hadn't had to get a job, I could have studied photography. It's not reliable though, is it?' Asher's tone was decidedly defensive. 'I mean, I suppose some people just luck into jobs, don't they?'

'He didn't luck into it,' I replied with equal aggression. 'He worked really hard. Being a photographer doesn't just happen – you have to do years as an assistant, you're always having to study new techniques and work with new equipment. And then there're the long hours and all the travelling. And if you're as good as Dan, it is reliable.'

Asher looked pissed off.

'Same for make-up artists,' I muttered into my wine glass. My phone was still dormant in my bag. Where the bloody hell was Emelie? If she was texting my brother instead of saving me from a night in the cells when I clubbed this idiot to death, there would be trouble. 'It goes a bit further than touching up people's lipstick.'

'Do tell,' he said, looking at his watch.

'You know, I would, but my friend just texted me and I really need to leave,' I said, knocking back the rest of my wine and throwing my bag over my shoulder. 'Thanks so much for tonight.'

'Did your friend really text you?' he asked, standing up but not looking particularly surprised.

'Nope,' I flounced past him. 'Bye.'

'You forgot your yoga mat,' he shouted after me across the loud and now busy bar.

'I don't care,' I shouted back.

Which was true until I got outside and remembered it wasn't actually my yoga mat and now I owed Matthew twenty quid. Bugger.

Best. First. Date. Ever.

CHAPTER FOURTEEN

'Oh, you know me so well,' Matthew shouted over the music and waved his present around gleefully. 'Can I put it on?'

'DVD yes, condoms no,' I replied.

Matthew's party was going better than I had anticipated. Having been desperate to eradicate all memory of the night before, I'd really thrown myself into the party planning. There were ridiculous amounts of booze in the kitchen, more food than would ever be consumed by the assembled masses and I'd even dug out the fairy lights to create a bit of interesting lighting. It was also something of a plus that the low lights meant you couldn't read 'Simon is a dick' on my living-room wall. Which you could in direct sunlight. Still. Everyone seemed to be enjoying themselves. Matthew was already worse for wear, Emelie was doing a fine job as secondary hostess keeping everyone's glasses full and I hadn't freaked out once. Result.

'So what did you do today?' I asked Matthew, taking a moment out of refilling the chips and dips to sit down on the sofa with the birthday boy. He wasn't bouncing off the walls as I might have expected. Worrisome. 'You don't seem your usual desperately self-involved birthday self?'

'Oh god, I don't?' he looked utterly stricken. 'Sorry, distracted.'

'I know, that's what's bothering me.' I ruffled his hair and tried not to look at my own TV screen. I assumed he was suffering First Birthday Without Stephen Syndrome and tried not to push it. 'Are you OK? Did you have a nice day?'

Matthew, on the other hand, could not tear his eyes away. 'Today? I slept, watched telly, had a wank. What's tall, dark and dickhead doing in the kitchen?'

He was of course referring to Dan. He'd arrived dead on the dot of nine with a bottle of whiskey, a bottle of vodka and a case of beer. Never let it be said that the boy could not take direction. And yet, since he'd walked through the door, we'd barely spoken. I was pretty much resigned to the fact that I'd misread the situation and he was just being friendly and supportive because I'd been dumped. And by 'resigned to', I of course meant 'relieved by'.

'He seems all right.' Matthew poured us both tumblers full of whiskey. He had eschewed the beer and wine options much, much earlier in the evening 'I forgot how hot he was.'

'Yeah anyway, back to you, birthday boy.' Whiskey was good. 'Is everything really OK? You just seem a bit down. As in more than your usual "everyone's a knob but me" down.'

'I know, I'm a miserable bastard,' Matthew threw back his drink and poured another. 'It's just, whatever. Birthday blues.'

'Watch your porno and be quiet then,' I ordered, giving him a kiss on the top of his head before marching back into the kitchen in search of the Doritos. It was a classy party.

'Matthew having fun?' asked Dan as I slid past. Tonight's ensemble combo included dark indigo skinnies, a checked white shirt, pale blue cashmere V neck and a skinny black tie. I had to admit, he looked really good. If a little warm. I was in my new sleeveless sky blue silk dress and I was roasting.

'Like the child that he is, he's fine now that I've told him he can put his video on,' I said, peering back into the living room. I knew Matthew wouldn't want me to go into his soul-wrenching heartbreak, so I didn't. Yay me. 'You OK?'

'Yeah, I was talking to Emelie. She seems nice when she's not punching out my date.'

'She is,' I said. Nice? Date? Were they back on? Argh. 'Are there any more crisps anywhere?'

'She's really hot.' Dan reached up to the top shelf where he'd hidden the snacks.

'She is.' There was no way on god's green earth he'd come to my party to hit on my best friend. Was there?

'No need to be jealous.' He set the crisps down and then turned to hold my gaze. 'You're hotter.'

I coughed, choking on a freshly acquired Dorito.

'Rach!' Matthew shouted from the living room. 'There's someone knocking at the door.'

'Then answer it,' I replied, not taking my eyes off Dan.

'I'm watching porn,' he yelled back. 'And it's my birthday.'

'I'll get it,' Dan said. I looked away quickly, just not quickly enough. 'Can you put the guacamole into that blue bowl? It's the green lumpy stuff.'

'You're so funny, I could wet myself.'

'Not in the kitchen, please.' He placed his hands on

my waist as he slid past me into the living room. Hmm, there was that funny flushing feeling again. He really needed to stop touching me. Or start doing it more regularly. I wasn't sure which. Whiskey made me very indecisive.

'This is a really great party.' Em replaced Dan in the kitchen, nibbling delicately on a carrot stick. Which was annoying given that I'd bought Mini Cheddars especially for her. 'There are so many people here.'

'Don't sound so surprised,' I replied. 'I'm very popular.'

'And you're wearing a dress again.' She gave me a half-hug, checked whether or not anyone was looking and inhaled a handful of dry-roasted peanuts. 'It's so pretty.'

'Thanks,' I gave her a little spin to make the full skirt flare out. 'I'm almost out of new outfits but nothing that survived the cull seemed appropriate.'

'Your old clothes weren't appropriate for milking cows,' she replied. 'There were fabrics in there I couldn't even identify.'

I stopped spinning and shoved a Mini Cheddar in her mouth. 'You threw away my wool coat. Aka my only coat.'

'Rach, my love,' Em said through a mouthful of cheesy biscuit. 'That was not a wool coat. It had never even been near a sheep. If that coat saw a sheep, it would climb off your body to go and take a closer look and ask you what the fluffy bah-ing thing was.'

'I still don't have a coat,' I grumbled. 'Glad you decided to come casual, though – wouldn't have wanted you to dress up too much.'

Emelie had gone all out for Matthew's party. Which was something of an understatement. Emelie had gone all out for the Notting Hill Carnival. At what point had she sat down and decided this was a good outfit in which to attend a house party, I did not know. In all her stylish wisdom, my best friend had teamed bright red sequined hot pants with fishnet tights and a slouchy striped T-shirt that sloped just low enough on her left shoulder to show off her new tattoo. Her glossy auburn hair was five times its usual size, a mass of haphazard curls pushed over one shoulder, and I assumed the black strappy patent platforms I could see by the sofa were hers. She looked like an off-duty Pussycat Doll. Or a very, very high-class hooker.

'I just thought it might be nice to try a bit,' she said, looking back into the living room where Dan was sitting on the opposite end of the sofa to Matthew, trying not to look as if he was interested in what was on the TV. Which, to be fair, was very interesting, regardless of sexual orientation. Who knew you could get that many people in a hot tub? I supposed they were all doing their best to squeeze together and make space. 'So, I was talking to Dan the man?'

'That must have been fun,' I said quickly. 'Do you know where the tzatziki is?'

'He's not going out with Ana any more.' She kept me locked in an even gaze. 'Apparently they had a massive row after . . . um, you set sprinklers on her and I smacked her in the gob.'

'Shocked.' How had she managed to get all of that out of him in five minutes at a party? I'd had him in my house painting for half an hour and hadn't been able to work out what the hell was going on with him and Ana. 'He told you all that, did he? Word for word?'

'Yeah . . . Funny how he's ended up here tonight,'

she replied. 'Hypothetically speaking, if he were interested, would you be interested?'

'If you're asking for permission to make a move, I won't remind you that you've agreed to go to my dad's wedding with my disgusting brother and I won't remind you that Dan is a massive, massive player.'

I chose to ignore the fact that I felt as though I'd just stabbed myself in the gut repeatedly with a rusty butter knife.

'Not me.' She paused to give Pete, my next-door neighbour and local middle-aged postman, a wink as he sidled past to get to the fridge. Poor Pete looked as if he was about to have a heart attack. 'You.'

'It's Dan.' I held my hands up to emphasize the weirdness of what she was proposing. 'I mean, *Dan*. We've worked together for years, we're friends. Sort of. I couldn't.'

'So?' Em refused to let it go. 'Things change. You've changed. And, more importantly, he's tall, he's gorgeous and he's here.'

She had a point.

'And I just want to get my hands in his hair.' She pulled her own hair and fluffed the ends. 'And the eyes, Rachel, the big brown eyes. Do not tell me you don't want a go on it.'

'Please, I'm eating.' I would have made a great politician. Probably.

'Rach?' Helena, my upstairs neighbour, appeared at my side with air kisses and a bottle of vodka. 'Is it me or does it say "Simon is a dick" on your living-room wall.'

'Sort of, yeah.' I gave a considered nod. 'I might have to give it another coat.'

'Shout if you need help,' Dan shouted across the room. 'She's not very good.'

Could he hear us? Could he hear Emelie? Shi-i-i-t.

'I'm amazing,' I countered. 'I totally did all the edging on my own.'

'Whatever.' He turned back to his conversation with Matthew. I turned back to Helena with slightly redder cheeks than I'd had before.

'So, um, I saw on Facebook that you two had broken up.' Helena hedged around her point awkwardly. 'Is everything OK?'

Helena was a great neighbour. She took the post in when we went away, she never made excessive noise and she always had milk and teabags. Unfortunately, she was not a star singleton role model. Despite being perfectly good looking, successful and – as far as I knew – disease free, Helena could not give it away and she was this close to turning 38. Given the way she was staring at Dan, I wasn't worried that this was because she was being too subtle in her approaches.

'Everything's fine.' I did not want to get into the break-up story at that second. It was Matthew's night. At least until midnight. Or until I finished the whiskey. Whichever came first. 'Thanks.'

'We should go out together,' she suggested with a friendly nudge. 'Unless you haven't already moved on.' Another pointed stare at Dan.

'No, I'm officially single now,' I replied. 'Professionally.'

'Brilliant.' She slid an arm around my shoulders and hiccuped. 'No one knows more about being single than me. Been single for ever, darlin'. I'll show you the ropes.'

I accepted her parting slap on the arse with a cheerful laugh. Single forever. Now there was a cheerful thought.

'Rach, your phone.' Em pointed towards a gently vibrating iPhone on top of the TV. Dashing past the

Jersey Whores, I grabbed my phone, ignored the mass jeers from the crowd that had settled on and around the sofa to watch and slipped into my bedroom. It was a message. From Ethan. I nudged the pile of jackets and cardigans over to one end of the bed so I could sit down and read it properly.

I'd replied to his 'I'd totally ask you out' message earlier in a fevered hour-long session of writing, deleting, writing, editing, deleting and eventually sending. The general gist of it was that he should be careful what he wished for, that I couldn't believe he was single and that I travelled a lot for work so a trip to Toronto wasn't out of the question. Which it wasn't. Sort of. I couldn't wait to see what he had to say. I really hoped it didn't include mention of a restraining order.

'Hey, hope you're having a fun Saturday night. Today was brutal. There was an incident with an oboe/light-saber battle. Being a teacher is tough sometimes.'

Too cute.

'Hmm, why am I single? Good question. I guess I don't know the answer or I wouldn't be! In the interests of full disclosure, I was actually in a pretty serious relationship until the beginning of this year but that didn't work out. She moved away, I didn't want to. And so, the singleness. I don't think I'm very good at it, though, otherwise I'd have more exciting plans than hanging out with my dog on a Saturday night. Any exciting plans your end that I should be jealous of?'

Tucking my hair behind my ears, I started my reply. Emelie would be mortified: imagine replying to a message from a boy Straight Away. But he was so sweet – how was it possible that he was still so sweet? I wanted to sound interesting and fun but not like a crazy party girl. I'd managed to keep The Savoy

Incident to myself – this one should be easy. Writing messages was so hard, how did anyone ever get together through internet dating?

'Hi! Happy Saturday!'

Good start, Redhead Rachel congratulated me. Now, let's just bang this one out and not take an hour like we did this afternoon.

'I do not like the sound of your job – lightsabre oboes? I hope you're getting danger pay. I'm having a party for my friend's birthday. He's currently sitting on the sofa watching gay porn while everyone brings him drinks. I think he's having fun.'

And then I was lost. We'd done all the 'but you're so cute!' parts – how did I carry this on without it just becoming about the weather and what he was eating for dinner. Should I carry this on? I knew it was point- less, long-distance email flirtations rarely ended well, but I wasn't ready to give up the kick I got every time my phone buzzed.

'Staying in with your dog sounds like a lovely Saturday night. Especially when you compare it to this gay porn birthday party. I hope you have some equally thrilling plans for the weekend?'

I sent it before I could think better of it and then lay back on the bed for a moment. I loved my friends and I loved that they'd all trekked over here on a Saturday night at short notice for the party, but I just needed a minute to myself. I was so tired. Being single was hard work. Throwing a party, getting tattoos, screaming at supermodels, going to yoga, dating morons, running, cutting and colouring your hair, breaking the law, selling your ex-boyfriend's ultra-rare vinyl and then spending the money on designer undies *and* painting your flat, all in one week, really took it out of a girl.

'Whatcha doin?' Emelie's head popped around the door. 'You're missing all the fun.'

'Am I?' I asked without sitting up.

'No, not really.'

The bed bounced lightly as she threw herself down beside me. 'This bed is comfy.'

'And now there's plenty of room in it.' I stretched out to grasp the opposite end of the duvet.

'That's one good reason why I don't allow sleepovers,' Em advised sagely. 'Always call them a cab before they get comfy.'

'I take it all back,' I said, eyes closed. 'You and my brother are a match made in heaven.'

'Ha,' she replied. 'We'll see about that.'

Em was quiet for a moment.

'Is everything OK?' she asked. 'In general? With you?'

'I think so.' I didn't bother opening my eyes. 'I just need a minute.'

'I'm really proud of you, you know,' she said, finding my hand and giving it a squeeze. 'You're handling this like a pro.'

'What kind of pro exactly?'

Before she could answer, my phone started vibrating on the bed between us.

'International number,' she said, standing up and slipping out through the door. 'Ooh.'

I sat up straight. International? Could it be?

'Hello?' My heart was absolutely racing and I had a terrible case of dry mouth, only partly due to the amount of whiskey I'd drunk.

'Rachel?'

It was Simon. Almost exactly eight days to the second since he'd done the deed, it was Simon.

'Hi,' I whispered. I wanted to hang up. I wanted to shout and scream but I couldn't. I just listened.

'I've been meaning to call all week,' Simon started slowly. 'See if you're all right.'

'It's Matthew's birthday.' I was determined to make it through in one piece. Where was Redhead Rachel when I needed her? 'We're having a party.'

'Well, tell him happy birthday from me.' He coughed awkwardly. 'Listen, I talked to an estate agent about putting the flat on the market today.'

He was already talking to someone about selling the house? I held the phone tightly, not saying anything, just feeling it getting hotter and hotter against my ear.

'So, if you want to buy me out, we can talk about that.' The same cold voice he'd used the last time we'd spoken was back. Obviously this was the business end of the phone call. 'I'd just like it sorted out sooner rather than later.'

Eloquent words at the right times had never really been my strong point. As my performance with Ana had proved, I'd never been a girl who excelled at lucid arguments and knocked her opponent down with a single sentence; but *nothing* . . .? I couldn't come up with *anything*? That was just rubbish. So I did the only thing I could do. I hung up. I just wasn't going to deal with this right now.

'Can I come back in?' Em asked once she was already back through the door. 'Was it Ethan?'

'Simon.' I stared at the wall in front of me. 'He wants to sell the flat.'

'*Enculé*,' Em bit a nail. 'What did you say?'

'I hung up.'

'Good girl.' She gave me a tight smile. 'What do you want to do?'

'It's a birthday party, isn't it?' I gave myself a mental and physical shake. He was not going to ruin my evening. 'Let's get our cake on.'

'Yay.' Em clapped and brushed down my dress. 'You look gorgeous by the way. Fuck that guy.'

'Fuck that guy,' I repeated. The words had a very comforting cadence, especially when repeated over and over and over.

'Happy birthday to you,' Em dimmed the lights and began singing as I stepped carefully through the living room, holding my amazing cheesecake aloft. Well, holding my slightly sunken on one side but surely still edible cheesecake aloft. It was the first cake I'd made since a pineapple upside-down cake in Home Ec and, god help me, this one had better be edible.

The party seemed to have thinned a little since my time out, but Dan was still there, albeit trapped in a corner by Helena, and Matthew was holding court on the sofa while his BFF and premier trolley dolly, Jeremy, furnished him with the appropriate drinks and snacks. Everyone else seemed to be smiling. This was officially a good party.

'Where did you get that?' Matthew's reaction to my culinary expertise was not exactly what I'd been hoping for. 'I hope you've got the receipt.'

'She made it, you knob.' Em cracked him round the back of the head. 'So shut up and eat it.'

'You made it?' His eyes glowed with love and booze. 'But you can't make tea?'

'I know.' I was too proud of myself to be offended. 'And I don't even think it's going to taste horrible.'

'I'll be the judge of that.' He steeled himself and cut a slice, avoiding the candles. The whole room was silent. Matthew stuck his fork in with impressive commitment and shovelled a giant mouthful towards his face.

'It's not horrible. Is it horrible?'

'It's not horrible,' he confirmed, taking another bite to prove his point. 'It's actually good.'

A sigh of relief echoed round my living room as everyone relaxed. I hadn't poisoned the birthday boy; they could go on with their evening.

'Good work, um, Rachel?' Jeremy said. I nodded confirmation that Rachel was in fact my name. He'd been Matthew's best gay buddy for years and he still couldn't tell the difference between Emelie and me. 'You'll make someone a lovely wife one day.'

'Yes, well, quite. If you would just excuse me for a moment.' I gave him my best dazzling smile, turned on my heel and marched straight into the bathroom. Where I let out the most pathetic howl I'd ever heard – and I'd been there when Matthew got his tattoo. The party responded accordingly with absolute silence.

'Jeremy, you knob,' I heard Emelie screech, before a far calmer version of the same voice spoke through the bathroom door. 'Rach? You all right in there?'

'Not really,' I replied from my elegant seat on the toilet.

I spun the toilet-roll holder around and around until all the specially purchased triple-layer Velvet was on the floor.

'Can we come in?'

'Probably not best.'

'Helena says she needs a piss,' Matthew said.

'Helena can go home and have a piss.' Oh my but my voice sounded a touch manic.

There was some mumbling outside the door, followed by footsteps, shuffling, doors banging and more mumbling. Rather than worry what people were thinking, I concerned myself with getting all that toilet paper back on the roll.

'Rach,' Em called, still on the other side of the door.

'Matthew and Jeremy want to go dancing so everyone's going to Popstarz.'

'Everyone?' I tried to imagine Postman Pete in the middle of a throbbing gay dance party. I suppose you never really knew your neighbours . . .

'Yeah, I'm a bit sleepy, though, so we can stay home and demolish the rest of that cheesecake. If there's any left.'

It was the most diplomatic way of saying 'everyone has left because you're mentally unstable but I'm staying on suicide watch' with a side of 'But hey, remember you made that cheesecake and it wasn't awful? That's your reason to live!' that I'd ever heard.

'No, you should go,' I croaked. 'I just need a minute. And then I'll come and meet you.'

'I'm not in the mood—'

'Emelie. You should go,' I said firmly. 'I just want to go to bed and I'm not in the mood for a sleepover.'

Further muffled debate outside the door.

'Hey, Rach, Em's coming to Popstarz so just get in a taxi and come if you want?' Matthew yelled. He actually sounded glad to escape. His mind hadn't been at this party from the beginning. If I wasn't losing my own tentative grip on sanity on the toilet, I might have thought more about where his was.

I smiled and ran a finger along the hem of my pretty dress. Sorry, dress. You deserved better than this, I thought.

'Get off you, daft cow,' Matthew hissed. It sounded like he was enduring some physical opposition to his declaration. 'Not you, angel. Just telling Emelie not to be retarded, I know you're fine. We'll see you later.'

'See you later.' I tried really hard to make it sound like I wasn't crying.

Waiting until I heard the front door slam shut, I stood up amidst a sea of bog roll and sighed unnecessarily loudly. It made me feel better. Redhead Rachel gave me a foul look in the mirror as I opened the door and peered out. Empty glasses, cans and discarded paper plates everywhere. Nothing like the aftermath of a party to make you feel like shit. I had to clean up. I had to take the dress off to clean up. Reaching around for the zip, I unfastened the dress and shucked it off. Such were the benefits of living alone: you could be in your underwear in your living room and no one saw. Or cared. I let the silk swoosh onto the living-room floor and stepped out of the puddle of pale blue prettiness. Just before I heard footsteps coming up the hallway.

'Oh, bloody hell.' Dan stood at the living-room door, shielding his eyes. I didn't know whether to be ecstatically happy or mortified that I was wearing my minxish new lingerie. I suppose it was better to flash someone in the lingerie of a burlesque performer as opposed to that of your average nan. He quickly pulled off his jumper and threw it in my general direction. It was just about within the scope of my understanding that I was supposed to put it on.

'I'm sorry,' I squealed, my head lost inside the soft fabric. 'I'm so sorry. I thought everyone was gone.'

'I came back for my keys.' He peered through his fingers. 'The door wasn't shut properly.'

I nodded at my toes. Well, this was awkward.

'You all right?'

I looked up. What a bloody stupid question.

'You're so much better than this, you know.' He gestured around the living room. Was he slating my decorating? Was he slating his decorating? 'You're not some prematurely middle-aged housewife. You're not boring. You're amazing.'

'I'm prematurely middle-aged?' It took a minute for the second part of the sentence to filter through. 'I'm amazing?'

'Yeah, like, you should still be doing better jobs,' Dan said quickly. 'Not just sticking to the local stuff because you've got to get home and cook your boyfriend's tea. I think this whole break-up thing is going to be good for you.'

'Right.' I ignored the crushing disappointment in my chest and pulled the jumper down to my knees. 'Well, maybe I like being at home to cook my boyfriend's tea?' This didn't feel like the time to mention the fact that I hadn't cooked Simon's tea once in five years.

'Or maybe you should come on the Sydney job with me,' he added. 'The people they've suggested so far are shit.'

Sydney! This was where I was supposed to be jumping up and down with joy but my feet were glued to the spot. The room was still lit by fairy lights and the remains of Mathew's cheesecake sat on the table between us. The birthday candle wicks, black and fuzzy.

'I talked to Veronica about it,' I said. 'She's going to put me forward, I think.'

'You'll get it. You're one of the best out there, you know,' he said, leaving the safety of the doorway and walking over to where I stood, swamped by his huge sweater. I really was a short-arse.

'And you're funny,' he went on. 'You're clever, you're unpredictable and, with some training, you could make a half-decent painter's mate.'

And I was lost for words. 'Thanks?'

'You don't need to check things off a list to teach you how to be amazing.' He was standing right in front of me. Close enough for me to notice he hadn't shaved.

226

Close enough for me to notice dark circles under his eyes. Close enough to smell his shampoo. 'You'll have a new boyfriend before you can blink.'

I blinked.

And then Dan kissed me.

It was short and soft and very brief but I still panicked. Pulling away sharply I clapped my hand over my mouth and locked my wide eyes on his. That was a definite kiss, not just an awkward swoop like at The Savoy. Definite lip on lip. But Dan didn't move. He just stood there, looking at me, all soft brown eyes, full lips and chocolate curls resting on his cheekbones. He didn't apologize; he didn't say anything. Instead, he took my hand in his, held it down by my side and kissed me again. And this time, I didn't stop him.

The hand that wasn't holding on to mine brushed my cheek before the fingers curled around my face, weaving themselves lightly into my hair. His lips were soft and the gentle kisses quickly began to build into something more as my body responded. My brain was still back in the bathroom trying to work out how to get the loo roll back on the holder, and I was quite happy for it to stay there. Its services were not required. My hands reached up around his neck, combing through his curls, my feet pushing me up onto tiptoes to better reach his kisses. This was insane. I was kissing Dan. But my heart was beating loudly in my ears, determined to drown out the voice in my head that kept saying this was stupid and whiskey-fuelled and that I'd regret it in the morning, I just couldn't find the words to make him stop. Because I really didn't want him to.

Instead, I let Dan pick me up until my toes were off the ground, and push me backwards against my big fluffy sofa cushions, the warm weight of his body settling on top of me. His lips were still firmly fixed

227

to mine but his hands began to wander, sliding underneath his whisper-soft jumper, settling on my lower back. At first.

'I have thought about this for so long,' he whispered, starting a trail of kisses from my ear all the way down my neck. I still didn't have words but my broken breath seemed to be enough. In lieu of words, I reluctantly pulled my hands out of his hair and ran them across his broad shoulders, tracing the muscles in his back. Lugging around all the camera equipment really had made for a great daily workout. He felt so solid and strong. Loosening his tie, he unfastened his top two buttons before putting his hands to work elsewhere.

'Oh,' I squeaked, opening my eyes in surprise. 'Cold hands.'

'Sorry,' he said, a small smile in his voice, but I could tell he didn't mean it. Mostly because he was too busy trying to take off the jumper that he'd given me to put on five minutes before. 'Do you wear this under those leggings every day?'

'No.' My voice sounded breathless and strange. 'Or yes? Actually yes.'

Compared to the other whoppers I'd been banging out lately, it was only a tiny white lie.

'Amazing.' His fingertips grazed the lace trim of my underwear before he went back to relieving himself of his own clothes. The sound of a fly being unzipped was apparently what it was going to take to bring me to my senses. Dan was my friend. I was very recently single. But his strong hands on my soft skin felt so amazing. I was upset about Simon's phone call. This wasn't real. My legs slid up around his waist while his jeans slid down towards the floor. I couldn't remember the last time I'd felt so wanted. The last time I'd wanted someone just as much. But this really was just about the stupidest thing I could do, besides going outside and dragging a stranger in from the street. I couldn't do this.

'I can't tell you how many times I've wanted to do this at work,' he said. 'Just drop my camera and push you up against the wall and just . . . for years . . .' Dan's words trailed off into low moans and I felt teeth on my earlobe. Rowr.

'Really?' I heard myself. I sounded surprised. Back in the bathroom, my brain acknowledged that yes, this was in fact a surprise. It also wanted to come back into the living room but I wasn't ready to let it in yet.

'Really.' He pushed himself up on one elbow and looked down at me with dark, heavy, dilated eyes. I pressed one hand across his chest, feeling his heart beating hard. This was it, last chance to be sensible. 'I've wanted to be with you for so long. I've waited for so long.'

Everything was just starting to get hot and loud and blurred when I heard my phone trilling loudly in the bedroom.

'Ignore it,' Dan murmured, pinning my wrists above my head.

'It's Emelie's ring.' I arched my back and felt a shudder run all the way down from the top of my head to my toes. 'I should answer it.'

'She'll get the hint.' He buried his face in my neck and oh, there was the earlobe thing again. This was wildly unfair. 'Please.'

But I knew Emelie wouldn't give in. And if I didn't tell her I was OK, she'd only come home to check what was going on. And that was the last thing I needed because, quite honestly, I had no idea myself. 'One second.' I reluctantly pushed his hands away and found the floor with my feet. 'Just one second.'

I picked the jumper up off the floor and pulled it on, readjusting my bra strap as I went. Worth every bloody penny, I thought as I dashed into the bedroom as fast as my wobbly knees would let me. My iPhone glowed in the darkness with three missed calls, all in the last five minutes, all from Emelie. As I picked it up, the phone buzzed into life.

'Hey,' I answered quickly. 'I'm fine, I just really can't talk right now, I—'

'Rachel, that cheesecake you made, did it have walnuts in it?' Emelie cut me off. 'Matthew's face is like, fifteen times bigger than it should be.'

'Oh, fuck.' I pressed my hand to my mouth. 'I didn't check the biscuits. I totally forgot about his nut thing.'

'He's going to be OK, we're on our way to the hospital,' she replied. 'I just need to know what to tell the doctor.'

'Hasn't he got his shot thing with him?' I ran past a semi-naked Dan and into the kitchen, looking for the spare epi-pen I kept in case of emergencies. Of which we'd already had two this year. Matthew wasn't nearly as careful as he should be, but I couldn't believe I'd been so stupid.

'He didn't bring it; he said his jeans were too tight and it made him look like he had a permanent skinny hard-on.'

'Of course he did. I'm on my way.'

'You don't have to come,' Em said. 'We're almost there.'

'Yeth thee doth,' I heard Matthew lisp in the background. 'I'm goin' to thlap her.'

'I'm on my way.' And back through the living room, ignoring the beautiful man on the sofa and into the bedroom. Jeans. I needed jeans. I'd poisoned my best friend on his birthday. This was a new level of fail.

'Hey, I – oh my.'

On my third trip back to the living room, I was greeted with the sight of Dan, stretched out on the sofa, shirt fully unfastened and revealing the previously unexpected chest hair scattered across. His jeans were gone, boxers on, but failing to completely conceal something else previously unexpected but hotly anticipated. Gosh.

'Everything OK?' he asked. He was obviously a comfortable semi-naked person. But, to be fair, he had good reason to be. 'Come here.'

'This is not good timing, I realize.' I was well aware that I was to go nowhere near the sofa. Instead, I clung to the doorframe, keeping a good and safe few feet between us. I must have picked my brain up somewhere en route. 'But I have to go. Matthew has this nut allergy and he was allergic to the cheesecake and he's on his way to hospital. I'm so sorry.'

I really, really was.

'Isn't Emelie with him?' Dan sat up and reached for my hand, pulling me back down towards him. My safety range was nearly safe enough. 'You look adorable in that jumper, by the way. Now take it off.'

'Dan, I really have to go, it's serious,' I sighed, weaving my hands into his hair. The theory was to stop him from moving his kisses anywhere more persuasive, but it just seemed to encourage him. I felt his breath on my neck and almost melted away altogether. 'Really, I have to go to the hospital.'

When I failed to reciprocate, he pulled away, the glazed glittering fading from his eyes.

'Seriously? You have to go right now?'

At last.

'I have to go right now.' I nodded, thankful I'd put jeans on before I came back into the living room. The more layers of fabric between us, the better.

'Fine, give me a minute and I'll go with you.' He started buttoning up his shirt.

'No, don't worry. You can let yourself out.' My handbag sat on the floor beside the sofa in its usual hiding spot. I picked it up, slung it across myself and quickly checked my cash situation. Just enough to get a taxi. If I could get a taxi. 'Um, I'll talk to you later?'

'Rachel, I want to come,' Dan said, shuffling into his jeans. 'My car is outside, I'll drive.'

'Don't be silly.' I already had a hand on the door. This was getting more awkward by the second. I obviously wasn't made for one-night stands, friends with benefits, or whatever the hell this would have become. 'Really, it's OK.'

'Will you just stop for a second.' He raised his voice just enough for me to notice. 'I want to drive you to the hospital. I want to come with you.'

I stopped for a moment. This was just too much. I needed to get outside, clear my head.

'You don't have to be all – like – decent.' As soon as the word was out of my mouth, I knew it was a mistake. 'This was, whatever, but I have to go.'

'I don't have to be decent?'

He grabbed his tie from the floor and shoved it into his pocket. I stared awkwardly at my tattoo. I would never regret getting it: what an amazing lifelong distraction.

'What is that supposed to mean?' he demanded. 'Am I not decent? Do you think I have to try to behave like a decent human being?'

'No, it's just that you don't have to do that,' I said to the floor. 'It's not like you're my boyfriend or anything. I can get to the hospital on my own.'

'What am I, Rachel?' he asked quietly. 'Tell me what I am to you exactly. What you think this is?'

'You're Dan,' I replied with a heavy sigh. 'And this is what you do. And we're friends and it was stupid of me to let it go this far. *Because* we're friends.'

'I'm Dan?' he laughed. 'I'm your dickhead mate, Dan. Good enough for a fumble on the sofa but not good enough to drive you to the hospital when you need someone. Not good enough to be your boyfriend because nothing means anything to Dan.'

'Don't.' I was itching to leave. And to stop feeling so incredibly horrible. 'I know you think—'

'How do you know what I think?' He forced his feet into his trainers. 'You haven't got a fucking clue what I think.'

'I need to go.'

That much was true. In the space of five minutes I'd gone from wanting to be as close as physically possible to this man, right through to as far away as human endeavour would allow. That and Matthew could be dead for all I knew. It was more likely that his tongue had swollen to the size of a double-decker bus and he was cursing my name, but still.

'Fine, but let me get this straight.' He pushed his hair back out of his face and came closer. 'So that, just then, it was just what – a quick shag?'

'Dan, don't.'

'Something to cross off the list?'

Had I missed something? Had it gone in?

This time my silence was not a positive.

'Wow. Thanks Rachel.' He pushed past me and headed straight for the front door. 'I really did not think you were like this.'

'I'm not like this!' I threw my hands in the air. 'I don't even know what this is. You're the one that's like this!'

'Like what exactly?' he said, opening the door. 'All I know is I'm an idiot.'

'Look. This isn't making a lot of sense. I need to leave. You obviously want to leave. Can we just pretend this never happened?'

'Maybe we should just pretend I don't even know you.' He gave me a filthy look from the doorway. 'Because, apparently, I don't.'

The door slammed behind him, making me jump. He got the last word as always. I didn't have time to try to work out what had just happened. Or almost happened. I had a fun Saturday night in A&E to look forward to.

CHAPTER FIFTEEN

Between the events on the sofa, the row, and a variety
of drunken dickheads jumping in front of my taxi at
every given opportunity, it took me the best part of
an hour to get to the hospital after Emelie called.
And by the time I'd convinced the receptionist to
tell me where they had stashed Matthew (I wasn't
family and, she'd met him, he blatantly didn't have
a girlfriend) he was already in a bed, wearing an
attractive green smock and with a face like swollen
thunder.

'Hi,' I said cautiously, holding out the epi-pen. It
was not going to be sufficient defence if he decided to
beat the crap out of me. 'How are you feeling?'

'Ike I migh' die,' he lisped. His light blue eyes were
red and puffy and his tongue was huge. If I hadn't
been directly responsible, it would have been quite
funny.

'He's exaggerating,' Em said. She sat on the other
side of him, her legs stretched out along the bed. 'The
doctor said it was a minor reaction, like the factory
that made the biscuits processed nuts rather than that
the cake had nuts in it. He's not going to die. He didn't

even have to stay in overnight, but he reckons A&E gets a lot of hotties at this time of night.'

'Gay danthing injurieth,' Matthew confirmed. His face was already starting to calm down. Disappointing, since I hadn't even taken a photo yet.

I settled into the hard plastic chair beside the bed and tipped my head back, eyes closed. 'Thank god. Honestly, I spent the entire taxi ride convincing myself you were going to die. All the way here, all I could think about was how I was going to explain to your mum that you died because I can't cook.'

'Are you all right?' Emelie asked, dropping her head on Matthew's shoulder, only to have it unceremoniously shoved away when a beautiful boy in skinny yellow jeans and a neon pink T-shirt was wheeled onto the ward, one leg propped up, the other clad in a matching pink Converse. 'I was worried you might have gone to find another supermodel to punch.'

'That was you,' I reminded her. 'No, tonight I settled for nearly giving Dan a quickie on the settee.'

Silence.

'Thpill,' Matthew demanded.

'He came back to get . . .' Bag? Keys? Couldn't quite remember. '. . . something and he sort of kissed me and then you called so I said I had to leave and he kicked off.'

'Because you had to come and visit your friend in the hospital?' I couldn't remember the last time I'd seen Emelie so excited. 'What a knob. But more importantly, how was it?'

'Weird, he was totally pissed off.' I frowned. 'Like, mad that I wasn't totally in love with him or something.'

'Not the argument,' she whined impatiently. 'The kissing? Was it just kissing? *Do* you love him?'

Matthew stopped checking out the neon fittie across the ward just long enough to raise his eyebrows at me. At least, I was fairly certain he was raising his eyebrows: it was hard to tell.

'Of course not. It's Dan. Remember, very tight jeans? Shags models? Is a dick?'

'Dumps supermodels for you? Turns up on your doorstep out of the blue? Snogs your face off?'

'Oh shut up,' I said. 'It's still Dan. He's hardly the father of my children, is he? He's the bloke you call after you've been to the doctor to ask if he's the reason you're itching.'

'Thath dithguthin,' Matthew lisped. 'Buh tru.'

'I can't believe I let it go as far as I did.' I tried not to think about just how far. Or how good. 'I can't believe I did it.'

'Were you wearing the underwear?' Em asked. 'You were, weren't you?'

'Yes.' I peered down the front of Dan's sweater. Thankfully I was still wearing it now. Just. 'How did you know?'

'That explains it.' She held her hands out, as though whatever she was getting at was obvious. 'It's the underwear's fault. Men think with their dicks because they're outside their body, leading them around all day long. They can't not think about them.'

'S'troo,' Matthew nodded fervently. 'S'juss there.'

'We don't because we're all neatly tucked away. It means we can get on with things without constantly thinking about sticking our genitals into something. But once you're wearing expensive, sexy lingerie? Game over.'

I liked this theory. It absolved me of all responsibility and explained why I couldn't shake the memory of Dan's warm, strong hands around my waist. We were past stomach flips. We were onto double somersaults from the top diving board, right off into a swimming pool full of you-bloody-idiot.

'That said, is he unbearably beautiful with his clothes off?' Em, as usual, completely ignored my request. 'Are his arms like little tiny barrels?'

'He's not Popeye,' I sighed. 'But yes, basically yes. I don't know, I just cocked up. He kept going on about how he didn't think I was "that kind of girl", and I was like, but you're that kind of boy! And then he got all defensive and angry and now I'm probably not going to Sydney.'

'I'm not entirely sure where Australia came into this.' Em tied her massive hair up in a high ponytail. 'And I know this is all new to you, but, honestly, when you're going to use someone for sex, you don't actually tell them you're going to use them for sex.'

'I wasn't going to use him for sex,' I replied, wildly offended.

'He'll get over it,' she tried to reassure me. 'I bet he's already called you.'

Ever the conscientious hospital visitor, I peeked at the iPhone I blatantly hadn't turned off when the nurse on reception had loudly reminded me I had to. No missed calls, but there was a Facebook message.

'No calls, new message from Ethan though.'

Lovely, uncomplicated, thousands-of-miles-away Ethan. Ahh, he said he'd be having a much better weekend if I was there. As long as he didn't have a nut allergy, maybe.

'Rach.' Em gave me her best serious look. 'This Dan thing. Are you sure there's nothing to it? You've been friends for years, after all, and he does seem to be making an awful lot of effort just to get into your pants.'

I considered her point for a moment. We were

friends, to a degree, and it was true, things had been different since I'd told him about Simon and me. And it wasn't as though I didn't think he was hot: getting up off that sofa had been one of the hardest things I'd ever had to do in my life. But he could be as funny and sweet and attentive as he liked – he was still Dan.

'You thud go and get thum theep,' Matthew lisped while I read. 'You muth be knackered.'

Realizing his attention was elsewhere, namely on the hot boy in the opposite bed, I accepted he wasn't just being kind and grabbed Emelie's hand. Time to leave.

'Home, James. Let's leave the invalid to it.' I gave Matthew a gentle hug goodbye. 'Talk tomorrow.'

Em patted him on the head. 'If you can talk tomorrow.' She turned to me with a wicked grin. 'Seriously, tell me *everything*.'

After giving Em, half the lower deck of the number 205 and anyone we happened to pass on Amwell Road a PG version of my assignation with Dan, I was incredibly happy to collapse on my sofa alone. Em had gone straight to the bathroom to brush her teeth for bed, the excitement of my evening altogether too much for her. Lying on the sofa alone, still wearing Dan's jumper, wasn't nearly as exciting as lying on the sofa wearing Dan. More so than lying there with Simon, but Simon wasn't exciting, he was Simon. He was sweet and clever and wonderful and funny and he'd dumped me on my arse because I 'wasn't the one'. A statement roughly translated from boy into English to mean 'I want to sleep around for a bit' or, at least, 'I want to sleep with someone else and I'm using this ridiculous terminology to absolve myself of blame. It's not my fault, it's yours for not being the one.'

I had been a brilliant girlfriend. I reminded him of his mother's birthday every year. I always made the bed. I shaved my legs every day. I dressed up in nothing but stockings and a Liverpool shirt on his birthday, even though my Man United-supporting dad would have spun in his grave if a) he'd found out and b) he had been dead. What was his problem?

And what was Dan's problem? He'd made all the moves. Surely he should be happy that I hadn't kicked him in the nuts and thrown him out the door. And even Ethan, what was he playing at? All these flirty emails that had no real intentions. Maybe I should invest my energies into something more potentially productive, like inventing a time machine to go back to the nineteenth century where I'd be married with four kids by now. Four kids and cholera, maybe – but still. Eurgh. Boys.

'Rach?' Em poked me in the shoulder. 'You've gone all quiet on me. You're not going to get hammered and start singing "*All By Myself*", are you?'

'I'm not drunk and I don't sing,' I replied. 'I'm just trying to work out how all of this happened.'

'Well, if you come up with an answer, remember to show the working out.'

'I think it's more of an essay question.' Ooh. I had an idea. 'I'll see you in the morning.'

'Night, beauty.' She kissed me on the top of the head and vanished into her room. She was ridiculously good to me. There was a perfectly wonderful one-bedroom flat in West Hampstead with a giant king-sized bed that had sat empty for a week now because she'd been sleeping on Ikea's second cheapest sofa bed just to make sure I didn't top myself. Now that was love.

Despite the fact that we were closing in on three a.m., I was wide awake. I pulled my writing set from the drawer underneath the coffee table. When my mum had bought me this two years ago, I'd responded by teaching her how to use Facebook. I don't know which of us was the stupid one. I hadn't written a letter since my Year Nine French pen pal decided to post me pictures of his penis, but she couldn't leave Facebook alone. And you can't defriend your mother. They get very, very upset about it. But this was a genuine pen on paper situation, the full Basildon Bond.

Dear Simon.

I shuffled into a sitting position and held my favourite turquoise pen over the paper. How to begin?

There are a couple of things I wanted to let you know that I really couldn't put into words the last time we spoke. Happily, I've had all of an hour to think about it now so it won't come out an incoherent mess and you will get the considered, eloquent response your recent actions deserve. You are a coward. A weak, sad little coward who doesn't deserve to be happy. You don't even deserve to be unhappy. You deserve to be miserable and alone and one of those sad little men who die in a house full of shit because no one cared enough to come around and check you were putting the rubbish out, and then, when they break in because they can smell your body from the street, they find bin bags full of takeaways dating back to 1997. And loads of cats. You deserve to die surrounded by angry cats.

I paused for a moment to breathe. This was coming out far too easily. Writing angry letters was fun. Especially when you'd had a couple of drinks earlier

in the evening but definitely were not drunk. Definitely.
I put the pen back to the paper.

I'm not angry because you broke up with me; I'm
angry because of the way you did it. You said it
was just a break, that we weren't breaking up. You
said that. Generally, when someone tells someone
something, especially someone they love, who they
live with, who they own a house with, it's what
they mean. Of course, this might not make sense
to you because you have a penis and I realize that
confuses you. Especially where right and wrong
and telling the truth and telling lies is concerned.
I should have made it easier for you. But you, you
horrible little cockweasel, were just too spineless
to tell me that you wanted to break up with me
so you just twatted around in that spare room,
waiting for me to get bored and break up with you.

Break for a quick fact check. Yep, all OK so far.

That's pathetic. You're pathetic. I'm angry because
you're pathetic. I really thought that we had a future
together. I thought you wanted to have kids and be
a family but, no, you want to shag your way around
London. I hope it really works out well for you and
I hope you don't catch something horrible that makes
your knob rot off. It's not OK to treat someone you
say you love the way you did. It's not OK to say
one thing and then change your mind two seconds
later. It's not OK to expect someone to be a mind-
reader. It's not OK to say come to Sydney or Toronto
and expect them to know what you mean.

I reread the last sentence. There was a slight chance

I'd gone off topic, but I didn't have any Tipp-Ex so it was staying in. Did people still use Tipp-Ex? Had the Conservatives looked into this? Was there a think tank on how we could get people from Tipp-Ex factories back to work? Anyway . . .

Anyway, all I wanted was for us to be happy. I'm sorry that wasn't enough for you. I'm sorry you're weak and emotionally retarded and that you basically just made the biggest mistake of your life but, let's be honest, you probably did me a favour. I'm pretty great. And pretty great is too good for you. Just so you know, next time I see you in the street, I'll be crossing the road and not waving. We're not friends. You're a cockweasel. Would you want to be friends with a cockweasel? No, didn't think so.

Have a nice life,

Rachel

It was even better than my A level General Studies essay and that was amazing. I folded the letter up neatly and slipped it into a corresponding envelope, writing Simon's name on the front and adding a flourish before setting it on the coffee table. Before putting the pen away, I took the napkin out of my handbag and crossed off 'write a letter'. All that was left on the list was to bungee jump, travel to a new country and find a date for my dad's wedding. It was like getting down to the toffee pennies and coffee creams in a tin of Quality Street.

Definitely time for bed.

When my phone buzzed into life the next morning, I was still unconscious and tangled in dreams involving chasing weasels through the woods near my mother's house while Dan followed, half-naked, waving a Canadian flag. Understandably, it took me a couple of seconds to work out what was going on when I opened my eyes.

I rolled across the bed to grab the phone off the floor and scream at whoever had disturbed my much-needed beauty sleep. Except it was Matthew.

'You're not dead then.'

'I'm not but I nearly was.' He sounded far too perky for, good god, seven a.m. on a Sunday. I'd had less than four hours' sleep. I wondered what exactly they'd given him at the hospital. And whether or not he had any left. 'And my near-death experience got me thinking. This to-do list thing is fine, but we need to step it up, Rach. I mean, any one of us could die any day.'

'Matthew, you've been allergic to nuts all your life,' I yawned. 'You've been hospitalized five times, one of those times because you ate a Walnut Whip on a dare. Besides, we're very much down to the step-it-up section of the existing list as it is. What do you want?'

'Nothing,' he lied. Matthew's normally laconic tones always got squeaky when he wasn't telling the truth. It was a symptom of the gay gene; he just wasn't as smooth a liar as straight boys. 'I just think we need to take more chances in life.'

'Can we take chances after I've had another three hours' sleep?' I gave myself a desultory sniff. 'And a shower?'

'You need to shower and you need to pack.' He sounded worryingly excited. East 17 reunion tour excited. 'I'll be round for you in an hour. We're going away.'

'What are you talking about?' It really was far too early for his madness. 'Away where? I've got to talk to my agent about getting back to work. I've had a week off already.'

'One more week won't hurt,' he said. 'You haven't had a holiday in ages and I've already put the tickets on hold. I can't save them for more than an hour. Tell Emelie to get herself sorted as well. I assumed you'd make me invite her. You need your passports.'

'Matthew, I need to hang around here in case Veronica manages to get me on that Sydney job, you know that,' I whined. Sydney. Sun. Sand. Half a planet away from Simon.

'Yeah, because Dan is absolutely going to take you to Australia on a job now, isn't he?'

Ohhhh. Good point, well made.

'Passports. One hour. I'm on my way.'

It took every ounce of strength not to remind Matthew that my estranged dad, whom I hadn't laid eyes on since I was two years old, hadn't died twelve months previously, leaving me with a gaping father-figure complex and buckets and buckets full of cash. I had to work for a living and to pay off my ever-increasing credit-card bill. But in the moment it took to decide that, no, he needed to be told, Matthew hung up. And that was that.

I flopped back down against my pillows, taking a moment to enjoy the massive empty bed before committing myself to standing up. Wherever we were going, there'd better be lots of opportunity to lie down.

Em was already in the living room, eating a slice of pizza that had clearly been left out all night after the party. She was disgusting sometimes. She was also reading my letter to Simon.

'Matthew just called telling me to get my arse into gear and not to forget my passport,' she shouted at me as I shuffled through to the kitchen for coffee. 'Did they give him the wrong drugs at the hospital? Has he got brain damage? Have you given Matthew brain damage?'

I turned around to see her holding up her hand for a high-five. I shook my head and she put it down again, disappointed.

'Apparently he's got some flight on reserve and he's coming to get us in an hour,' I explained. 'That's all I know.'

'It's not that I don't love being friends with an ex-trolley dolly,' she began. 'It's just that he never calls and says, I'm taking you to Honolulu, does he? If it's Düsseldorf again, I'm not going.'

'Düsseldorf was OK,' I reminisced privately over a particularly good schnitzel. 'I mean, as a place, it was lovely.'

'Düsseldorf was OK?' Emelie raised an eyebrow. 'Whatever.'

'I'm not really in a rush to go anywhere.' I leaned against the fridge with my coffee. 'Especially not in the next hour. Can't we just watch *Hollyoaks* and then get twatted over Sunday lunch like normal people?'

'Amen, sister,' Emelie nodded. 'You can tell him that when he gets here. After you've finished apologizing for poisoning him.'

'Hmm,' I sipped the lukewarm cup of Nescafé. 'Maybe I'll go and pack . . .'

When Matthew's keys rattled the lock, I was sitting on the sofa, looking at my mini-suitcase and glugging down a second mug of coffee. It was still only eight a.m. and I wanted to be awake when Matthew announced we were going to the arse end of Norway for a week. Em was in the other room, screaming at a pair of 'piece of shit Jimmy Choos' that refused to fit in her bag.

I could have offered to put them in mine, but listening to her yelling at inanimate objects while Simon Rimmer and two of McFly failed to make a risotto on the telly was far more entertaining. It was terrifying how much stuff she'd carted over here in the space of the last week. She had more clothes here than I now owned. Which had made packing something of a piece of piss for me.

'Who's ready for an adventure?' Matthew threw himself on the sofa and looked at me with wild eyes.

I pressed my lips together and gave him a narrow-eyed look. 'You made me spill my coffee.'

'You poisoned me,' he replied with an equally catty look. 'Even?'

'Maybe,' I relented. 'So where are we going?'

'OK.' He rubbed his palms on his jeans. 'So, the whole nearly dying because you don't know how to make a cheesecake thing sort of got me thinking. I know we're trying to train you up to be a good single girl, but I think it's also important that we start taking chances. So we're going to Canada.'

'We're not going to Canada,' I responded immediately. Almost as quickly, Emelie's head appeared around the door.

'Canada? No way.' She shook her head. 'There's no way we're going to Canada. I have a busy week.'

'You, why not?' he said to me. 'And you, you haven't had a very busy week since 2003.'

'I work very hard,' she said. 'Just because I work from home, doesn't mean I don't work. I have to approve all the new Kitty Kitty products; I'm developing new style-guide art; I'm working on—'

'Wah wah wah,' Matthew made a very unflattering quacking gesture with his hand. 'Whatevs.'

'Children, inside voices please. Matthew, we can't

go to Canada. Ethan will think I'm a mental if I just turn up on his doorstep.'

'We're not just turning up on his doorstep,' he sighed. 'You're going to Vancouver for work, so you're just stopping over in Toronto. See? I've thought of everything.'

I looked at Matthew's excited face. And then at Emelie's angry face. I wondered what face I was pulling. Who actually packed a bag and left the country? OK, so I didn't have anywhere I needed to be for the next few days. And no, it wasn't like anyone was counting on me doing anything. And Matthew would have paid next to nothing for the tickets. No one could deny that putting some distance between myself and the flat could only be a good idea, and god knows Sydney was definitely off the books. A week away and then back for Dad's wedding, ready to start work again. Matthew had definitely had worse ideas. Like Düsseldorf.

'It'll be a good break, get you away from all of this,' Matthew promised. 'It'll be fun.'

'It would be nice to get away,' I admitted. Redhead Rachel was already dragging her case down the street and hailing a cab. 'And it is on the list.'

'Seriously?' Matthew looked as though he didn't quite believe me. 'We're going? I'm not going to have to give you the rest of my very convincing argument?'

I pointed at my suitcase and waved my suitcase at him. 'Before I change my mind.'

'You're not really going?' Em pointed at me with a stiletto. 'We're not really going to go?'

'Right, either you admit that you're wanted for murder over there or you shut your face and get in the taxi that will be here in three minutes,' Matthew snapped. 'I'm not dragging you off to Guantanamo Bay, I'm taking you on a first-class flight to a beautiful city to stay in a nice hotel for a couple of days with your best friends. Or supposed best friends. Can you please get over yourself for one minute and say thank you?'

Em pressed her lips into a tight line. I didn't know what she was going to say but I knew it wasn't going to be good.

'Rachel shagging some random from when she was sixteen isn't going to make Stephen come running back to you, you know.'

Oh, wow. The big guns.

Matthew didn't have an answer for that. But his breathing became audible and his grip on my Snoopy mug became dangerously tight. When the doorbell rang, it seemed like the loudest sound I had ever heard. Silently, Matthew stood up, pushed Emelie out of the way and headed to the door.

'I literally have no idea why you said that,' I whispered. 'Why, *why* would you use the "S" word?'

Em's face was completely white. 'You need to talk to him about that.' She shook her head. 'I know he hasn't told you.'

'Hasn't told me what?' There was something I didn't know? What? I was missing something and I didn't like it.

I heard the front door slam shut as quickly as it had opened and Matthew marched into the living room, grabbed a pile of letters from the coffee table and marched back out again. He was recycling my junk mail before we went on holiday? And there was me thinking how mad my mum would be if she knew I hadn't bleached the toilet.

'Matthew?' I gave Em a quizzical look but she just shrugged, Jimmy Choo still in hand. 'Can you see him?'

'I think he's gone outside,' she said, peering down the hallway. 'He's not on the stairs.'

'If he's gone to set himself on fire or something, I'll be well annoyed,' I muttered from the sofa. 'Now, seriously, what's going on with you two? What don't I know?'

But Matthew wasn't giving her an opportunity to answer. He opened the door, slammed it shut behind him and marched back up the hallway.

'Emelie, stop bloody whining, put your shoe in your handbag and get downstairs,' he ordered. 'Rachel, that was Simon.'

'At eight in the morning?' Em looked confused. 'On a Sunday? Is he ill?'

'He always gets up early on a weekend,' I said blankly. 'He's got football practice.'

'He came for his post,' Matthew clarified. 'He has now got his post and will not be bothering you again. He will also not be talking to estate agents about selling your flat until you tell him he can. Now, the taxi's here, shall we leave?'

I stared, speechless. Matthew Chase. Man of action.

'Better get a move on then.' Em slipped her shoe into her handbag and pulled up the handle to her suitcase. 'Canada it is.'

There really was only one thing for it. I left regular Rachel with her ex-boyfriend, her blonde hair and her Sky Plus box full of *Glee* repeats sitting on the sofa watching *Something for the Weekend* and let Redhead Rachel drag my suitcase down the hallway and out to the black people-carrier on the street.

Canada, it was.

CHAPTER SIXTEEN

Fourteen hours, one first-class flight and several glasses of champagne later, Redhead Rachel was in Toronto and ticking 'travel' off her to-do list. I leaned over the desk that ran the length of the room and stared out of the window. I couldn't quite believe it. Granted the view of another building and a couple of garages wasn't very grand, but it certainly wasn't Islington either. We weren't in Islington. We were in bloody Canada. The hotel itself was, as Matthew had promised (on the recommendation of international jetsetter, Jeremy), absolutely gorgeous if terrifyingly trendy. It was a bit like checking in to the set of *Mad Men* while being surrounded by the cast of *Gossip Girl*. Once we were safely up in our room, Emelie threw herself across the squishy mattress.

'OK, I'll see you two later,' she said, closing her eyes. 'You crazy kids have fun, I'm knackered.'

'Get off your arse.' Matthew grabbed her leg and dragged her down to the foot of the bed. 'We're going down to the bar; it's only –' he looked at his watch, realized he hadn't reset it and shrugged – 'well, it's early.'

Em looked to me for support but I was too busy

sitting cross-legged in the big square chair checking out the room service menu. 'There's a four-hundred-dollar vibrator on here.' I felt all the colour drain from my face. 'Where have you brought us?'

'I bet it's not real. I bet no one has ever ordered it.' Matthew waved away my fear. 'It's just one of those trendy hotel things. I bet they wouldn't have one if you called down for it.'

'Right,' I wasn't convinced. 'Um, is it me or is that the shower? In the middle of the room?'

Em and Matthew both looked up.

'Why is there no shower curtain?'

Apparently international jetsetter Jeremy had failed to mention that the rooms didn't have bathrooms. They had shower cubicles in the bedroom. At the end of the bed. Clear glass shower cubicles three feet from the edge of the bed. Not even a trace of frosting to protect your modesty.

'You are not getting naked in front of me,' Matthew looked horrified. 'I'll wait outside.'

'You're really going to sit outside the room every time one of us wants a shower?' Em asked.

'Well I'm not going to sit and watch, am I?'

Poor gay Matthew.

'Better look away now then.' She stood up and started stripping off. 'I always feel disgusting after flying.'

I launched myself into her spot on the bed and grabbed the remote control. 'Bagsy I go after you.'

'Oh dear god,' Matthew held his hands over his eyes and headed towards the door. 'I'll be in the bar getting drunk enough for this not to bother me. You might need to carry me back to bed.'

Post-shower, Emelie promptly lay down and passed out. Refusing to listen to my anti-jetlag advice, she was already tucked up in the great big bed before I got in the shower. By the time I stepped out, she was fast asleep. Or at least pretending to be so she didn't have to go down to the bar and watch Matthew do his bit for international relations. Why did I always have to be mother? I looked at my sparse wardrobe options. It was Sunday evening. No need to go over the top but – given what I'd seen hanging around reception when we walked in – a little effort might be required. At least lipstick. Maybe eyeliner. Ensemble-wise, I went for cropped black Capri pants and the longest stripy T-shirt in my collection, hoping I could pass for continental chic and not a bit tired and lazy. There was a good enough argument to support either if you could be bothered to look for it. Slipping my room key into my big old bag, I locked a loudly snoring Emelie in on her own. And tried not to be jealous.

Even though it was a Sunday, the Sky Yard was packed with people; even after two loops, I couldn't spot Matthew. Once I felt sufficiently awkward, I shuffled towards an empty table in the back and played people-watching while I waited for a waitress. Everyone in there was irritatingly cute and hipster but there was not a single mountie or lumberjack in sight. My mum would have been so disappointed. Matthew, however, would surely have been delighted: my gaydar was going off in a big way. Hopefully he hadn't ditched me before I even got there. After a couple more minutes, I gave in and took out my phone to text him. I'd been avoiding looking at it for fear of a message from Simon or Dan, but there was nothing from either of them. Rather than entertain the sick part of me that was disappointed, I invested in the part that was excited to see a new message from Ethan. I'd messaged from the airport to tell him about my last-minute job in Vancouver, including two-day layover in Toronto to meet the stylist. It seemed like a plausible excuse – or at least one that a male high school teacher wouldn't question.

The message loaded slowly but, at last, there it was, right next to that adorable picture of Ethan and his dog.

'Hey, you're coming to Toronto? Actually, I guess by the time you read this, you'll be in the city. That's amazing! Will you have time to hang out? Crazy that you're coming just when we got back in touch. Give me a call when you get into town, my schedule is pretty clear.'

He wanted to hang out. He was only mildly suspicious. He'd actually given me his mobile number. These were all good things. If he hadn't been suspicious at all, I'd have worried he was backwards or religious or something. But I wasn't quite ready to call him; instead I tapped out a text saying I had the entire next day free and that I'd love to hang out. A tiny electric thrill ran up my spine as I pressed send. This was very exciting.

'Someone looks pleased with herself.' A painfully pretty creature sat herself in the empty seat opposite me. 'Is this seat taken?'

'Um, not right now?' I watched as she sat herself down with complete ease.

Was this the done thing in Canada? People just sat down with you in bars? And I was really selling this girl short by referring to her as people; she was clearly some sort of glamazon, sent by the gods of the to-do list to make me question whether or not I was really trying. Glossy, coffee-coloured curls, olive skin, perfect manicure and fresh, glowing make-up. I immediately assumed pro. Make-up artist that was, not the other kind of pro who hung out in hotel bars.

'Cute shirt,' she looked me up and down. 'American Apparel?'

'Topshop.' I was too confused and English to come up with a return compliment before the waitress appeared at our side, but her outfit was effortlessly classy: black cigarette pants, dove grey T-shirt, tasteful jewellery. Maybe she was a fashion editor.

'Drinks, ladies?' The waitress looked appropriately bored through her layers of eyeliner.

'Uh, wine?' I peered at the menu in front of me. 'White wine?'

'We have a great chardonnay,' she suggested.

'No they don't,' my tablemate answered for me. 'She'll take the sauvignon. Me too. In fact, we'll take a bottle.'

'On its way.' The waitress turned on her high heel.

'The chardonnay is that bad?'

'Intervention bad,' she nodded. 'I'm Jenny, by the way.'

I hoped to God that Em didn't decide to venture downstairs. If these two were ever in the same place at once, the world might just implode or something.

'Rachel. Are you from Toronto?' I asked.

'Oh god no. Canada would never lay claim to me.' She pushed her hair back from her face. 'I'm not nearly nice enough. I'm just here for work.'

I nodded, still not entirely sure what to say.

'I'm not a hooker,' she replied, no trace of a smile on her face, 'if that's what you're thinking.'

'Oh, no, I didn't think that. I didn't. Really.' I hadn't thought it! I hadn't!

'Relax, I'm fucking with you.' She placed a super-soft hand covered in elaborate cocktail rings on my arm and tried not to laugh. 'Brits, you're all so sensitive. No, I am here for work, I'm from New York. Way too much of a bitch to pass for a Canadian.'

'So what do you do?' I asked, scanning the bar for Matthew or our wine. I wasn't bothered which came first as long as it came fast.

'I'm a stylist.'

'No way.' I looked down at the Facebook exchange between myself and Ethan. I loved it when fate worked out to make me not a liar.

'Yeah,' Jenny replied. 'I know, it's retarded. I dress people for a living.'

'Not at all,' I assured her. She was right, the sauvignon was good. 'I'm a make-up artist.'

'Really? That's awesome.' She raised her glass. 'You're here on a job?'

My phone buzzed on the table between us. Ethan had replied already.

'No, I'm just here with friends.' I looked around for said friend but fate was working against me this time. 'And, maybe there's a boy. Sort of.'

'When isn't there a boy?' she asked. 'But a sort of a boy in a foreign country? That sounds like the kind of story you want to share with a complete stranger in a hotel bar on a Sunday night.'

I smiled. Usually I wasn't great at making small talk with new people. Or even people in general, but it was impossible not to like this girl. Over one and a half glasses of wine, I gave her the mid-length version of the Ethan story, including the list, leaving in Simon, leaving out Dan, and then we read the text message. He suggested brunch at my hotel.

'So say yes already,' Jenny gave me a killer grin. 'Brunch can't hurt, right?'

'Can't it?' I paused for a second before replying with a restrained 'see you then', and stuck my phone back in my bag.

'Depends what you think is gonna happen with this

guy?' Jenny pulled her hair back into a ponytail-slash-semicontrolled explosion. 'Is this just a fun rebound hook up or are you thinking along the lines of a more life-changing fairy-tale happily ever after?'

'Potential fun hook-up?' Even I didn't sound convinced. 'Given that life-changing fairy-tale-type affairs are usually just that.'

'OK, couple of things. One, don't count out the fairy tales, especially concerning Brit girls and foreign guys.' She counted her points off on her decorated fingers. 'Two, don't take this the wrong way, but you really don't seem like the random hook-up kind of gal and, three, any idea what his expectations are?'

I carried on sipping my wine. She raised an excellent point. 'I have no idea what he's thinking.'

'So if he was thinking: awesome, here's this cool chick I had a crush on in high school and I'm recently single and she's recently single and she's just in town for the night, so why not? How would you feel about that?' She templed her fingers on the table. 'Good or bad?'

'Maybe not great?'

'Right?' She raised both eyebrows. 'And what happens if you meet, you have some crazy connection and you realize he's the one?'

'The one?' I tucked my hair behind my ears with a smile. 'Is there such a thing?'

'There really is,' Jenny assured me. 'And not to sound like a complete dick but, when you meet him, you'll know.'

I gave her a disbelieving look.

'Oh yeah,' she went on. 'Sweaty palms, nausea, racing heart and, for most of us modern girls, an utter conviction that he is absolutely, positively, not the one. It's usually that guy.'

We sat in silence for a moment while I tried to convince myself there was no way she talking about Dan.

'So you ticked off everything on the list?' Jenny asked.

'I have two things left.'

'Anything I can help with?'

I frowned, wondering how she'd feel about a lovely Saturday afternoon at a church in Godalming. 'I have to do a bungee jump or something similar and I have to find a date to take to my dad's wedding next Saturday so I can turn up looking amazing with someone amazing. At this point, the bungee jump is going to be easier. Says the girl who can't climb a stepladder to paint her ceiling without getting dizzy.'

'It actually might be.' She looked so happy. This girl really was a problem-solver. 'I'm pretty sure they've got one of those slingshot bungee-ball things at Niagara Falls and they start on the ground so you don't even have to climb up anything to do it. It's not that far from here. Would that count?'

If I knew what a bungee ball was, I would be calling them up and booking myself in. This girl was amazing.

'It might.' I scribbled 'Bungee ball – Niagara Falls' in my notebook. I hadn't even thought about Niagara Falls being close by – we had to go. I'd been obsessed with them ever since *Dirty Dancing*. Although the reference to Acapulco in the same scene had been ruined for me by the Phil Collins song. I had no interest in going loco down in Acapulco or anywhere else with Phil. 'I will be so happy when I've crossed everything off this list. There's a chance I also need to make an appointment to see someone about my OCD. Not that I'm turning light switches off fourteen times or anything.'

'I love making lists. Objectives. Resolutions. Really,

I totally get you,' she said. 'But now you've got to work out how to put what you've learned into practice. No point writing a list, ticking it off and then forgetting about it. You gotta start living it every day.'

'Well, I wasn't planning on getting a tattoo and crashing a charity ball every week but, yeah, I think it's encouraged me to branch out a bit,' I agreed. 'I was blonde until a week ago.'

'No way? See, you're gonna be fine.' She waved a hand to dismiss my concerns. 'Great job, great friends, totally cute. You've got it all figured out.'

'Really?' I laughed. 'Please tell my mother that. Are you single?'

Jenny took a deep breath, swirled her glass and then drank the rest of her wine down in one.

'I am single.'

'Can I ask why?'

She smiled but it didn't make it up into her eyes. 'Guy I love doesn't love me. He just moved in with someone else actually.'

'Do you think anyone actually chooses to be single?'

'Yeah, sure,' she said. 'But choosing it and wanting it, two totally different things. I think a heap of people sit down and think, hey, I need some me time, but I don't buy the idea that they go to bed alone every night with a smile on their face. I'd rather be single than be with the wrong guy, but I don't think anyone wants to be alone. I don't want to be alone.'

'You remind me of one of my friends,' I said, trying to commit her wisdom to memory to repeat back to Em and Matthew.

'You remind me of one of mine,' Jenny replied. 'So, what's the real deal, you want to get back with the ex? Is he the love of your life?'

'No,' I said without thinking. 'He isn't. He was just

there. I was too busy getting on with every day; I wasn't paying a lot of attention to what was going on at the time. Really it should have ended ages ago.' Hearing myself saying those words was so strange. Because they were so true. How had I not realized before now?

Jenny leaned her head to one side and pulled a random strand of hair straight out before letting it spring back into a coiled curl. 'Happens to the best of us, honey. Don't beat yourself up over it. My trick is to worry so much about what I don't have, I don't realize what I've got. And it's only when he gets up and leaves that I miss him. Now that sucks.'

'I wish I had some sage advice for you.' I took my third glass of wine.

'I find "don't be a dick" works in most situations,' she replied. 'I'm just not good at following my own advice.'

'Do you know what you want now?' I asked.

'Yeah, I just want to be with him but he's moved on. I can't do anything.'

I couldn't imagine anyone not wanting this girl. She was sweet, she was beautiful and she was so clever. What was wrong with this man?

'I want to say never give up, if that's what you want.' It was rubbish advice but it was all I had. 'Just tell him how you feel.'

'Maybe,' Jenny focused her gaze back on me. 'And what is it you want? Now you know all this awesome new stuff about yourself?'

'I want to be with someone who wants to be with me.' I really didn't think before answering. 'Someone who wants me to be happy. Who wants the best for me.'

Like Dan? Asked the voice in my head.

'So just a super-cute, good guy who loves you – and is exciting but trustworthy, fun but dependable, and would be there for you no matter what?' Jenny suggested. 'Yeah. The dream. I wish I could say he definitely exists.'

Except maybe he does repeated that annoying little voice.

I pushed it away and raised my glass to hers. 'Is that too much to ask?'

'Yes,' Jenny replied, checking her watch and sinking her drink. 'This is super-fun, honey, but I've got to run. I'm in room three-oh-seven. Give me a call if you're around tomorrow, OK? I feel like there's more work to be done here.'

'I appreciated the therapy session. You have a fun evening.' I couldn't help but feel a little sad that she was leaving.

'The therapy session was my fun,' she threw a beautiful, expensive looking bag over her shoulder and leaned across the table to kiss me on both cheeks. 'And god knows, you British girls need it more than most.'

The crowd around the bar parted like magic as I watched her hair bounce off towards the exit. Well, that was interesting. Even more interesting was that it had now been near enough two hours since Matthew had left for the bar and I was officially giving him up for dead. Bed was calling. Which I imagine was sort of what had happened to Matthew, he probably just wasn't sleeping in it.

CHAPTER SEVENTEEN

'I can't believe you're actually going on a date with your school crush.' Emelie was merrily munching on pastries in bed, despite my repeated warnings not to get crumbs under the covers. I was busy trying on every outfit I'd brought with me. Nothing felt right. Redhead Rachel had, for some reason, failed to show up this morning and I was as nervous as an X Factor auditionee who was only there because my dead dad had made me promise to try.

'It's going to be so awesome. You're totally going to marry him.'

'Nothing like putting pressure on a situation,' I muttered into the mirror on the back of the door. 'This? Is this OK?'

I'd opted for the strappy, pale yellow sundress decorated with a tiny white swallow print that fell just above my knee, together with white ballet flats and, because I was having to play this one without my overconfident alter-ego, a cardi. Just in case.

Em nodded, swallowing a mouthful of croissant.

'It's fine.' She moved on to pulling apart a mini-muffin. 'You're going to marry your childhood sweetheart and

I'll probably end up marrying your slutty brother. It'll be like a movie.'

'Don't even joke about it.' I fussed with my hair, pulling bits back, letting them drop around my face and then pulling them back again. Why did nothing look right? Why was this so hard? 'You know I wouldn't wish that on my worst enemy.'

'I don't know,' Em replied. 'I reckon he and Ana would make a good couple. If I don't get in there first.'

'Emelie,' I whined. This conversation was not helping me be my most calm and wonderful self. 'Out with it. Do you really like Paul or is this just some desperate cry for help?'

She pulled her most attractive truffle-pig face and concentrated hard on a muffin. 'I don't know.' She popped a piece of muffin in her mouth. 'I know you think it's disgusting, but don't you think it's time I gave the whole boyfriend thing a go?'

'Yes, but not with my brother.' I swiped a tiny little Danish from the breakfast tray before she cleared it. 'And not because it's gross but because he's not good enough for you.'

'He could be sitting outside my bedroom window serenading me every night and you wouldn't think he was good enough for me,' she pointed out. 'You'll never see past him being your brother.'

I thought back to what Jenny had said about 'The One' in the bar the night before. Was that how she felt about Paul? Had I been standing in the way of them being together for years? If it didn't still turn my stomach, I'd feel just awful. But it did so I didn't.

'Jesus Christ, I love this city.' The door swung open towards me as Matthew crashed through it, still in the clothes he'd worn to travel in on Sunday morning. And with the five-hour time difference, that was well over twenty-four hours ago. Although, by the looks of the outfit and Matthew's face, they'd both clearly spent some time on the floor overnight. 'I met someone.'

'You don't say.' I held my arms out and spun for approval.

'You look lovely,' he said, shedding his clothes and walking towards the shower. 'I'm sure you look lovely.'

'Um, what's with the nudity?' Em shouted across the room as his boxers hit the floor. 'I'm eating. And I thought you were the world's biggest prude?'

'Just because I don't want to see you naked doesn't mean you should be denied the privilege of this,' Matthew bowed with a flourish before ducking into the shower cubicle. 'Where are you going?'

'Brunch with Ethan,' I took one more deep breath, blew it out and picked up my bag. 'Is it warm out?'

'Don't know, I never left the hotel,' he shouted over the running water. 'Met a delightful artist downstairs. His name's Dallas; he stays here when he's in the city. Lives in some godawful place where they have to kill things to eat them.'

'You *have* to kill them?' Em sounded sceptical.

'I'm not saying there isn't a Tesco's around there somewhere but you get the idea,' he said, soaping up. 'It was a brilliant pick-up line anyway.'

'I'd better go,' I said, looking at my watch and trying to ignore the gut-churning nausea in my stomach. Really, butterflies would have sufficed. 'Really, do I look all right?'

'You look very cute,' Emelie confirmed. 'If I hadn't seen you since I was sixteen, I'd be very impressed.'

'I was a total loser at sixteen.' I fussed with my hair one last time before throwing my bag over my shoulder and checking for the hotel room key. 'Braces, Sun-In, three-inch turn-ups on all my trousers. Not good.'

'Then you're already on a winner.' She settled back on the bed and turned on the TV. 'He's expecting sixteen and gross. He's getting twenty-eight and amazing.'

'True,' I muttered. 'Wish me luck.'

'Good luck,' she said with a wave. 'Text me, let me know what you're doing.'

Matthew drew a smiley face in the steam on the shower door and waved. And then drew a giant penis and gave me a thumbs-up. I took that as my cue to leave.

Even in the crowded café, I spotted Ethan immediately. Amongst all the flannel-shirt-wearing, beanie-hat-sporting hipsters, his big blue eyes, bright blond hair stuck out like a very attractive sore thumb. He looked exactly the same. Until he stood up. While I'd spent the last ten years playing house and powdering super-model's arses, it looked as if Ethan had spent a decade bench-pressing bears. He was big. Really big. He met my eyes, did a second take on the hair, which I suddenly remembered was bright red instead of dark blonde, and then gave me a wave. And suddenly I was Body Shop White Musk, Robbie Williams and a packet of Chipsticks all over again.

'Rachel?' As soon as I was within grabbing distance, he wrapped his arms around me in a massive hug. So absence really did make the heart grow fonder. I couldn't even pass him sheet music without blanching before. 'It's so good to see you.'

'You too.' I was almost too afraid to sit down. He was so pretty. The Facebook photos really hadn't done him any justice; he was just a very handsome man.

Really, he looked so incredibly clean-cut, I kept expecting him to pull a piece of wood out from under the table and start sandpapering, or for a giant golden Labrador to bound up and lick his face. If I didn't do it first. Not my usual type, but beggars can't be choosers. Especially when the choice was Adonis or nothing.

'You look great,' Ethan reached out for the glass of water in front of him. 'I don't think I would have recognized you on the street. You were always such a tomboy. And the hair! Wow.'

I was sitting in a café in Toronto with Ethan Harrison. The Ethan Harrison. As in 'Rachel Loves Ethan 4 eva IDST', Ethan Harrison. Sigh, swoon, thud.

'You look just the same.' Aside from the muscles and the lack of braces and the muscles and the extra foot in height. And the muscles. I couldn't quite look him in the eye so I stuck to the collar of his white polo shirt and promised myself I'd try to work my way up. 'You sound a bit different though.'

'Yeah, I suppose I've picked up the accent,' he laughed. 'My dad is Canadian so I'd always had a twang at home. Once we got out here, it just came out of nowhere.'

'One of my best friends is from Montreal, I'm totally used to it.' I ordered a coffee and built up to his chin. Good, solid, square jaw. His straw-blond hair was just starting to curl around his ears and, while it was a lot shorter in the front than it used to be, my heart fluttered at the thought of there being just enough for me to reach over and brush it out of his eyes. If I weren't sitting on my hands. In a café in Canada. Opposite Ethan Harrison. Where *was* Redhead Rachel? Sixteen-year-old Rachel was not qualified to handle this.

'Isn't it strange?' Ethan scratched his head and his bicep strained against the cuff of his T-shirt. His arms were even bigger than Dan's. Not that I was thinking about Dan. 'If you'd told me ten years ago that you and I would be sitting here now, I would never have believed you.'

'That has been a recurring theme lately,' I agreed, pushing all thoughts of London out of my mind. 'Although, to be fair, if you'd told me a week ago I'd be sitting here, I wouldn't have believed you.'

'It was a last-minute job?' he asked. 'In Vancouver?'

I stared at him for just a second too long. 'Yes. Vancouver. Last minute. Job,' I nodded. 'It's a shoot. For a magazine.'

'And you're a make-up artist?' He sounded surprised but he was still smiling. 'That's so strange. I just don't remember you being one of those girls.'

'One of what girls?' I was always curious to hear what other people thought of me. Apart from Dan. I didn't need to hear what Dan thought ever again. Because I wasn't thinking about Dan. Eurgh.

'Oh, I don't mean anything bad.' His cheeks burned with an adorable embarrassed blush. Ahh. 'It's like, there was a whole group of girls who wore so much make-up at school. The Lip Gloss Girls. That was what I called them.'

'The Lip Gloss Girls?' I laughed, knowing exactly who he was talking about. I had been insanely jealous of each and every one of them. 'That's awful.'

'You know, Louise and Claire and all those others – they were, like, constantly putting on that gross lip gloss.' He pulled a face as a very pretty waiter in a black knitted cap brought over coffee. Professional experience said male model. Ordering-from-male-models-posing-as-waiters experience said he would absolutely get our order wrong. 'I remember thinking it looked like they had glue all over their mouths. Who would want to make out with that?'

'Yeah, I wasn't really into all that stuff then,' I pressed my own lip-glossed lips together and willed the sticky shine to Go Away. 'I love it though. I meet a lot of interesting people.'

'Really?'

'No,' I replied immediately. 'Nearly all people are horrible. Just awful.'

'You always were funny,' Ethan placed a hand over mine. I tried not to have a stroke. 'It's really good to see you. I got to say, I'm loving the internet right now. This totally makes up for all those godawful online dates I've been on.'

'Big fan of Match.com?' I tried to sound casual, but really I was desperate to know. There must be something horribly, horribly wrong with him that I couldn't see. Nazi sympathizer? Video-game geek? Puppy kicker? There had to be something wrong with either him or all the women in Canada. I was this close to proposing with an onion ring.

'Not hardly.' He let go of my hand. My heart shattered into a million tiny pieces. And there was a chance I was suffering from an epic case of internal monologue hyperbole. 'I haven't been single that long. Me and my ex broke up earlier this year and I sorta spent all summer sulking. Now it's almost time for school again. I'm just way too busy to really date properly. It's hard work out here.'

But you wouldn't be too busy for a long-distance relationship with your childhood sweetheart, I thought. Wonder what he's doing next Saturday? Possibly getting a little bit ahead of myself.

'What about you?' He gave me a look. 'Lots of online action?'

'Ha,' I snorted. Very sexy. 'Not quite. I haven't been single that long either, though.'

When I actually added it all up, after drinks with my new BFF in the bar the night before, it had been less than two months in twelve years. I'd started going out with my first boyfriend in the October of Year Twelve, and Simon and I had been broken up for eight days. There was no wonder I needed help.

'This place is pretty great.' He waved a hand around at the café after we'd ordered breakfast. I'd gone for the breakfast sandwich, exactly as it was advertised on the menu. Ethan had attempted to request a couple of substitutions to something resembling a fry-up and been greeted with repeated confusion from the hot server. As a waiter, he made a great model. I expected to be doing the make-up on his Armani underwear campaign any day. 'Some friends of mine hang out in the bar sometimes but I've never been.'

'Yeah, I heard it was a nice spot,' I agreed. I'd already decided to keep to myself the fact that I was only staying at The Drake because my gay best friend's gay best friend got a shag every time he visited. Why blow the mystique?

'So what are your plans while in Toronto?' Ethan reached across the table to give my hand another squeeze. I was definitely going to have a stroke. 'You're here today and tomorrow, right?'

'Yep. Two days and then on to Vancouver.' I was actually a very passable liar when I had my story straight. I imagined this would come to work in my favour should I ever need to explain Simon's mysterious disappearance. 'I don't really have any plans while I'm here, though. I ended up meeting the stylist when I got in last night.'

That wasn't so much a lie as a grammatical error. Technically. Jenny was *a* stylist.

'So, you want me to show you around?' He gave me another flash of that big white grin and I felt myself flush from head to toe. 'I'm not much of a tour guide, but I'm sure I can do the sights.'

I was very satisfied with the sight in front of me as it was, but it was always nice to show willing.

'Sounds brilliant,' I confirmed. 'I'd love to.'

It didn't take me long to fall in love with Toronto. Between my charming tour guide and the almost offensively friendly people, not to mention the abundance of maple syrup shoved sideways into every foodstuff available, it was nearly impossible not to. By mid-afternoon, I was ninety-five per cent sugar. And I was perfectly happy with that.

After breakfast, we came out of the hotel and hit the street. Ethan pointing out little art galleries, vintage boutiques and every single dog that went by. Everything about the morning was horribly cute. Even though the neighbourhood had adopted a New York sort of attitude, all artfully distressed fabrics, buildings covered in political graffiti and every shop manned exclusively by skinny boys in plaid shirts and fertility impairing tight jeans, they all maintained their native hospitality. I couldn't remember the last time I'd said hello to so many strangers. And as a dyed-in-the-wool Londoner, I wasn't sure how I felt about that, until I'd had my second maple syrup macchiato, at which point I more or less felt brilliant about everything.

By the time we'd crossed everything off Ethan's sightseeing list (sadly it wasn't a physical list) we'd visited the CN Tower, the Hockey Hall of Fame, walked down the boardwalk, considered going inside the

Royal Ontario Museum but settled for just judging the bizarre architecture (it looked as though a spaceship had crashed into the V&A), and eventually set up shop in the rooftop bar of the Thompson hotel, where I could see all of Toronto laid out in front of me. (Despite my terrible lemming tendencies, I had to admit the view was beautiful. And as long as I stayed away from the edge, I was OK. Ish.) I'd drawn a line at checking out the Bryan Adams star on the Canadian walk of fame, but I did appreciate his enthusiasm for his heritage. I was also knackered and very much wanted a little sit-down. Em and Matthew had both texted to say they'd spent the entire day sitting on their arses on the roof deck of our own hotel, slowly getting drunk and eating everything on the menu. Despite the fact that I'd had a lovely, lovely day, I couldn't help but be a little bit jealous.

Ethan had been a wonderful host. He opened doors, he pulled out my chair and he wouldn't let me pay for a thing. Every word out of his mouth was funny or sweet and always interesting. He was aware, he was intelligent; I found out he loved his career as a teacher, spent as much time reading and researching lesson plans as he did going hiking with Sadie, his golden retriever, and every thought that passed through his mind was spelled out on his honest face. There was no pretence, no guessing games. I asked a question, he answered it. He asked a question, he wanted to know the answer. Ethan Harrison was, to all intents and purposes, the perfect man.

So all I could hope was that it was the jetlag that was leaving me feeling completely and utterly unaffected by his attention. We were sitting side by side on the corner of a high table, not too close to the edge of the deck. I stole a glance at my date, the sun setting in the sky behind him, lighting up his hair and casting shadows on his handsome face. Why didn't I feel anything? Once I'd got over the initial buzz and potential heart attack, something strange had happened. Nothing. I liked Ethan but I didn't *like* him. Try as I might, there was just nothing there.

'You really set the fire alarm off at The Savoy?' he asked over a giant plate of what looked like chips and gravy covered in baby food. It was not the most appetizing thing anyone had ever put down in front of me, but I was assured poutine was a delicacy. I couldn't see how the chef could work maple syrup into it and, therefore, I was officially not interested.

'I did,' I confirmed. 'Unless the Metropolitan Police happen to ask. In which case it was an accident and nothing to do with me.'

Given how I'd come to be in touch with him again, I'd left the single girl's to-do list out of our conversation so far but, now we'd settled in one place, we were running out of conversation. Fast. I wasn't into ice hockey; he didn't follow football any more. He loved to hike. Surviving in the great outdoors without a corkscrew was one of my greatest fears. Ethan didn't watch TV. Didn't. Watch. TV. What option did I have left?

'You're insane.' Ethan smiled across at me with crinkly blue eyes. 'I knew you were cool but now I see you're completely crazy.'

'Not really.' I rubbed the tattoo on my right wrist. It was almost completely smooth again. 'Mostly incredibly ordinary. According to some people, I'm actually very boring.'

'I don't believe it,' he said. 'Who would ever think you were boring?'

I rested my elbow on the table and covered a small smile with my hand. I'd only had a couple of sips of my drink but my head was swimming already. The perils of jetlag and cocktails. Jetlag and cocktails. Nice to mix things up from the usual Monday routine.

You know what's wrong here, whispered Redhead Rachel, appearing out of nowhere. You know exactly what's wrong with this situation.

Nice of her to show up at the end of the bloody day. This might be the only instance where it was better never than late.

'Really, I'm a big fan of the quiet life.' I chose to ignore my bitchy alter ego but, even as I said the words, I knew it wasn't true any more. 'I don't need to be out punching supermodels in the face every Wednesday.'

OK, that part was true, but I didn't want to spend every Thursday night making spaghetti bolognese for a man who didn't deserve it either. I'd rather just make it for myself. Possibly for Emelie. I'd never be cooking for Matthew ever again. Ethan's expression suggested he was still stuck on the 'punch a supermodel in the face' part of our conversation.

I picked up a chip that seemed relatively gravy- and cheese-curd-free. 'That was Emelie anyway.' I bit into the chip. I put the chip back down. Bleurgh. 'I just set off the fire alarm.'

'I can't believe how much you've changed.' Ethan started on the poutine with much more commitment. 'You know you're kind of amazing, right?'

You are amazing. Redhead Rachel yawned at my side. And he's completely and utterly dull.

Redhead Rachel was a bit mean. But worryingly correct.

'Really, not amazing. We should have caught up a month ago.' I raised an eyebrow. 'Things were very different.'

But of course we wouldn't have been able to catch up a month ago because, without the list, I would never have thought to look him up. Matthew would never have messaged him. I would never have been sitting in a bar in Toronto. I would have been watching *Match of the Day* with half a Domino's Tunion and the best part of a bottle of white wine giving me indigestion.

'So, Rachel Summers, high-flying international make-up artist,' Ethan held an imaginary microphone out to me. 'Where do you see yourself in five years?'

'Another answer that would have been very different a month ago,' I replied, wondering what the answer was now. 'Tough question, Mr Harrison.'

'How so?'

'A month ago I would have freaked out at the thought of how old I'll be in five years. Thirty-three. Scary.' I closed my eyes and swallowed. 'And I'd definitely have said I'd be married with a baby. Maybe two. That's it probably.'

Ethan smiled happily. 'Sounds like my answer.'

'I'm just not sure it would be mine any more.' I rubbed my tattoo and pushed my hair back behind my ears, letting it fall back around my face. 'Thirty-three doesn't seem nearly as scary as the idea of having kids right now.'

'So what do you want?' he asked.

I laughed out loud and smiled at my answer. 'I don't know. I really don't know. Just getting a clearer idea of what I don't want.'

'Do you think you'll stay in London?' Ethan asked as I turned in my chair to look out at the sun setting over the city. It had never occurred to me that it would be so pretty here. In fact, like so many things, Canada had never really occurred to me at all. I was glad

Matthew had made me come; I was a frog in a well. Or a slightly more flattering animal. The lights of the CN Tower were just starting to stand out against the powdery sky and Lake Ontario glittered in the distance. 'I hear Toronto is running very short on make-up artists.'

'Really?'

Boring, the redhead whined, he's cheesy and boring. Aren't we over that?

'Really.'

It would have been the perfect time for a kiss. Sitting there shoulder to shoulder, knees touching under the table, sharing a drink at the end of a wonderful day after all these years apart but, when it came down to it, my butterflies had fluttered off somewhere else.

'You probably wouldn't realize how much you'd miss it unless you left,' Ethan broke the tension and pulled away. 'I think that's the thing about cities – you get used to all the things they offer you, then you really don't think about it until it's taken away. I lived in New York for a summer after college and, when I got back to Toronto, things here just seemed so slow, like it took forever to get anything done. But now I wouldn't leave for anything. I just want to go to work, come home, walk my dog and chill out.'

'Sounds nice,' I said. Rachel from one week ago would have genuinely considered that blissful. Redhead Rachel was gagging with her fingers down the back of her throat. And, somewhere in the middle, the real Rachel knew this wasn't the life for her. As wonderful and romantic as it would have been to run away with my teenage dream, it just wasn't going to happen.

He rubbed a hand over his face and rested his forehead against his fist. 'I can't even start to wonder how boring my life must sound to you. I don't mean I just sit in my house every day waiting to go to sleep. I just mean this is a great city if you don't want to be constantly freaking out. It's a great place.'

'It's beautiful.' I fingered the change in the pocket of my sundress, no idea what to say next. 'And you have animals on your money.'

Ethan smiled. I wondered when I'd become mentally unstable.

'Yes we do.' He leaned in towards me and loosened the hair behind my ear.

'Beavers,' I held it up to show him. 'And, is that a moose? Funny.'

'I guess I never thought about it.' His smile was just a little bit crooked even though his post-braces teeth were perfect. Why wasn't I falling for this? I was clearly defective. 'I guess I never thought about a lot of things.'

Out of the mouths of fools and babes, Redhead Rachel commented while inspecting her nails to my left.

'I've been thinking about something.' Ethan leaned in for the kill.

His lips were only on mine for a moment. It wasn't even really a kiss, more of a test-the-waters peck and, as soon as I'd got used to them being there, they were gone. It was soft and sweet and a perfect first kiss.

It just wasn't Dan.

'I totally just got off with Rachel Summers,' Ethan blushed, placing his hand over mine and gently squeezing it. 'Wait until I tell the lads.'

'Only took you twelve years,' I said quietly, trying to smile. What was wrong with me? Why was I thinking about Dan? I tried to imagine how I'd be feeling if we were round the back of the sports hall, his Lynx Java mingling with my Impulse Vanilla Kisses instead of on the rooftop of a posh hotel, my Marc Jacobs Daisy and his nothing at all. The whiff of dog food on chips didn't help, but that really wasn't the problem here.

I'd been trying so hard to make this Ethan thing real I was completely ignoring a far more worrying situation. And it wasn't the chips. 'So what do you want to do now?' he asked. 'We could catch a movie maybe? Dinner? You're not really feeling the poutine, right?'

'I'm so sorry but I'm sort of knackered.' I yawned to demonstrate my point. 'I really just want to go to bed.'

'Bed?' If he spent any more time blushing, he'd be no use to anyone in the bedroom anyway. Every ounce of blood in his body was making a beeline for his cheeks.

'My bed,' I clarified hastily. Wow, way to leave a sentence open for entirely the wrong interpretation. 'I should go to my bed and sleep. Jetlag.'

As soon as the words were out of my mouth, it was as if my body just gave up. As the sky above us turned from powder blue to a soft, dusky purple, my ability to keep my eyes open began to fail and all I wanted was my bed. Maybe my judgement was just impaired by the shroud of sleepy. I needed to rest. When I had a clear head I'd be able to work out what exactly was wrong with this picture. Or at least what was wrong with me.

Redhead Rachel was already standing by the lift, tapping her watch. She seemed to know exactly what was going on. If only she would let me in on it.

'Jeez, you must be totally jetlagged.' Ethan looked a little bit disappointed but, ever the gentleman, he signalled for the bill and gave my hand another squeeze. 'I had a lot of fun today. It was great to catch up.'

'Definitely.' It had been fun. It just hadn't been the

whirlwind romance I'd built myself up for. 'Thank you so much for showing me around.'

'Let's get you back to your hotel.' He threw a couple of notes on the bar and flashed the waitress a goodnight smile. The dimples I'd wanted to tweak so desperately in Year Eleven returned with a vengeance. I really wished I could pin down what was wrong with me. Surely it wasn't just that he didn't watch TV?

'Thanks.' I hopped down off my bar stool and let him wind his fingers around mine, hoping to feel something gooey and lovely in my stomach. All I could feel was that one rancid chip rattling around. Truly it was the stuff great love stories were made of.

'So this is you.' Ethan's very practical car pulled to a stop outside the shiny black fascia of The Drake.

I unbuckled my seatbelt and gave him my best sleepy smile. At least I hoped it was a good sleepy smile and not just cross-eyed. 'Thanks so much, it was fun.'

'It was.' He turned off the engine and wrapped his hands around the steering wheel. Ruh-roh, that was a very serious face. 'I know you have to leave on Wednesday but do you have plans tomorrow?'

'I don't know,' I lied. 'Can I text and let you know?'

'Of course.' He shifted in his seat until he was facing me. 'I'd really like to hang out. Today was awesome.'

'Right.' I turned quickly, one hand on the door handle, leaned in to plant a kiss on his cheek and then bolted out of the door. 'Night, Ethan.'

I slammed it shut behind me and was safely inside the hotel before I even heard his engine turn over.

'Hi, Miss Summers,' the receptionist gave me a wave. 'Good evening?'

'Yes?' I offered. She looked as convinced of that as I did. Em had texted me to say she and Matthew were in the bar and to come and join them, but since I clearly couldn't be trusted to deal with people, I headed straight up the stairs to bed. It would be nice to have a shower without an audience.

'Well, sleep tight,' she called after me.

'Yeah, whatever,' I chuntered, mounting the stairs. Fat bloody chance of that.

CHAPTER EIGHTEEN

I crawled into bed, still in my sundress, and got under the covers. There was no time for a shower. I didn't care if my face felt a little bit sunburned. I didn't care if I woke up with panda eyes. Why had no one worked out that jetlag and messy-stressy boy nonsense was the cure for OCD? Wrapping myself up in the duvet, I couldn't even find the energy to flick off the light switch. By the time I'd rolled myself up against the seasonably warm weather, I was right in the middle of the bed. Fuck it, Emelie was just going to have to roll me over when she got in. As soon as I was down, I turned into lead, and like lead I sank into a deep sleep the second I closed my eyes.

It was daylight again when I opened them.

'Morning.' Matthew was stretched out on the chaise lounge, reading a French magazine. Matthew didn't speak French. 'You were sock on when we got in last night.'

'I was knackered,' I said quietly, so as not to wake Emelie. 'We walked around all day. What time is it?'

'Ten-ish?' Matthew replied. 'I thought you were never going to wake up. Give sleeping beauty a tap; the car's booked for eleven thirty and I have to eat something before my stomach lining starts digesting itself.'

'Car?' Getting up was an epic struggle. My limbs felt as though they'd been chopped off and replaced with sausages. Nothing seemed to work.

'Em was telling me about that bungee-ball thing at Niagara Falls.' He stood up and hauled me out of bed. 'So I looked into it. We're going.'

'We are?' I looked down at my crumpled dress and up at Matthew's shocked expression. 'I slept in my clothes.' I explained.

'So I see.' He held my shoulders and walked me over to the shower. 'Good date?'

'Feels like a car conversation,' I pulled at the zip on my dress and wrapped a towel around me to avoid burning Matthew's retinas with my boobs.

'That bad?' He turned on the water, testing the temperature with his hand. 'Are you OK?'

I picked up my special redhead shampoo, ready to wash some sense back into my hair.

'Let's just say I've picked the right day to jump off the top of a tall building.'

'Road triiiip!' Emelie yelled, throwing a plastic bag full of treats across the back seat and then distributing huge Starbucks cups to Matthew and me in the front seat. He'd taken driving dibs and I was playing navigator, which left Em in charge of entertainment although, as far as I could tell, my role was mostly holding the iPhone where Matthew could keep his eye on the TomTom app while Em stretched out on the back seat and ate crisps. I'd definitely drawn the short straw.

Much to Em's delight, Matthew was doing his best to rev the engine of the Mini Cooper when my phone switched out of its map mode and flashed up with a private number.

'It's probably Ethan,' I said, opening the car door and hopping out onto the pavement. 'Give me a minute.'

'You've got one minute,' Em shouted through the window. 'Road triiiip!'

'Hello?' There really was no good reason not to see him, other than I'd already made plans to jump from a great height with a bit of elastic tied around my ankles. It wasn't as if he was going to propose. Probably. He had talked an awful lot about his friends' babies. If ever there were a marrying kind, it was him. And I supposed – until a week ago – me. Stupid bloody timing.

'So, I read your letter.'

Simon never bothered with hello. It was one of his less pleasant habits. Like clipping his toenails in the living room, eating Marmite sandwiches before bed and keeping his hands down his pants during *Match of the Day*. Actually, during any TV show after eight p.m. And these were the things of which I needed to keep reminding myself.

'Why are you reading my letters?' I was more than a little bit confused. 'And why you didn't your number come up? Have you changed your number?'

'You changed the locks without telling me,' he replied. 'It seemed fair.'

'You left.' I found a bus shelter and sat down. Pacing wasn't going to help my blood pressure. I nodded good morning at the two old ladies waiting beside me. They nodded back. Lovely people. 'Why are you reading my post?'

'I'm not reading your post.' He sounded pissed off. 'I'm reading the letter you wrote, addressed to me. The one in which you repeatedly refer to me as a cockweasel.'

It took me a minute but I got there eventually. The letter. The letter I put on the coffee table. That Matthew must have picked up when he went to get Simon's mail. Cockweasels.

'Oh.' It was a good job I was already sitting down although, really, lying down might have been better. 'That letter.'

'That letter,' he replied. 'Matthew said you were going to Canada?'

I looked around at the two old ladies in the bus stop, the cars driving over tramlines on the wrong side of the road and the funky black and white stripy building opposite.

'I'm in Canada,' I confirmed. 'Toronto.'

'For work?' He was starting to sound slightly less pissed off and slightly more curious.

'Nope.' Why give him any more details than he deserved?

'Fine. Look, this is costing me a fortune so I'm just going to say it,' he said after a moment's pause. 'That letter really fucked me off.'

'Imagine that,' I replied. If he started giving me shit, I could just hang up again. What was he going to do: come to Canada to shout at me in person?

'Yeah. It wasn't very nice to read but, after I read it, I thought . . . You were right. There were parts of it that made me feel like shit. I can't really blame you. You're right about everything.'

Well, this was a turn-up for the books.

'What I did was shit and cowardly and you didn't deserve it.'

I leaned back against the wall of the bus shelter. Really?

He took a deep breath and I could have sworn I heard a heavy sniff. 'Rachel, I'm sorry. I know I shouldn't ask and I know you should say no, I know you're going to say no but, god, I really want to see you.'

I stared across the street as a tram rattled by. Trams. Canada was funny.

'Rachel, are you there? You know I can't tell if you're answering me in your head when we're on the phone.'

'I'm listening,' I replied. 'You want to see me.'

'I know I'm an idiot cockweasel who doesn't deserve it but I want to come home,' he said quickly, tacking a nervous laugh on the end for good measure. 'I've been sitting here looking at my phone, reading that letter all day. It's taken me until now to get the guts up to call you.'

What was I supposed to say? What was I supposed to do? I nibbled on the corner of my thumbnail.

'OK, I'll just keep talking and you don't hang up, deal?'

In five years, I'd only seen Simon cry twice. Once when his granddad died and again when Chelsea won the double, but it sounded as if he was having a go at hitting the triple himself.

'I don't know what I was thinking, changing jobs, meeting new people, coming up to thirty, whatever,' he went on. 'I convinced myself I was missing out on something. It was like, I looked at you and started seeing a mortgage and pension plans and university fees and weekly trips to the supermarket and just being old. I stopped seeing you. But I was wrong.'

I was a weekly trip to the supermarket? I stopped biting my nail. He looked at me and saw pension plans?

'I've had a bit of time to think about it and I was wrong. I can admit that now. I *was* a cockweasel but now I want to come home. I love you.'

'You do?'

'I do.'

'Even though I'm boring?'

'Even though you're boring,' Simon tried to laugh. 'But boring's not that bad when you think about it, is it? I really miss you, Rach.'

I breathed in and then breathed out. I was calm. I was totally, totally calm. I was not about to hulk out on Queen Street West.

'But what if I don't want that any more?' I asked. We were this close to Rachel go smash-smash. 'What if I'm different?'

'You're still Rachel,' he replied. Someone was getting annoyed that I hadn't rolled over like a dead dog. 'Look, when are you back? Shall I pick you up at the airport? I'll make dinner and we can sort everything out.'

I puffed out my cheeks and looked back at the car. Em was hanging out of the window making 'wrap it up' hand gestures in between scoffing handfuls of Ruffles. I gave her a wave and a two-minute sign. Or at least I thought it was a two minutes sign. I might have actually flashed her a V.

'Rach?' Simon's voice on the other end of the line.

'No.' My voice. My word.

'No I shouldn't pick you up?'

'No to all of it.' I stood up and started pacing. Threat of stroke be damned. 'No, you can't pick me up. No, you can't pretend none of this happened. No, you can't come home. It's not your home any more.'

Saying it made it true. I'd done too much in the last ten days to just go back. Of course it would be easier to write it off as an extended mad half-hour, but since when was anything worth doing easy? I wasn't in love with Simon any more. I hadn't been in love with Simon for a long time. I was in love with not being on my own, with having someone there at the end of the day and now I knew I didn't need that. My heart wasn't broken over him; it was breaking for the things I had wanted from him. And I didn't want them any more.

'Rachel?'

'You are a coward. And a cockweasel.' I winced and mouthed an apology at the old ladies. One of them shook her head, the other smiled. 'What if I'd come home three months ago and said, all right Simon, I reckon I might want to shag about for a bit but once I'm bored of sleeping on my mate's settee, I'll come back. It'll be on my terms and I'll call you up and insult you first, though. Does that sound OK? What exactly would you have said?'

'Rach—'

'I'll call you when I'm back and I've decided what I want to do with the flat. I have to go now, I'm about to throw myself off a bridge or something.'

I pressed end and called Simon a very bad word in a very loud voice. The old ladies sitting beside me in the bus shelter looked somewhat startled.

'Oh, sorry,' I covered my mouth with my hand and apologized again. 'I forgot where I was for a minute.'

'Don't worry,' one in a fetching orange mac replied. 'We've come across more than one cockweasel in our time, we just never used that name for them.'

'Do you remember Donald Tyler?' the other chuckled as the bus pulled up. 'Now he was a real cockweasel.'

I wiped away the beginnings of tears, pleased that they had never made it all the way out, and smiled at the two ladies as they boarded the bus. Forty years from now, that would be me and Emelie. Matthew would doubtlessly be too busy cruising around Miami in his toy boy's convertible. Scratching my tickly nose, I walked back to the car and jumped back in.

'What's up?' Matthew took one look at my face and pulled me into a hug. 'You all right?'

'It was Simon,' I mumbled to the wet patch my tears had started on his T-shirt. 'He wants to come home.'

'Oh my god.' Em launched herself and the Ruffles through the gap in between the seats to get in on the hug action. 'What did you say?'

'I told him no.' First order of business, I took the Ruffles and dropped them in the foot-well. I was going to be needing them soon enough. 'I don't want him back. It's not his home any more, he left.'

'Amazing.' Matthew untangled himself from the hug and held his hand up for a high-five. 'Good. You're better off without him.'

'You're totally owning this single thing,' Em agreed. 'Men of the world watch out.'

'Hmm, yeah.' I rested my head on her arm. 'Rachel Summers, international heartbreaker.'

That title might have more credibility if I could stop thinking about one very specific heart I'd at least bruised recently. And it did not feel good.

'You still need to fill us in on that story,' Matthew reminded me once he'd wrangled Emelie back into her seat and convinced her to fasten her seatbelt. 'Do you want to rain-check on this? We could do it tomorrow?'

The last couple of days had been tiring and confusing. The jetlag had put Redhead Rachel right off her game and, basically, I needed to be back on it. Which meant only one thing. I buckled my seatbelt, took my to-do list out of my handbag and waved it at Matthew. 'If I'm ever going to do this, it's going to be today.'

'Yes ma'am,' he nodded, turning the key in the ignition. 'Niagara Falls it is then.'

'Whooo!' Em bellowed out of the window again. 'Road triiip!'

'Yeah, Em,' Matthew spoke into the rear-view mirror. 'That's going to get really tired, really quickly.'

'WHOO.' She leaned forward and repeated herself, twice as loud, right in his face. 'ROAD TRIP.'

'Shall we just get going?' I suggested, tucking the manky-looking napkin away. Maybe it wouldn't be such a bad thing if I didn't survive the bungee jump. A broken neck had to be better than four hours in a car with these two.

I wasn't entirely sure what I was expecting from Niagara Falls but Alton Towers meets Blackpool Illuminations dropped in the middle of a National Trust park really wasn't it. The place was terrifyingly tacky, the complete opposite of tasteful and modern Toronto. It took twenty minutes to crawl through the neon signs, past the waxwork museum, the bowling alley, funfair and four different Starbucks before we were waved off into a car park. And by car park, I mean great big gravelly field. Em bounded out from the back seat like an over-enthusiastic puppy as soon as the car had rolled to a halt.

'Come on, it's this way,' she yelled, bouncing up and down, face turned up to the sun. Anyone would think we kept her in a box in the cellar. 'I can't wait for you to see it.'

Matthew unfolded his giant frame from the tiny car with slightly more dignity and stretched. Vanity was pain. Hiring the coolest car in the garage wasn't always a good idea if you were technically a giant.

'Come on.' He wrapped an arm around my shoulders and we followed Em and the hordes of other visitors across the car park. 'It's going to be fine.'

The en-route Ethan discussion had been relatively brief. Still shaken by SimonGate, I couldn't really sit there and make excuses as to why I'd spent a wonderful day with a wonderful man and felt nothing. Em was clearly wearing her hopeless romantic hat and blamed everything from nerves and jetlag through to the jeans he was wearing and the far too early introduction of her beloved poutine. If nothing else, I had discovered her secret shame of adding melted cheese slices to chip-shop chips and gravy when no one was looking. Matthew, on the other hand, was much more fatalistic. Ethan wasn't the one. It was a fun crush, long-distance things often were, he told me, but when it came down to it the chemistry wasn't there.

'It's not your fault,' he'd told me as we cruised along the highway listening to Bryan Adams. When in Rome. 'You're not going to fall hopelessly in love tomorrow. If Ethan was some bloke you'd got off with in a bar one night, it wouldn't matter that you didn't want to marry him within fifteen minutes of meeting him. And maybe if he lived in London you wouldn't be putting so much pressure on it.'

'I suppose so.' I stared at the Facebook message I'd sent and tried not to feel like a shit.

Hey Ethan,
Thanks so much for yesterday, I had a really great time. Toronto is amazing. It was so, so great to catch up but I'm going to have to pass on today. Unexpected work stuff. Let's stay in touch and if you ever come back through London, you have to give me a shout.
    Love,
    Rachel

It really wasn't worthy of him; he was such a great guy and I had a feeling that this was what was commonly known as the short shrift, but what was I supposed to do? It wasn't as if we were engaged. We hung out once. He kissed me once. We both knew I was leaving in forty-eight hours. And I told myself that over and over until I'd managed to almost completely bury the fact that I felt awful for leading him on. He hadn't replied yet. I decided to believe this was because he and Sadie were hiking somewhere without a phone network and not just because he was busy making a redheaded voodoo doll. It wasn't as though he needed to curse me: I was en route to giving myself a fatal heart attack anyway. Number nine, bungee jump.

'Everything's going to be fine,' Matthew had promised. 'Sooner or later you're going to find someone who knocks you right off your feet. Someone who makes you feel alive. Someone who kisses you and makes your knees weak. Relationships are complicated enough as it is. It's not worth settling for anything less.'

'Fact,' Em had agreed. 'And nothing feels more amazing than meeting someone who drives you crazy. You need a little passion in your life, Ray Ray. Toe-curling, lip-bruising passion.'

At that point I wasn't sure what was scarier. The thought of the bungee jump, settling for less, or that the only person to have made me feel that way in my entire life was Dan Fraser, seventy-two hours ago when he knocked me right off my feet and onto my back.

Since my eyes had been scarred by the hideous tourist-trap extravaganza on the way into the falls, and my mind was full of nonsense, I was completely unprepared for the ridiculous level of natural beauty that lay in front of me when we finally caught up with

Emelie. With every step, the rush of water got louder and louder, the view more and more spectacular. It was absolutely breathtaking. Hopping up to sit on a low stone wall, I ignored the growing lemming tendency that told me I was awfully high up, and snapped a million photos; but not a single picture would ever be able to replicate how I felt at that second. I looked over my shoulder at the neon monstrosities behind us and then back at the falls. No wonder the shops were fighting so hard for my attention, but it wasn't even really a competition. Unless you were wearing a bum bag and your name was Billy Bob. The falls were immense. Epic. More impressive than the wonder room at Selfridges. Almost as thrilling as the first time I saw my red hair. I had forgotten that there were things in nature that could stun me into silence, things that had been here for centuries, things other than Sky Plus. As soon as I'd regained my composure, true child of the twenty-first century that I was, I took a picture on my phone and texted it to my mum. She would have loved it. In fact, she would love it. I made a mental note to come back with her sometime soon.

'It's amazing,' Matthew said after a few minutes of quiet. 'Sure you don't want to find a barrel and go over the top? I'll totally accept that as an alternative to the bungee jump.'

Oh yeah. I wasn't here to be stunned into silence by nature. I was here to lock myself in a giant hamster ball and get volleyed a billion feet into the air and back down again to my splattery death. There really hadn't been any point in sending Ethan that email. I could have just died quietly and let him live on in blissful ignorance.

'I'm going to pass.' I peered over the edge into the rush of white water where the falls crashed into the river. Vapour rose up to mist my face lightly, numbing the sick feeling in my stomach. It was strange to feel something so delicate coming from something so powerful. And yet still, sitting here in front of Niagara Falls with my two best friends, in a foreign country, with red hair, a tattoo and very nearly a criminal record, all I could think about was Dan. There really was only one course of action. But there weren't any barrels handy.

'Right.' Back to the falls, I jumped off the wall and dusted down my arse. 'Where's this bungee ball?'

'Oh for fuck's sake.' I closed my eyes as I felt the straps of a very intimate harness being tightened around my denim cut-offs. 'Do I really have to do this?'

Of all the items on my to-do list, this was the one that was bothering me the most. Get a tattoo, fine. Break the law? There were a million ways to do that without actually getting into trouble on a daily basis. I would rather sign something that said my head would explode if I didn't go running every day for the next ten years than give the bungee-ball operator, who incidentally didn't look qualified to be operating a ping-pong ball, a thumbs-up. My fear of heights had never been that debilitating because I'd made a point of never having to deal with heights. Really, when in life did you have to be up high? Simon changed all the light bulbs, I stayed on the bottom deck of the bus and I never went upstairs in Urban Outfitters. Easy. This was not something I'd ever worried about. I didn't like heights. I didn't like confined spaces. I didn't like teenagers in charge of machinery that could kill me. Really, it was like my three biggest phobias had come together. Basically, the only thing that could have made this a more terrifying experience would have been if they'd strapped a tarantula to my face.

I'd made Em, Matthew and their giant ice creams stay at the bottom of the platform, supposedly to take photos, but really it was just so there would be as few witnesses to my nervous breakdown as possible. Plus, their morbid fascination with watching me go to my death had put a fever in their eyes that I did not like seeing. Matthew in particular was enjoying this altogether too much. The pinging catapult and crashing noises he'd been making for the very, very long forty minutes we'd spent waiting in the queue had not helped. By the time I was strapped in, every part of me was dripping in sweat and I was fairly certain I was hyperventilating.

'So, I'm like, gonna set the ride and then I'll like totally signal to you and then,' the kid in charge of a dubious-looking control desk wiped his nose with the back of his hand and looked to the skies to like totally remind him of his lines. 'Slingshot passengers are propelled over one hundred metres into the skies above Niagara Falls at speeds of up to one hundred and sixty kilometres per hour.'

He coughed. Spat something onto the floor and started up again.

Oh my god, I was actually going to die.

'You should not ride the slingshot if you are pregnant, have a heart condition or, uh, there's some other stuff,' he shrugged. 'You're like, not knocked up though, right?'

'Really not, just mentally unstable,' I replied through a bright smile. I just had to get it over with. Like ripping off a plaster. A deadly plaster that would come loose of the mechanical arms and hurl me over the falls to a watery grave. Any second now. 'Can we please just do this?'

'Yeah, uh, I think that's OK. We've definitely had

people who have been mentally retarded before.' He shuffled back to the controls. 'Although I'm not supposed to say retarded when I'm working the ride.'

I really wished he would stop calling it a ride. Ride suggested it was going to be fun. You rode donkeys on the beach. You rode a rollercoaster. This was me strapping myself into a giant metal death machine, operated by the son of Mr Bean. There wasn't even a prize for completing everything on the to-do list. Just that sweet, sweet sense of completion, I told myself. That was a prize. Unless I died and then all I would have to show for my endeavours would be a visit to the police station, cramp, and a manky, scribbled-on napkin. If I hadn't started this nonsense, I wouldn't be here now. If we hadn't made that list, I wouldn't be trying to work out why I couldn't stop wondering where Dan was, what he was doing and with whom. It wouldn't bother me that he hadn't tried to get in touch with me. It wouldn't bother me that – wait? Was that the signal? I tried to lean forward against the harness to get a better look at Bean Jr, but no, he was too busy hunched over the controls with half a taco hanging out of his mouth.

Grabbing onto the harness, I braced myself and prepared for my imminent demise. I imagined if Elvis had been given the choice between checking out on the shitter or in front of one of the natural wonders of the world, he, well, he probably would have chosen the shitter. Besides, there was a weight limit on this thing. But there were worse ways to go than with an amazing view of Niagara Falls; it was sort of wonderful. I could see both waterfalls from here: rushing white water, vibrant green trees, electric blue sky. Such pretty colours. Such a shame that, as soon as I turned around, all I could see was the screaming neon Bowlerama sign. I supposed it had its own charm, just . . . not really.

Canada was underneath my feet, or at least underneath the capsule and, right there, just across the water, was America. To be honest, I was more shocked that the tack-fest was on the Canadian side than that it existed. The US side of the falls seemed incredibly dignified by comparison and I was at least glad I'd got to see something so beautiful before I died. Because I was utterly convinced I was about to die.

I heard the click before I felt anything. Half a heartbeat later I was being thrown into the sky, the waterfall millions of miles below me. Or at least one hundred metres away. It was bizarre; I couldn't feel anything, physical or otherwise. All I knew was that my stomach and Niagara Falls was somewhere below me and, any second now, this glorious soaring sensation was going to be replaced with a terrifying plummet to my untimely death. But now. And to think, under any other circumstances, I loved being right.

CHAPTER NINETEEN

'ohmygodthatwasamazing,' I exhaled, as Dougie Howser's backward brother released me from the sling-shot capsule to an audience and Emelie and Matthew's cheers. My legs gave out almost instantly, but luckily there were two pairs of arms waiting to scoop me up off the floor as Mr Bean Jr stepped out of the way and let me fall.

'We're not allowed to touch customers,' he commented above me. 'We hope you enjoyed your slingshot experience.'

My eyes were wide open but I was completely blind. All I could see were blurs of colours and everything seemed very loud. I was alive. I felt very, very alive. I imagined this was as close as I'd ever get to knowing how it felt to be born – disoriented, deafened, and with a rapidly building urge to start sobbing at the top of my lungs. I wanted to sit down. I wanted to tick bungee jump off the list. I wanted to never, ever do that again.

'I am so proud of you.' Em threw herself at me in a huge hug. 'That was incredible. Matthew videoed the whole thing.'

'I did,' he confirmed. 'Might set it to a soundtrack

or something before we show your mum. Either the sound on this is incredibly sensitive or your colourful language was unbelievably loud.'

'Bit of both?' I suggested, taking a Bambi-on-ice step forward. 'That was incredible.'

'Still scared of heights?' Em asked, helping me down from the platform while two roaring frat boys were strapped into the capsule in my place. Should they be drinking beer in there?

'Petrified,' I confirmed. 'But it's done. I did it. I feel like I could do anything.'

'And what exactly do you want to do?' Matthew asked.

I paused for a moment to really consider his question and give the appropriate answer. I'd just achieved something life-changing. I'd faced my fear head on. I had climbed Everest. I'd sailed the Atlantic. I'd found the Louboutins in the Selfridges sale.

'I'd take your arm off for a burger,' I replied.

Once we'd secured all the appropriate evidence that the bungee ball had in fact happened – photos, T-shirts, keyrings, the works, Emelie helped me hobble over to a bench while Matthew was voted hunter/gatherer and sent off in search of food.

'Do you feel amazing?' Em asked, flicking through my souvenirs. They weren't terribly attractive but I was too proud of myself to worry about being vain. For the moment. There was always Photoshop.

'I do,' I confirmed and, with a very shaky hand, I dug around in my giant bag for my to-do list and dutifully crossed out 'bungee jump'. Just one item left. I shoved it into my pocket and tried to will my stomach to settle. 'A bit sick but amazing.'

'I bet everyone that does something as amazing feels

a bit sick afterwards,' she replied, giving me a sideways hug and then utching a few inches away just in case. 'Like, people who walk on the moon or climb mountains or touch Johnny Depp.'

Unsure of whether or not she was taking the piss, I gave her a tiny laugh and rested my head on my knees, waiting for my heart to stop pounding. The feeling in my legs I could do without, but I'd be much happier if I wasn't convinced I was on the verge of having a stroke. My blood pressure really had been tested enough for one day.

'Here you go, superstar.' Matthew reappeared a few minutes later with three giant brown sacks from Wendy's. 'Three number sevens, extra large, with fries, onion rings and Diet Cokes.'

He set a cardboard tray down on the neighbouring bench and opened up the bag. Dear god, it smelled good. I took out the silver wrapped sandwich and took a bite before even asking what a number seven was. As it turned out, number seven was code for the most delicious chicken burger I had ever, ever put in my mouth. I'd hoovered mine down and started on the fries while Em and Matthew were still picking the chunks of tomato out of the bun. And that probably explained why I threw it straight back up into the nearest bin two minutes later.

'Are you all right?' Matthew asked once we'd swapped benches and I'd spent fifteen unpleasant minutes sorting myself out in a Starbucks toilet. 'Honestly?'

'I don't know,' I replied, staring out at the water. 'I feel weird.'

'Weird how?'

'Like I really could do anything.' I tried to process how I was feeling while I spoke. It wasn't often, at twenty-eight, you had to deal with an entirely new emotion. 'And that's sort of scary. I feel like I've opened a door without checking what was behind it. Like I've got no excuses any more.'

'Wow,' Emelie was still going at her chips. 'That's deep for you.'

'Yeah,' I agreed. 'I don't like it.'

'It's been a big day,' Matthew replied. A stiff breeze came off the falls and blew my hair all over my face. I pushed it away and behind my ears, waiting for Matthew to put it back, but he didn't. He also did not mention the fact that I was wearing a giant hoodie emblazoned with a hockey-playing moose. Puking always made me feel the cold and it genuinely had been the best option in the gift shop.

'I've got something for you.' He pulled a small square of blue tissue paper out of the inside pocket of his jacket. 'It's from me and Em. We got it while you were buying twenty-five Toblerones in duty-free.'

'I bought two,' I muttered, taking the package. 'What is it?'

'Open it and you'll find out, fatty.' He turned back to take in the view.

'I picked it,' Em chimed in on my other side.

Inside the tissue was a small, pink leather notebook. The cover was engraved in gold with the words, 'Bliss List'. I looked up at my friends. They were both smiling.

'Because you've almost finished your list,' he nodded towards the notebook. 'I've got you started on a new one.'

Right there, on the first page of the book was a number one, circled in silver pen alongside the instruction, 'Buy Matthew dinner'. I turned the delicate pale blue page. There it was again on the second page. And the third. And the fourth.

'I got bored after a couple of pages.' He leaned right over, resting his chin on his hands. 'There were some other fun things I wanted to put in there but Em told me I wasn't allowed.'

'It's your new single girl to-do notebook,' Em explained. 'All part of the transformation. New notebooks, new start.'

'Appreciated.' I wrapped the book back up in the tissue paper and slipped it into my bag. 'Thank you, really, it's amazing. You're amazing.'

'I was worried you were going to go all *The Shining* on us if you didn't start putting together a new list soon.' Matthew shrugged. 'Can't fight who you are, beautiful.'

'You don't think the list thing makes me a bit, well, mental?' I asked. The sun was starting to set behind us and the sky above the falls began to darken.

'Would I be friends with you if you were mental?'

'Yes,' I replied. 'Because you've been friends with me for ages, I have video footage of you crying at *An American Tail: Fievel Goes West* and I know you get a fake tan every week. Seriously, do you think I'm mad? Or boring?'

Emelie punched me in the arm considerably harder than was necessary. 'What's brought this on?' she asked. 'Do you even remember what you were doing ten minutes ago?'

I gave her a hard slap back. 'Cleaning my teeth in a Starbucks bog because I'd just thrown up?'

'Before that,' she pointed out, rubbing her arm. 'The bungee ball. The list. The fact we're in Canada. What happened to the new you? Did you just puke her out?'

'No.' I took the list out of my pocket. 'She's still here. I'm just a bit worried she won't be once I tick off this last thing. What do I do then?'

'Date for the wedding.' Matthew leaned over my shoulder. 'Someone in mind?'

'Actually, I was going to ask you,' I replied. 'It's not tragic to take your best friend to a wedding. Em's going to be there, I'm going to be there, you should be there.'

'In that case, I'd be very honoured.' He gave me a little bow. 'So do it. Tick it off.'

Taking a very deep breath, I pulled the black pen out of the bottom of my bag and crossed it out. There.

It was done.

'There.' Emelie ruffled my hair and whooped loudly enough to attract the attention of everyone in a fifteen-metre radius. Which really was quite a lot of people. 'You did it. You're officially single.'

'I suppose I am.' I looked up. Nope, sky hadn't fallen in. No flying pigs.

Everything was exactly as it had been two seconds before. Almost.

'I couldn't have done it without you two. I would've been face down on my mum's settee if you hadn't made me do all this.' I stared at the list triumphantly. 'It's going to sound weird, but I've had more fun in the last week than I have in the last five years.'

'You haven't exactly had the average dumpee's week,' Matthew reminded me. 'And you've spent a lot of time with me. I am sort of awesome.'

'And me.' Em grabbed the list for a quick review. 'I can't believe I punched that girl in the face.'

'I can't believe you're going out with my brother.' I screwed up my face, fighting off another wave of nausea. 'It'll just be me and Matthew singing "Single Ladies" at the wedding reception, I can already see it.'

'Really?' she cocked her head to one side. 'Anything you want to share at this point, Matthew?'

I turned altogether too quickly for my delicate stomach.

'Oh Emelie, you giant tactless cow.'

Unfortunately for Matthew, looking at the floor didn't work as an avoidance technique. He was so huge and I was so tiny, I could always see his face.

'I'm missing something, clearly.' I jabbed him in the hip. 'What's going on?'

'Fine.' He stuck his hands deep into the pockets of his jeans and gave Emelie the filthiest look he could muster. 'Following my recent near-death experience, which let us all remember you were the cause of, I may or may not have seen Stephen.'

'Woah. What?'

'Like, totally woah,' he rolled his eyes. 'Whatever. I called him and poured my stupid heart out and the long and the short of it is, he came and got me from the hospital and we sort of decided to try again when I get back.'

'Is that where you've been disappearing to?' I finally put two and two together and got four, instead of putting two and two together and coming up with 'where is Matthew and why is he not here with me?'. 'You're back together?'

'Sort of.' He sucked the air in through his teeth. 'Maybe. We're taking it slowly.'

'The sort of slow where you still shag random men in Canada?' I couldn't quite believe I was hearing this. Stephen had destroyed Matthew. Ripped his heart out and left him sobbing on my sofa bed for six straight months and now they were just getting back together as if nothing had happened?

'I'm trying to be sensible,' he replied. 'Granted my kind of sensible and your kind of sensible might not be exactly the same thing. But, for the record, I didn't actually shag the mountie. I'm all talk.'

I squeezed his giant arm. Matthew really was a very tall man. 'Why didn't you tell me?'

'Didn't really seem like the right time,' he replied. 'And I didn't know if it was definitely going to happen, we've been talking for a while, then we got a drink, then, well. He was going to come on my birthday but he freaked out and didn't. Then I called from the hospital and he said he needed a bit of time and nothing passes time like leaving the country.'

There were no words. He'd sold me on a grand romantic adventure, flown me halfway round the world and thrown me millions of miles up in the air to distract himself from his ex-boyfriend's indecision?

'I know I should have told you and I know you'll never approve,' he attempted to explain. 'But I know he's the one and if he hadn't agreed to give me a second chance, I don't know what I would have done.'

'You really believe in that?' I asked quietly.

'Because it's true. He's the only one I'll ever feel this way about. Whatever he does.' He nodded. 'No one has ever given you butterflies? No bolt of lightning out of the blue?'

'The thing about that is eventually the lightning strikes the butterfly and all you're left with is a nasty worm,' I pouted. 'Butterflies don't last. No one should act on butterflies.'

'So there have *been* butterflies?' Matthew started to smile. 'Em, get the camera out, I want her face preserved for all eternity when she admits this.'

I closed my eyes. 'I'm going to say this really quickly and neither of you are allowed to comment on it ever.'

Em jumped around in a close approximation of the Snoopy dance while Matthew clenched his fists, eyes wide.

'Let's just say . . .' I paused to see if they could keep

303

up their end of the deal. Shockingly, they remained silent. '. . . If I was having those sorts of feelings about someone – the scary, gushy, can't-stop-thinking-about-them feelings: isn't there just a really good chance that it's all reboundy and that I shouldn't act on it?'

'No,' they answered simultaneously. It never wasn't annoying when they ganged up against me.

'It's Dan, isn't it?' Em pressed. 'Tell me it's Dan.'

I pressed my lips together.

'Rachel Lulu Summers,' Matthew looked as if he was about to burst. 'Is it? Are you in lurve with Dan?'

'I suppose, oh god, I suppose the more I think about it . . .' I couldn't quite meet their eyes. I'd just let some spotty oik teenager toss me a hundred metres up into the air and I couldn't look at my best friends. What hope was there? 'I suppose I sort of keep thinking about him.'

I closed my eyes and waited patiently for the two of them to stop whooping and high-fiving. It was not dignified behaviour.

'You're not helping.' I raised my voice, just ever so slightly. 'I don't know how else to explain it.'

'Butterflies? Lightning?' Matthew suggested. 'Ring any bells? Church-type ones?'

'That's the thing, though,' I started to nibble on my thumbnail. Really, someone was going to have to make a second Wendy's run. 'Butterflies and lightning, yes, church bells, no. Dan isn't someone you get serious with.'

'Dan isn't what you had in mind,' Matthew said after one more round of whoops. 'But it doesn't ever really work out like that, my love.'

'Are we not evidence enough of that?' Em pointed towards the two of them. 'I've had a crush on your idiot brother for ten years, and Matthew's going back to the cheater. No offence.'

'None taken.' Matthew said with a slap. 'She might

be horribly tactless but she's right. You can't choose who you fall in love with, any more than you can choose when it happens.'

'But I don't know what to do.' Now I'd started talking about it, I couldn't stop. 'I really like him, I just never realized. But since the thing at The Savoy, then after you left the party and we, you know, oh my god. It was like a punch in the face. I've fucked up so badly and I've known him for all these years and now it's all new and I'm confused and he's like a different person, and-oh-I don't know. What if he doesn't feel the same? What if it was just a thing for him?'

'You haven't fucked up; you're just going to have to tell him how you feel,' Matthew sighed, resting his arm around my shoulders. 'Oh young padawan, you have so much to learn.'

'You have to call him,' Em produced her phone and held it out. 'Right now.'

'I've got my own bloody phone, Emelie,' I replied, waving the evidence in her face. 'I just don't know if I can.'

'Bottom line,' Matthew held his hands out. 'Are you happier when you're with Dan than when you're not?'

'Maybe.'

'What if he was just nice Dan? Not shouty Dan. What if it was just the kissing part?'

'I can't pretend that idea fills me with horror.'

'Then you call him and tell him that.'

I looked up at my giant, Teutonic beastie.

'I love you.'

'Love you too,' he kissed the top of my head. 'Even if you're a moron.'

I looked at him and Emelie. They didn't move. In fact, they seemed to settle in and get comfy.

'Do you two want to fuck off a minute?' I suggested,

pointing towards Blackpool in the distance. 'If I promise not to throw it up, will you bring me another burger?'

'I could go another one actually.' Em patted her tiny belly and dragged Matthew away with a smile. 'You've got five minutes.'

Staring out at the water, I watched *Maid of the Mist* boats glide along the placid surface of the water before turning in towards the Canadian side of the falls where they were suddenly bounced along like tiny toys. It didn't look fun. More fun than calling Dan, but less fun than sitting quietly in a corner and eating a burger.

Bloody men. Maybe I shouldn't just stay single, maybe I should go the whole hog and give celibacy a try. It seemed to be working out OK for the Jonas Brothers. Britney hadn't fared so well, though. Hmm. I knew too much about celebrities. Maybe I should just be alone and get a cat. Maybe two cats. I would call them 'tragic' and 'spinster' and they would be my babies. I would dress them up in nappies and bonnets and push them around in a pram.

Dear god, I'd finally gone insane. Probably the best time to make the call.

'Hello?'

'Dan? It's Rachel.'

I wasn't expecting a chorus of angels to greet me on the other end, but the near minute of complete silence was a bit awkward.

'Dan, without wanting to be an arsehole, I'm on an iPhone 3 and the battery on this thing is rubbish,' I said finally.

'Fine. What?'

OK, it was a start.

'I just thought I'd give you a call.' I searched for the

right words but nothing seemed like a sure-fire winner. 'Say hello.'

'You waited until midnight to call to say hello,' he asked. 'Are you drunk?'

I looked at my watch. It was almost seven. Which did in fact make it almost midnight in London. Cock.

'I'm in Canada,' I explained. 'Sorry, I totally forgot about the time difference. I didn't wake you, did I?'

'Canada?'

'I'm visiting a friend,' I fudged. Had I told him about Ethan? I couldn't remember. I couldn't remember anything. 'It was all a bit last-minute.'

I was not making a very good job of this. Dan was right to assume drunk – I wished I was. Why would anyone attempt to have this sort of conversation sober?

'I was wondering if we could have a chat when I'm back?' I just wanted him to put me out of my misery. I was fairly certain I actually preferred it when he was shouting at me in car parks.

'You and me?' He didn't sound as charmed as I'd hoped he would be. 'A chat?'

'Yes?'

'What can't you say right now?' Dan asked. 'Or can you not speak in front of your Canadian boyfriend?'

He didn't have to make it sound so stupid.

'No,' I swung my legs, hoping the movement might pump some sense back into my brain. 'I need to talk to you about the me and you stuff. The stuff you said the other night.'

I heard a loud sigh followed by a swallow. Well, at least someone had a drink in their hand.

'When are you back?'

'Thursday?' I was fairly certain that was right. 'Dan?'

'I won't be here on the Thursday,' he replied matter-of-factly. 'I've booked a job in LA. You remember jobs?'

I bit my lip hard and drew blood.

'You're going to LA? Before Thursday?' I touched my lip gingerly, feeling the sting. 'For how long?'

'Don't know. I've got a work visa, might stay for a while.'

'A while?'

'Yeah, it's the weirdest thing,' he replied. 'I told this girl how I'd liked her for years and she fucked off to Canada to see another bloke. So I made this list to help me get over her. It basically says: go to California, shag a load of models and never speak to her again.'

I couldn't usually argue with a list but it really didn't sound like this one was going to work out well for me.

'Dan, don't, I'm trying.' I'd done so well not to cry for so long but, after everything I'd been through in the past week, I was past caring. 'Don't be like this.'

'Don't you remember Rachel? This is who I am. This is what I do. Have fun in Canada.'

He hung up before I could even say what I wanted to say. Whatever that was. I redialled straight away but the call just cut off. It didn't even go to voicemail. And this was why falling for the butterflies was never a good idea. I didn't feel all bubbly and excited now. I felt cold and broken and empty. I was all of the parts that never made it into love songs or Mike Newell films. Mike Leigh maybe.

'Rachel?'

I looked up to see Matthew and Emelie holding out fresh food. Their shiny hopeful faces fell when they saw mine.

'Did you talk to him?' said Matthew.

'What did he say?' asked Emelie.

'Nothing good.' I took the brown paper bag and began shoving chips into my mouth. Ahh, lovely salty chips, unburdened by gravy and cheese curds, clogging up my arteries all on their own. Chips never let me down.

'Are you crying?' Matthew poked my cheek with a rough finger. 'You're crying. Stop it please.'

'Can't,' I mumbled through a steady stream of tears and fried potato. 'I don't know why I'm doing it.'

'Brilliant, we've got PMT to deal with on top of all of this.'

'It's not PMT.' I gave him a weak laugh to show willing but it just dissolved into a very pathetic choked sob. 'Since you're so interested, I'm not due for—'

'Rule twenty-four in the straight/gay friendship handbook, your monthly visitor is not up for discussion.' He gave me another giant hug while Emelie squatted at my feet and held the bag of chips. I felt like a junk-food-craving horse. 'Tell us exactly what he said. What did you say?'

'I didn't really get much of a chance to say anything.' My bitten lip began to sting from the salty chips. I let it. 'I said I wanted to talk to him when I got back and he said he didn't want to because he's going to LA on Thursday. For "a while".'

'Oh Rach, that's shit,' Matthew doubled the hug. 'When?'

'He just said he wouldn't be around on Thursday,' I mumbled. 'He's going for a while.'

'Then we have to get you home tonight,' Em reasoned, looking up at Matthew for approval. 'Right? We just get her home before he leaves?'

'It's as good a plan as any,' he agreed. 'Why the fuck not? I'll give Jeremy a ring, see if he can change our flights.'

I sat on the bench, eating my chips and trying not to start hyperventilating while Matthew marched up and down the footpath trying to get through to Jeremy.

There was no way he was in bed at midnight. I wasn't even sure if Jeremy slept at all.

'It'll all be all right, you know,' Em promised, stealing a chip.

Not if you take any more of my dinner, I thought, but rather than threaten my sort of amazing friend, I nodded and smiled. And then shoved another handful of potato-ey goodness into my mouth before she could get back in the bag.

We sat there for nearly an hour while Matthew made arrangements. Normally I would have had to get involved, be writing things down, generally sticking my nose in, but this time I was perfectly happy to sit on my bench, eating my chips and snuggling inside my sweater. And, by happy, I did mean emotionally dead and physically exhausted.

Tourists came and went, snapped pictures in front of us and then left, drawn away by the siren song of the WWE gift store or, on my frequent recommendation, a Wendy's number seven chicken sandwich.

Just as Matthew returned, looking very pleased with himself, Niagara Falls officially got tired of being ignored. The moment he took his seat on the bench, fireworks exploded in the sky over the waterfalls, echoing like thunderclaps and lighting the water with pretty patterns.

'Oh my god,' Matthew sat down slowly, never taking his eyes off the skies. 'Look at it.'

And we did look at it. For fifteen straight minutes the three of us sat in silence and watched the display play out over Niagara Falls, deaf to the oohing and ahhing taking place around us. Em put down the bag of chips and reached for mine and Matthew's hands. The waterfalls were beautiful on their own but, for such a longtime firework whore as myself, this was the icing on the cake. I was sure there would be purists who would say it was gilding the lily, but they were wrong. No case to be argued. Fireworks over Niagara Falls, a completed to-do list and my two best friends. What more could I possibly, possibly ask for? Plus, it was the quietest the three of us had been in each other's company without a television being present for as long as I could remember. This was monumental for so many reasons.

I was about to burst into tears again when I heard a very loud, very masculine sniff at the side of me. And another less manly sob to the other side.

'Are you crying?' I asked, checking both sets of tear-stained cheeks. 'Both of you?'

'It's just so beautiful,' Matthew wailed. 'And I'm just really happy.'

'I know,' Em agreed tearfully. 'I know it was your list and everything but I feel a bit like we've all been on some bullshit caring-and-sharing learning adventure.'

And I knew exactly what she meant. Without Emelie and Matthew, I'd be a quivering wreck, hiding out in my mum's spare bedroom. Or, worse, I'd be back with Simon. Now we could do anything. I could do anything. I could colour my hair, I could start running, I could get a tattoo, I could hunt down my first crush, I could buy myself something obscenely expensive and selfish, I could write Simon a letter that explained exactly what a knob he was, I could bungee jump-ish, I could break the law, I could travel to a country I'd never visited before and I could find a date to my dad's wedding who made me feel fantastic about myself because he was my best friend. The point of the list wasn't just to tick items off and forget about them, it was to learn something new. And the most important thing I'd learned was that I could do anything. Maybe realizing how I felt about Dan was just another lesson. A bloody harsh one but still. I'd get over it somehow because I could. I knew I could.

Once the fireworks and chips were finished, we hauled ourselves up off the bench and made our way back to the car. It was almost physically painful to leave the falls. I was still absolutely elated but simultaneously terrified of losing the feeling. Jeremy had managed to get all three of us on a flight out from Toronto first thing in the morning that would get us back to London for ten p.m., twelve hours earlier than our original flight. I just hoped that would be enough.

The drive back to the hotel was considerably more subdued than the drive out, mostly because Emelie was asleep in the back and snoring loudly instead of yelling 'road trip' and signalling for truck drivers to sound their horns at every opportunity. I sort of missed it. Staring out of the window in silence, I felt a strange sense of optimism creep over me. Yeah, I'd told a boy I liked him, or at least I'd tried, and he hadn't said it back, but at least I'd said it and now I was doing something about it. I wasn't sitting around hoping everything would get better on its own because I realized now that doing nothing was the only sure-fire way to be certain that nothing would happen.

We arrived back at the hotel incredibly quickly, Matthew having subscribed to my list a little and destroyed the Canadian speed limits more or less all the way back to Toronto. A two-hour journey so easily became a ninety-minute drive when you put your foot down. After handing the car over to the valet, he dragged Emelie out of the back and resigned himself to carrying her up the stairs while I took care of the bags and bags of snacks still littering the car.

'Ms Summers?' The same receptionist from the night before called me over as I attempted to sneak past her up the stairs. 'I have a package for you.'

'A package?' I was genuinely flummoxed. Unless Ethan had left me a horse's head, I had no idea what this could be. I was still a little surprised that he hadn't even replied to my Facebook message, but I couldn't imagine he was the dead-puppy-in-a-box-type either. I set the bag of snacks on the counter and opened up the great big blue box with my name on it. Inside, sitting on a bed of beautiful gold material, was a note. It was from Jenny.

Rachel, I read, Sorry I couldn't stay and talk longer. It was fun hearing about your list! Here's a little something I hope will help you out at that wedding, date or no date. Knock 'em dead. Jenny xoxo

The receptionist was almost more excited than I was. I laid the card to one side and picked up gold fabric. Only it wasn't just fabric, it was a stunning pale gold dress, high boat neck, three-quarter-length sleeves and a full tulle skirt that looked as if it would fall a little way below my knee, fluffed out with more layers than I could possibly count. It was the most beautiful dress I'd ever seen in my entire life. I held it up in front of me and looked up to see the receptionist with her hand clapped over her mouth, tears in her eyes.

'It's just so pretty,' she breathed after a moment.

'I know,' I replied in exactly the same voice.

That just settled it. Jenny hadn't been real after all; she was my fairy godmother. I held the dress out in front of me and stared into the mirrored wall of the hotel lobby. Yes Cinders, I watched as the colour of the fabric lit up my skin and made my bright new hair shine, you shall go to the ball.

CHAPTER TWENTY

'I'm coming!' I yelled, dashing up the hallway in my beautiful gold dress and delicate borrowed Jimmy Choos, clutch bag wedged into my armpit, one diamond stud in my ear and one in the palm of my hand. But the knocking at the door didn't stop.

'But Miss Summers, you look beautiful.' Matthew stood at the front door, resplendent in a new grey suit and pale gold tie, purchased especially to complement my dress. 'Really, you look amazing.' He leaned in to give me a delicate air kiss on the cheek that wouldn't smudge my make-up.

'You scrub up all right yourself,' I commented, while he did a twirl. 'I'm almost ready. Why didn't you let yourself in?'

'Just wanted to make a grand entrance,' he called from the hallway. 'You put the pictures up all by yourself? They look great.'

'I am capable of hammering a nail into a wall as it happens,' I replied, applying one last coat of mascara in the living-room mirror. 'I put them up yesterday.'

After arriving back in London, I'd made a last-ditch dash over to Dan's place, calling en route and hoping

I'd make it before he left for LA. But he wasn't home. And, according to the neighbour who'd come out to see what exactly all the racket was about, he hadn't been home in a day or so. I was too late, he'd gone. Instead of throwing myself off Waterloo Bridge, I got back in the taxi and let him drive me back home. There was nothing I could do until he decided to talk to me, whenever that might be. Until then, I'd decided to keep myself busy.

Once I'd prised myself out of bed sometime on Thursday afternoon, I went for a run, then came home and gave the hallway a fresh coat of paint to cover up the sad shadows where mine and Simon's photos had once hung. And, on Friday, after another mid-morning run, I took myself to Ikea and came back with a cartload of new picture frames to fill. There was the photo I'd taken on my phone of my new do, a ticket from the charity do at The Savoy and even the scrap of paper bearing Asher's number. I'd framed my Agent Provocateur receipt. I'd taken a photo of my, Emelie's and Matthew's tattoos and framed them as well. I put up what felt like several thousand photos of me in the slingshot bungee ball and several thousand more of me and my two best friends at Niagara Falls. In two short weeks, I'd been able to rewrite my entire hallway. And, in the living room, in prime position over the sofa, was a worse-for-wear-looking napkin, covered in scribble, mounted in a huge black wooden frame.

'Emelie's already gone?' Matthew wandered into the living room and picked my new *Mad Men* DVD up off the top of the TV. 'She's not coming with us?'

'She went home last night.' I gave myself one last look in the mirror. Hair was shiny, dress was spotless, make-up pretty, fresh and – as experience had taught me was essential – waterproof. 'I don't think she wanted Paul to pick her up from here.'

'Fair enough,' he smiled at my artistic masterpiece. 'I suppose she has to go home anyway, with you abandoning us so callously.'

'Well yeah,' I agreed. 'If she's going to be alone in anyone's house, it might as well be hers. Besides, there's no way she's getting it on with my brother here. I'm not that OK with it.'

'When do you leave again?' he asked.

About ten minutes after I'd given up banging Dan's door down, Veronica had called to tell me I'd got the Sydney job. The make-up artist the magazine had originally booked had quit when she'd heard Dan had pulled out, and Dan had only pulled out because he thought I was going. There wasn't a single verse in Alanis Morissette's entire songbook to deal with the irony of the situation. Because Dan had let them down, I was getting to go to Australia. Because I had let him down, I got the opportunity of a lifetime. Or had he let me down? Either way, neither of us had seemed very happy the last time we'd spoken and now we were both going to be on opposite sides of the planet because he wouldn't listen. I was prepared to accept some responsibility but, quite frankly, not a lot.

'I'm going tomorrow night.' I picked up the wedding invite from the arm of the sofa and held out my arms to indicate I was all done. 'Flight's at ten.'

'I'll drive you.' Matthew held out his arm. 'You have to bring me back some Vegemite.'

'All right you two, ready?' Stephen poked his head around the living-room door and Matthew lit up like a Christmas tree. 'The car's double parked. Rachel, you look amazing.'

Lucky lady that I was, I had two escorts to the

wedding. And, given the way they were smiling at each other, there would be another wedding to go to soon enough. God knows Stephen had spent every waking moment working me and Emelie over for approval since we got back from Toronto. And rightly so. Matthew might be ready to give him a second chance, but Emelie and I had agreed he was on a six-month probation period as far as we were concerned. One wrong look and we took his balls.

'Shall we go?' Matthew asked, holding out his arm.

I checked the list in my little pink notebook – invite, directions, card, present – yep, I had everything.

'We shall,' I gave him a tiny curtsey and took the offered appendage. Since I was sworn off men for the time being, it was likely to be the only appendage I'd be manhandling for a while.

Emelie and Paul were waiting for us outside the church and, as much as it pained me to admit it, they both looked incredibly happy to be together. Paul had clearly washed his Ewok hair and Em, wearing my pale blue silk number and cute little white lace gloves, was glowing. It was just unfortunate that they weren't the only people waiting for me outside the church.

I spotted Simon before anyone else. I put it down to the fact that spending five years of being with someone gave you something of a Spidey sense as to when they were present. His car, our car, was parked a little way down the lane from the church and he was leaning against a gravestone a few feet away, decked out in his best suit, his slightly-too-long dark blond hair combed down flat. He'd clearly missed his monthly haircut appointment.

'Don't worry,' Matthew said as Paul pushed up his suit sleeves. 'We'll get rid of him.'

'No.' I held my hand over my eyes to shield them from the sun. I could tell he wasn't there to start trouble. He looked so sad. 'I'll talk to him. Wait for me inside.'

Seeing I was serious, the four of them set off up the path to the church while I turned in the opposite direction. This wouldn't take long.

'Simon?'

'Rachel?' He squinted at me and then did a double take. 'Is that you?'

'I realize it's been a while but I wouldn't have thought you'd have forgotten what I look like.' I crossed my arms in front of me. 'What are you doing here?'

'Your hair.' He continued to look me up and down until we passed right through ignorant and onto completely obnoxious. 'You look great.'

'Thank you,' I replied. At least I actually did, which was a weight off my mind. We were a long way from baggy boxers and his dirty old T-shirt in the hallway. 'What are you doing here?'

'Well, you wouldn't talk to me on the phone,' he said. His tie flapped awkwardly in the breeze. He never could tie them properly and the skinny end was far too long. 'And I know you hate coming to family things on your own. I wanted to come with you.'

'I'm not on my own, though.' I pointed out Matthew and Paul, who – against my instructions – were attempting to look menacing on the steps of the church. They weren't quite pulling off the Mitchell brothers. Chuckle Brothers maybe, but that probably wasn't quite the effect they were going for. 'And if I wanted to talk to you, I'd have called you.'

'I didn't recognize you,' he said. 'From over there, I didn't realize it was you. Your hair?'

The hair. Always the hair.

'Simon, we're at my dad's wedding, don't you think

today's going to be enough of a pain in the arse for me without you pulling this shit?' I shook my head. 'Just go home.'

'Rachel, listen.' He shuffled a little bit closer. I didn't move an inch. 'I know you're pissed off, you're right to be pissed off, but I really am sorry. Can't you give me a second chance? Whatever it takes, I'll do it.'

Wow. Whatever it takes. I wondered if he'd get in a barrel and let me throw him over Niagara Falls? I sighed and looked at the sorry state of my ex-boyfriend. The former love of my life. The man I'd accepted would be the father of my children. Before I knew better than to settle. I had no doubt he meant what he was saying: he was a complete mess. If I took him back, I was certain he'd spend a good six months at least on his best behaviour; maybe he would even propose. And it would be wonderful to have someone back in my bed at night, someone to be there when I got home at night, someone to take care of me.

But it wasn't going to be him. And until I'd worked out who it was, I was more than capable of taking care of myself.

'I'm sorry, Simon.' I stepped in closer, gave him a hug and sorted out his tie. 'It's not going to work out. Go home.'

'But the flat? The car? Croatia?' he said with desperation.

Hmm. Weren't they my arguments once upon a time?

'My mum says she'll buy you out of the flat,' I replied, thankful that my mum was a lot better with money than I ever would be. 'The car is yours; I never drive it anyway. We'll take whatever it works out to off the cost of the flat. And you'll have to go to Croatia without me. I'll be in Sydney.'

'Sydney, Australia?' Desperation petered out into

defeat and Simon shrank back into himself. I felt myself grow taller in my heels.

'I have a job there,' I nodded. 'I'll call you when I get back. We can sort out the house stuff then.'

And, with one final kiss on the cheek, I turned and walked back up the path to the church, took Matthew's hands and closed the door on Simon. Which would have been an incredibly dignified and elegant end to our relationship if Paul hadn't gone back outside and chased him all the way to his car and screamed obscenities down the lane, in front of the vicar, until Simon drove away in tears.

My brother, my protector.

My dad's wedding, just like the previous two I'd attended in non-foetus form, was beautiful. But you'd think, by the time you'd made it to your fourth, you'd have it down to a fine art. I had to give the man his due: he really did seem to look as though he meant what he was saying, while he was saying it. And he couldn't be completely evil, I reasoned, otherwise my mum and Theresa, his second wife, wouldn't be sitting in the back of the church nattering away after the ceremony. Maybe his last wife would make it to the next wedding. Give her a bumper marriage in the middle to get over the disappointment.

'Rachel Summers,' a familiar voice crowed over my shoulder outside the church. 'Don't you look a vision?'

'Aunt Beverley,' I acknowledged, wondering what the wedding etiquette was on pushing an elderly relative over and then hiding behind the headstones. Probably not OK at aged 28. Maybe I could pay one of the younger cousins to do it. Or just ask Matthew. He'd totally do it.

'That dress really is splendid,' she said, holding my

hands out to my sides so she could get a proper look. A proper look as to where to stick the knife. 'Almost a wedding dress, isn't it? And yet I still don't see a ring on that finger. Such a shame. You're what? Thirty now? Thirty-one?'

Ahh, she'd gone straight in with a direct blow. Only one way to fight back really, and Redhead Rachel wasn't afraid to fight passive-aggressive bitchiness with passive-aggressive bitchiness.

'Oh shit, has it fallen off?' I snatched my hand away and theatrically inspected my left hand. 'Matthew'll be ever so mad.'

'You're engaged?' She looked a little bit confused. But then she was old; she always looked a little bit confused. 'To that young man?'

We both looked over to where that young man was pawing Stephen and completely blowing my cover. The one condition of him bringing his boyfriend to the wedding was that he acted as my Aunt Beverley cover and he'd failed. Oh, young love.

'No, I'm only joking.' I turned back to my aunt and gave her my biggest, brightest smile. 'We're just fuck buddies, you know?'

'Oh,' she let go of my other hand. 'Rachel.'

'Yeah, well, he's a massive poof really, but you know what men are like, never satisfied. He'd probably put it in a goat if it let him.' I leaned over to give her a far-too-tight hug for far too long. 'Bye, Bev. Love to Uncle Alan.'

I strolled off across the lawn with a smile on my face and a song in my heart. Turned out I didn't need a date to make this wedding tolerable. Veronica had been right, as long as I had my own balls, who needed a man?

By nightfall, the wedding had been declared a huge

success and, more importantly, everyone loved my dress. I'd have felt guilty for stealing the bride's thunder but, given that most of the people in attendance, including Paul, couldn't even remember her name, I chose not to. And besides, she seemed more pissed off at the presence of my mother and Theresa to notice what her eldest stepchild was wearing. Not that I was sure she knew who I was: my dad had so many kids now we were practically the Von Trapp family, except without musical talent and considerably better dressed.

'How long do you give this one?' my mum asked, taking the empty seat next to me at a table right by the dance floor. 'I like her, she's got a good energy.'

'A year? Two?' I suggested.

'Generous,' she said. 'First anniversary max.'

'I thought you liked her?'

'That's why I'm only giving them a year,' she smiled. 'Far too good for your father.'

'And the two of you claim to be friends.' I sipped my billionth glass of champagne and smiled at Em as she and Paul joined my dad and his newest wife for their first dance. They'd been inseparable and quite frankly, insufferable all day long, but even I had to admit they looked great together. I'd never seen Em so smitten with a boy and I'd never seen Paul so attentive. Maybe they were meant to be. But still. Ew. 'I can't believe she's here with Paul.'

'He's been taken with her for some time, you know.' Mum accepted a top-up on her champagne and clinked my glass. 'You might have to get used to this. I know I'd be much happier with Emelie for a daughter-in-law than some of the young ladies I've heard about in the past.'

'Young ladies?'

'Exactly,' Mum replied. 'And Matthew is back with Stephen?'

'He is,' I confirmed. 'Apparently sometimes a break can work. I've never seen either of them so happy.'

'And you?'

I turned in my chair to give her the full effect of my dazzling smile and jazz hands. 'Haven't you heard? I'm in a three-way relationship with two gays. It's been the talk of the wedding.'

Aunt Beverley hadn't been slow in getting the gossip out.

'Well, yes, I'd heard that,' she sighed. 'I told Bev I'd had you all over for Christmas dinner last year and they both call me Mum.'

I loved my mother.

'But really, what's going on? Are you OK?'

'I am,' I replied. 'Or at least I will be. But yeah, work is good, my friends are happy, my brother is going out with someone he won't catch anything from and you're smiling. What more could I want?'

'I saw Simon outside earlier.' She ignored my comment about Paul, just as she had been ignoring them for the last twenty-seven years. 'Are you . . .?'

'Absolutely not.'

'Good.'

'Why would I waste my time on a Scorpio?' I gave her a nudge and sipped my wine while my alleged gay lovers joined in the slow dance. Cue mass murmurs around the room. 'I'm going to give boys a miss for now. No point wasting time on the wrong one.'

'Glad you've finally come round to my way of thinking,' Mum said. 'Being alone doesn't mean being lonely. We're made of stronger stuff, you and I. A man can't make you happy if you're not happy with yourself, you know.'

'I know,' I said, setting my champagne down and

giving her a hug. 'I'm sorry I've given you such a hard time in the past. I didn't really understand before.'

'You forget you'll always be my baby,' she said, hugging back. 'You might think you're all grown up, but you've still got a lot to learn before you're as wise as your old mum.'

'Point taken.' Did it ever get any easier to accept your parents were right and you were wrong?

'Ms Summers?' Matthew appeared and held out his hand to lead me to the dance floor while Stephen offered the same to my mum. 'Quick spin and then home?' he suggested, spinning me out and then whirling me back in. 'That really is a fabulous dress. Remind me to take you somewhere worthy of its presence.'

'Thanks.' I gave my dad a wave over Matthew's shoulder. He looked happy. 'I might take you up on that. Anywhere in mind?'

'I'm feeling another list coming on actually.' He dipped me low on the dance floor. 'Ten more stamps in the passport? A country from each continent? Visit every state in America?'

'Shall I get Sydney out of the way first and we can take it from there?' I suggested.

'Done and done,' he said, pulling me in close. 'Love you, Rach.'

'I love you too,' I said, nuzzling into his chest. Across the floor, I saw a tall, dark middle-aged man cut in on my mum and Stephen. It wasn't anyone I recognized, but I was familiar with the glint in her eye. There was hope for her yet. 'And if a little old lady in a navy suit asks, we're doing it.'

'Gotcha,' he nodded.

And after another verse chorus and verse of the wildly inappropriate 'Three Times a Lady', he gestured for us to make a move. A plan I backed wholeheartedly.

At my request, we listened to Magic FM all the way back to London, Matthew and Stephen belting out power ballads as though their lives depended on it, while I attempted to harmonize. We had just put in a spectacular version of 'Total Eclipse of the Heart' when our hire car pulled up outside my flat.

'Night beautiful,' Matthew kissed me on the cheek through the driver's side window. I shoved myself halfway across him to give Stephen a sloppy kiss on the cheek that I still wasn't sure he deserved, before turning on my heel and heading for the door. I was happy my friends were happy. I was happy my family was happy. I was happy I was drunk. Until I got home and saw a tall dark figure loitering around my doorstep. Why had I sent Matthew home without seeing me in the door? Now I was going to be murdered in this beautiful party dress and Aunt Beverley would tell everyone at the funeral I was having relations with a gay man.

'Hi.'

I didn't think it was usual for murderers to say hello.

I didn't think it was usual for murderers to bring a suitcase.

But then I hadn't counted on the murderer not being a murderer at all but in fact being a very tired-looking, two days' worth of beard-wearing Dan. On my doorstep. At midnight.

'Hi.' I stayed at the bottom of the steps, my heart pounding and climbing up my throat. 'You're in LA.'

'And you're drunk,' he replied, pointing to the case beside him. 'I haven't left yet. I'm on my way now.'

'Oh.' Heart crashing back down to my feet. 'You didn't call me back.'

'No.' He tipped his head to one side, his curls sliding across his forehead, covering up his eyes. 'I had some thinking to do.'

'Dangerous,' I replied. This Mexican stand-off was starting to become a problem. I was drunk, it was cold and I really needed a wee. The unholy triumvirate of doorstep dilemmas.

'Yeah, thing is,' he said, peeling off his jumper and holding it out to me. This one was black, cashmere again. If we kept this up, I'd have quite the collection soon enough. 'I'm in love with this girl who isn't in love with me and I don't really know what to do about it.'

'Right.' I skipped up the steps as lightly as possible given that the balls of my feet were burning. And I really, really did need that wee. 'How do you know she's not in love with you?'

'Because if she felt the same way I did, I'd know.' He took a deep breath and sat back down. I was just going to have to hold it. Afraid to stop him mid-sentence, I sat down beside him.

'I knew it from the first day we worked together but I didn't know what to do about it. I'd never, ever felt that way about anyone before, but she really didn't seem that impressed by me. And she had a boyfriend, although that had never stopped me before if we're being entirely honest.'

'You were wearing a baseball cap,' I said in a completely flat voice, praying for my cloudy brain to clear up. I was going to need all my wits about me for this one. 'That first day. It was a *Cosmo* shoot.'

'And you told me you couldn't take me seriously while I was wearing it,' he went on. 'But I remember thinking that, sooner or later, you'd break up with your boyfriend and realize that we were meant to be together. So I threw away all my baseball caps.'

Jaw on the floor. That was hands-down the most romantic thing anyone had ever done for me. Even if I didn't know it at the time.

'You did?'

'I say all. Most of them,' he shrugged. 'But I never wore one on a shoot with you ever again. I just waited for you to break up with your boyfriend. But when you did, by the time I'd heard about it, you'd got another one.'

'I was a bit of a fast worker,' I acknowledged. This was bizarre; I'd had no idea for six years. Talk about playing it cool.

'Luckily, that one didn't last,' Dan kept talking. 'But I told myself to wait because I didn't want to be your rebound fling. So I waited, just a bit too long, because as soon as you'd told me you'd broken up with one bloke, you'd met Simon and you practically moved in together right away. Once you bought the house, I thought it was all over, so I started dating Ana to try to distract myself. But then . . . well, but then. And now we're here.'

Even if I'd had any grasp over my vocabulary, I wouldn't have been able to speak for all the butterflies dicking about in my stomach. What was it butter-flies actually did, anyway? Besides make me feel as if I was absolutely, positively about to throw up? What was pretty about that?

'Rachel?' Dan took hold of my hand. 'I would feel really good if you could join in with something right now. Anything really.'

'I went to Canada to see a boy,' I started, forcing the butterflies under control. Now if I could just hear myself over my own heartbeat. 'He was my first crush.'

'I know I said say anything, but I'm not sure I meant this,' Dan interrupted. 'Anything else?'

'Shut up,' I ordered. His hand was so hot around mine. Hot and big and solid, like him. I had long fingers but, compared to Dan, I had tiny hands. 'I went to Canada to see this boy and it was lovely. He was lovely. But the whole time I was there, all I could think about was you.'

'Oh,' he nudged me with his knees. 'That sounds better.'

'And then I did a bungee jump at Niagara Falls and called you to tell you but you didn't want to listen and then I came home to see you but I thought you'd gone to LA which you bloody hadn't,' I added. 'So I sort of gave up.'

'Oh yeah.' He wrapped his other arm around my shoulders, rubbing my back absently. Boom. The butterflies took cover from the uncontrollable lightning bolts. 'Sorry about that. Hang on, you did a bungee jump?'

'Kind of. It was on my list.' I turned my face up to look at his. 'I came back a day early. When you wouldn't answer your phone, I flew back a day early to see you but you'd already gone.'

'I panicked.' He pushed my hair out of my face, then traced a fingertip along the neckline of my dress, brushing my collarbone. 'But I'm here.'

'But you're leaving,' I pointed out, wrapping my fingers around his and putting them back on his knees. This was going to be hard. 'Tonight?'

'I'll be back in a week.' Dan squeezed my hand but I shook it free. 'Or you could come with me. Go in and pack a bag. Just come.'

'I can't.' My voice wasn't even really a whisper. 'I'm going to Australia.'

'You booked the Sydney job.' He closed his eyes and retracted his hands. The lightning subsided for just one minute. 'Of course you did.'

Old Rachel wanted to tell him she'd blow the job off, that she'd just tell them she was sick or stuck in Canada or something and run off to LA with Dan, but I just couldn't. New Rachel wouldn't let her.

'How long are you gone for?' He fiddled with the hem of his T-shirt before looking up and turning those big brown eyes on me. 'I'll be back next Sunday.'

'I'm staying for a month. At least.' This time, I was the one who took hold of his hand. 'Veronica booked me some jobs, I'm going to travel for a bit.'

It was as though I'd just gone to tell Bambi the bad news about his mum.

'I thought you'd gone, Dan,' I said. 'I thought this wasn't happening. Getting away for a bit was the best idea.'

'My timing is shit. 'He pushed his too-long curls out of his eyes.

'It's not brilliant.' A tiny fluttery laugh escaped from my throat. Probably wasn't the right time for giggles, but if I didn't laugh, I was absolutely going to cry. 'What time's your flight?'

'Not until morning.' Dan rapped a fist against his case. 'To be honest, it was either convince you to come with me or go out and get totally hammered. Tried-and-tested method of dealing with rejection.'

'It's not rejection,' I said after a few too many moments of silence. 'I'll be gone for a month. In the greater scheme of things, it's really nothing.'

Didn't feel like nothing, though. From my perspective, it felt like this was really not meant to be. I was right in the first place: never give in to the butterflies, they just make you sick. I couldn't even begin to imagine what Dan was thinking.

'Can I stay tonight?' he asked.

Oh. So that's what he was thinking. I suppose six-year epic unrequited love or not, he did still have a penis.

'I really want to say yes,' I whispered, my forehead resting against his. 'But I don't think it's a very good idea.'

'I think it's a very good idea.' His breath tickled my ear and my resolve wavered as that now-familiar feeling shivered all the way down my spine.

'I need a bit more time.' The words didn't come out easily but I knew they were the right ones. 'I don't want to mess you about but I'm not ready.'

'Right.' He pulled away abruptly and leapt to his feet. 'Plan B then, I'll go and get hammered. Have fun in Sydney.'

'Dan, wait.' I tried not to keel over as he vanished from my side.

'I'm done waiting,' he called back, dragging the case noisily down the street. 'Maybe you can put "call Dan" on your list when you get back from Australia.'

Of course, the grand romantic gesture would have been to kick off my heels, forget that I was desperate for a wee and run down the street after him. But New Rachel didn't run after men. New Rachel stood on her own two feet, high heels attached, and unlocked the door to my house.

Four weeks later . . .

It only took one ten-hour layover at LAX to remind me why I hated flying. I shifted in my crappy chair and waited for the feeling to come back into my left arse-cheek while I pondered another run round duty-free. There was no such thing as too many cheap Toblerones.

The airport was a bit of a shock to the system after the month I'd had. The magazine shoot had been great; I'd made lots of excellent new contacts and one job led to another and to another and another. Before I knew it, I was flying out to New Zealand with a group of models from London, swimming through caves lit up by glow worms and re-enacting scenes from *Xena: Warrior Princess* before spending happy drunken nights hanging out on the beach. Most amazing of all, I even had a bit of a tan. So to go from the wide-open spaces of Australia and New Zealand to the confines of an airport was a bit much. I wanted to be home. I wanted to be in my bed. I wanted to find out just exactly what Emelie was thinking when she and my brother changed their Facebook status to 'in a relationship' last week. She'd been strangely un-Skype-able since the announcement. It was still taking some getting used to, but I was trying.

On the other hand, Matthew and Stephen couldn't leave me alone. I took my iPhone out of my pocket and read his last message. I couldn't remember the last time I'd seen him this happy and he really, really wanted to share that joy. Every day I got an update of their adventures – nothing sordid, thank god, but they never left the house without letting me know where they were off to. And I suppose I was supposed to be honoured that they'd named their new kitten Red for me, but I just had everything crossed that they would never ask me to look after it.

The only person I hadn't heard from was Dan. Matthew had tried to convince me that it didn't mean anything, his arguments flipping from 'he's cooling off because he thinks you rejected him' to 'he's giving you space to think', depending on which suited my mood. I'd sent him a couple of emails, a couple of texts, but got nothing back. If this was Dan cooling off, they should consider using him in the fight against global warming. Just thinking about him made me feel positively chilly.

I flicked through my text messages one last time. I could call my mum. She'd love a chat. It was only, oh, four a.m. in London. Maybe not then. Besides, she was another one who had apparently jumped on the love bandwagon while I was out of town. The last time I'd called she was out at Pizza Express with the 'gentleman friend' she'd met at the wedding. My first instinct was to be pissed off that she'd taken him to 'our' place, but then I remembered I wasn't thirteen and she was allowed to go to eat overpriced pizzas without me. It was too early to call anyone in England. Too soon to call anyone in Australia. And I was too full to eat another Panda Express.

I could call Ethan, who, having got over my callous abandonment – in that he was dating the chemistry teacher at his high school and, it turned out, hadn't been taking the whole thing quite as seriously as I had in the first place; my ego was adequately deflated – had turned out to be a fairly constant email buddy. It was nice to have a straight boy to fire questions at, even if his answers were often lacking in tact. Really, though, what did I expect?

Giving up on communication with another human

being, I put my phone away and closed my eyes. Just another two hours to go.

'Is that an iPhone in your pocket or are you just happy to see me?'

My eyes snapped open.

'iPhone,' I replied. 'Definitely an iPhone.'

Dan Fraser stood in front of me. He clearly had not spent the last eight hours hunched up in an unpadded chair. Rather than crumpled, cramped and crappy, he looked fresh, tanned and far happier than he had any right to be.

'Ouch.' He picked my giant handbag up out of the chair next to me and replaced it with himself, cradling the bag in his lap. 'What do you keep in here? It's like the Tardis. Except bigger. And bluer.'

'What are you doing here?' I tried to funnel my shock into rage but instead I was having a minor stroke as to the state of the carry-on baggage under my eyes. What was the protocol on me running for the lavs to pop on some Touche Éclat before he answered?

'Funny story.' He opened my bag and peered inside. Cheek. Of. The Devil. 'I ended up staying out here for a few weeks to try to clear my head but for some reason, I just could not stop thinking about you.'

'And yet you were unable to return my messages.'

Hi, my name is Rachel and I make snarky comments at inappropriate moments when I don't know what else to say.

'And yet I was unable to return your messages,' he agreed. 'Because whenever I wrote down what I was thinking, it came out wrong. And because I had no idea what you were actually saying in your messages, given that they made no reference to our last conversation whatsoever.'

I thought back to my emails. There was a chance I'd

gone a little too far with the 'I'm breezy' school of communication. It was hard to pour your heart out on a medium that could so easily be printed out and used against you at a later date. As I'd learned.

'So I decided it was time to come home, get on with my life, when I was on the phone to Veronica and she mentioned you were coming home and that your flight connected in LA.' He pulled four full-sized Toblerones out of my bag and raised an eyebrow. 'And here we are.'

'You're on my flight?'

'I'm on your flight.'

He really had to stop sneaking up on me when I was knackered, jetlagged or drunk. I was indecisive at the best of times but, right now, I had no idea what I was going to do. All I knew was that, now he was here, sitting beside me, I had missed him so much more than I'd let myself realize.

'Bit convenient, isn't it?' I asked, not quite ready to look him straight in the eye.

'Not really.' He replaced the chocolate and took out my notebook and a pen. My heart stopped – and not in a good way. 'It took me a lot of time and a lot of money to casually run into you in a departures lounge halfway round the world, but I thought the cool thing to do would be not to mention that.'

'Fair enough.' I bit my lips, trying to will some colour back into them. Oh god, my hair. What must my hair look like? I had Heidi plaits. Why did I have Heidi plaits?

'Lots of new lists, he said, leafing through the pages. 'You really do have a problem.'

'This is not news,' I pointed out, still trying to work out exactly what was going on. Was he just trying to make friends? 'What are you writing?'

He turned the book around to show me. It was a short list.

Accept Dan's apology.

Give Dan a Toblerone.

Kiss Dan.

Without even trying to accomplish the first two tasks, Dan wove his fingers into my hair, pulling me towards him until, finally, his lips were on mine. Every firework from Niagara Falls went off in my stomach, obliterating the butterfly population and putting the lightning in the shade. It just felt right. So this was why Matthew was prepared to take Stephen back. Why Emelie had held out for ten years for me to give her permission to go out with my brother. I would have waited a lifetime for another kiss like that but, luckily, I only had to wait a couple of seconds.

'I'm sorry I was a dick that night on your doorstep,' he murmured, his hand tangled up in my messy plaits. 'I thought I was out of options.'

'I really did just need some time,' I whispered back, not caring who was watching. 'But I know that's not the easiest thing in the world to ask for.'

'But it should have been,' he countered. 'So what do you reckon? Shall we give it a go?'

'Well,' I ummed and ahhed for a moment. 'I suppose it is on the list—'

'It is on the list,' Dan leaned in for another kiss, cutting me off.

He always did have to have the last word.

But, it *was* on the list.

When Lindsey asked her Facebook fans to write their very own single girl's to-do lists she was inundated with emails full of hilarious, empowering and touching lists.

Turn the page to read Lindsey's four favourites and to find out more about Lindsey's other books.

Line Sehested Laursen's
Single Girl's To-Do List:

1. I use the whole bed when I'm sleeping. At first, it was kind of awkward to spread my body all over a double, but soon enough I will be forced, and expected, to stick to my side of the bed. So I'm enjoying all of the bed while I can!

2. I plan my future wedding! When you're in a relationship - and you're not engaged - it is kind of weird to fill up notebook after notebook and cover the whole wall with wedding inspiration. It will probably make a S.O. (significant other) run away in to the night screaming their lungs out, because they feel pressured in to something they're not ready for. So that's why I'm researching my wedding now. No spending limit and you don't have to consider if a potential S.O. would like the pink table cloth.

3. I try to travel and "enjoy" ☺ everything the world has to offer - this includes food and boys and everything else. I will never be as young and as free again as I am now, and I definitely think that it is important to do this while you can - so I do! On my trips around the world, I've seen amazing things that have changed me and my life for the better - things I wouldn't have be able to see if a relationship was holding me back!

4. I want to learn how to cook! Not because I think that girls should do the cooking in a relationship - I am as feminist as you get - but because I enjoy cooking. I'm just not very good at it. And let's face it, you **are** more likely to get a great husband if you are a great cook. That's just how it is. But he needs to be amazing at cooking too, so we'll share the chore!

Katie Turner's Single Girl's To-Do List:

1. Meet Seth MacFarlane (Done!)

2. Marry Seth MacFarlane.

3. Divorce Seth MacFarlane $$$.

4. Become a Hollywood make-up artist.

5. Retire early and geek-out watching 'Doctor Who' all day long.

Stacey Cosens's Single Girl's To-Do List:

1. Travel the world with your best mates, and share exciting girlie adventures!

2. Save up and go on an unashamedly ridiculous spending spree in New York.

3. Get really drunk and show everyone in the club you haven't forgotten those Spice Girls dance moves.

4. Drag your friends up on stage to sing the cheesiest girl anthem you can think of, at a karaoke night.

5. Eat everything in sight on a girl's night in, without feeling guilty.

6. Dance on a bar top, without being removed by security.

7. Go out with your girlfriends in themed fancy dress.

8. Get a dramatic haircut.

9. Attempt to bake.

10. Learn a new craft, such as knitting, dressmaking or embroidery.

Gemma Critchley's Single Girl's To-Do List:

Pay a visit to Book Marc in New York and treat myself to some lovely, lovely, pointless-yet-beautiful Marc Jacobs goodies.

Get invited to some sort of marvelous celebrity party (an invite to the Royal Wedding should cover it. I'd even settle for an evening do invite).

Go to said party wearing something that Stella McCartney created just for me. Or Holly Fulton, if Stella's busy. I'm not fussy.

Learn about wine. And I don't just mean honing my talent for knowing which supermarket has a 3-for-a-tenner-deal on.

Live outside of Yorkshire. Technically I have done this a bit but I keep coming back to these rolling hills. I need to get out of the country, I reckon.

Get promoted to 'Queen of the Internet' at work. I don't think that technically exists as a job title at the moment but I'm sure I could speak to HR about it.

Go on at least one adventure every week, even if it's only to a different pub after work. I often forget how amazing new adventures are until I leave it too long and then get taken by surprise by one.

Finish my 'one a day' blog project this year and manage to write stuff that is semi-engaging and coherent. If you want a nosy, you can have a look here: http://beatifnik.wordpress.com

Learn to not be bothered that my four younger siblings are all married, engaged and having babies. Become comfortable with being the 'black sheep' due to not being shacked up with kids at the age of 28. Black shearling is fabulous anyway, come Autumn/Winter'11 I'll be laughing all the way to Topshop...

Win at life in general; have fun, care less about the little things that don't matter and get on with it with a smile. If I can manage that, the other to-dos should come naturally.

Thank you to everyone who sent in their lists!

I heart New York

It's official. Angela Clark is in love –
with the most fabulous city in the world.

Fleeing her cheating boyfriend and clutching little
more than a crumpled bridesmaid dress, a pair of
Louboutins and her passport, Angela jumps on
a plane – destination NYC.

Holed up in a cute hotel room, Angela gets a
New York makeover from her NBF Jenny and
a whirlwind tour of the city that never sleeps.
Before she knows it, Angela is dating two sexy guys.
And, best of all, she gets to write about it in her
new blog (Carrie Bradshaw eat your heart out).
But there's one thing telling readers about your romantic
dilemmas, it's another figuring them out for yourself…

Angela has fallen head over heels for the big apple,
but does she heart New York more than home?

I heart Hollywood ♥

Angela Clark can't believe her luck...

She's living in New York, the most FABULOUS city on earth. And, she's bagged the perfect job at hip magazine *The Look* along with a sexy boyfriend – singer Alex Reid.

When Angela's editor sends her off to Hollywood to interview hot actor and fellow Brit James Jacobs, she doesn't exactly jump at the chance. The trip is going to test her new relationship with Alex to the max.

Angela doesn't fall for Hollywood right away. It's not as glossy and shiny as she had imagined and she doesn't feel like she fits in. Despite his lady-killer reputation, the only person who seems genuine is James Jacobs and Angela is suprised to discover they have lots in common.

But then a paparazzi snaps Angela and James in a very compromising position. Will the people Angela trusts come through – or will they believe everything they read?

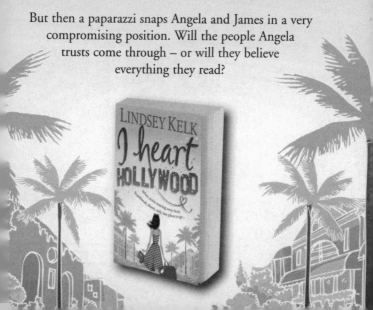

I heart Paris ♥

Angela is in the city of love – but romance is
taking a nose dive…

When Angela Clark's boyfriend Alex suggests a trip to Paris
at the same time as hip fashion mag *Belle* asks her to write a
piece, she jumps at the chance.

But even as she's falling for the joie de vivre of Paris,
someone's conspiring to sabotage her big break.
And when she spots Alex having a tête-à-tête with his ex in a
local bar, Angela's dreams of Parisian passion all start
crashing around her.

With London and her old life only a train journey away,
Angela can't decide if she should stay and face the music
or run away home…